MURDER ON UNION SQUARE

MURDER ON UNION SQUARE

A Gaslight Mystery

Victoria Thompson

BERKLEY PRIME CRIME
NEW YORK

BERKLEY PRIME CRIME

Published by Berkley

An imprint of Penguin Random House LLC

375 Hudson Street, New York, New York 10014

Copyright © 2018 by Victoria Thompson

The Edgar® name is a registered service mark of the Mystery Writers of America, Inc.
Penguin Random House supports copyright. Copyright fuels creativity, encourages
diverse voices, promotes free speech, and creates a vibrant culture. Thank you for
buying an authorized edition of this book and for complying with copyright laws by
not reproducing, scanning, or distributing any part of it in any form without
permission. You are supporting writers and allowing Penguin Random House to
continue to publish books for every reader.

BERKLEY is a registered trademark and BERKLEY PRIME CRIME and the
B colophon are trademarks of Penguin Random House LLC.

Library of Congress Cataloging-in-Publication Data

Names: Thompson, Victoria (Victoria E.), author.
Title: Murder on Union Square / Victoria Thompson.
Description: First edition. | New York : Berkley Prime Crime, 2018. |
Series: A Gaslight mystery ; 20
Identifiers: LCCN 2017052494| ISBN 9780399586606 (hardback) |
ISBN 9780399586620 (ebook)
Subjects: LCSH: Brandt, Sarah (Fictitious character)—Fiction. | Malloy,
Frank (Fictitious character)—Fiction. | Murder—Investigation—Fiction. |
Private investigators—New York (State)—New York—Fiction. | BISAC:
FICTION / Mystery & Detective / Historical. | FICTION / Mystery &
Detective / Women Sleuths. | GSAFD: Mystery fiction.
Classification: LCC PS3570.H6442 M879 2018 | DDC 813/.54—dc23
LC record available at https://lccn.loc.gov/2017052494

First Edition: May 2018

Printed in the United States of America
1   3   5   7   9   10   8   6   4   2

Cover art by Karen Chandler

This is a work of fiction. Names, characters, places, and incidents either are
the product of the author's imagination or are used fictitiously, and any resemblance
to actual persons, living or dead, business establishments, events,
or locales is entirely coincidental.

*With thanks to the real Bill Jonson
for giving me the idea for this book.*

MURDER ON UNION SQUARE

I

"WHAT DO YOU MEAN, WE CAN'T ADOPT CATHERINE?" Sarah asked the attorney.

Michael Hicks gave her a look that told her he shared her frustration. "I'm sorry—"

"I thought Mr. Wilbanks settled all of this in his will," Sarah's husband said. Frank Malloy reached over and took her hand, giving it a reassuring squeeze. They'd come to Michael's office today expecting good news. Plainly, they were going to be disappointed.

"I thought David had settled everything, too," Michael said. "And I know he certainly intended to as well. My father-in-law was a very careful man, but you see, I didn't draw up his final will. Estates are not my area of expertise, and it would be unethical for me to prepare a will for a family member in any case, so I referred him to a colleague of mine, Bill Jonson."

"Are you saying this colleague made a mistake?" Malloy was angry now but trying not to take it out on poor Michael. Sarah understood completely.

"Not a *mistake*." Michael was being very diplomatic. "My father-in-law was careful but also very private. He didn't believe he needed to tell Mr. Jonson all the sordid details about Catherine's birth."

"Which ones did he leave out?" Malloy asked.

Michael winced. "I, uh, I've asked Mr. Jonson to join us, if you don't mind, so he can explain it all to you." He got up and went to his office door to admit a man who had obviously been waiting for this summons.

Michael introduced Mr. Jonson, who was a distinguished-looking man of middle age wearing a conservatively cut, tailor-made suit and immaculate shirtfront. When they were all seated again, Michael said, "Bill, I have informed Mr. and Mrs. Malloy that they cannot adopt Catherine, but I haven't explained exactly why yet. I thought you could do that better than I."

"Of course." Mr. Jonson gave them his best reassuring smile. "You see, Mr. Wilbanks told me that Catherine was the illegitimate child he had with his mistress, an actress named Emma Hardy. However, he didn't think it necessary to explain that Emma Hardy also happened to be married to a Mr. Parnell Vaughn at the time of their affair. He probably thought it was none of my business."

"But what difference does that make?" Sarah asked.

"Even Mr. Vaughn admitted he couldn't possibly be Catherine's father because he and Emma were separated when she met Mr. Wilbanks."

"Which is why Mr. Wilbanks didn't think it necessary to mention Mr. Vaughn at all," Jonson said. "Unfortunately, the law is rather unforgiving when it comes to matters of paternity."

"What does that mean?" Malloy asked.

"It means that the law considers a woman's husband to be the father of her children, regardless of any evidence to the contrary."

"But that's ridiculous," Sarah tried.

"In some cases, yes, but it is nevertheless the law."

"So you're telling us that the law considers Parnell Vaughn to be Catherine's father?" Malloy asked, no longer bothering to hide his anger.

"Yes," Michael said, "and that's one reason why David decided to leave part of his estate to Frank rather than directly to Catherine."

"You mean he knew about this paternity law?" Sarah asked.

"No, I'm sure he didn't," Mr. Jonson said. "And I certainly didn't explain it to him because I had no idea Miss Hardy was ever married to Mr. Vaughn. Rest assured, I would have made sure to settle the matter prior to Mr. Wilbanks's death. Even without knowing about Mr. Vaughn, I was already very concerned that if he left Catherine a great deal of money in her own right, she'd be a tempting target for any greedy family members Emma Hardy may have had or anyone willing to pretend to be her family member. A large inheritance would also make her a target for fortune hunters later in life."

"But after seeing how much you loved Catherine, Frank," Michael said, "David decided you were the man who could and would protect her from both of those dangers."

Malloy winced and glanced at his wife. "He should have left the money to Sarah."

"I'm afraid David was also old-fashioned. He would never trust a female with so much money, and besides, Sarah had already told him she wouldn't accept it." Michael smiled slightly. "I must also tell you that Mr. Jonson did not approve of David making you one of his heirs, Frank."

"I certainly did not," Jonson said. "Even though Mr. Wilbanks's will instructed you to become Catherine's legal guardian, there was no way to compel you to do so. Such a provision causes an attorney great concern."

"Yes, it does," Michael said. "Bill was almost apoplectic about it."

"So was I," Malloy said. "I wish I'd suspected he was going to do it so I could have threatened to refuse it like Sarah did."

"Which is why he never informed you, I'm sure," Michael said.

Mr. Jonson still looked distressed. "You see, after you received your inheritance, you could have abandoned Catherine completely, and even now you have no obligation to share any of the money with her."

"But we would never abandon Catherine," Sarah said.

"David believed that, I know," Michael said, "which is

why he did what he did, but the fact remains that he has put you in a difficult position. You can't adopt Catherine as long as Vaughn is legally her father."

"You might get a judge to name you as her official guardian," Jonson said, "but it would mean a court case and publicity you'd find distasteful and a scandal that could follow her all of her life. You'd probably win in the end, although there's no guarantee of that, but even if you did, you still wouldn't be able to adopt Catherine, and Vaughn would always be there."

"You might never hear from him again, of course," Michael said, "but whenever there's money involved, people do tend to make nuisances of themselves. There's no telling what he might do, and after what happened before . . ."

"You don't think he'd try to kidnap her?" Sarah asked in alarm, remembering the horror of her first encounter with Catherine's blood relatives.

"It wouldn't legally be kidnapping," Michael said. "In the eyes of the law, he's her father, so he could be entitled to custody."

Sarah couldn't help groaning.

"So what can we do about this?" Malloy asked impatiently. "I know you lawyers always have an answer for everything."

Michael glanced at Jonson, who said, "We do try, but there isn't always an *easy* answer for everything. In this case, you would need for Vaughn to relinquish his parental rights. I could have the documents drawn up and when he has signed them, you could then proceed with the adoption."

"And Vaughn couldn't come back later to reclaim Catherine?" Sarah asked.

"No, he couldn't."

"I wonder how much he'll want in exchange for his signature," Malloy said.

"Uh, that's another thing we need to discuss," Michael said uneasily. "It's illegal for you to pay him to give up custody."

"What?" Malloy nearly shouted. "Why would that be illegal?"

"Because it's considered selling a child, and selling human beings is illegal in the United States, I'm happy to say."

Sarah wanted to weep. "So we're supposed to convince Mr. Vaughn to sign Catherine over to us out of the goodness of his heart?"

"I'm afraid so."

"And if he doesn't have any goodness in his heart?" Malloy asked.

Michael and Mr. Jonson exchanged looks again. "Let's just hope he does."

"WHAT ARE WE GOING TO DO?" SARAH ASKED MALLOY the moment Michael's office door closed behind them.

"We're going to find Parnell Vaughn and convince him to sign Catherine over to us."

"What are the chances he'll do it?"

Sarah didn't like Malloy's expression one little bit. "Very small, I'd guess."

Sarah wanted to weep again. "He'd do it if we paid him, I'm sure."

"I know, which is why I think we'll have to pay him."

"But Michael said that's illegal!"

"Which means we're stuck either way."

"What do you mean?"

"I mean, when Vaughn finds out he's legally Catherine's father, he'll probably decide he'd be a fool to sign her over. He'll know that as long as he has the right to claim her, we'll be willing to keep paying him off to keep him from doing so."

"But if he signs the papers . . ." Sarah said.

"Which he won't do unless we pay him, and if he knows that's illegal, he'll always have that over us, too. If we don't keep paying him, he'll accuse us of 'buying' Catherine and try to get her back again."

"So, we're back to my original question: What are we going to do?"

"I'm going to find Vaughn. We can't decide anything until we've talked to him."

He was right, of course. "He's probably touring in some theater company, though." Vaughn was an actor, too, which was how he'd met Emma Hardy. "How will we track him down?"

"Same way we did before, and with any luck, we'll find out he drank himself to death since we last saw him."

"Oh, Malloy, we don't really wish him dead," Sarah said, although she couldn't help thinking how Vaughn's death would make everything so much simpler.

"Mr. Malloy is right," Maeve said. "If Vaughn was dead, that would make everything so much easier."

Sarah gave her nanny a look meant to chasten her, although she was sure such efforts were wasted on the girl. "We do not wish Mr. Vaughn ill, Maeve. We simply want him to sign some papers." Sarah had gone straight home after their meeting with Michael Hicks, while Malloy had gone to find out what he could about Parnell Vaughn. Maeve had just returned from the Lower East Side, where she was supervising the workmen who were turning the old house Sarah had purchased into a maternity clinic that would provide services free of charge to women in need. She'd wanted to tell Sarah how she'd outsmarted the workmen yet again and terrorized them into doing exactly what she demanded, but she'd forgotten all that when Sarah told her about their meeting with the attorney.

"Oh no, I don't wish Mr. Vaughn any misfortune," Maeve assured her with just the right amount of sincerity. "But I'm afraid your lawyer is right. People act strange when money is involved."

"Then we'll deal with that when we must. In the meantime, tell me how the clinic is coming along."

"Women are still coming to the door every day wanting to know when we're going to open," Maeve said.

"I know. You've told me that before. I'm sure everyone knows the midwives have moved in, too, so that probably doesn't help."

"Those two women you hired are going to be perfect, and having them move in to make sure the place is occupied at night was a very good idea. They're already making home visits, and Miss Hanson delivered a baby last night."

"She did?" Sarah couldn't have been more delighted. "Oh, I do miss those deliveries." Sarah had made her living as a midwife for years before her marriage.

"I already told them they'll need to let you deliver a baby every now and then."

"Thank you," Sarah said with a grin.

"Oh, and I almost forgot, you'll never guess who I saw today."

Sarah didn't particularly care, since her mind was still focused on Catherine and their situation, in spite of Maeve's best efforts to distract her. "Who?"

"That fortune-teller, Serafina Straface."

"Serafina? Really?" Sarah asked in surprise. "How long has it been since we saw her?"

"A couple years, I think."

"What did she want?"

Maeve gave her a pitying look. "The same thing all the other women want."

"Oh!" So Serafina was expecting.

"Yes. Apparently, she's still telling fortunes or whatever it was she did."

"She's a medium."

Maeve rolled her eyes at such a notion. "So she says. Then I guess she's still a medium, but I gathered she's looking for a private place to have her baby."

"I suppose she married her young man, Mr. DiLoreto."

"You can suppose that all you want, but when she told me her name, she said it was Straface."

"Oh dear." The world was not kind to unwed mothers.

Then she remembered. "In Italy, women don't take their husband's name."

"Really?"

"Yes, really."

"That's interesting. But I guess in America, actresses don't either. Emma Hardy didn't."

"You're right, she didn't. So Serafina is interested in using the clinic?"

"I think she was just interested in using you as a midwife. She said she went to your old house, and they sent her to the clinic to find you."

"Our neighbors have been very good about not telling people where we live now," Sarah said.

"Yes, they have, and it sure cuts down on the number of people coming here looking for a handout," Maeve said with a smirk. "She didn't tell me when, uh, she'll need the clinic, but she seemed glad to hear it should be ready in a few days."

"Do you think so?" Sarah asked in surprise.

"If I have anything to say about it, it will. I have those workmen terrified of Mr. Malloy, especially after they tried to pretend they didn't know they were supposed to fix the wall in the back today."

"Maeve, you missed your calling."

"I know. I should've been a man. I would've been good at it, too. Better than most men, anyway."

Sarah couldn't help laughing, in spite of everything, which she guessed had been Maeve's intention. "I didn't mean that. I meant you should have been a . . ."

Maeve waited a few seconds while Sarah tried in vain to

think of some profession to which a woman could aspire that would use Maeve's talents. "See? You can't think of anything. I was right. I should've been a man."

"But instead you're going to help other women."

"I suppose, and maybe someday Mr. Malloy will let me work for him."

FINDING PARNELL VAUGHN TURNED OUT TO BE MUCH easier than Frank had anticipated. As an actor, Vaughn often worked for touring companies, and he might have been anywhere in the country. The last time they'd tried to locate him, he'd just been returning to New York from a tour. Frank tried the theatrical agent who had helped him then, only to discover that agents represented shows, not actors, and Vaughn was no longer appearing in any of that agent's shows. Frank had to visit only a couple more agents, however, before he found his quarry.

"Oh yes, Parnell Vaughn," Mr. Dinsmore said with obvious distaste. "He's having quite a successful run with Mrs. Hawkes at the Palladium Theater."

"Mrs. Hawkes?" Adelia Hawkes was one of the most famous actresses in the country. "Are you sure? It's *Parnell* Vaughn I'm looking for. Maybe you have him confused with someone else."

Mr. Dinsmore smiled grimly. "I see you know Mr. Vaughn."

"We're acquainted, yes."

"Then you probably know that he has always been a very talented performer."

"I've, uh, never actually seen him on the stage," Frank admitted.

"Well, then, let me assure you that he is." Oddly, Mr. Dinsmore didn't seem pleased to admit this. "But like many creative individuals, he has a serious problem with, uh . . ."

"Yes, he drinks," Frank said, sparing Mr. Dinsmore from finding a polite way of saying it.

"Or rather, he did. It seems he's turned over a new leaf in the past year or so. He met a lady who has been a stabilizing influence on him, and his career has prospered as a result."

So much for Vaughn drinking himself to death. "I'm glad to hear it. He's performing at the Palladium, you say?"

"That's right. I'm sure you can find him there Tuesday through Saturday evenings and on Wednesday, Saturday, and Sunday for matinees."

"Would you happen to know where he lives? He might not want to discuss our business at the theater."

"I wouldn't have any idea. Actors are notoriously migratory."

"How do you find them when you need them, then?"

"Oh, they stop by weekly when they're in town. They check in with all the agents, just to let us know they're available. Then when we have a need, we send them to audition."

"That doesn't sound like a very efficient system," Frank observed.

Dinsmore did not seem to appreciate Frank's opinion. "Perhaps not, but it works."

Frank thanked him for his time and made his way back to the street. Like most of the agents, Dinsmore's office was in a building just off Union Square, which was the central location for theaters as well. He couldn't see the Palladium Theater from here, but he knew where it was. He wondered if Sarah would like to see a play tonight.

"I THOUGHT SHE WAS SUPPOSED TO BE HIS MOTHER," Malloy said in disgust as they waited in their seats for the crowd to disperse when the show was over. "And then he started making love to her."

"Everyone knows Mrs. Hawkes always plays the romantic lead," Sarah said. "I thought Mr. Vaughn was very good."

"He'd have to be good to make people believe he was in love with a woman twice his age."

Sarah glanced around and was relieved to see no one was close enough to have overheard. Most of the audience had gone and the remaining few were moving toward the exits. It hadn't taken long, since the crowd hadn't been large to start with. "I don't think she's *twice* his age."

"She's got at least fifteen years on him, though."

He was right, so she didn't bother to dispute it. "I think we could head backstage now."

They rose from their seats and made their way to the front of the theater. A few generous tips to crew members bought them directions to Parnell Vaughn's dressing room. The door stood open and the sound of laughter spilled out into the hallway. Two young women emerged. Sarah recognized them as minor characters from the play. They gave Sarah and Malloy a curious glance before making their way to their own dressing rooms.

Sarah stepped up to the open doorway and saw a comfortable but cluttered room. Vaughn sat in a slipper chair, his back to the mirrored dressing table littered with pots and jars, and a young woman lounged on a worn love seat nearby. They both looked up in surprise. Sarah recognized the young woman from her role as the maid in the play. Vaughn got to his feet. He obviously didn't know who Sarah was, and of course he wouldn't since they had never met. Then Malloy came in behind her, and Vaughn's expression changed instantly.

"Mr. Malloy, isn't it?" he said, putting out his hand. He'd stiffened ever so slightly, but he was a good enough actor that his expression revealed only pleased surprise at his visitor. They had not parted on the best of terms at their last meeting.

"Yes. It's nice to see you again, Vaughn. May I introduce my wife, Sarah?"

Vaughn took her outstretched hand, but instead of shaking it, he sketched a little bow and gallantly kissed it. He was a strikingly handsome man with soulful dark eyes and a mane of dark hair artfully styled. He was even more impressive up close than when he was on the stage. When he raised his head, Sarah realized why women fell under his spell.

Then his expression, designed to charm, changed slightly to recognition. "Sarah, did you say? Are you by chance the little girl's, uh . . . ?"

"Foster mother? Yes, I am." Couldn't he even remember Catherine's name?

His gaze darted from her to Malloy and back again as he put the clues together. "And you and Mr. Malloy have married."

"Yes, we have," Malloy confirmed.

Having overcome his initial surprise, Vaughn now eyed them both more critically, taking in Sarah's expensive gown and Malloy's tailor-made suit. "And you've obviously prospered in the meantime."

Sarah blinked in surprise. They'd assumed Vaughn would know what had happened and that Malloy was now a wealthy man, but it seemed he did not.

Fortunately, Malloy also realized this. He smiled broadly. "Yes, we have. I've started my own detective agency." He pulled out a card and handed it to Vaughn.

"Nelly, who are these people?" the young woman on the love seat demanded crossly.

"Oh, pardon me, my dear. May I present Miss Eliza Grimes? Eliza, Mr. and Mrs. Malloy."

Eliza rose gracefully from her seat and offered Malloy her hand quite regally. Malloy made a point of not kissing it, Sarah noted fondly.

"His fiancée," Miss Grimes informed them, slipping her arm through Vaughn's possessively.

Did Vaughn wince a tiny bit? Sarah wasn't sure, but she found it odd he hadn't identified her as his intended when he introduced her. Seeing them together, Sarah couldn't help thinking they probably shared about the same age difference as Vaughn and Mrs. Hawkes, or nearly so. Eliza Grimes certainly hadn't reached her twentieth birthday yet.

"Congratulations," Malloy said without much enthusiasm.

"You also seem to have prospered, Mr. Vaughn," Sarah said quickly.

He brightened at that. "Did you see the show?"

"We did indeed and enjoyed it very much. We thought you were excellent."

"Thank you, Mrs. Malloy. It's a great honor to work with Mrs. Hawkes."

"I'm sure it must be. She's legendary."

"But much too old, of course, to continue playing the romantic lead," Eliza said.

"Now, Eliza," Vaughn said gently.

"And you are an actress, too, Miss Grimes," Sarah said.

Eliza lifted her chin. "Yes, I am. I'm Mrs. Hawkes's understudy."

And much more suited to the role, age-wise, but Sarah didn't say that.

"Eliza has a bright future ahead of her," Vaughn said.

"I'm sure she does," Sarah agreed.

No one had a reply to that, and an awkward silence followed. Finally, Eliza said, "Now, who are you really, and what do you want with Nelly?"

Vaughn patted her hand where it was wrapped around his arm. "You remember I told you about Emma's little girl."

Eliza rolled her eyes. "Oh yes, *Emma*."

"Yes, well, Mrs. Malloy is the lady who took her in."

"Then he must be the copper who arrested you," Eliza said, unimpressed.

"And I'm also the copper who let him go," Malloy said with a small smile.

"But that doesn't explain what you're doing here now," Eliza said.

"No, it doesn't," Malloy said. "We need to discuss something with you, Mr. Vaughn."

"About the little girl?" he asked with a frown.

"About Catherine, yes," Sarah said, unreasonably annoyed that he couldn't say her name.

"But maybe you'd like to meet at my office tomorrow," Malloy said. "Since it's a private matter."

"No," Eliza said before Vaughn could answer. "You're here now, so you might as well get it over with."

Malloy looked at Vaughn, who reluctantly nodded. Plainly, he didn't want to talk to them at all.

Malloy glanced at the girl. "Is it all right to speak in front of Miss Grimes?"

"Of course it is," she replied for him again. "We're going to be married. We have no secrets."

Sarah doubted that very much, but she said, "We should at least close the door. I'm sure you don't want anyone else knowing your business."

Malloy, being the closest, did the honors. Vaughn found a straight-backed chair half-hidden by the rack of costumes along one wall. Malloy took it while the two women sat on the love seat, and Vaughn sat back down in the dressing table chair.

"You make this sound ominous, Mr. Malloy," he said with a strained smile.

"Not at all," Malloy said. "Now that Sarah and I are married and Catherine's parents are both dead, we would like to adopt her legally."

"That's very kind of you."

"But why are you telling us about it?" Eliza asked, still suspicious.

Malloy cleared his throat. "It has come to our attention

that, even though you and Miss Hardy weren't living together at the time, because you were married to Emma Hardy when Catherine, uh, came along, the law still considers you Catherine's father."

"What?" Eliza cried, turning on Vaughn. "You swore to me that child wasn't yours."

"She isn't," Vaughn assured her. He turned to Frank. "I can't take care of a child. Surely you can see that."

"That's not what we're asking, Mr. Vaughn," Sarah said quickly. "In fact, it's just the opposite. We do want to take care of Catherine. We want to adopt her as our own, but we can't because of this legal technicality. However, our attorney assures us that it's possible for you to relinquish your parental rights by simply signing a paper. That would free you of all responsibility for Catherine and allow us to adopt her."

Vaughn needed only a moment to consider. "Oh well, in that case, I'd be more than happy to help you. I don't suppose you've got the paper with you?"

"Wait a minute," Eliza said, and all of them turned to her. "What's in this for Nelly?"

"I'm doing them a favor, Eliza," Vaughn said.

"Yes, you are, so they should do something for you in return."

This was exactly what Sarah and Malloy had been afraid of. "What did you have in mind, Miss Grimes?" Malloy asked. He wasn't using his friendliest tone, but Eliza didn't seem intimidated.

"You want this little girl, but you can't have her without

Nelly's help, so I think you ought to give him some token of appreciation."

Vaughn sputtered a protest, but Malloy stopped him with a gesture. "How big of a token would you consider appropriate?"

Plainly, Eliza had not expected to succeed so easily. For a moment her mouth hung open in shock, but she recovered quickly. Without so much as a glance at Vaughn to confirm her decision, she said, "A thousand dollars."

Equally plainly, from the requested amount, neither of them had an inkling of just how wealthy Malloy had become. For his part, Malloy managed to wince, probably because it hadn't been too very long since such an amount would have been impossible for him to raise. A thousand dollars probably equaled Parnell Vaughn's annual income as an actor, but only if he worked regularly.

"But we can't—" Sarah began, but Malloy stopped her with a gesture.

"That's a lot of money, but Catherine means a great deal to us."

"Really, Mr. Malloy, there's no need . . ." Vaughn said faintly.

"You're entitled to it," Eliza insisted. "You could refuse to sign their paper and then where would they be?"

"We appreciate your help in this matter, Mr. Vaughn," Malloy said, his expression suitably grave. "Our attorney can have the papers drawn up by Wednesday. Can I meet you here before your matinee and get your signature?"

"And we'll get our money, too?" Eliza said.

"Of course," Malloy said.

"Then yes, we'll meet you here on Wednesday afternoon, won't we, Nelly?"

Parnell Vaughn looked far from committed. "I . . . I suppose so."

Before anyone could reply, the door burst open.

"Parnell, darling, I've been wait—" Adelia Hawkes stopped mid-word at the sight of Vaughn's visitors. She did not appear to be pleased by it. "I didn't realize you were having a party."

Frank and Vaughn had risen to their feet. Sarah had to resist the urge to do the same. Adelia Hawkes seemed to fill the room with her presence and demand obeisance. She'd changed from her costume into an ensemble most would have considered outlandish. Her lavish brocade coat glittered with gold threads and an intricately wound turban of patterned silk completely covered her hair and sported a peacock feather that trembled with her every move.

"It's hardly a party, Adelia," Vaughn said. How odd. He sounded a little defensive. "These are some . . . old friends who came to see the show tonight and wish me well."

"Old friends?" She eyed Frank and Sarah much the way Vaughn had done earlier.

"We were so impressed when we heard Mr. Vaughn was appearing with you that we had to come," Sarah said. "You were absolutely fantastic in that role, Mrs. Hawkes."

Her disapproval vanished. "Did you think so? How lovely. One can never judge one's own performance."

"Oh yes, and Mr. Vaughn was just telling us how honored he was to be cast as your leading man."

Mrs. Hawkes cast Vaughn a fond look before turning back to Sarah. "Perhaps your friends would like to join us, Parnell. A few of us usually have a little supper together after the show," she added to Sarah.

"Thank you, but I'm afraid we're committed elsewhere," Sarah said. It wouldn't be a good idea to get too cozy with these people. Someone might figure out who they really were and tell Vaughn. Or worse, tell Eliza.

"A pity. Perhaps next time. Parnell, are you ready?"

"Almost," he said.

"Good. We'll go on ahead, then. Lovely to meet you," she added to Sarah, and then she was gone.

For a second she seemed to have taken all the air in the room as well, but they recovered quickly.

"I'm afraid I must go. Duty calls," Vaughn said with forced brightness.

Eliza made a rude noise, and Sarah realized Mrs. Hawkes had not even acknowledged her. For her part, Eliza had sat perfectly still, almost as if frozen, during Mrs. Hawkes's brief visit.

"You know you're welcome to join us, Eliza," Vaughn said.

"Oh yes, so the great Mrs. Hawkes can subtly insult me all during the meal. No thank you. I'll see you later." She rose and started for the door, but she stopped when she reached Malloy. "Don't forget to bring the money when you come. Otherwise, you can go whistle for your signature."

When she was gone, Vaughn tried a conciliatory smile. "She's very young and hasn't learned the art of discretion yet."

Malloy nodded. "Mr. Dinsmore—do you know him? Wylie Dinsmore, the agent?—he told me you'd met a lady who had been a good influence on you and that your career had flourished as a result."

Vaughn didn't seem pleased that Dinsmore had shared confidences about him, but then his expression cleared. "Yes, Eliza has encouraged me, and she wants me to succeed. I don't think Emma ever did."

"We're very happy for you, Mr. Vaughn," Sarah said. "And I know you want to stay in Mrs. Hawkes's good graces, so we'll be on our way now. Thank you for being so understanding about the situation with Catherine."

"I'm happy to help. I have nothing to offer a child, especially one who isn't even my own."

"We understand completely," Sarah assured him.

"And, Mr. Malloy," Vaughn added a little sheepishly. "I couldn't take a payment for helping you, so just ignore what Eliza said."

If Malloy was surprised, he didn't show it. They arranged a time to meet next Wednesday before the matinee.

Sarah and Malloy took their leave, and one of the stagehands escorted them out a side door into an alley where the other actors were making their way to suppers or entertainments of their own.

"Why do you suppose she calls him Nelly?" Malloy asked when they were out on the sidewalk and away from anyone who might be interested in their conversation.

"I think it must be a nickname for Parnell, at least in her mind."

Malloy shook his head. "When Dinsmore told me Vaughn had found a woman who helped him, I was picturing somebody like you."

Intrigued, Sarah said, "Like me in what way?"

"Oh, I don't know. Somebody sensible, I guess. And nice, at least. Instead, she's just like Emma except she's convinced Vaughn he's a good actor instead of convincing him he's not, just to keep him in line."

"Do you think that's what Emma did?"

"She never had a kind word to say about him, as far as I could see, and she encouraged him to drink. Why would a woman do that if not to keep a man under her control?"

Sarah couldn't imagine doing that to someone she loved, but then, she wasn't Emma Hardy, either. "You're probably right. At least Miss Grimes's influence has had good results."

"She's still trying to keep him under control, though. Did you notice the way she answered for him?"

"Of course, and did you notice she's the one who said they're engaged?"

"And he didn't look too happy when she did," Malloy said. "I wonder how long it will last, though."

"What do you mean?"

"You couldn't see Eliza's expression when Mrs. Hawkes came in. She might have inspired Vaughn's success, but she's jealous of it, too."

"Oh, I understood that perfectly," Sarah said. "Those remarks about Mrs. Hawkes being too old for the part were telling."

"They were also perfectly true. I can't imagine Mrs. Hawkes likes having Eliza around to remind her that she's getting a little long in the tooth."

The image surprised a laugh from Sarah. "You don't think Eliza says that to her face, do you?"

"No, she's too smart for that, but she doesn't need to say anything. She just needs to sit there and smile."

Sarah sighed. "She won't be smiling if we don't pay Vaughn the thousand dollars."

"Don't worry. I'll have it with me just in case."

"But if we pay Vaughn to sign the papers—"

"I said, don't worry. I won't be paying Vaughn. If Eliza insists, I'll give the money to her, not him. That way, if they come back later and try to blackmail us, I'll remind her of that."

"Do you think that's all right legally?"

"I think it's legal enough to convince them. And if Vaughn continues to be successful, he probably won't need to come back to us anyway."

"I hope you're right. He really does seem to be a good actor."

"He is if Eliza can keep him from drinking."

"And he'll have to help her become successful, too." Sarah shook her head. "That's a lot of uncertainty."

"I think all actors live with uncertainty, so he's probably used to it."

"I suppose so, and if he's willing to sign that paper, I will wish him all the best."

Malloy smiled. "So will I."

. . .

THE NEXT MORNING, SARAH AND MAEVE TOOK THE ELevated train down to the Lower East Side so Sarah could see for herself how close they were to opening.

The two midwives were out doing home visits. After Maeve and the foreman had taken Sarah on a tour, the two women settled down in the newly completed kitchen for a cup of tea.

"There doesn't seem to be much left to do, and all the furniture is here. How soon do you think we can open?" Sarah asked.

"A few days, I'd say. They're just finishing that last room and they'll have to clean up, although the midwives and I have been doing a lot of that ourselves. I've already had to turn people away, but they know they can return as soon as we hang out the sign." Maeve nodded to the neatly painted board leaning against the wall by the back door.

"Should we have some sort of event to announce that we're open?"

Maeve smiled. "I don't think that will be necessary. Everybody in the neighborhood knows we're here and what we do."

"I guess they're as anxious to get started as we are. My goal is to never turn anyone away."

The sound of footsteps drew their attention, and they looked up to see a young woman standing in the doorway.

"Mrs. Brandt, I was hoping you'd be here," she said.

Sarah rose and looked more closely, not quite trusting

her eyes. "Serafina, welcome. Maeve told me you'd stopped by."

They had met the beautiful Italian girl a few years earlier when a séance she'd been conducting had ended in murder. Serafina stepped into the room. Even though the September weather was still pleasant, she wore a cape and had buttoned it closed in front. Then Sarah remembered what Maeve had said about the girl, and she knew what Serafina was hiding.

"I'm afraid we haven't opened the clinic yet, but if you need a place to stay . . ."

"Oh no, I do not need a place to stay. I am still living in the same house on Waverly Place."

"Still doing séances?" Sarah asked.

"Of course. I have some very loyal clients, and I have done well for myself even after . . . Well, since I saw you last."

"Is Mr. DiLoreto still helping you?" Sarah asked, deciding that was the most tactful way to inquire if Serafina and the young man she had been in love with were still together.

But Serafina's polite smile vanished and her eyes filled with tears. "No, I . . . Nicola has died."

"*Died?*" Sarah echoed in surprise. "I'm so sorry. I had no idea. Please, come over here and sit down and let us get you a cup of tea."

When the girl was settled, still wearing her enveloping cape and sipping her restorative tea, Sarah said, "Was Mr. DiLoreto ill?"

"Yes, he . . . He was very sick. We called in a doctor, but there was nothing he could do. We were planning to marry, but I was so busy with my clients and we did not think we needed to hurry . . ." She shook her head. "After he was gone, I found out about the baby." She opened her cape to reveal her swollen stomach.

"And you've continued with your work?" Sarah asked, wondering how she had explained her condition and the absence of a husband to the society people who came to her for help contacting dead loved ones.

Serafina smiled sadly. "I wear robes now. Flowing robes. And I have stopped going out."

"Except to come here," Maeve reminded her.

"My time is getting close. I cannot give birth at my house. Everyone will find out and my clients will stop coming."

"What are you going to do?"

"I have told my clients that I will be going on a holiday soon. I had hoped to come to you and stay until the baby is born. Then I found out you were opening this clinic. If I could come here, no one would know. I would pay you, of course. I do not need charity. Then, when I am well again, I will return to my home. I will hire a servant who has an infant that she will bring with her into my house."

"Oh, Serafina, that is such a wonderful plan. I was afraid you were going to give your baby away."

"Never. And did Maeve not tell you? I have changed my name. I am Sarah now, too. Sarah Straface. I want to be completely American."

"It's a lovely name," Sarah said.

Serafina smiled, but her smile quickly became a grimace, and she clamped a hand to her side.

"What is it?" Sarah asked. "Is the baby kicking?"

"No, I . . . I have been having pains. I know you are not ready yet, but I could not stay at home." Her lovely dark eyes were pleading.

"Oh dear!" Sarah said, but she wasn't thinking "oh dear," not at all. Excitement skittered through her at the realization she was going to deliver a baby again after all these months. "Maeve, can we get a room ready?"

Maeve's eyes were like saucers. "Of course. I'll go make up the bed."

On the appointed Wednesday, Frank got to the theater just after noon. Early enough, he hoped, to be in and out before most of the cast arrived to prepare for the matinee. He entered through the side door the cast used. The door was unlocked and although a stool stood nearby, obviously for a guard who would monitor who went in and out, no one was around. In fact, the halls were eerily quiet, in stark contrast to the busy bustle he'd encountered after the performance the other night. He caught a glimpse of a woman disappearing into one of the dressing rooms at the end of the hallway, but he saw no one else before he reached Vaughn's dressing room.

Frank hadn't noticed the other night that the door bore Vaughn's name and a small wooden star had been nailed beneath it. Frank knocked and waited, but no one responded. He tried again, more loudly. Still nothing. He glanced up and down the hallway to see if Vaughn was in sight, but he still saw no one. He tried the door and the knob turned easily. Thinking he'd simply wait for Vaughn inside, he pushed the door open.

The first thing he noticed was the sharp metallic odor, and then he registered the body crumpled on the floor. And the blood. So much blood. Vaughn stared up at him, his eyes wide with terror and a silent plea for help. Frank went to him instinctively, kneeling down, heedless of the blood pooled around Vaughn's head. But Vaughn's gaze didn't move. He still stared fixedly up at the door, and when Frank felt for a pulse, he found none. The body was still warm, though, which meant the killer might still be nearby. They should seal off the theater in case he was hiding somewhere.

Frank pushed himself to his feet and started toward the door. Just as he reached it, Eliza Grimes appeared in the doorway.

"Mr. Malloy," she said with some satisfaction. "I hope you don't think you're finished with your business. I know what Nelly said, but—"

"Miss Grimes, we need some help. Can you go find a guard or someone in authority?"

"A guard? What for? What's going on? And don't think you can trick me into leaving you alone with Nelly!"

"Miss Grimes, please," he tried, reaching out to her, but that was a mistake. His hand was covered in blood.

"What's that? What's happened? Nelly!" she shouted, and tried to push past him.

"Don't go in there!" He did his best to hold her, but she wrenched free and managed to get her head around him enough to see.

"No! Nelly!" she cried, and began to scream.

In moments people appeared from every direction. Actors still in street clothes and stagehands still carrying their tools and an officious-looking man in a suit who demanded to know what all the fuss was about.

Before Frank could tell him, Eliza threw herself into the man's arms. "Oh, Mr. Hawkes, he's killed Nelly!"

2

At first Frank had thought they'd quickly realize their mistake. He hadn't killed Vaughn and no one with sense would think he had. Except Eliza Grimes kept screaming that he'd done it and the people in the theater had no reason to doubt her, so they'd put him in another dressing room and held him there until they found a policeman. The policeman happened to recognize Frank's name and sent for a detective from Police Headquarters because Frank used to be a detective at Police Headquarters, and the one they sent turned out to be someone who didn't know Frank all that well.

He apparently didn't like Frank all that well either.

"Why'd you kill him, Malloy? Was he diddling your wife?"

"Don't be an idiot, O'Connor. I didn't kill anybody."

O'Connor hadn't been a detective sergeant very long so he must've thought he had to act tough. "The girl said she saw you do it."

"I doubt she said that since she didn't get there until after I did, and Vaughn was already dead when I got there. Look, I wasn't in there long enough to figure out what happened, but I did see blood everywhere. Whoever killed him would be covered with it."

O'Connor looked meaningfully at Frank's bloody hand, which rested on his bloody knee.

Frank sighed. "When I saw him, I thought he was still alive, so I knelt down beside him to check. That's how I got blood on my pants and my hand, but you'll notice I don't have it anywhere else. How did he die?"

"I figured you could tell me, Malloy, since you killed him."

"That isn't funny, O'Connor. From the way the blood was splashed around, I figured somebody beat him to death. Did you find a weapon?"

"You know we did. It was right where you left it."

Frank ground his teeth in an effort to control the urge to throttle O'Connor. He was a strapping lad who could probably more than hold his own and at least a few years younger than Frank, which was another reason Frank resisted the urge to use violence. "Haven't you bothered to wonder why I would want to murder Vaughn in the first place?"

O'Connor smiled smugly. "I didn't have to wonder. The girl told me the minute I got here. It seems you and your wife want to adopt his kid, and you need him to sign some kind of paper so you can do it, but she says Vaughn changed his mind. He was going to keep the kid, so you killed him."

That was so ridiculous, Frank could only gape at him. Had Eliza really said that? And if she had, why would she lie? The last thing Vaughn wanted to do was keep Catherine. "That's not true," he finally managed.

"What's not true? That you didn't want to adopt Vaughn's kid?"

Frank sighed. "No, that part is true. She's not really Vaughn's child, but the law thinks she is because he was married to her mother."

"What?" O'Connor looked appropriately confused.

"Lawyers are involved, so it's complicated. At any rate, Vaughn isn't the child's real father, so he was perfectly willing to relinquish his rights to her and let us adopt her. I brought the papers for him to sign today, and he was expecting me."

"The girl said you were going to pay him."

"*She* wanted me to pay him, but Vaughn told me he didn't want any money."

"Or maybe he did want money and you wouldn't pay him so—"

"O'Connor, you know the rumors about me. They're true. I'm rich. I could easily afford to pay Vaughn off if I had to."

O'Connor didn't like that, although Frank wasn't sure which part he didn't like. Frank knew perfectly well that a lot of the cops he used to work with were jealous of his good fortune, which was only natural. Others had just never cared for him in the first place and the money was another good excuse to hate him. O'Connor probably fell into one of those two groups, maybe both. Even if he didn't, he was enjoying tormenting Frank over this murder.

"Look," Frank tried in a reasonable tone, "I tried to convince everyone to close off the building in case the killer was still here hiding somewhere. They wouldn't listen to me, so he's probably long gone, but it's worth searching the place, just to be sure. He'll be covered with blood and—"

"I don't need to search anything. I've got you right here, Malloy, and it's going to give me great pleasure to take you in. Every time a cop goes bad, it makes it harder on the rest of us."

"You're making a terrible mistake, O'Connor," Frank tried. "And even worse, you're letting the real killer get away."

"That's my problem, isn't it, Malloy?"

"And you're making it my problem by arresting me."

O'Connor just shook his head, that same smirk on his broad, Irish face as he called for the uniformed coppers to take him away.

"At least let me telephone my wife and tell her what happened," Frank said as they were taking him out.

By now all the actors and stagehands had arrived for the matinee performance that would not take place. They lined the hallway, watching in silence as the cops took Frank out. He scanned the crowd for a friendly face but saw none. Eliza Grimes would be off somewhere, either being questioned by police or comforted by friends.

There was no help for it now. He'd be booked and mugged and charged and jailed. At some point along the way, he'd manage to let Sarah know what was happening so she could bail him out. Until then, Frank resigned himself to being thoroughly humiliated by his former colleagues who would take great delight in his downfall.

. . .

THE SHRILL RING OF THE TELEPHONE STARTLED SARAH as it always did when it stabbed through the peaceful harmony of her home. Not that she'd been enjoying much harmony this afternoon while she waited for Malloy to return home with Vaughn's signature. He should have been back hours ago, but this telephone call was undoubtedly him.

Just as she stepped into the entry hall to answer it, the front door opened and Maeve came in. "I think the workmen are finally finished, but you won't believe what they tried to convince me they still had to do," she told Sarah in the silence between the telephone's ringing.

Sarah held up her hand to signal Maeve that her tale would have to wait on more pressing matters. The telephone rang again, and Sarah picked it up and lifted the earphone to her ear.

The response to her greeting was a lot of noise she couldn't identify and finally Malloy's voice. She couldn't make out much of what he said except for the word *arrested*.

"Arrested? Who's been arrested?" she shouted into the mouthpiece.

"I have," he said, his outrage apparent even over the bad connection.

"For what?"

"Murder. Vaughn was murdered. Come to the Tombs and bail me out."

"Murder?" she cried, but the line went dead, and when Sarah frantically clicked the switch hook, the operator came on to tell her the party on the other end had hung up and did she want to try to call them back.

"No, thank you." Calling back to the Tombs would be a futile effort. She'd have to go herself to find out what on earth had happened.

"What is it?" Maeve demanded. She'd been removing her hat and gloves but had stopped with one glove off when she heard Sarah say the word *murder.*

"Malloy has been arrested for murder." Even saying the words aloud couldn't make them make sense.

"Murder? Who is he supposed to have murdered?"

"Parnell Vaughn, apparently."

"Dear heaven," Maeve said.

"Yes, and I need to go down to the Tombs and bail him out, he said."

"Well, you aren't going alone. I'll telephone Gino and have him meet us there. And I'll telephone Mr. Nicholson."

"Who is Mr. Nicholson?"

"The best defense attorney in the city. He's the one I hired for . . . Oh, it doesn't matter. Go get changed while I contact them. Where is Mrs. Malloy?" she added, glancing at the door that led to Frank's mother's suite of rooms.

"She's upstairs with the children. I'll tell her what happened."

By the time Sarah had changed into street clothes and informed her shocked mother-in-law, out of earshot of Catherine and sight line of Malloy's son, Brian, that Malloy had been arrested, Maeve had contacted Malloy's partner, Gino Donatelli, and the attorney she thought so highly of.

"They'll both meet us at the Tombs," Maeve reported when Sarah made her way downstairs again. They hurried out into the early fall evening.

"Let's take the El," Sarah said. "It will be faster than a cab."

"What do you suppose happened?" Maeve asked as they walked toward the Seventh Avenue elevated train.

"I have no idea. Malloy was supposed to meet Mr. Vaughn at the theater today around noon to get his signature. I was worried when he didn't return home and didn't telephone, of course. We were planning to have a bit of a celebration this evening and tell Catherine the news, and he was supposed to come straight back after he saw Mr. Vaughn."

"How was this Vaughn killed?"

"I don't know. I'm afraid I don't know anything. All he was able to say was he'd been arrested for killing Vaughn and I should come bail him out."

"It's all some kind of terrible mistake, I'm sure," Maeve said, but Sarah heard the question in her voice.

"We might have been afraid Vaughn wouldn't sign the papers, but Malloy certainly wouldn't have done anything drastic."

"I don't think he did, but they must have some reason for arresting him. Maybe there was some kind of accident."

Sarah didn't want to think of any reason whatsoever that Malloy might be responsible for the death of Parnell Vaughn. "There's no point in our arguing about it. We'll find out soon enough."

. . .

"**M**R. MALLOY?"

Frank had been expecting to see Sarah. Instead his visitor was a corpulent gentleman in a very loud checked suit. "Yes."

"I'm Henry Nicholson, Esquire, at your service. Your wife has retained my services to expedite your release from incarceration."

Of all the strange things that had happened to him today, this was probably the strangest. "My wife?" How would Sarah know someone like him?

"Well, more accurately, your, uh, employee, Miss Smith."

"Maeve hired you?"

"Yes. Her grandfather and I were old friends, so naturally, when she telephoned and told me of your predicament . . ."

Frank might not have recognized Nicholson's face, but he certainly knew his reputation. "You're a criminal defense attorney." And one universally hated by policemen and prosecutors alike.

"I most certainly am, and you are charged with a criminal offense, so I expect we shall soon be good friends."

"Where's my wife?"

"I sent her and Miss Smith and your associate, Mr. Donatelli, to my office, which is just across the street. The Tombs is no place for ladies, as I'm sure you will agree. Now, I have convinced the judge to see us and set your bail immediately. There is no reason why a gentleman of your stature and reputation should be held in jail another moment."

What he meant, of course, was a gentleman of Frank's wealth. But Frank had no desire to spend another moment in the stinking, moldy, filthy New York House of Detention, known affectionately as the Tombs, so he didn't argue. "All right."

"Then let's go see the judge, shall we?"

Nicholson's office was as ordinary as Frank's detective agency office, and Frank understood exactly why. Nicholson's clients came from all income levels, and he didn't want the poorest to think they couldn't afford him, nor did he want the wealthy to think he wasted their fees on unnecessary luxury. Nicholson probably lived in a splendid mansion, but his office gave the impression he was barely scraping by.

"Sarah," Frank said with relief when he found her in Nicholson's inner office. He hated the fear he saw in her eyes and cursed himself for being the cause of it.

"Are you all right? What on earth happened?" she asked.

"I'm fine, although I'm furious."

Maeve and Gino were there, too, and they had to fuss over him for a minute or two as well. Then Nicholson came in and invited them all to sit down and tell him what he needed to know.

Between them, Frank and Sarah explained the situation with Catherine and why Parnell Vaughn was considered to be her legal father and why they were trying to get Vaughn to relinquish his parental rights. Then the rest of them fell silent as Frank described arriving at the theater today to find Vaughn dead and having Eliza Grimes accuse him.

"Why would she say she saw you do it when she didn't?" Sarah asked.

"I'm not sure she did. That's just what O'Connor said. Detectives often lie to get a suspect to confess," Frank explained.

"Or maybe she did say it," Maeve said. "People often lie when it suits their interest."

Nicholas cast her an admiring glance. "Miss Smith is right, of course. We have to consider that Miss Grimes may have killed Vaughn herself in a fit of jealous rage, so naturally, she would want to implicate someone else. She did arrive at a suspiciously opportune moment."

"She knew I was coming to see Vaughn, which is why she came just then," Frank reminded him. "And she didn't have any blood on her."

"She would naturally have cleaned herself up before appearing in public," Nicholson said with a small smile.

"Is it possible she did it?" Gino asked. Frank's handsome, young partner was obviously furious at this injustice to the man who had taught him everything he knew about solving crimes. "How was he killed?"

"Beaten, like Nicholson said," Frank said.

"Could a woman have done that?" Sarah asked.

"A woman *has* done it," Frank reminded her. "Remember, Emma Hardy used to hit Vaughn, and he never fought back."

"No gentleman should," Nicholson said. "Unless his life is endangered, of course. It appears Vaughn made a costly miscalculation there."

"But could a woman have killed him?" Maeve pressed them. "Did the killer use a weapon?"

"Yes," Nicholson said. "It appears Mr. Vaughn was beaten about the head and shoulders with a quail."

"A *quail*?" Frank echoed incredulously. "You mean a bird?"

"Not a real quail. A brass one, it seems. Satisfyingly solid."

"Oh yes, I saw them on the shelf over the sofa in his dressing room when we went to see him in the play," Sarah said. "It was a family of quail, three different sizes. They were . . . lovely."

Nicholson smiled benignly. "Apparently, the largest member of the family fit nicely into the killer's hand and was heavy enough to crack Vaughn's skull."

"He was hit more than once," Frank added. "There was blood splashed on the walls and ceiling."

"Mr. Malloy, please," Nicholson cautioned. "There are ladies present."

Frank glanced at Sarah, who bit back a grin. "My wife is a nurse, Mr. Nicholson, and Maeve is . . . well, Maeve is Maeve."

"And I'm terribly shocked, of course," Maeve assured them. "But I'm also wondering how blood would get on the ceiling."

"I'll explain it to you later," Frank said quickly.

"Yes, the important thing now is getting this ridiculous murder charge dropped so the police can find the real killer," Sarah said.

But when she looked at Frank expectantly, he couldn't quite meet her eye.

"That's what we need to discuss, Mrs. Malloy," Nicholson said. "You see, the police aren't interested in finding the real killer because they have Mr. Malloy."

"But surely—"

"Don't worry," Nicholson said quickly. "He will never go

to trial. We can make sure that his case is pigeonholed, and no one will ever bother him again."

"Oh yes, I know all about that," Sarah said in disgust. "The right person is bribed and the charges go into a file and are never seen again, but that's for people who are guilty and know they'll be found guilty if they're tried. Malloy is innocent."

"Of course he is, as anyone who knows him will believe," Nicholson said without as much conviction as Frank would have liked.

Sarah's blue eyes fairly sparked. "But lots of people *don't* know him, and they'll think he's a murderer."

"She's right," Frank said when Nicholson would have argued. "It's fine for some gangster to get his case lost. What does he care about his reputation? If anything, it would get him more respect, but not with the people in society."

"Are you in society now, Mr. Malloy?" Nicholson asked with some interest.

"No, but my in-laws are and Catherine might want to be someday. She shouldn't have some terrible story about a murder that was covered up in her background."

"He's right," Sarah said, "and Malloy needs to have his name cleared as well. He doesn't deserve to have this shadow over him for the rest of his life."

Nicholson frowned. "Are you suggesting we go to trial? Because I can assure you there's a good chance a jury might decide Mr. Malloy had a very good reason for wanting this Parnell Vaughn out of the way. You practically admitted it with the story you told me."

"He won't need to go to trial," Gino said, "because we're

going to find the real killer. Then the police can drop the charges against Mr. Malloy, and everyone will know he's innocent."

Nicholson looked far from impressed. "And how will you do that, young man?"

Gino gave him a dazzling smile. "We're detectives, Mr. Nicholson."

THE FOUR OF THEM TOOK THE EL BACK UP SEVENTH Avenue and then walked the rest of the way to the house on Bank Street. By the time they got home, night had fallen and the children were ready for bed. Sarah took Malloy upstairs to tuck them in. Kissing Catherine good night was bittersweet when she thought of all the tragedy that had surrounded the poor, innocent child since the moment of her birth. Now another person from her past was dead, and the man who most wanted to keep her safe was accused of his murder. At least she was blissfully unaware of it, for the moment, at any rate.

Their cook, Velvet, had kept their supper warm, and they gathered around the dining room table to eat it. Hattie, their maid, served them and then withdrew, granting them privacy. Malloy's mother had joined them, even though she had eaten earlier with the children, and they quickly brought her up to date.

"What's this 'pigeonholing' you keep talking about?" she asked when he'd finished.

Malloy frowned. "When somebody is charged with a crime and gets out on bail, if you pay off the right people, your case gets put into a pigeonhole-shaped filing case and just never removed."

"Does this happen a lot?" she asked.

"Unfortunately, yes, so there are a lot of criminals walking around loose. I guess some people will think I'm one of them."

"How do you get yourself into these messes, Francis?"

"I wish I knew, Ma."

"He doesn't do it on purpose," Sarah said.

"Are you sure?" Mother Malloy asked.

"It doesn't matter," Malloy said impatiently. "What matters is getting out of it. I might be free, but I also want to clear my name, and that means finding the real killer."

"What do we know about Vaughn?" Gino asked. "Is there any reason somebody might want to kill him?"

"Somebody besides Francis, you mean?" Mother Malloy asked.

Everyone pretended she hadn't spoken.

"I don't think we know much about him at all, do we?" Sarah asked.

"We know he was married to Catherine's mother and that she used to hit him," Maeve reminded them. "And he used to drink. A lot."

"He'd apparently stopped drinking, at least," Sarah said.

"That's what I'd heard," Malloy said. "This theatrical agent told me he'd met a woman who straightened him out, and he'd gotten a part in a play with Mrs. Hawkes."

"Mrs. Hawkes?" Mother Malloy said, obviously impressed.

"He played her romantic lead," Sarah told her. "Even though he's at least ten years younger than she is."

"Fifteen," Malloy said. "And we know that Eliza was jealous."

"Jealous of what?" Maeve asked.

Sarah turned to Malloy, and she saw the same uncertainty in his eyes. "I'm not sure."

"Neither am I," Malloy said.

"Why aren't you sure?" Maeve asked.

Sarah shook her head. "When we went to Mr. Vaughn's dressing room the other night, Eliza was there, too. We explained the situation, and he agreed to sign the papers."

"After Eliza insisted we pay him a thousand dollars for his trouble," Malloy added.

Maeve grinned. "So she's jealous *and* greedy."

Sarah pursed her lips to keep from smiling. "And then Mrs. Hawkes came in. She was summoning Mr. Vaughn to join her and some other people for supper, but Malloy and I both noticed how unhappy that made Eliza."

"Wasn't she invited?" Gino asked.

"Vaughn said she was," Sarah recalled, "but she said she wouldn't go because Mrs. Hawkes would just insult her all evening. Then she left in a huff."

"And you thought she was jealous?" Maeve asked.

"She clearly was," Sarah said, "and we thought she was jealous of Mr. Vaughn's success, because she's just starting out in her career."

"But maybe she was jealous of Mrs. Hawkes's interest in Vaughn," Malloy said.

"Does she have an interest in him?" Maeve asked. "Besides the fact that he's acting in her play, I mean."

"I'm not sure," Sarah said, trying to remember. "She was obviously fond of him and wanted his company at supper."

"But isn't she married?" Mother Malloy said. "Her husband is her manager."

"How do you know that, Ma?" Malloy asked with great interest.

She gave him the look that had sent him running for cover when he was a boy. "Everybody knows that."

Maeve gave a suspicious little cough that might have been a snort of laughter.

"She could still be more than merely fond of Mr. Vaughn," Sarah said. "Enough to make Eliza jealous, at least."

"And actresses do have a reputation for infidelity," Gino said.

"Not Mrs. Hawkes," Mother Malloy decreed righteously.

No one was going to contradict her.

"But Eliza is young and probably not very sure of Mr. Vaughn's affections," Sarah said. "She might have imagined Mrs. Hawkes was a threat to her romantically."

Gino nodded eagerly. "Which could mean she was the one who attacked Vaughn, and that would explain why she lied about seeing Mr. Malloy kill him."

"Or maybe she never said that at all," Maeve reminded him. "We need to find out for sure."

"And how do we do that?" Gino asked.

"We ask her," Maeve said. "If she said it, there's no reason for her to deny it."

"And if she didn't say it, she'll be surprised," Malloy said.

"We just need to figure out who besides Eliza could give us more information about Vaughn and who else might have killed him."

"Wait a minute," Sarah said. "When we were in Mr. Nicholson's office, he told us the killer used the brass quail to beat Mr. Vaughn, and Malloy mentioned how much blood there was."

"That's right," Maeve said. "You were going to explain how it got on the ceiling."

"The ceiling?" Mrs. Malloy echoed in horror.

"Ma, maybe you should go upstairs," Malloy said.

"Don't be silly. How did blood get on the ceiling?" she demanded.

Malloy sighed with a long-suffering air. "The killer must have grabbed the quail—"

"It was a figurine," Sarah added to Mrs. Malloy. "Made of brass. It was sitting on a shelf in his dressing room."

Frank cleared his throat to draw their attention back. "He was hit many times with the quail."

"His killer was very angry," Maeve observed.

"Yes, I think we can assume that. And with each blow, the killer would bring his arm back and then strike again." He demonstrated the action. "The quail would get blood on it and the blood would fly off and get on the walls and the ceiling."

"And the killer," Sarah said. "The killer would have been covered with blood!"

"He would've had some on him, at least."

"Why didn't anybody see him, then?" Maeve asked.

"Probably because he had plenty of time to get away while the police were busy arresting me," Malloy said in disgust.

"And if it was one of the actors, their dressing rooms were right there," Sarah said. "All they had to do was change their clothes and wash their face and hands."

"But they'd still have to get rid of their bloody clothes," Maeve said.

"That's probably not too difficult," Malloy said. "If it was someone from outside, they could just put on an overcoat and leave. Or an actor could hide the bloody clothes in a dressing room or someplace else in the theater. It's a big place."

"So it could be anyone," Maeve said with a sigh.

"Which is why we need to find out who might have had a reason to be very angry with Parnell Vaughn," Malloy said.

"I'm sure everyone in the play knows all the gossip about everyone else in the play," Sarah said. "We just need to start asking questions."

"And how do we do that?" Maeve asked.

"What do you mean, 'we'? Aren't you already busy with the clinic and the children?" Malloy asked her.

"The clinic is almost done. I can take a few hours here and there."

"And I'll watch the children," Mother Malloy said. "I'm already taking them both to school and bringing them home since Maeve is at the clinic so much." Mother Malloy usually dropped Catherine off at Miss Spence's School for Girls on her way to spend the day with Brian at the New York Institution for the Deaf and Dumb, where she volunteered in exchange for the opportunity to learn American Sign Language along with her grandson.

"I can go to the theater and see who's willing to talk," Gino said.

"And I can go with you," Sarah said. "Some of the women might not want to talk freely to a man."

"Are you serious?" Maeve said slyly. "They'll all want to talk to Gino."

This pleased Gino immensely. "Are you jealous?"

Maeve smiled sweetly. "Yes, and if you aren't careful, I'll hit you over the head." She was instantly contrite when everyone groaned. "Oh, I'm sorry! That was a terrible thing to say."

"Yes, it was," Gino said gravely, although the sparkle in his dark eyes gave him away. "Somebody will need to talk to Mrs. Hawkes, too."

"I'll do that," Malloy said.

Everyone gaped at him.

"Why not? I'm the most logical one."

"Won't she be afraid of you? She'll think you killed Mr. Vaughn," Sarah reminded him.

"She will until I explain that I'm investigating because I didn't kill him and want to find out who did."

"All right, but she's bound to be a little nervous just the same," Sarah said. "I should go with you at least."

"I was hoping you would."

"So how do you propose we find her?"

Malloy frowned. "What do you mean?"

"I mean, surely they'll close the play with their leading man dead, so we won't find her at the theater."

"They won't close the show," Mother Malloy said. "Haven't you ever heard the old saying 'The show must go on'?"

Everyone stared at her in surprise.

"Where did you hear that?" Malloy asked his mother.

"Everybody knows that. They'll have an understudy for this Vaughn person, and he'll take over the role."

"Ma, you seem to know an awful lot about the theater for somebody who has never been to a play."

"What makes you think I've never been to a play?" she asked, obviously insulted. "I wasn't your mother my whole life."

Maeve coughed again, but she managed to say, "Magazines often have stories about famous actors and actresses."

Sarah couldn't imagine her staid mother-in-law being interested in reading about such people, but apparently, she was mistaken. "Is there anything else we should know about theater people, Mother Malloy?"

"They're very superstitious, or so I'm told. Do you know they won't say the word *Macbeth* inside a theater? It's very bad luck."

"Did Mrs. Ellsworth tell you that?" Malloy asked. Their neighbor was a fount of information about superstitions.

"Everyone knows that," she said haughtily. "They call it *the Scottish play* instead. And don't forget everybody there is an actor, Francis, which means they'll probably be good liars, too. Keep that in mind."

Malloy promised he would.

3

For all her willingness to help, Maeve had to check in with the workers at the clinic the next morning because they were still managing to not be quite finished. Malloy and Sarah headed to the theater, and Gino was to meet them there. Mrs. Malloy had warned them—from her vast knowledge that included information about Mrs. Hawkes's legendary eyes—that actors were not early risers, so they made a late start.

Even still, they found the theater locked up tight. Their determined knocking on the side door finally produced a lone guard who had apparently been sleeping somewhere in the building. His graying hair stood up at odd angles, and he was scratching his scrawny chest.

"Don't nobody get here until late afternoon when there's no matinee," he informed them.

"We really wanted to see Mrs. Hawkes," Sarah told him, figuring a respectable matron was the only one of the three of them who stood any chance at all of getting information from him. Malloy, for all his fine clothes, was still Irish, and Gino was still Italian.

"She'll be here later, ma'am," the guard said.

"But she's an old friend of mine," Sarah lied. "We went to school together, and I wanted to express my condolences to her over Mr. Vaughn's death. Could you possibly tell me where she lives?"

The guard had obviously succumbed to Sarah's charm and decided to be helpful in his own way. "She don't live nowhere that I know of. She's on tour most of the time."

"But she must be staying somewhere in the city while she's in this play," Sarah tried.

The guard blinked several times while he considered this. "Oh yeah. They stay in the Marquis Hotel, her and Mr. Hawkes. He's her manager, you know."

"Oh yes, I did know that." Which she certainly would if she were good friends with Mrs. Hawkes. "She's so fortunate to have him looking after her affairs."

The guard's eyes widened in shock. "I don't think he knows about her affairs, ma'am, and it's best you don't mention them to him."

Sarah just gaped at him for a moment, but Malloy immediately came to her rescue. "We certainly won't. Thanks for your help."

He took her arm and steered her back to the sidewalk with Gino in their wake.

"Did that guard say what I think he said?" Sarah asked.

Gino, she was annoyed to see, was grinning like a loon while Malloy was biting back a smile.

"Looks like Mrs. Malloy's magazines don't tell her everything about Mrs. Hawkes," Gino said.

"So maybe Eliza did have a reason to be jealous," Malloy said.

Sarah tried to recall exactly how Mrs. Hawkes had acted when she came to Vaughn's dressing room that night they were there. She and Vaughn had obviously been on good terms, which Sarah would expect since they were performing together. "Did you think Mrs. Hawkes was annoyed to find us in Mr. Vaughn's dressing room the other night?"

"What do you mean?" Malloy asked as they strolled through Union Square on their way to the Marquis Hotel.

"I'm trying to remember exactly what she said. She accused Mr. Vaughn of having a party, I think."

"A party?" Gino echoed. "Because the two of you were there?"

"And Eliza. It's a small room, so maybe it looked like a crowd to her," Sarah said.

"Or maybe she just didn't like Vaughn having visitors at all," Malloy said.

"Is it possible that she and Vaughn were lovers? Do you really think Eliza had a reason to be jealous?" Sarah asked.

Neither man replied, but Gino was grinning again.

The hotel was in the next block beyond the park. "Oh, it's a pun," Gino said when they saw the sign.

"What do you mean?" Sarah asked.

"When he said 'marquis,' I thought he meant a 'marquee' like a theater has."

Sarah smiled at the play on words. "I suppose with so many theaters in this neighborhood, they cater primarily to actors."

"I'd guess not many actors could afford to stay in a nice place like this, though," Malloy said. "When I called on Vaughn and Emma Hardy last year, they were staying in a real dump."

"I remember," Gino said. "I wonder where he was staying now."

"Maybe Mrs. Hawkes can tell us," Malloy said.

"Do you want me to wait for you?" Gino asked. "I don't expect you want me to go inside."

"No, we don't want her to think we're having a party," Malloy said, making Sarah smile.

"Why don't you go down to the clinic and meet Maeve," Sarah said. "The two of you can go to the theater later when she's able to get away."

Gino obviously thought this was a splendid idea, but he glanced at Malloy for approval.

"Just be sure you actually go to the theater," was all Malloy said. When Gino was gone, he turned to Sarah. "You don't need to encourage them, you know."

"I feel sorry for Gino. She's going to lead him a merry chase."

"Oh, I think he enjoys it. So what do we want to ask Mrs. Hawkes?"

They discussed that topic for a few minutes and then entered the hotel's lobby. A uniformed doorman held the door for them and seemed particularly interested in the fact that they didn't have any luggage. Malloy ignored his raised eyebrows and escorted Sarah to the front desk.

The lobby was small but spotlessly clean and comfortably furnished. No one sat on any of the sofas and chairs scattered around the room. Maybe it was still too early for actors to be up and about. The wall behind the front desk counter was pigeonholed for mail and room keys. Sarah tried not to think about pigeonholes.

An officious clerk looked down his nose at them, which was amazing considering how short he was.

"We're here to see Mrs. Hawkes," Malloy said. "She's expecting us."

This took the clerk aback, but he rallied quickly. "She didn't mention that she was expecting visitors."

"Poor Adelia is probably too distraught to do much of anything," Sarah said. "That's why we're here. You know what happened, of course."

"Of course. Everyone's talking about it. Poor Mr. Vaughn."

"Did he live here, too?" Malloy asked.

"Oh no. He lived in a rooming house, I believe. Most of the actors do. Only the stars are guests here. And producers, of course, like Mr. Hawkes."

"Perhaps you could announce us," Sarah said.

He frowned, uncertain, and then Malloy slipped him a silver dollar and he became much less uncertain. "Whom should I say is calling?"

"Mr. and Mrs. Malloy," she said. "Remind her we met in Mr. Vaughn's dressing room a few days ago."

While the clerk made the call, Sarah exchanged an anxious look with Malloy. Of course, if they were refused, they could always seek her out later at the theater. But to their relief the clerk informed them Mrs. Hawkes would see them.

Armed with the number of her suite, they allowed the elevator operator to take them up.

Mrs. Hawkes herself answered their knock, a slightly puzzled smile on her famous face. "Pardon my dishabille. I wasn't expecting visitors," she said as she admitted them. Indeed, she wore a frothy peignoir over an even frothier nightdress, although Sarah noted her hair was perfectly styled. Her face, however, without the heavy stage makeup, showed every one of her years.

"Thank you for seeing us," Sarah said. "You remember my husband?"

"Of course." She produced a lace-edged handkerchief from somewhere and dabbed at her eyes, although Sarah saw no trace of moisture there nor any indications she'd been weeping at all. "You were visiting poor, dear Parnell the other night. Please, come in."

The suite was large and comfortably furnished with over-stuffed sofas and chairs and tables set conveniently nearby. The room overlooked the street, although they were high enough that the noise of the traffic was muffled.

"I ordered some coffee sent up," she said. "Please, have a seat."

They sat on the sofa and Mrs. Hawkes positioned herself in a chair opposite them, taking a moment to arrange herself to best advantage. Was she always so conscious of how she appeared? And was that a consequence of her profession or just natural vanity? And how odd that she felt so comfortable entertaining a strange man in her nightclothes.

"We were very sorry to hear about Mr. Vaughn," Sarah said, "and we wanted to express our condolences."

"But I should be offering mine to you," she protested. "You were old friends, were you not?"

Sarah didn't dare glance at Malloy. "Not exactly. We only knew Mr. Vaughn slightly."

Mrs. Hawkes frowned, obviously confused. "But he introduced you as old friends."

"He was being kind," Sarah said. "In fact, we only knew Mr. Vaughn through his late wife."

"Emma?" Mrs. Hawkes said. "How on earth did you know *her*?"

How to explain their unique relationship with Emma Hardy? "Through her daughter, whom we are trying to adopt."

Did Mrs. Hawkes know about Catherine? And Vaughn's part in their little domestic drama? Apparently so, judging from the rapid change in her expression from confusion to horror. Then her horrified glance shifted to Malloy. "You're the one who killed Parnell!"

Malloy held up his hand as if to stop the accusation from reaching him, but Sarah quickly explained before he could say anything that might alarm their hostess.

"That's just it, Mrs. Hawkes. My husband did *not* kill Mr. Vaughn, and in order to clear his name, we must find out who did."

Mrs. Hawkes did not appear to be convinced. "How dare you come here!"

"We dared because we thought you would be as anxious as we are to find the real killer."

"Of course I am," she said, indignant but more confused than ever. "But Eliza said . . ."

"What exactly did Eliza say?" Malloy asked, speaking for the first time.

Mrs. Hawkes had to consider this for a moment. "I . . . I don't really know. I'd just arrived at the theater, and Baxter, my husband, was tending to her. She was hysterical, you see, after finding poor, dear Parnell . . ."

"I'm the one who found him, Mrs. Hawkes," Malloy said. "I tried to stop her from going into the room."

"But what were you doing at the theater in the first place?" Mrs. Hawkes demanded, as if that were the most outrageous detail of the whole story.

"Vaughn had agreed to sign some papers that would allow us to adopt Catherine. I'd brought them with me."

"So that's it. My husband said something about papers, but I had no idea what he meant. And Eliza said Parnell had refused to sign them, so you killed him."

"Mr. Vaughn was only too happy to sign the papers," Sarah said. "He isn't Catherine's father, so he had no interest in her."

Mrs. Hawkes frowned. "If he isn't her father, why was he involved at all?"

Sarah quickly explained the legalities.

"Good heavens, how unreasonable," Mrs. Hawkes concluded.

"Yes, but the law is the law, and Mr. Vaughn wanted to be relieved of his responsibility for the child," Malloy said.

"Or so you say," Mrs. Hawkes said. "How can I trust your word?"

"Eliza was there when he agreed," Sarah said. "In fact, she insisted that we pay Mr. Vaughn a consideration to reward him for agreeing. It was only later, after Mr. Vaughn was dead, that she claimed he had changed his mind, and of course we would have had no way of knowing whether he did or not since he was already dead when my husband found him."

"But Eliza said he'd changed his mind," Mrs. Hawkes reminded them. "And that you were so angry, you killed him."

"You're an intelligent woman, Mrs. Hawkes," Malloy said. "Is it likely Vaughn would refuse to give up his claim to a child who isn't even his in exchange for a thousand dollars?"

Mrs. Hawkes's expressive face expressed surprise. "A thousand dollars! Is that what the little baggage asked for?"

"Yes," Malloy said with some satisfaction.

"Good heavens. You're absolutely right, Mr. Malloy. That does seem unlikely."

"And my husband is very anxious to discover who really did kill Mr. Vaughn, which is not the usual behavior of a murderer, Mrs. Hawkes."

Mrs. Hawkes raised her hands in surrender. "I don't have a lot of experience with murders, but I have to assume you are correct. You have convinced me, Mrs. Malloy, and I am also eager to find out who killed poor, dear Parnell. He was a fine actor, and I'd become quite fond of him. He had a brilliant future ahead of him, and now he's lost to us. The person responsible must be caught and punished."

"Then you'll help us?" Sarah asked.

"How on earth can I help you? In fact, how on earth can you hope to succeed in such a quest?"

"I'm a private investigator, Mrs. Hawkes. I've brought many a killer to justice, and I'm especially motivated to find this particular one."

She blinked in surprise. "Of course you are. But what is it you think I can tell you?"

Before they could reply, someone knocked on the door.

"That will be the coffee I ordered." Mrs. Hawkes went off to answer the door, and a waiter brought in a large tray with a coffeepot, cups and saucers, and a plate of petit fours.

The waiter poured their coffee and served them before he left.

When they were alone again, Mrs. Hawkes said, "Oh dear, where were we?"

"You asked how you could help us, so first of all, did Vaughn have any enemies or anyone who might wish him harm?"

Mrs. Hawkes frowned as she considered the question. "I can't imagine anyone wanting to actually kill him, but there is a . . . a situation in which someone might be angry with him."

Malloy actually leaned forward a bit and Sarah felt her own interest piquing. "Anything at all might help," he said.

"Well, you see, a couple of years ago a group of . . . of theater owners and managers formed a syndicate. They control most of the theaters in the country and they arrange the national tours. Actors can only perform in the plays the

Syndicate assigns to them. They no longer have control over their own careers."

"Why would this have put Mr. Vaughn in danger?" Sarah asked.

"Oh, of course. You wouldn't know. Because, you see, I have refused to join the Syndicate. My husband and I still control my bookings and my tours. They have tried for years to coerce me into joining them, but I have resisted. They are especially angry at me because I have recruited other actors to the cause."

"Mr. Vaughn being one of them," Sarah guessed.

"Exactly. He had been a part of it and then left the Syndicate to perform with me. He brought Eliza Grimes and several others with him. I know the Syndicate saw it as a mutiny, and they must have been furious at poor, dear Parnell."

"Furious enough to kill him?" Malloy asked doubtfully.

"I . . . Well, you'll have to ask them, I suppose. Businessmen do get upset when things don't go their way."

"How many actors have, like you, declined to join this syndicate?" Malloy asked.

Mrs. Hawkes stiffened at this. Or perhaps she was just straightening her spine with pride. "Alas, not many have held out against their power. They control virtually all the large cities and most of the smaller theaters along the touring routes. I was extremely fortunate to find a theater willing to book me here in New York. Others who were not so fortunate have been forced to join the Syndicate in desperation."

Sarah glanced at Malloy and saw he was as unimpressed

as she was with the idea that this syndicate might be responsible for Vaughn's death. If anyone was a threat to the Syndicate's success, it was Mrs. Hawkes herself, not her hapless leading man. "I got the feeling that Eliza Grimes was jealous of Mr. Vaughn," she tried.

Mrs. Hawkes stiffened again, and this time Sarah was sure she had taken offense for some reason. "What do you mean?"

What *did* she mean? And what kind of jealousy would have offended Mrs. Hawkes? "Of his success, perhaps," she tried.

That seemed to placate her. "Of course she was jealous of his success. She was jealous of everyone in the play. That's the problem with young actresses. They think they deserve instant fame. They have no idea how hard one must work to reach my level in this business."

"Was she jealous of your attentions to Mr. Vaughn?" Malloy asked mildly.

"My attentions?" Mrs. Hawkes asked with some outrage. "I'm sure I don't know what you're talking about."

Malloy shrugged. "I noticed you invited him to join you for supper after the play. She wasn't happy about that."

"She wasn't happy about anything Parnell did, I'm sure. She probably wanted him all to herself, but an actor must mingle and meet the right people if he hopes to have a career. I was only being kind by including him in my party, and he appreciated it, I know."

Sarah wanted to ask another question about her relationship with Vaughn, but the sound of a key in the lock distracted them all, and the door opened to reveal a portly middle-aged man in a rumpled suit. He wore a derby that he'd pushed to the back of his head to reveal a receding hairline. His luxuriant mustache twitched at the sight of the Malloys.

"I didn't know you were expecting anyone, Adelia," he said, making his disapproval obvious.

"This is Mr. and Mrs. Malloy, Baxter. They—"

"I know who they are," he said, coldly furious. "He's the one who killed Parnell."

Malloy was on his feet, and Sarah rose, too, but Mrs. Hawkes remained seated, serenely confident. "Don't be ridiculous, Baxter. If he'd killed Parnell, do you think he'd be here?"

"I don't have any idea where he'd be, but Eliza said he killed Parnell."

"And Eliza is a fool, as we both know. Quite the contrary, my darling. Mr. Malloy not only did not kill Parnell, but he is determined to find out who did, in order to stop these ugly accusations."

"And exactly how do you know he didn't kill him?" Hawkes asked.

Mrs. Hawkes smiled sweetly. "Because he told me."

Hawkes glared at his wife, but she didn't seem to notice. Or maybe she just didn't care.

"I was explaining to the Malloys that someone from the Syndicate might have killed Parnell as a way of discouraging other actors from leaving them."

Hawkes made a rude noise. "If the Syndicate killed every actor who tried to leave them, they wouldn't be able to fill a single touring company."

"Then maybe you can think of someone who really did want to kill Vaughn," Malloy said.

Hawkes pulled off his derby and ran his fingers through his thinning hair. "Is that coffee?"

"Yes, darling. Sit down and I'll pour you some and you can stop upsetting our guests," Mrs. Hawkes said.

Hawkes dropped his hat on a table by the door and joined them, taking the chair next to his wife's, leaving Sarah and Malloy to resume their seats. When his wife had handed him a cup of coffee, Hawkes took a long sip, then looked up expectantly.

"We were actually just discussing how Miss Grimes was jealous of Mr. Parnell," Sarah said.

Hawkes's gaze went immediately to his wife, who returned it with total innocence. "They think she was jealous of my attentions to poor, dear Parnell. I explained how important it was to have friends in this business."

"Friends, yes," Hawkes said, his gaze never wavering from hers. "You were a good friend to poor, dear Parnell."

Sarah blinked at the sarcasm in his voice, but Mrs. Hawkes didn't seem to notice he was not sincere.

"I hope so. He needed friends, and Eliza was simply using him to her own ends. She never would have been cast as my understudy without his recommendation."

"We were lucky to get her," Hawkes said impatiently. "Not many actresses want to go against the Syndicate."

"Tell me, Mr. Hawkes," Sarah said, hoping to forestall an argument, "did Miss Grimes actually say she'd seen my husband kill Mr. Vaughn?"

Hawkes had turned to her with obvious reluctance and

it took him a moment to focus on her question. "That she'd *seen* him do it? No, I don't think so. I mean, if she had, she would've tried to stop it, wouldn't she? Or at least screamed and . . ."

"And distracted the killer," Malloy said helpfully. "Killing Vaughn wasn't the work of a moment, I'm afraid. He was struck several times, so if she'd seen the killer—"

Mrs. Hawkes gave a tiny cry of distress and pressed her handkerchief to her lips.

"Have a care, man," Hawkes cried, jumping up, but he didn't go to her. He went to a sideboard where several liquor bottles sat and poured a splash of amber liquid into one of a collection of glasses and carried it back to her. "Drink this."

She did, gulping it like medicine. "Oh dear," she said weakly. "How dreadful."

"I'm sorry, Mrs. Hawkes. I didn't mean to upset you," Malloy said, although Sarah didn't think he was all that sorry.

"What do you want from us?" Hawkes asked, angry now. "We don't know who killed Vaughn. Eliza said it was you, and that makes the most sense to me. Anybody else who was at the theater that day was depending on him. He was the leading man, and without him, we're going to have a hard time keeping the play going. The only person there that day who had anything to gain from his death was you."

"But since I didn't kill him," Malloy said, "you're wrong about no one else having anything to gain. We just need to figure out what it was."

"Then you'll have to do it without our help, Mr. Malloy. I'm going to have to ask you both to leave."

. . .

"If I could talk Mr. Malloy into buying a motor-car, I would have picked you up in it," Gino told Maeve as they stood side by side on the crowded Third Avenue elevated train, watching the second-floor windows of the buildings that lined the street go flashing by. Gino usually liked being close to Maeve but not with so many other people around.

"What makes you think he'd let you drive his motorcar?"

"Because he'll be afraid to drive it himself. That's the only reason he hasn't bought one yet."

"So you think he'd buy one just so you could drive it?"

"I'd be like a chauffeur. Rich men always have one."

"I thought you were his partner? Wouldn't being a chauffeur be a demotion?"

Gino sighed. Why did she always ruin his pipe dreams? "Maybe I'll buy my own, then."

She just rolled her eyes at that, knowing as well as he did that he'd never be able to afford it. "Who do you think we'll see at the theater?"

"I don't know. Lots of pretty actresses, I hope."

As he'd expected, she reacted to that, but of course not as he'd hoped. She laughed. "And maybe some handsome actors, too. Maybe I'll have to use my charm."

"I'd like to see that," he said quite honestly.

From the look she gave him, he wasn't going to see it ever.

At long last, they reached their stop on 14th Street and spilled out of the crowded car with several dozen other travelers. From there, they only had to descend the stairs to street level and walk a few blocks to the theater. The streets were much busier now than they had been that morning. Old Mrs. Malloy was right, actors were late risers, and they seemed to enjoy promenading on the streets around Union Square, especially along Broadway.

"It's funny how you can tell who the actors are," he remarked as they passed a cluster of handsome, fashionably dressed young people who had stopped on the sidewalk to chat.

"Yes, they love the attention and they do anything to attract it," Maeve observed. He thought she disapproved, but he didn't mention it.

"I wonder what makes some people want to go on the stage," Gino said. "I'd be afraid of making a fool of myself."

"I imagine it's the same thing that makes them parade up and down Broadway in their fancy clothes. They like having people look at them, even if they're being foolish."

That didn't make any sense, but Gino let it pass. "I'm thinking you should talk to the men and I should talk to the women."

Maeve frowned. "Are you going to tell them we're detectives?"

What was wrong with that? "Of course. Why wouldn't we?"

"Because you're not with the police anymore, and they don't have to talk to you. In any case, I'm pretty sure they won't want to say anything to get one of their fellow actors in trouble."

"Then how do you propose we get them to talk to us?"

She smiled sweetly. "By telling them we're reporters. They'll want to see their names in the newspapers. That's good publicity."

Why hadn't he thought of that? "I suppose that could work."

"That and your charm." Maeve grinned as they turned into the alley beside the theater.

Gino tried the side door before knocking and found it open, so he escorted Maeve inside. Gino noticed a chair where someone could sit and watch to make sure no one unauthorized could enter, but it was empty. The groggy guard they had met earlier was nowhere in sight.

"Quick, before somebody sees us," he said, taking Maeve's arm and hurrying her along the deserted corridor. It led to a longer hallway lined with doors. Some were open and some were closed.

A young man stood in the corridor, staring at one of the doors. He turned in surprise when he heard them. "Hello, who are you?"

Maeve gave him a smile Gino would have killed to get. "I'm Mazie Dobbins from the *World*. Could I ask you a few questions about . . . ?" Her gaze drifted to the door at which he had been staring. It bore a star and the name of the dead man. ". . . poor Mr. Vaughn?"

"Oh, I probably shouldn't say anything," he said, although from the way he was smiling back at Maeve, he'd be telling her everything she wanted to know in about three seconds.

Gino didn't wait around to find out. He casually walked on down the hallway, glancing at each door he passed. He saw Mrs. Hawkes's name on one of them along with another star. Some of the doors had no star, just a name, and others had neither. Behind one he heard female voices, so he stopped and knocked.

The voices instantly fell silent and the door opened just a crack. A female eye peered out at him. "Who are you?"

Gino gave her the smile he hoped would one day soften Maeve's heart. "I'm Dave Shook from the *World*. I was wondering if you could tell me something about the actor who got killed, Parnell Vaughn?"

The door opened a little wider and the female inside took a good long look at him. "Hey, girls, give this one a gander." Without another word, she grabbed his lapel and pulled him inside, slamming the door behind him.

"WHAT WOULD YOU LIKE TO KNOW, MISS DOBBINS?" THE young man asked Maeve as Gino sauntered away. He was handsome in a showy way, with brown wavy hair brushed back off his broad forehead and a smile that showed strong white teeth. His suit was cheap and flashy, but his voice was like liquid gold. He must be quite impressive on stage.

"Just whatever you can tell me about Mr. Vaughn. We're doing a story about him, so we need to know as much as possible. Is there someplace we could talk?"

"My dressing room is just down here," he said, gesturing.

"Oh, I thought this might be your dressing room now." She nodded at Vaughn's door.

"Not yet, although . . . Well, I was Parnell's understudy, so I suppose it will be mine now." The thought apparently pleased him. So much for grieving poor Parnell.

Maeve followed him down the hall. "How fortunate for you."

"Yes, it's an ill wind that doesn't blow somebody some good, although I would never have wished anything bad for poor Parnell. He was always, uh, a good friend to me."

He opened one of the unmarked doors and motioned her inside. The tiny room was filled almost to bursting with a rack of clothing on one wall and a dressing table and chair on another. The third wall held a small dresser and another straight-backed chair. He pulled it over closer to the dressing table for her, although that meant moving it only a few inches. "Please make yourself comfortable, Miss Dobbins."

Maeve sat, noticing he'd closed the door behind them. She wasn't too worried, though. She figured Gino would come running if she screamed. She reached into her purse and pulled out the small notebook and pencil she used to make herself notes about the clinic construction project. When she'd opened it to a blank page, she looked up expectantly. "I don't think I caught your name, Mr. . . ."

"Winters. Armistead Winters."

"What a wonderful name for an actor, Mr. Winters."

"Why, thank you," he said, as if he'd invented it himself, which he probably had.

"Had you known Mr. Vaughn very long, Mr. Winters?"

He frowned a little, as if trying to remember. "A little over a year, I'd say. We met when we were on tour together."

"Were you his understudy then, too?"

Winters laughed at that, a theatrical chuckle that seemed a bit forced. "Not at all. I was the leading man in that show, and Parnell . . . Well, let's just say he wasn't quite himself at that time."

"Was this shortly after his wife died?"

Winters's well-shaped eyebrows rose at that. "Why yes, it was. Emma, I think her name was. She was a real harridan by all accounts."

"You didn't know her?"

"No, not at all, but the theater world is small. I knew her by reputation."

"And Mr. Vaughn was still drinking at this time, I assume."

This time Winters frowned. "You seem to know a lot about him, Miss Dobbins."

Maeve didn't even blink. "I told you, we're doing a story about him. I've been gathering information. He had somewhat of a reputation himself, it seems."

"Yes, he did. Don't misunderstand. Vaughn was a fine actor, even when he was drunk. Some said he was actually better when he was drunk. But no one was ever going to cast him in a leading role if he wasn't dependable."

"And then he met Miss Grimes."

For just an instant, anger flashed in his dark eyes, but he recovered quickly. "Yes, he met Miss Grimes."

"Was she on the same tour with you, by any chance?"

"As a matter of fact, she was," Winters admitted with apparent reluctance.

"How fortunate that Mr. Vaughn met her when he did. I understand she was a very good influence on him."

"Yes, quite good. She . . . she brought out the best in him, it seems."

"And he stopped drinking," she prodded.

"Oh yes. Eliza will not be denied when she sets her mind on something, and she had set her mind on Parnell Vaughn." This fact did not seem to please Mr. Winters.

"It sounds as if you know her well, Mr. Winters."

"Yes, we were . . . great friends."

"And more than friends, I would guess," Maeve said.

Armistead Winters's expression hardened. "You're very perceptive, Miss Dobbins. Yes, we were more than friends. Before she met Parnell Vaughn, Eliza and I were to be married."

4

A CHORUS OF FEMININE SQUEALS GREETED GINO'S ENtrance into the crowded dressing room. Two other girls jumped up from where the three had apparently been sitting in a semicircle in front of a long shelf that must have served as a shared dressing table to the minor female cast members. The three females surrounded him.

"He's a fine-looking creature," the blonde observed. They were all prettier than most any girl in the city except perhaps Maeve, and their appreciative expressions were more than gratifying.

"Thank you, miss," he managed as they turned him around so they could each get a good look at him from all angles.

"And who might you be?" the brunette who had opened the door asked.

"I told you, I'm from the *World*."

"That's right, Davy something. He's a reporter, girls."

"And who are you?" he asked, well aware he was grinning foolishly but unable to help himself. If only Maeve could see this.

"I'm Sally," the brunette said.

"I'm Verena," the blonde said.

"I'm interested," the strawberry blonde said.

That made them all laugh, but Verena said, "Put a sock in it, Angie. This here fella is gonna make us famous!"

"I'll certainly try," Gino said. "That is, if you've got anything good to tell me about Parnell Vaughn."

That made them all giggle with delight.

"Oh, we do, don't we, girls?" Sally asked. "Pull up a chair for Davy here."

Someone dragged another chair into their circle and Sally pushed Gino down onto it. He pulled out the small notebook and the pencil he used to take notes when questioning a suspect. He supposed what a real reporter did wasn't so very different.

When the girls were settled around him, he took a minute to look each of them full in the face, mostly so he would be able to recall every detail of this delicious moment when he told Maeve about it later. "So what do you have to tell me?"

This set them to giggling again, but soon they sobered enough to speak. After exchanging a few meaningful glances, they silently appointed Sally as the spokesperson. "It's not really so much about Mr. Vaughn. It's more about Mrs. Hawkes."

"Something about Mrs. Hawkes that got Vaughn murdered?" Gino asked in surprise.

The girls grinned knowingly. "She and Vaughn were lovers."

Gino managed to hide his surprise. Hadn't old Mrs. Malloy already told them how respectable Mrs. Hawkes was? "But Vaughn was engaged to Miss Grimes, wasn't he? And Mrs. Hawkes is married to . . . to Mr. Hawkes."

But they weren't the least bit chastened. "That's what makes it such a scandal, silly," Sally said. "You can't say you heard it from us, though."

"Oh no," Verena confirmed. "Mr. Hawkes would send us packing, but we didn't give you our real names anyway."

"Except for Angie. So you can't say where you heard it, but it's true," Sally said.

"Are you saying Vaughn and Mrs. Hawkes were in love?"

For some reason this made them laugh uproariously.

"Oh no," Sally assured him when she could speak again. "Not at all! It's just that Mrs. Hawkes, well, she . . . uh, she, uh . . ."

"She likes a little diddle before every show," Angie said.

Gino blinked in surprise. "A . . . *diddle?*"

"You know. A roll in the hay."

"Before *every* show?" Gino asked just to make sure he understood.

"Six days a week and twice on Wednesday and Saturday," Verena gleefully confirmed.

"But . . . but, she's married," Gino tried.

"Mr. Hawkes?" Sally said dismissively. "He's too old to perform like that."

"That's why Mrs. Hawkes likes them young," Verena added.

"Oh yes," Angie said. "She'd just love you, Davy."

Gino ignored that. "So Vaughn and Mrs. Hawkes . . ."

"Yes, he serviced her," Sally said.

"And he must've done a good job of it because she made him the leading man," Angie said.

Gino felt a little dizzy at his good fortune. Suddenly, Eliza Grimes had a very good reason to be jealous of Mrs. Hawkes, and a very good reason for being angry with Parnell Vaughn. "So that was his reward for . . . for . . ."

"Oh no," Sally said, laughing at him again. "That was his *duty* as the leading man."

"And heaven help him if he didn't, uh, fulfill it," Angie added, making them all burst into laughter again.

"And you can't say you heard it from us," Verena reminded him.

"And we didn't give you our real names," Sally added. "Except Angie."

But Gino wasn't finished. "What about Mr. Hawkes? Did he know about this?"

"Of course he did," Sally said. "How could he not?"

"Although nobody ever mentioned it to him, not if they valued their job," Verena said.

"Sometimes," Angie said with a wicked grin, "he had to wait outside her dressing room for them to finish up."

How humiliating that must have been, to have to stand there while his wife and her lover were . . . Good heavens, if that wouldn't drive a man to murder, what would?

. . .

"You were engaged to Eliza Grimes?" Maeve asked, somehow managing not to let her excitement show.

Winters smiled sadly. "Well, perhaps not formally, but we were in love, or at least I was, and I had every reason to believe she shared my feelings. We had discussed marriage, which is very important because marriage can interfere with an actress's career in ways it doesn't with an actor."

"In what way is that, Mr. Winters?"

"Children, Miss Dobbins. A man can simply go off on tour and leave his children, but a woman cannot."

Oh yes, Maeve should have figured that out herself. She imagined actors would simply desert their wives and children if they interfered with a career. Men did that all the time, actor or not. Actresses, on the other hand, would most likely be dropped from the company when a pregnancy got too noticeable. "I see. And what had you and Miss Grimes decided about her career?"

"Why, that we would not have children, Miss Dobbins. Unlike many young women who try their hand at acting, Eliza was serious about her career. She and I agreed that we would support each other instead of having her sacrifice her dreams for my sake."

"How very noble of you, Mr. Winters," Maeve said with apparent sincerity, although she seriously doubted he was.

He smiled modestly. "Why should the world be cheated out of Eliza's talents by my selfishness? Besides, I don't need a child to create my legacy."

"Oh no," Maeve said, managing just the right amount of admiration. "Your work will do that for you."

"How kind of you to say that."

"But you must have been devastated when Eliza, uh, turned to Mr. Vaughn."

Anger once again flared in his dark eyes, but his voice never faltered. "It was painful, of course, but perhaps not as bad as you imagine. You see, Eliza is young and not very sophisticated. She doesn't understand . . . Well, she doesn't understand many things."

"Such as?"

"Drunks, for one thing."

"And what doesn't she understand about drunks?"

"That they never really reform. Vaughn may have made an effort for her sake in the beginning—and been rewarded with a leading role—but it was never going to last."

"Mr. Hawkes must have thought it would if he cast him in this play."

"Hawkes does whatever his wife wants, and she wanted Vaughn in this play. Don't ask me why. Oh, I know what the critics say about him now, but they weren't very kind to him when he was staggering onto the stage and throwing up behind the potted ferns."

"Oh dear."

"Yes, oh dear. I've covered for him many a time when we were on tour. But Eliza thought she could save him. I couldn't compete with that, Miss Dobbins. No man can. So Eliza set her heart on saving Vaughn, and I decided to wait her out."

"Wait her out?"

"I told you, I knew his reformation would never last. Sooner or later, Vaughn would start drinking again, and when he did, Eliza would be heartbroken, and I would be standing by to comfort her."

"And that's why you're in this play?"

He smiled, grimly this time. "I'm in this play because Baxter Hawkes was desperate for actors. His wife refuses to join the theater syndicate—do you know what that is?"

"I . . . I've heard of it," Maeve lied.

"Adelia Hawkes is a fool. She thinks she can continue to control her own career even when the Syndicate runs all the good theaters from here to California. She'll never be able to hold out against them, of course, and in the meantime, she and Baxter have to beg actors to reject the Syndicate and join their company."

"And they begged you?"

"They didn't have to," Winters said bitterly. "Baxter lured Vaughn by offering him the male lead opposite Mrs. Hawkes, which no Syndicate company would do, so Eliza came along because she wanted to stay with Vaughn."

"And you?"

"I'm the most pathetic one of all, Miss Dobbins. I came because I wanted to stay close to Eliza."

"And you stayed on, even after Eliza and Mr. Vaughn became engaged."

Winters gave a snort of laughter. "Who told you they're engaged?"

Maeve didn't have to pretend to be confused. "I . . . Someone told me."

"Eliza, probably. She'd started telling people that, but

Vaughn never acknowledged it. Oh, he didn't deny it. He didn't want to embarrass her, but he had no intention of ever marrying her. I think Emma Hardy cured him of marriage."

"Emma Hardy? Was she his wife?"

"Yes, and . . . Well, I'm done speaking ill of the dead. None of them can hurt me, in any case."

"And Eliza must be sorely in need of your comfort now," Maeve guessed, although she couldn't help thinking what a poor basis for renewed romance that would be.

Winters must have shared her concern. "Yes, she must be," he said with no enthusiasm whatsoever.

GINO KNEW HE WAS BLUSHING WHEN THE GIRLS SAW HIM out of their dressing room. They were laughing and teasing and running their hands over parts of him that no female had touched since he'd been in diapers.

"Come back and see us, Davy!"

"You can be my leading man anytime you like!"

"And once on Wednesday would be enough for me!"

He should really go find Maeve, but he let the girls tease him for another minute before turning away, and when he did, he saw her farther down the hall, watching the little scene with apparent interest. The girls were still laughing and teasing and reminding him they'd be happy to welcome him back anytime as he made his way to Maeve. For some reason, he couldn't seem to wipe the smile off his face.

Maeve, on the other hand, was not smiling at all, and that made Gino even happier.

"What happened to your actor friend?" he asked, glancing around.

"He got to crying about losing his good friend Parnell Vaughn and I had to leave him. What have you been up to?"

"Oh, uh . . ." He glanced back down the hall to see the girls going back into their dressing room. "Asking questions."

"Is that what they call it now?"

But nothing could wipe the smile off his face, because he was thinking, no, now they call it *diddling*. Of course, he couldn't say that to Maeve. In fact, he couldn't in all decency tell her any of what he'd found out about Vaughn and Mrs. Hawkes. "Did your actor tell you anything interesting?"

Before she could answer, a portly, middle-aged man came bustling down the corridor. "Who are you and what are you doing here?"

Maeve brightened immediately. "I'm Mazie Dobbins from the *World* and—"

"I already told your people I wouldn't buy any more advertising from them if they sent more reporters, now get out of here or I'll have your jobs! Both of you, out! Right now!"

They could have argued, but that wasn't likely to get them in to see any of the other actors, so Gino took Maeve's arm and hustled her back down the corridor toward the alley door.

"Who do you suppose that is?" Maeve whispered.

"I don't know, but it doesn't matter."

When they reached the door, they found the guard back on duty and looking rather sheepish. "How did you folks get in here? I've been sitting here every minute," he said, glancing nervously back down the hall at the middle-aged man.

Gino didn't bother with a reply. The guard opened the door and saw them out before slamming it closed again. Gino would have bet it was now locked, too.

They paused to catch their breath, then set off toward the sidewalk.

"So what did you find out?" Maeve asked.

"I, uh, I can't tell you."

"What do you mean, you can't tell me?"

The heat in his face had reached his hairline. "I mean . . . I need to tell Mr. Malloy first, to see what he says."

"He'll say to tell me and Mrs. Malloy," Maeve said.

"If he does, he can tell you himself."

"*What?* Gino, you're being much too mysterious!"

"No, I'm not. What did your actor have to say?"

Maeve set her chin. "I'm not going to tell you."

"Why not?"

She looked mad enough to spit. "Just to annoy you."

And she did, all the way to the Malloys' house.

"AND TWICE ON WEDNESDAY AND SATURDAY?" FRANK repeated, not quite sure he'd heard Gino correctly. They were in the butler's pantry, where Gino had drawn him to share his news privately before they joined Maeve and Sarah in the parlor.

"That's what they said. Do you think it's true? Would a woman really demand that? And would her husband tolerate it?"

Frank could only shake his head. "The older I get, the less I'm surprised, but this is pretty strange."

"And if it's true, it gives Eliza a reason to be jealous and it gives Mr. Hawkes a reason to want Vaughn dead."

"If he minded, and from what those girls said, he might not have."

"How could he not? She's his wife."

Frank scratched his head. "I'd be pretty mad if it was my wife, but you haven't met them. They're an odd pair."

"They'd have to be. So are we going to tell Maeve and Mrs. Frank?"

"Why wouldn't we?"

Gino's cheeks turned pink. "Because, well, you know . . ."

"It's shocking?"

"Yes!"

"Don't worry. I'll tell them. I want to get a female's perspective on this."

"On whether it could be true, you mean?"

"Yeah, that, too. Come on."

Frank led poor Gino back to the parlor, where the women waited. The parlor windows were open to the late-September breeze, and they sat on the sofas placed in front of the cold fireplace. "Sarah, why don't you start by telling them what we found out from Mr. and Mrs. Hawkes?"

Sarah did, taking a moment to answer Maeve's questions about the theater syndicate.

"The fellow I talked to mentioned it," she said. "I told him I knew what it was, and it explains why . . . Well, I'll wait for my turn."

"That's about all they actually said," Sarah concluded,

"but we got the definite impression that Mr. Hawkes didn't care for Mr. Vaughn and that Mrs. Hawkes wasn't mourning him too much."

"That's very strange," Gino said, earning a curious look from Maeve.

"Maeve, what did you find out?" Frank asked.

"I talked to an actor named Armistead Winters. He plays the brother, or at least he did, and he's Vaughn's understudy, which I gather is a step down for him. He was the leading man when he first met Vaughn on tour."

"When was that?" Sarah asked.

"A year or so ago, he said. After Emma died, at least. He claims he was engaged to Eliza when they both met Vaughn."

"A spurned lover," Sarah said with approval. "That makes him a good suspect."

"He claims he knew Eliza's interest in Vaughn wouldn't last, but it has to have been hard for him to watch."

"Wait a minute," Gino said. "If Eliza threw him over for Vaughn, why is he in the play with them?"

"He said it was because he wanted to be near her when Vaughn threw her over. He was able to get a part pretty easily because Mrs. Hawkes refuses to work for the Syndicate, so they have a hard time finding actors for their plays."

"That doesn't make sense," Gino said.

"Yes, it does," Maeve said. "Mrs. Frank already explained how actors don't want to go against the Syndicate."

"Not that," Gino said. "The part about Winters being in the play with them."

"Why not?" Frank asked.

"Because what man would follow a woman around after she threw him over? Doesn't he have any pride?"

"Maybe he's in love," Maeve said with a smirk.

"Then he's an idiot."

"Men in love often behave like idiots," Sarah said. "Women, too."

Gino had no answer for that.

Maeve grinned. "Did Mr. Malloy give you permission to tell me and Mrs. Frank what you found out?"

Gino didn't actually groan, but he did run a hand over his face and threw Frank a pleading look.

"Gino learned something very interesting about Vaughn and Mrs. Hawkes," Frank said.

"I knew it!" Maeve said. "They were lovers."

Frank and Gino exchanged a glance. "Yes, but not in the usual way."

"I didn't know there was an unusual way," Maeve said.

Gino gave her a pitying glance. "There's a lot of things you don't know."

Frank held up his hands to stop their bickering. "Just listen and then you can decide. It seems that there's a reason Mrs. Hawkes likes her leading men to be young. In addition to being in the play, they are also required to, uh, to *pleasure* her before every performance."

"Does that mean what I think it means?" Maeve asked, wide-eyed.

"I'm sure it does," Sarah said. "*Every* performance?"

"It relaxes her," Gino said grimly.

"Who told you this?" Maeve scoffed. "Those girls?"

"Didn't your actor mention it?" Gino replied. "Even the

guard who answered the door at the theater this morning said something about Mrs. Hawkes's affairs. It must be common knowledge."

Maeve glared at him. "I'm sure Mr. Hawkes doesn't know it."

Gino shrugged. "According to the girls, Mr. Hawkes would wait outside her dressing room until they were finished."

"Could this possibly be true?" Sarah asked in amazement.

Frank shrugged. "Anything is possible, and if it's true, it explains why Eliza was jealous of Mrs. Hawkes and why Mrs. Hawkes didn't want Eliza to join her and Vaughn for supper after the show."

"But if Vaughn was having an affair with Mrs. Hawkes," Maeve said, "why would Eliza keep insisting she was engaged to him?"

"I don't think they were having an affair," Sarah said.

"So you think those girls were lying?" Maeve asked a little triumphantly.

"No, they may well have been telling the truth. In fact, it's such an outlandish story, I can't imagine they could have made it up. Somehow it doesn't sound like a *love* affair, though."

Gino turned to him. "Is this the female perspective you wanted?"

"Yes, it is. Tell us why you don't think it's a love affair, Sarah."

She gave him a wry smile. "All right. Bearing in mind that I've no personal experience with affairs, it is my impression that they begin because two people are infatuated with each other and fall in love."

"But you don't think Mrs. Hawkes and Vaughn were in love?" Maeve asked.

"He didn't seem particularly enamored with her the night we saw them together after the play, but admittedly, that was only for a few moments. But today, Mrs. Hawkes was clearly not deeply mourning him the way you would expect a woman in love to be mourning."

"Or even the way you'd expect somebody to be mourning a friend," Frank added, remembering he'd found that strange at the time.

Sarah nodded. "Also, people engaged in a love affair generally attempt to keep it a secret from their spouses."

"Or fiancées," Gino added.

"Exactly. Yet it appears Mr. Hawkes knew about it, and I can't imagine why he would be as tolerant as people have indicated he was."

"Oh, I see," Maeve said. "For whatever reason he didn't mind his wife and Vaughn . . ." She gestured vaguely.

"Diddling," Gino supplied.

"What?" Maeve asked.

"That's what those girls called it," he replied helpfully.

Maeve did not seem to appreciate his assistance. "But why would a husband allow another man to . . . to . . ."

"Diddle?" Gino offered.

". . . his wife?" Maeve continued valiantly.

"Because," Sarah said, "while he may not have liked it—and I think we can assume from the way he referred to Mr.

Vaughn today when we met with them that he did not like it at all—he tolerated it for some reason."

"Because it relaxed her," Gino said.

"And Mr. Hawkes has to keep his wife happy, since she's the one people come to see," Maeve said finally.

Frank was putting this all together now. "So she needs a man to, uh, relax her before each performance, and she chooses young leading men to, uh . . ."

"Perform the duties," Gino supplied, obviously beginning to enjoy this.

"But Vaughn is no threat to his marriage because Mrs. Hawkes isn't in love with him."

"And she can replace him with the next leading man if necessary," Sarah said.

"That would be your actor, Winters," Gino told Maeve.

"I wonder if he knows," she replied, making Gino grin.

"When I first heard this, I was sure it was a good reason for Mr. Hawkes to kill Vaughn, but now I'm not so sure," Gino said.

"But she is still his wife. It had to have bothered him," Frank said.

"Oh, I'm sure it must have," Sarah said. "Especially if it was common knowledge, as Gino believes. He has his pride even if he had no reason to be jealous."

"And people would be laughing at him behind his back. He had to know that, too," Frank said.

"Then why would he tolerate it?" Maeve asked. "Why didn't he just"—she glanced at Gino—"relax her himself?"

"I'll explain that to you later, dear," Sarah said to Frank's relief. How did they get into these discussions? "The question is, did Eliza know and how did she feel about it?"

"You said she was jealous of Mrs. Hawkes," Maeve said.

"Yes, but that could have just been professional jealousy and a bit of envy for the attention Mr. Vaughn got from her and everyone else because he was the lead actor," Sarah said.

"She must have known, though. You didn't see those girls who were talking to Gino. She would see them every day. They would have been gossiping like magpies and taking great delight in telling her all about it."

"Maeve's right," Gino said. "They would've been only too happy to tell her every detail."

"But wouldn't she have been angry with Mrs. Hawkes?" Maeve asked.

"I'm sure she was, but she couldn't say anything for fear of losing her job," Sarah said. "And she'd certainly be angry at Mr. Vaughn for not resisting Mrs. Hawkes's advances."

"But wouldn't she know he didn't have any choice?" Gino asked.

"Jealousy doesn't tend to be logical, Gino," Sarah said. "She could be equally angry at both of them. And if she killed Mr. Vaughn, she would have had a good reason to accuse Malloy of doing it."

"How on earth are we going to figure this out?" Gino asked. "None of these people are going to tell the truth, and all they have to do is not say anything at all."

"Don't worry," Frank said, as much for his own benefit as for Gino's. "Somebody saw something. Or heard something."

"But how will we find out?" Maeve asked. "Gino and I

got thrown out of the theater, and they aren't going to be too happy to see Mr. Malloy back there anytime soon because they think he's the killer."

"Gino, do you think those girls would talk to you again if you saw them outside the theater?" Frank asked.

Gino perked right up. "Sure."

"And how about your actor friend, Maeve?"

Not to be outdone, Maeve said, "Of course."

"Then Gino and I will go see the play tonight. Gino will bring the girls flowers and take them to supper." Gino was very happy now. "And I'll follow your actor friend to find out where he's living so we can arrange for Maeve to encounter him someplace tomorrow."

"And I'll see if I can encounter Mrs. Hawkes," Sarah said.

"Do you think she'd see you again?"

"Probably not, but I've been thinking. My mother telephoned earlier, as soon as she heard Mr. Vaughn had been killed. She doesn't know anything about the adoption problems, of course, and the newspapers didn't have Malloy's name yet, so she doesn't know he's suspected, but I'm sure she will be happy to help when she understands the situation."

Frank couldn't help groaning. "Your father made me swear I wouldn't let her get involved in another case."

"Even he will want to get involved when he knows what's at stake," Sarah said. "At any rate, I think Mrs. Hawkes will be happy to see Mrs. Felix Decker when she finds out the wealthy Mrs. Decker might be interested in investing in her theater troupe."

"Your father would never . . ." Frank began before he noticed Sarah's expression. "Oh, I see. It's just an excuse."

"Yes, and of course I'll go with her."

"What if she throws you both out?" Maeve asked, much too delighted by this whole idea.

"I don't think she'll throw us out. I think she'll be happy to talk about Vaughn's murder when her husband isn't around to stop her. I also think Mr. Hawkes might talk to you if you're a little forceful with him."

Frank frowned. "Why should he?"

"Either because he wants you to find out who killed Vaughn or because he did it and he wants to make sure to mislead you into thinking someone else did it. Either way, he'll see the wisdom, I think. Besides, refusing to help find the killer makes him look guilty, which you will certainly point out to him."

"And someone needs to talk to Eliza," Maeve said.

Frank frowned. "I think we should leave her for last. She's the one who accused me, so she isn't going to want to see me or Sarah."

"I'm sure Gino would love to charm her," Maeve said with a grin. "But I could probably get her to talk if I pretend to be a reporter."

"Let's see what Winters says about her first. I also don't think we should talk to her at the theater where Winters or somebody else might try to interrupt, so we'll need to find out where she lives so we can catch her alone."

Maeve cast Gino a meaningful glance. "I'm sure those girls could tell you where she lives."

Gino grinned back. "I'm sure they could."

. . .

Aʀᴍᴇᴅ ᴡɪᴛʜ ᴛʜʀᴇᴇ ʙᴏᴜǫᴜᴇᴛs, Gɪɴᴏ ᴡᴀɪᴛᴇᴅ ᴏᴜᴛ ɪɴ the alley beside the theater with all the other stage-door johnnies hoping to escort one of the actresses to a late supper and an even later assignation. Gino's hopes were even higher, although Frank doubted all three girls would accept his invitation to supper.

Meanwhile, Frank waited in the shadows with his hat pulled low, hoping to escape recognition if someone who had met him walked by. Gino had already left with one of the girls on his arm when Frank saw the actor who had taken Parnell Vaughn's place come out. Frank had half expected him to be with Mrs. Hawkes and whoever else accompanied her to supper, so he was surprised to see him with Eliza Grimes instead.

He shouldn't have been surprised, though. If Winters and Eliza really had been engaged or at least involved when they first met Vaughn, she might naturally turn to Winters now, since he was obviously still in love with her and would welcome her back.

Frank had also been surprised to see Eliza on stage so soon after Vaughn's death, but apparently, his mother was right about theater people: The show must go on. Eliza had looked a bit strained during the play, but he doubted anyone who didn't know her circumstances would have noticed, and her part was small enough that even a poor performance wouldn't have mattered much. Now she made no attempt to hide her grief. She clung to Winters's arm and kept her gaze lowered, carefully avoiding any attention that might come her way from the men who remained in the alley with their bouquets and high hopes.

Frank waited until they had reached the end of the alley and turned onto the sidewalk before following them. At the next corner, they turned down a side street, heading toward the blocks of rooming houses and cheap hotels where the actors lived when they were in the city. A block later they stopped outside a small café and had a discussion Frank was too far away to overhear. Apparently, Winters wanted to go in but Eliza was shaking her head. Finally, he gave up trying to convince her, and they walked on another block to a row of older houses where lights burned brightly in most of the windows in spite of the late hour.

Winters and Eliza stopped in front of one of the houses and had another discussion. Eliza shook her head *no* several times, and Winters finally seemed to accept her decision. He walked her to the front door and left her there with a chaste kiss on her forehead.

Frank wondered how strict these rooming houses were about renting to unmarried couples. Most rooming houses catered to only one gender or the other for fear of gaining a reputation as a house of ill repute. Actors and actresses had a reputation for loose morals, though. Did that carry over to the people who served them as well? Frank didn't particularly care about their morality, but he'd like to know if Eliza and Vaughn had been living together. He'd make sure Maeve found out.

When Eliza was safely inside, Winters left, sauntering back down the sidewalk the way he had come. Maybe he was going to join Mrs. Hawkes and her party for supper after all or maybe he was just going to his own room somewhere else. Unfortunately, Frank had been loitering while he watched the couple and now had no time to look as if he had a purpose for standing in the middle of the sidewalk. He started walking in the opposite direction from Winters, and Winters gave him a curious glance as they passed, but Frank simply nodded and kept going. When he reached the next corner, he turned and walked until he was just out of sight, then quickly looked back to see where Winters was heading.

But he had disappeared.

What? He'd hardly had time to reach the other corner, much less walk far enough to be out of sight. Frank walked quickly back, scanning the street but seeing no sign of him. He glanced at Eliza's rooming house as he passed but saw no sign that Winters had gone back there. Had he entered one of the other houses? Frank was looking up at the next one, trying to see any signs of activity within when something struck his shoulder and sent him plummeting facefirst onto the sidewalk.

5

Gino left the theater alley with only Verena on his arm, but he was still the envy of most of the other swells standing around, trying to catch the eye of a pretty young actress. Sally and Angie had accepted his flowers, but they had already promised their company to other fellows, so Miss Verena Rose had him all to herself. She suggested a Chinese restaurant a few blocks down Broadway, so they went there.

Gino was well aware of the interested glances they were getting from the after-theater crowd. Verena still had on her stage makeup and her blond hair was done up in an enormous Gibson girl bouffant. He only wished Maeve was there to be jealous.

He waited until the waiter had taken their order before getting down to business. He was still trying to decide what to ask her when she said, "I didn't see anything in the *World* about what the girls and me told you."

"The *World* isn't the kind of paper to publish sensational stuff like that," Gino said.

Verena gave an unladylike snort. "Since when?"

"Well, they wanted more information before they published it," he tried.

"Ah, so that's what brought you back. What other information do you need, because I'm not sure what else I can tell you. They do close the door before they go at it."

Gino felt the heat rising in his cheeks and knew from Verena's wicked grin that he'd turned red. He couldn't let his personal humiliation stand in the way of getting the information he needed, though. "You said Mr. Hawkes, uh, knew what was going on with Vaughn and his wife."

"Everybody knows. She's got a reputation all over the country, at least with show people."

But not with her fans, if Mrs. Malloy was any measure. "So Eliza Grimes knew, too?"

Verena laughed at that, and it wasn't a nice laugh. "You're wondering because she claimed she was engaged to Parnell."

"Wasn't she?"

"Who knows? She kept saying they were going to get married, but I never heard him say it, not once."

"He didn't deny it, though, did he?"

Verena frowned as if trying to remember. "No, he didn't, but that doesn't mean anything. He was the kind of man who'd avoid a fight anytime he could, even if it was other people doing the fighting."

"You mean he'd walk away?"

"No, I mean he'd try to settle the people down. He didn't like shouting or arguing. Sometimes he'd agree with somebody just to keep the peace. I think that's one reason Mrs. Hawkes liked him so much. He'd do whatever she wanted—and I don't just mean the diddling—to avoid an argument."

"I guess he didn't argue with Mr. Hawkes, either."

"And not with Eliza, even though that girl could get a rise out of Saint Peter himself. So Parnell wasn't going to tell people they weren't engaged, because there was nothing more likely to set her off."

"Not even diddling with Mrs. Hawkes?"

Verena shrugged. "That was different."

"How was that different?" he asked in amazement.

"Oh, I'm sure she didn't like it, but Parnell told her he didn't like it either. And it's not as if he was in love with Mrs. Hawkes or anything."

Was it possible to have that much congress with a woman and not have feelings for her? Gino would probably never know. "It must have been embarrassing for Mr. Hawkes, too."

Verena just shook her head. "He's used to it by now, I'm sure. It's been going on for years with all her leading men. Saves him a lot of trouble, too. She's testy when she doesn't get what she wants."

Luckily, the waiter brought their food just then, so Gino didn't have to think of something to say to that. Gino had ordered a bottle of wine to go with their dinner, and Verena seemed very pleased. He asked her about herself and found out her mother had been a chorus girl in her youth. Verena wanted to be a serious actress, though, so she had taken a part in this play because the Syndicate wanted her only for singing and dancing. She thought the Syndicate would take her more seriously in the future if she had some acting experience.

"Who do you think killed Vaughn?" Gino asked later as they were walking back to her rooming house. The streets were still busy, although the huge theater crowds had dispersed to their various suppers and parties. The electric streetlights in this neighborhood made it easy to navigate even this late at night.

Verena considered his question. "I don't know. If it was anybody else in the cast, I could probably guess two or three people, but Parnell? He was just so sweet and nice to everybody."

"There must be some gossip backstage, though. What are other people saying?"

"They think it was that Irish fellow who came to see him. That's what Eliza said, and who else could it be?"

But Gino knew it wasn't the Irish fellow. "What about that actor who got his part in the play?"

Verena laughed at that. "Nobody would kill for a part in this play."

"Why not? And wasn't that Winters fellow engaged to Eliza Grimes himself? That would give him another reason not to like Vaughn."

"Oh, you have been busy if you found that out," Verena said, impressed. "I can't imagine anybody committing murder for Eliza Grimes, but there's no accounting for taste, I guess."

"So you think he might've wanted to get Vaughn out of the way so he could be the leading man and get Eliza back?"

"And have the privilege of servicing Mrs. Hawkes into the bargain?" Verena scoffed. "I'm sorry, my dear boy, but I'm afraid a man faced with all that would be more likely to commit suicide than murder."

FRANK THREW UP HIS HANDS TO KEEP HIS FACE FROM hitting the concrete, but the flash of pain and the shock of the attack still stunned him. He managed to roll, expecting a kick, but none came, and when he was faceup, he saw his attacker standing over him with arms akimbo. His face was in shadow with the streetlight behind him.

"Who are you and why are you following me?"

Frank recognized the voice. He'd heard a lot of it during the play that evening. He pushed himself up to a sitting position. "Frank Malloy, private investigator. I'm trying to find out who killed Parnell Vaughn."

Winters muttered something that might have been a curse. "Do you think I did it?"

"I thought you might know something," Frank said, deciding discretion was the better part of valor.

"Then why didn't you just ask me?"

"I was going to, but I needed to find out where you live so I could call on you tomorrow."

"You could've come to the theater."

"No, I couldn't. Would you give me a hand?" Frank reached up, and Winters took his hand and helped him to his feet. His palms stung and were probably bleeding, but he couldn't see well in the shadows. He gingerly reached for a handkerchief, hoping he wouldn't get blood on his coat, and wiped his hands just in case. He didn't want to explain to Sarah how he happened to be bleeding.

"Why couldn't you come to the theater?" Winters asked.

"Because people there think I'm the one who killed Vaughn."

Winters leaned in to get a better view of Frank's face in the darkness. "You're that swell who came to see Parnell."

"That's right, the one Eliza said killed him, but I didn't. I just found him when he was already dead. But now I have to find out who really killed him in order to clear my name."

Winters gave an exasperated sigh. "I'm sorry I knocked you down, but I thought you might be trying to rob me or something."

"No harm done. Say, can I buy you supper and find out what you know about Vaughn? I saw you trying to convince Miss Grimes to stop and eat on your way home, so you must be hungry."

Winters had to think it over for a minute, but then he said, "I suppose that would be all right. I don't think I can help you, though. I have no idea who killed him."

Winters led Frank back to the café where he'd stopped with Eliza earlier. The decor was simple and the fare cheap, and it obviously catered to the poorly paid actors and not the more affluent theatergoers. Frank got some curious glances from the patrons, most of whom probably knew one another well. When they'd given their orders, Frank took advantage of the washroom to clean his scraped hands and brush himself off.

Winters still looked disgruntled when Frank rejoined him at their table.

"I used to be better at following people," Frank said. "I'm getting rusty, I guess."

"Why should I believe you didn't kill Parnell?"

"Because I'm trying to find out who did."

"Maybe you're just trying to figure out who else you can blame it on."

That was fair. "Except I really didn't do it, so that means somebody else really did. Somebody you know. Somebody who might've killed Vaughn because he was engaged to Eliza Grimes or because he had the leading role in this play or because he was involved with Mrs. Hawkes."

"I'm not involved with Mrs. Hawkes," Winters said, although Frank could see the color had drained from his face.

"Aren't you? I thought she liked to get the, uh, attentions of her leading man before every performance."

Now the color flooded back into his face. "Who told you that?"

"Someone who knows. But maybe Mrs. Hawkes hasn't informed you of all your duties yet."

"That's none of your business."

"Not unless it's the reason Parnell Vaughn was killed."

"It wasn't. Nobody cares about that."

"Except maybe Mr. Hawkes."

Winters laughed mirthlessly. "He's the one who arranges it. Mrs. Hawkes likes to pretend her leading men simply find her irresistible."

Frank hoped his astonishment didn't show on his face. This situation was even stranger than he'd thought. Time to change the subject. "What about this theater syndicate? I hear they were angry at Vaughn for joining Mrs. Hawkes's play."

"Maybe they were. Maybe they were mad at me and Eliza and everyone else in the cast, but if they were going to kill anyone, it would be Baxter Hawkes. He's the one keeping this company going in spite of their best efforts to shut us down."

"So nobody would want to kill Mrs. Hawkes?"

Winters snorted. "Not likely. Everybody loves her. She's the one people pay to see, and she's the one the Syndicate really wants to come into their little family so they can make money off her."

"So killing Vaughn wouldn't help them, I guess."

Winters shrugged. "Unless somebody thought killing the leading man would kill the play and Mrs. Hawkes would be so upset she'd decide to join the Syndicate."

"Was that likely?"

"Not at all. She didn't care anything about Parnell. She's had dozens of leading men through the years, and she'll have dozens more before she's through. She'll always find somebody willing to . . ." He sighed and looked away.

Willing to do whatever she wants in exchange for a leading role, Frank thought but he didn't humiliate Winters by saying it.

The waiter brought their food, and neither man had anything to say for a few moments while they started eating. Frank took the opportunity to rack his brain to think of something else Winters might know that could be helpful. Finally, he decided on a tactic. "I guess Eliza is pretty upset about Parnell."

Winters's head jerked up and his eyes narrowed. "Leave her out of this."

"That's hard to do since she's the one who accused me of killing Vaughn."

"She didn't mean that," he admitted reluctantly. "She knows you didn't do it."

This was news. "What makes you say that?"

"She told me."

"Then why didn't she tell the police?"

Winters took a long minute to cut up his steak before he answered. "She will. She was just upset that day. You can't blame her, seeing Parnell like that. It was pretty shocking."

"I know, I saw him, too, but I didn't accuse an innocent person of doing it."

"But she saw you with him. She saw blood on your hands."

"From checking to see if he was alive. The real killer would've been covered with blood."

Winters's head jerked up again. "How do you know that?"

"From experience. From fifteen years of being a cop. From the amount of blood splashed on the walls and ceiling. Tell me, Winters, were you in the theater when it happened?"

"I . . . How should I know? I don't even know when it happened."

"Not very long before I found him, so not very long before Eliza came to the door and started screaming. Were you there then?"

"I . . . Yes. I heard her."

"And where were you when you heard her?"

"In my dressing room, minding my own business."

"How long had you been there?"

"I don't know. Not long."

"Did you see anybody acting suspicious?"

"You mean did I see anybody running out of Parnell's dressing room covered in blood? No, I didn't see that," Winters snarled.

"Not even Eliza?"

Winters threw his fork down. "What are you implying? Eliza couldn't have killed him."

"Are you sure?"

"Of course I'm sure. It must have been a man to overpower him like that."

"He wasn't overpowered. Somebody picked up a brass statue and hit him on the head in anger when he wasn't expecting it. When Vaughn fell down, the person just kept hitting him over and over until he got tired. Or *she* got tired."

"But Parnell would have fought back."

"Would he? I knew his wife, Emma Hardy. She used to beat on him all the time, and he never fought back."

Winters didn't know what to say to that. He just gaped at Frank for a long moment.

"So Eliza could have done it," Frank said.

"But you said she would've been covered with blood and there wasn't a drop on her."

"She could have cleaned herself up."

"How? Where?"

"The theater has washrooms, doesn't it?"

"Of course, but—"

"And she'd have clothes in her dressing room to change into."

"But what would she do with her bloody clothes?"

"Hide them, I'm sure. Whoever killed Vaughn had to

hide their bloody clothes. I've been backstage at the theater. There must be a thousand places to hide things."

"Eliza didn't do it," Winters said. "I know she didn't."

"How do you know?"

Plainly, Winters did not want to answer that question, but he said, "Because she was counting on Vaughn to take her with him when he moved on."

"Moved on? Where was he going?"

"He was going to be a star," Winters said, not bothering to hide his bitterness. "She thought this play was going to make him famous, because everybody would see how good he was. Then when he got a role in a Syndicate play, he would make sure she got a part, too, a good one."

"Could he do that?"

"Probably, but he'd have to get himself a role first. Nobody else thought it was likely to happen, at least not until Parnell had proved he was reliable over the long term, but Eliza was sure it was. She'd pinned all her hopes on him. That's why she insisted they were going to be married, so he couldn't leave her behind."

"And you think that proves she didn't kill him?"

"Of course it does."

He seemed very sure, and Frank couldn't blame him because Winters clearly still loved Eliza and wanted to believe she was innocent. But Frank couldn't help thinking that if Vaughn had somehow found the courage to tell Eliza he wasn't going to marry her or even that he wasn't going to promote her career, she would certainly have been angry enough to kill him. Unfortunately, no one except Vaughn and Eliza would know if that conversation had taken place.

. . .

THE NEXT MORNING, MAEVE WAS VERY DISAPPOINTED to learn Malloy had already questioned Winters. That left her with nothing to do but travel down to the Lower East Side and check on the progress at the clinic.

"Be sure to tell Serafina I'll be down to visit her as soon as I can get away," Sarah told her.

"Her little girl is so beautiful," Maeve said. "All that dark hair. Serafina keeps asking how long she can stay, though."

"We're not going to put her out, if that's what she's worried about. She'll want to start seeing clients again as soon as she goes home, so she should stay a few weeks, at least."

"And of course she's paying, unlike your other patients," Maeve said.

"How many are there now?"

"Four, counting Serafina, and I expect there will be more by today. I don't think they've even hung up the sign yet because the workmen are still dragging their feet about being finished."

"It's just like I imagined," Sarah said, remembering the joy of holding up Serafina's newborn baby for her to see for the very first time.

"Except for the workmen. I need to put the fear of God into them today."

Sarah wished her well, but Maeve didn't get far. A small cluster of reporters had just congregated on the doorstep, asking questions about a dead actor.

Malloy sent them away with a few well-chosen words, informing them that even if he'd killed Parnell Vaughn, which he hadn't, there was no scandal involved—no illicit affairs, no missing funds, no political shenanigans. They were more than disappointed.

When Malloy had effectively cleared Bank Street of the press, Maeve headed downtown, Malloy went to meet Gino at the office of their detective agency, and Sarah went to visit her mother.

Because Sarah had telephoned to let her mother know she was coming, Elizabeth Decker was dressed and anxiously awaiting her daughter's arrival long before she would normally have left her bedroom. In spite of the relatively early hour, Sarah thought she looked beautiful. Her golden hair was growing more silver each year, but her face showed little evidence of the passing of time and her figure was still as slender as a girl's.

She greeted Sarah with a kiss when the maid escorted her into the back parlor. The comfortably furnished room served as the family's sitting room, with the more formal front parlor reserved for guests. "I was planning to visit the children tomorrow, but of course I'm always happy to see you anytime," she said. Sarah's mother adored little Catherine and Malloy's son, Brian, even if neither of them was really her grandchild. "Now, sit down and tell me why you're here. You were so mysterious on the telephone."

"Not mysterious," Sarah said, laughing. "I was merely being discreet. The operators listen in, you know."

"Of course I know, but what could you have to say that they would be interested in?"

"Oh, I imagine they'd be very interested to hear something about Mrs. Adelia Hawkes."

"The actress?" her mother cried in delight. "Don't tell me she's hired Frank to solve Mr. Vaughn's murder."

Sarah could only wish. "Not exactly."

"Then what, exactly?"

"They've accused Malloy of being the killer."

"What?"

"I guess you didn't see the newspapers this morning."

"Certainly not. I had to get up and dressed at this ungodly hour, so I didn't have a chance."

She was wasting her time trying to make Sarah feel guilty. "Malloy was the one who found Mr. Vaughn's body."

"I thought he was killed at the theater."

"He was, and Malloy had gone there to . . . Well, I suppose I need to explain the situation with Catherine." She did, as briefly as she could.

"That's ridiculous! How could anyone refuse to let you and Frank adopt little Catherine?"

"Easily. The law isn't very logical sometimes."

"Most times, I suspect," her mother said. "At any rate, you said Mr. Vaughn had agreed to give up his right to her."

"Yes. His, uh, fiancée had insisted that we pay him for his cooperation, but he had told Malloy privately that he didn't really want any money."

"I should hope not."

"So when Malloy went to the theater to get Mr. Vaughn's signature, he found him dead in his dressing room. Then Mr. Vaughn's fiancée came in and saw him and accused him of being the killer."

"How horrible! No one believed her, I hope."

"Everyone believed her. They arrested Malloy."

"Good heavens! Do we need to do something to get him out of jail?"

"No, we already did, but I'll be sure to let him know that was your first thought."

"Of course it was my first thought. So they realized their mistake?"

"No, or at least not yet. We paid his bail, though, and hired an attorney."

"But surely, he's not going to trial or anything like that."

Sarah sighed. "As you probably know, the justice system can be easily manipulated by people with money."

"What a vulgar term, Sarah, and how would I know how to manipulate the justice system?"

"Because you've been helping Malloy solve crimes for a while. I thought perhaps you'd figured that out by now."

"Oh, you mean things like bribing the police to investigate."

"What a vulgar term, Mother."

Her mother ignored her. "Do you mean you can bribe them *not* to investigate, too?"

"Of course, and you can bribe other people to make sure the case never comes to trial. It's all very neat for people with, uh, the means to pay the bribes."

"And I suppose many criminals have the means."

"Yes, ill-gotten though they may be. So our attorney suggested we do just that, except that Malloy is worried about your reputation."

"My reputation? Why would any of this affect *my* reputation?"

"Well, yours and Father's. Because Malloy would always

have a cloud of suspicion over him if his name is never cleared."

"Oh, I see, and he's our son-in-law."

"We wouldn't want people to snub you because of this."

Her mother smiled slyly. "We might actually become celebrities because of this, but I must say, I'm touched by Frank's concern."

"And of course he's concerned about me and the children as well. Even though I don't care what society might think of me, someday Catherine and Brian might."

"Yes, they'll both want to make good marriages, and some families can be so stuffy about things like murder."

Sarah wasn't sure if she was joking or not and decided not to ask. "So I've come for a favor."

Her mother brightened right up at that. "You need my help?"

"Yes. I need to call on Mrs. Hawkes, but I don't think she'll be willing to see me."

"Does she know you?"

"Yes, we met at the theater the night we met with Mr. Vaughn and asked for his help. Then Malloy and I called on her yesterday to find out what she might know about Mr. Vaughn's death, but her husband threw us out."

"Threw you out? How interesting. I've never been thrown out of anyone's home. How does one do it?"

Sarah managed not to roll her eyes. "He just asked us to leave and we did, but he was very angry, so we probably aren't welcome back."

"I see. And how can I help?"

"You can go to see her and take me with you."

"You know I'd do anything to help you and Frank, but what possible excuse could I have for calling on her?"

"I was thinking you could offer to finance a show for her."

"What a marvelous idea! Is that something people do?"

"I think it's something rich men do for their mistresses when they are actresses, but I'm sure respectable people must do it, too."

"Mrs. Hawkes is rather old and far too respectable to be someone's mistress, isn't she?"

Sarah decided not to disabuse her mother of that opinion. "If you're worried someone might think she was Father's mistress, I don't think you need to be concerned."

"I wouldn't care, of course, but your father would take some ribbing at his club, and he wouldn't like that."

Sarah was sure he wouldn't. "At any rate, you aren't really going to do it. That's just what you're going to say so she'll meet with you."

"I see. And you'll go with me, and you'll end up questioning her or whatever."

"That's right, and of course we won't mention any of this to Father."

"Of course. Unless I decide it really would be a good idea to invest in a show, in which case I'll certainly mention it to him."

"Of course," Sarah said, once again not certain if her mother was serious or not. "So how do you think we should go about this?"

"Let me see, I can write her a note to request a visit, but . . . Now that I think about it, if I were offering to do something for her, she should come to me."

"I didn't want to invade your privacy."

"Pish tosh. If my son-in-law has been falsely accused of murder, my privacy is already invaded. Besides, she can't throw us out if she's here, can she?"

"And her husband can't interrupt us either," Sarah said. "Which is what happened when Malloy and I visited her."

"Good, that's settled, then. Shall I ask her to come this afternoon?"

"That would be lovely. She doesn't have a matinee on Friday and she doesn't have to be at the theater until this evening."

"I can have someone deliver my note so we don't have to worry about the mail. They'll place it right into her hand and wait for her reply."

"Very clever, Mother."

"Not clever, Sarah. It's just common sense. Now, help me write the note so she can't possibly refuse."

The note was the work of a few minutes, owing to her mother's vast experience with saying things she didn't mean to people she barely knew (or didn't know at all), which is mostly what went on in society, according to her mother.

"So you don't think Winters killed Vaughn?" Gino asked.

Frank considered the question carefully. "He didn't act guilty, if that's what you mean, but he's an actor. I have to consider that. In fact, almost everybody who might've killed Vaughn is an actor. Which means I can't trust my usual instincts about whether people are telling the truth or not."

"And neither can I," Gino said.

"Did you find out anything useful from the girl?"

"I think so. She said everybody knew about Mrs. Hawkes and Vaughn. Show people, I mean, from all over the country. She's been doing this for years with all her leading men, and Hawkes knows it and doesn't care."

"That's what people keep saying, but how can he not care?"

"Don't ask me, but maybe he does whatever he has to just to keep her happy. She's the one people pay to see, according to Verena."

"Maybe," Frank said doubtfully. What kind of a man could stand by while his wife . . . ? Well, Frank couldn't, at least.

"Verena also said Eliza didn't care, which I found hard to believe, but she was sure, because everyone knew Vaughn didn't have any real feelings for Mrs. Hawkes. Could that be true? I mean, if they were, well, you know."

"You're too romantic, Gino," Frank said kindly. "Do you think men fall in love just because they've had a woman? That would mean men would fall in love with prostitutes."

"But that's different. I mean, you don't really know a prostitute, do you?"

"Not the way Vaughn knew Mrs. Hawkes, I guess, but sometimes knowing a woman makes you like her less."

Gino grinned at that. "I guess you're right, and maybe that's what happens with Mrs. Hawkes and her leading men. Verena said she can get testy when she doesn't get what she wants. Eliza must not be much better, either. Verena also thinks Eliza and Vaughn weren't really engaged."

"She does? Why?"

"Because she never heard Vaughn say it, and he was . . . Well, we know what kind of a man he was. He wasn't going to get into an argument, was he?"

"I expect Eliza would be a little feisty if she didn't get her way, too."

"Verena said Vaughn would do anything to avoid a fight or even stop other people from arguing. So if Eliza said they were engaged, he'd go along."

"Unless he'd finally decided to tell her he wasn't going to marry her," Frank said.

"In which case, she could very well be the killer."

Frank nodded. "We need to talk to her."

"I don't think she'll have much to say to you."

"Winters claims she knows I didn't kill Vaughn, but I'm not going to take his word for it, so I'm not going to even try to talk to her."

"She knows Mrs. Frank, too."

"So she isn't likely to confide in her, either. That leaves you and Maeve. Was Maeve right? Do you think your charm would work on her?"

Gino frowned. "I don't know. She's still mourning Vaughn, and Winters is trying to win her back, so she's got more than enough men to think about right now. As much as I hate to say it, I have to agree with Maeve. I think she's the one who should see Eliza."

"We can't let Eliza know Maeve works for us, though."

"No, she can pretend to be a reporter, like she said. If Eliza is as ambitious as we think, she might be excited over some publicity."

"You're probably right. So, do you want to go down to

the clinic and rescue the workmen from Maeve's wrath again?"

Gino grinned. "Of course. I'll be happy to deliver her to Eliza's doorstep, now that we know where her doorstep is. What are you going to do?"

"I'm going to see if I can find out more about the Theatrical Syndicate and if anybody connected with it might really have wanted Vaughn dead."

"I'M GOING TO TELL MRS. FRANK TO MAKE MR. MALLOY buy an automobile," Maeve said as they walked toward Eliza Grimes's rooming house.

"Make sure she knows I'm supposed to drive it," Gino said with a grin.

"Who knows? I might learn to drive it myself."

As usual, Gino couldn't tell if she was serious or not. "Females can't drive automobiles."

"Why can't they?"

"Because . . ." For a horrible few seconds, he couldn't think of a single reason. Then he said, "Because they'll never understand how the engine works."

"Do you understand how the engine works?"

Maeve could be so exasperating. "An automobile is a very powerful machine. It might run away with you."

"Like a horse, you mean? Women ride horses all the time, and they even drive wagons."

"It's not the same thing."

"No, it's not. You never have to worry about an automobile getting spooked and throwing you."

How did he manage to get into these conversations with her? "What are you going to ask Eliza?" he asked to change the subject.

"I don't know. I thought I'd start by asking her where she hid her bloody clothes after she killed Vaughn."

This time he knew she wasn't serious. "Do you want me to wait for you?"

"Of course, but not on the street where she could see you. I'll meet you at that café around the corner when I'm finished."

"All right. This must be the place." They'd stopped outside the rambling house on the quiet street just off Union Square where Gino had delivered Verena home last night. "Good luck."

She gave him a dazzling smile that reminded him only that she didn't need it.

6

FRANK FIGURED HE'D START WITH THE THEATRICAL agent, Wylie Dinsmore. He'd seemed to know a lot about the Syndicate, and he certainly knew Parnell Vaughn, since Dinsmore was the one who had told Frank where to find him.

Mr. Dinsmore wasn't nearly as happy to see Frank this time as he had been the last time. "I see you located Parnell Vaughn."

"Yes, I did, but I didn't kill him, if that's what you've heard."

"Of course you'd say that."

Frank bit down hard on his anger. Getting mad at Dinsmore wasn't going to help anything. "I can understand why you don't want to talk to me, but I'm a detective, and I'm trying to figure out who really did kill Vaughn. If I killed him, why would I do that?"

"Maybe to find someone else you can blame it on."

This time Frank didn't bother to hide his anger. "I'm a rich man, Dinsmore. All I have to do is put a little money in the right hands, and nobody will ever worry about who killed Parnell Vaughn again, so if I really was guilty, that's what I'd do."

Dinsmore considered Frank's argument and apparently decided it made sense. "So you're really trying to find out who killed him?"

"Yes, I am, and I'm hoping you know who might have wanted Vaughn dead."

Dinsmore gave a bark of laughter. "You won't find anybody like that on Union Square. Dead actors don't make money."

"Is that the only value actors have to you, Mr. Dinsmore?" Frank asked mildly.

Color blossomed in Dinsmore's fleshy face. "I just meant . . . Nobody wanted Vaughn dead."

"Not even the Syndicate?"

Something flashed in Dinsmore's squinty eyes but was gone before Frank could identify it. "Of course not the Syndicate. Why would they?"

"Maybe because he wouldn't cooperate. I heard he refused to join."

"So what if he did? The Theatrical Syndicate isn't very interested in the likes of Parnell Vaughn. Handsome young men are a dime a dozen in this business."

"Who *are* they interested in?"

"Adelia Hawkes. And they certainly aren't interested in killing her."

"I don't suppose they are. They want her to join the Syndicate and make money for them."

"Of course they do. Believe it or not, Mr. Malloy, theater owners like making money just as much as anyone else."

"And they could make a lot off Mrs. Hawkes, I guess."

"She's one of the most popular actresses of our time. I've been begging her for over a year to join."

"*You* have? Why you?"

Dinsmore jerked back guiltily. "I didn't mean me personally—"

"Yes, you did. You said you'd been begging her. Why you? I thought you told me agents don't represent individual actors, so why is getting her into the Syndicate so important to you?"

Dinsmore's face was scarlet now. "I'm going to have to ask you to leave."

"Ask all you want. I'm not leaving until you answer my question."

Dinsmore glared at him for another full minute, but Frank wasn't the least bit intimidated. He'd been stared down by truly dangerous men enough times to know a phony when he saw one. Finally, defeated, Dinsmore said, "I work for the Syndicate."

"You mean you get actors for their shows?"

"Of course I do. That's what all agents do."

"Ah, but you do something more," Frank mused, making Dinsmore glare even harder.

"They hired me to convince Adelia to join the Syndicate," he said through gritted teeth.

"Why did they choose you in particular?"

Plainly, Dinsmore was insulted. "Because we're . . . old friends."

"Or lovers," Frank guessed.

"That's a filthy thing to say."

"Is it? I know about Mrs. Hawkes's reputation for carrying on with her leading men."

"She doesn't carry on."

"I was being polite. I know she expects her leading men to, uh, relax her before each performance."

"That's a lie!"

"Is it?" Could Dinsmore possibly not know?

Dinsmore opened his mouth to defend Mrs. Hawkes's honor but no sound came out. Then he closed his mouth with a snap and he seemed to deflate as all the anger drained out of him.

After another moment, Frank asked gently, "Are you in love with her?"

"She's the most . . . amazing woman," he said, his voice little more than a whisper.

"You must have known her for a long time."

"Since she first started in the business. I got her her first important role. She was the ingenue in some play. I can't even remember the name of it. But all the critics could talk about was her performance. Those eyes of hers . . . Well, she stole the show completely. The other actors hated her, of course, especially the leading lady, who was getting a little too old to . . ." He paused, then shook his head. "I just realized, she must have been about the age that Adelia is now."

"And that's what people are saying about Adelia now, that she's too old."

"Are they? It's no wonder, I suppose."

"So you were trying to convince her to join the Syndicate," Frank prodded.

"Of course I was. It's for her own good, too. The actors benefit from it just as much as the theater owners."

"How do they benefit?"

"Because until the Syndicate organized them, every theater in the country booked its own acts and theater companies had to deal with each individual theater separately. They might arrive in a town to discover the theater had closed or had booked another show for the same dates or they might perform and then not get paid. Many times troupes ended up stranded someplace with no money and no way to even get home. It was a terrible system."

"And the Syndicate fixed all that?"

"Yes, the theater owners work together to organize tours now. The actors know they'll have a place to perform and that they'll get paid and that they won't get stranded. It's been a godsend for everyone."

Frank wasn't so sure. "Then why won't Mrs. Hawkes join?"

Dinsmore sighed gustily. "It's Hawkes. He's the one keeping her out."

"Why?"

"Why do you think? Money, of course."

"But wouldn't she get more work if she joined the Syndicate?"

"That's the irony," Dinsmore said, furious again. "The Syndicate controls all the good theaters now. When she goes on tour, they have to book the third-rate ones and sometimes she has to perform in church halls and even once in a skating rink. It's humiliating."

"But if they'd make more money with the Syndicate . . ."

"Hawkes claims it's artistic freedom. The Syndicate not only books the theaters, it also chooses the plays and the actors who will perform in them. Adelia would have to take the parts they give her."

"And they probably wouldn't make her the ingenue anymore."

Dinsmore smiled mirthlessly. "Exactly."

So vanity was apparently a big part of artistic freedom, and maybe Mr. Hawkes wasn't really the one behind Adelia's refusal to join the Syndicate. "What arguments were you using to convince Mrs. Hawkes to join?"

He shook his head. "It doesn't matter. None of them worked. She wants to choose her own plays and her own parts."

"And her own leading men, I assume."

Dinsmore scowled. "Adelia chooses the entire cast."

"I guess that explains why all the men in the cast are so handsome," Frank tried.

"Actors tend to be handsome."

"And young, I gather. How much younger was Vaughn than Mrs. Hawkes?"

"I can't see that's any of your business."

"Still, it did seem odd when such a young man made love to her."

"How dare you! I told you—"

"I meant onstage," Frank quickly corrected him. "But you're wasting your time defending her virtue. I'm told everyone in the theater business knows about her, uh, requirements for her leading men."

Dinsmore sighed, sadly this time. "I told you she was an amazing woman."

"So you *were* lovers."

"Years ago, before she married Hawkes. He ruined her."

"What do you mean?"

"She used to love the work, but all she cares about now is the attention. I think that's why she won't join the Syndicate. She's afraid she'll just be cast as someone's mother."

Which she probably would. And she might have to give up her young lovers, too. No wonder she found the Syndicate less than appealing. "So you don't think Parnell Vaughn had any influence on her at all?"

"No one influences her except Hawkes."

"Then why would someone kill Vaughn?"

"That, Mr. Malloy, is not my concern."

M AEVE HAD TO KNOCK SEVERAL TIMES BEFORE ANYONE came to the rooming house door. She was just wondering if she should try the back door when a girl answered. She looked to be about Maeve's age, and she plainly hadn't been awake long enough to even comb her hair. She wore a housedress and her feet were bare. "Who are you?" she asked, peering at Maeve through bleary eyes.

"Mazie Dobbins from the *World*. I'd like to interview Eliza Grimes, please." Maeve knew better than to wait for an invitation, and she took advantage of the girl's surprise to push past her into the foyer. The house had been grand at one time, with mahogany paneling and silk wallpaper and an impressive staircase climbing up to the second story, but now the wood paneling was scuffed and the wallpaper was shredding in places, and the staircase sagged slightly. "Just tell me which room is hers and I'll show myself up."

"Wait a minute," the girl said, scratching her head through the tangles in her blond hair. "Who did you say you were and what do you want with Eliza?"

"I'm from the newspaper. I need to talk to Eliza about Parnell Vaughn's murder."

Maeve started for the stairs but the girl grabbed her arm. "Mr. Hawkes said not to talk to reporters."

"He didn't mean me," Maeve said brightly and pulled loose of the girl's grip. "Don't worry, I'll find Eliza."

"Verena?" a voice called from upstairs. "Who is it?"

Ah, so this was the famous Verena. Maeve was not impressed. At least not much.

"Some girl reporter, she says," Verena replied.

"Eliza?" Maeve called, remembering her mission and starting up the stairs. "I just need to ask you a few questions. Your picture will be in the newspaper."

"My picture?" A face appeared over the upstairs railing. "What newspaper?

"The *World*," Maeve said. "We sell more newspapers than anyone."

"Mr. Hawkes said not to talk to any more reporters," Verena called up behind Maeve.

"It's publicity for the show," the girl upstairs said. Maeve was now sure she was Eliza.

"Would you like to talk in your room or someplace else?" Maeve asked when she reached the top of the stairs. Eliza had also not been awake very long. She wore a silk kimono over her nightdress, and her hair hung over her shoulder in a braid.

Eliza glanced down to where Verena was staring up at them from the bottom of the stairs. "My room."

She led the way down a short hallway and into one of the doors lining it. Maeve followed, and Eliza closed the door behind them.

Eliza was younger than Maeve had expected, probably no more than eighteen. She was pretty enough, Maeve supposed, and stage makeup would probably make her striking.

The room was like a thousand other rooms in cheap lodging houses, with an iron bedstead supporting a sagging mattress, a washstand, a chest of drawers, a row of pegs on the wall for hanging things, and a single stuffed chair. The bed was unmade and clothes lay over the chair. Eliza scooped them up and dumped them onto the bed. She gestured vaguely to the chair, and Maeve sat while Eliza perched on the edge of the bed.

"I'm very sorry about Mr. Vaughn, Miss Grimes," Maeve said, pulling the small notebook and pencil from her purse. "I know you want to see his killer caught and punished."

"He's been caught," Eliza said sullenly.

Maeve raised her eyebrows in mock surprise. "He has? Who is it?"

"That rich fellow, Malloy."

Now Maeve didn't have to act surprised. Mr. Malloy had told her what Armistead Winters had said about Eliza knowing Malloy was innocent. "Isn't that the man they arrested? But I thought they let him go because he didn't do it."

Eliza thrust out her chin like a thwarted child. "Who told you that?"

Maeve pretended puzzlement and flipped a few pages back in her notebook. "Armistead Winters. He said you knew this Malloy fellow was innocent." It wasn't even a lie. Winters really had said that.

Eliza frowned. "He's got no business saying things about me."

"Then why don't you tell me what you really think? I'll make sure the newspaper publishes the truth."

Eliza stared at Maeve for a long moment, and then her lower lip began to quiver and a small sob escaped her lips. She covered her mouth delicately with one hand as her eyes filled with tears. Maeve watched in fascination as the tears swelled and swelled until one eased gently over her bottom lid and rolled down the smooth curve of her cheek.

Maeve had never seen anyone cry so artistically, and that was when she realized it was a show being staged just for her benefit. Resisting the urge to applaud, she said, "You were engaged to marry Mr. Vaughn, is that right?"

"Of course it's right. That's why you're here, isn't it? Because I was his fiancée."

"How long had you known Mr. Vaughn?"

Eliza blinked, sending another tear down her face, but she made no effort to wipe either of them. "I . . . a little over a year."

"You met him when you were on tour, I understand."

"Yes, we were in Kansas, I think, when we . . ."

Maeve pretended not to notice her near-confession. "And you were already engaged to Mr. Winters at the time."

"What? Who told you . . . ? Oh, Army, of course. He'd like to think that, but no, I was never engaged to him."

"Army?"

"Armistead. I call him Army."

Of course she did. "Mr. Winters never proposed to you, then?"

"Of course he did, but I never accepted. He talked about it all the time, making plans. I never realized he thought I'd agreed until I told him I was going to marry Nelly."

"Nelly? Oh, Parnell," Maeve said, scribbling something into her notebook.

"Nelly actually did propose, and I did accept," Eliza said. She could be confident now that Nelly could never contradict her.

"You must have loved him very much."

"Oh yes! He was . . . He was the most beautiful man I've ever known."

Maeve didn't ask how many men she'd known. No sense in being insulting. "Did you know Mr. Vaughn had a daughter?"

"I knew his wife had one, but she wasn't his child. He'd told me all about how Emma had left him for a rich man. He was the father, the rich man, I mean. Nelly didn't have anything to do with the little girl."

"So this Malloy fellow was the little girl's father?" Maeve asked, pretending confusion.

"No! Where'd you get that idea?"

"You said Malloy was rich and—"

"There's more than one rich man in this city. No, somehow this Malloy decided he wanted to adopt the little girl. He was going to pay Nelly to sign some papers so he could."

"But if Nelly wasn't the little girl's father—"

"I don't know anything about it," Eliza insisted impatiently. "It was something legal, so you'll have to ask a lawyer. All I know is this Malloy wanted Nelly to sign papers so he could adopt the kid."

"Then why kill him?"

Eliza gave her a pitying look. "Nelly wanted a thousand dollars to sign the papers, so if Nelly was dead, he wouldn't have to pay it."

"But if he's rich—"

"All I know is Nelly is dead and this Malloy fellow was there when it happened."

"I see," Maeve said, nodding sagely. "Did you notice anyone else at the theater that day?"

Eliza frowned. "What do you mean?"

"I mean if someone else was there, they might have seen or heard something. I know you didn't actually see this Malloy kill Mr. Vaughn, but if someone else did . . ."

"Oh." Eliza considered for a moment. "Lots of people were there, getting ready. We had a matinee."

"Then they probably saw you and saw Malloy coming out of Mr. Vaughn's dressing room."

"I . . . I don't know. I don't remember seeing anyone."

"What about earlier? How long had you been there before you went to Mr. Vaughn's dressing room?"

"Not long. Well, that's not true. I got there early so I

could be there when Malloy came. I wanted to make sure he paid Nelly the money."

"Did you think Mr. Vaughn wouldn't ask for it?"

Eliza's pretty face drooped into a frown. "He was too nice. People took advantage of him."

"People like Mrs. Hawkes?"

Eliza stiffened. "What do you mean?"

Maeve smiled sympathetically. "Everyone knows about Mrs. Hawkes and her leading men."

"It was disgusting," Eliza sneered, anger flaring in her eyes. "Everyone thought so. A woman that old . . ." She shuddered delicately.

"I can understand you being jealous," Maeve tried.

"Jealous? Why should I be jealous? It didn't mean anything, not to him. In fact, he hated her."

"He did?" Maeve asked with renewed interest. "Had he told her? Had he refused to keep on, uh, obliging her?"

"Of course not! He'd lose his job. But he'd told me. He'd promised me."

"What had he promised?"

Eliza's bowed lips puckered, as if she were trying to hold back her words, but once again, it was only an act. "He'd promised we would start our own company when this play closed. I'd be his leading lady then."

"Really? Is it that easy to start a theater company?" Maeve asked with even more interest.

"Well, no, not really," she admitted reluctantly, "which was why he needed to get some money from that Mr. Malloy. He needed investors."

"And did he have other . . . *investors?*"

"Not yet, but it was only a matter of time. Nelly was a great actor. Anyone could see that. He could have been as famous as the Booths."

"That makes his death doubly tragic," Maeve said with as much sincerity as she could feign. "Do you really think this Malloy fellow killed him?"

To her credit, Eliza took a moment to consider her answer. Finally, she said, "It could've been somebody else, I guess, but who would want to kill Nelly?"

"You were closer to him than anyone," Maeve said. "You must have some idea."

Eliza shrugged.

Maeve managed not to sigh and continued patiently. "You said you weren't jealous of his relationship with Mrs. Hawkes, but it must have been embarrassing for you."

"Embarrassing? You don't know the half of it!"

Maeve leaned forward to encourage her. "Everyone knew, I suppose."

"Of course they did! She *tells* people!"

Maeve didn't have to pretend to be shocked. "You mean she brags?"

"She wants everyone to think she's irresistible, but nobody believes it. They knew Nelly didn't have a choice. And poor Nelly, half the time he couldn't . . ." She looked away.

"Couldn't what?"

Eliza was so furious, Maeve could almost imagine steam was coming off her lovely head. "He was always too tired to make love to *me!* Can you imagine?"

Maeve supposed she could. Mrs. Hawkes was extremely demanding. "How dreadful."

"We couldn't wait to get away from her, and now . . ." Tears filled her eyes again, but Maeve didn't bother to watch them artfully fall this time.

"Think hard, Miss Grimes. Did you see anyone behaving strangely the day of the murder? Someone running down the hall or carrying a bundle or spending a long time in the washroom?"

"A bundle?"

"Yes, a bundle of clothes, maybe. They would have needed to get cleaned up and get rid of their bloody clothes."

"I did hear someone running," she said with a frown, her tears forgotten.

"When was this?"

"Earlier, before I went to Nelly's dressing room."

"Was it a man or a woman?"

"I . . . I have no idea. I just heard someone running. I figured it was one of the stagehands."

"And you didn't see them?"

"Of course not. I was in my dressing room, putting on my makeup. I wanted to be ready before that Malloy fellow arrived."

"Which way were they running?"

"How should I know? And what does this have to do with your story? I thought you were going to write about me in the newspaper."

Maeve quickly smiled. She'd have to be more careful. "Sorry. I was just thinking how much fun it would be if the

World solved the murder before the cops. I'd probably get my own column."

"Aren't you going to ask me about myself? What plays I've been in and all that?"

"Of course." So she did and dutifully took notes, even though no one would ever see them. Fortunately, Eliza's career hadn't been very long, so the notes were short. Eliza obviously enjoyed talking about herself, though. She even mentioned Parnell Vaughn a time or two.

"And be sure to say that I'm available after this play closes," she added when Maeve had exhausted her supply of questions.

"I guess Mr. Vaughn was very popular with the rest of the cast," Maeve tried.

"I suppose. Except for Army, of course. Army was very jealous of me."

"Jealous enough to kill?"

"Oh no," Eliza insisted, instantly frantic at her mistake. "I mean, he adores me, but he'd never . . . He's just not that kind of man."

"I've been wondering . . . You said you weren't jealous of Mr. Vaughn and Mrs. Hawkes, but what about her husband? Surely, he was."

Eliza frowned, apparently unwilling to make a hasty judgment this time. "I don't know . . . I mean, he knew, of course. How could he not? But . . . Well, Nelly said Mr. Hawkes was the one who arranged it."

"Arranged it?"

"Yes, he . . . Well, he told Nelly he had to go visit Mrs. Hawkes before every performance."

"Didn't Parnell think that was strange? Didn't *you* think it was strange?"

"Of course, because it *was* strange, but . . . I don't suppose Nelly minded so much, at least not at first." She shrugged one shoulder. "He's a man, isn't he? Wasn't he, I mean. Men have a different attitude toward things like that."

So much for her claims that he didn't enjoy it. "When were you and Mr. Vaughn going to get married?"

"I . . ." She literally squirmed. "We hadn't set a date yet."

"I suppose it's difficult with your schedules."

"Yes, we . . . Being an actor is very demanding."

"And what about Mr. Winters?"

"What about him?"

"He told me he still has a fondness for you."

"Oh, I'm fond of him, too, but it's much too soon to even think about another man."

"Of course, I just . . . Well, you're fortunate to have someone to look after you."

"Yes. Yes, I am." She didn't seem too happy about it, though.

"Do you think Mr. Winters will be as successful as Mr. Vaughn? He's very handsome."

"Yes, he is, but . . ."

"Isn't he as good an actor as Mr. Vaughn?" Maeve tried when Eliza hesitated.

"He's fine, and with Mrs. Hawkes promoting him, he'll probably do well."

But she obviously didn't think he'd do as well as Parnell Vaughn would have, and maybe she didn't think Winters would take her with him when he moved up. Or maybe she just didn't think he'd move up at all.

"I've been told," Maeve said, thinking she should get back to what she really wanted to know, "that the killer would have been covered in blood."

Eliza's lovely eyes widened. "Who told you that?"

"The police," Maeve said vaguely. "Could someone have managed to get rid of bloodstained clothing at the theater?"

"I don't know. I suppose."

"I was in the backstage area of the theater when I interviewed Mr. Winters. I thought there would be lots of places to hide things there."

"I guess there are, although I've never had anything to hide."

"And a place to wash up."

"We have several washrooms."

"And lots of dressing rooms where people change their clothes," Maeve added. "I'd think it would be easy for someone to get cleaned up."

"Unless someone saw them."

The skin on the back of Maeve's neck prickled. "Did you see someone?"

Eliza smiled benignly. "No, I told you. I only heard someone running."

"Didn't you look out to see who it was?"

"No," she said too quickly. "Why would I? People run down the hallway all the time."

"Do they?" And if so, why had she remembered this time in particular?

"I'm really very tired. I haven't slept well since Nelly died. I think you'd better leave now."

Maeve couldn't think of anything else to ask that she thought Eliza would answer truthfully, so she took her leave. When she stepped out into the hall, she was surprised to see the girl who had opened the door to her standing nearby. Had she been listening?

"Are you really from the *World*?" she asked.

"Of course," Maeve lied. She was very good at lying.

"I heard what you asked her, about seeing anybody that day."

"Did you see someone, Verena?" Maeve asked, remembering to be nice even though she wasn't too fond of Verena.

"You said you were doing a story about Eliza. Maybe you'd like to do a story about me, too."

"Of course I would." Maeve pulled the notebook and pencil out of her purse.

"It's Verena Rose, like the flower."

Maeve jotted down Verena's name even though she wanted to forget it. "Who did you see?"

"I saw a lot of people."

"Anybody who didn't belong there?"

"That depends on what you mean by *belong*."

"Did you see someone who wasn't involved with the play?"

"That rich fellow, the one Eliza said killed Parnell."

"Anyone else?"

Verena glanced around and then motioned Maeve to follow her down the stairs. When they reached the foyer, Verena stopped and turned to face her.

"You're not a reporter."

Maeve never blinked. "Who do you think I am?"

"I don't know. Not a copper. They don't have women coppers."

"No, they don't, so I'm not with the police."

"Then why were you asking her all those questions about who was there and what she saw?"

"You must have also heard me say I want my newspaper to find the killer before the police do. That'll sell a lot of newspapers. I could be the next Nellie Bly."

Verena seemed impressed. She glanced up as if checking to see if anyone was listening from upstairs. Satisfied no one was, she said, "Don't pay any attention to Eliza. She wasn't really engaged to Parnell."

"But she said—"

"I know what she says, and I know Parnell never said they weren't, but he had his reasons."

"Do you know what they were?"

She pursed her lips as if trying to decide whether to reply or not. Then she glanced upward again. When she returned her gaze to Maeve, her eyes were hard. "Everybody thinks there was nothing between Mrs. Hawkes and Parnell, but that's not true."

"I know they were, uh . . ." What was that word? ". . . diddling."

Verena gave a mirthless laugh. "Yes, they were, and everyone knew."

"But she did that with all her leading men."

"Yes, she did."

"Then what are you saying?"

"I'm saying that maybe Mrs. Hawkes always carried on with her leading men, and maybe Mr. Hawkes knew it and didn't care, but this time was different."

"How different?"

"This time, Mrs. Hawkes wanted more from Parnell than an occasional diddle."

"Was she in love with him?"

"I don't know what she called it, but Parnell was special to her. She really cared about him. You could tell by the way she looked at him."

"And what about him? Did he care about her, too?"

Verena gave her a wicked grin. "Parnell was a gentleman. He didn't kiss and tell, but . . ."

"But what?"

"But he never proposed to Eliza, no matter what she claims, and she was always complaining that he never had the energy to make love to her."

Maeve needed a moment to absorb all this. "So you think that Parnell Vaughn and Mrs. Hawkes really were lovers?"

"I'd bet on it."

"Did Mr. Hawkes know?"

This time Verena's smile was mysterious. "You'll have to ask him."

7

ADELIA HAWKES HAD IMMEDIATELY REPLIED TO MRS. Felix Decker that she would be delighted to call upon her that afternoon, and she had arrived promptly at two o'clock. Elizabeth Decker received her in the formal front parlor and served her tea and cakes while Sarah listened through the door that had been left ajar. They chatted amiably about the weather and how much Mrs. Decker had enjoyed the play she had not actually seen yet. Apparently, women in society also had to lie well in person, as well as in writing.

Mrs. Decker went on to explain that she had always loved the theater and had only recently learned that one could support it in more ways than simply buying a ticket and attending a performance. She hoped Mrs. Hawkes could tell her more.

"Of course I don't usually concern myself with the business side of things," Mrs. Hawkes demurred. "My husband takes care of all that, but I'm sure he would be happy to meet with you and Mr. Decker to discuss the matter more thoroughly."

"I'm afraid I haven't actually spoken to my husband about this yet. I wanted to meet you first and find out what would be involved. Socially, I mean. Would we have a box at the theater, for instance?"

"I'm sure that could be arranged," Mrs. Hawkes said, although the request had obviously surprised her.

"I'd adore having a box. We could bring our friends, you see. They would be so impressed that we actually know you."

"I should enjoy meeting them, I'm sure," Mrs. Hawkes said with apparent sincerity. "Perhaps you could make it fashionable to invest in theatrical productions."

"Oh my, I hadn't thought of that. I've never had the opportunity to make something fashionable before."

Sarah decided she should rescue Mrs. Hawkes before she became convinced her mother was completely brainless. She pushed the door open and stepped into the room.

Both women looked up.

"Sarah, what a delightful surprise," her mother said, lying again.

Mrs. Hawkes was truly surprised, but not at all delighted.

Before she could bolt, Sarah's mother said, "Mrs. Hawkes, may I present my daughter, Mrs. Sarah Malloy?"

"Mrs. Hawkes and I are acquainted, Mother," Sarah said.

"As I'm sure you know, Mrs. Decker," Mrs. Hawkes said

coldly. "I suppose there's no need for me to ask my husband to speak to yours about investing in our theater company, is there?"

"Please forgive us for our subterfuge, Mrs. Hawkes," Sarah said, taking a seat on the sofa beside her mother. "My mother was a reluctant participant, but she is as anxious as I to clear my husband's name."

"Please accept my apologies for getting you here under false pretenses," her mother said. "My admiration for your work is completely sincere, however."

"Thank you, Mrs. Decker, but I'm sure you'll understand when I say that—"

"And please accept my condolences on the loss of your dear friend Mr. Vaughn," her mother continued relentlessly. "He was a marvelous actor, and his absence will be felt very keenly."

"I . . . Thank you." Mrs. Hawkes's anger had suddenly drained away, leaving her a bit uncertain. "Now, if you'll excuse me—"

"As you may know, Mr. Vaughn was connected to our family in a rather roundabout way," her mother went on as if she had no idea Mrs. Hawkes was trying to make her escape. "His late wife had a daughter, as you may know, and Sarah and her husband hope to adopt the child."

"Yes, I believe I heard something—"

"Mr. Vaughn was not her father, of course," her mother continued, "but the law is so peculiar about things, so Sarah and Mr. Malloy had to ask Mr. Vaughn's permission, you see. He was so very kind to them and more than willing to do whatever was necessary to ensure the little girl's happiness. I shall always be grateful to him for that. He must have been a wonderful man."

"Yes," Mrs. Hawkes said faintly. For some reason the color had completely drained from her face. "Yes, he was."

"I never thought of it before, but a theater troupe must be something like a family," her mother said. "You spend so much time together that you're bound to become close, and losing a member of that family must be very difficult, like losing a loved one."

"Please," Mrs. Hawkes said as the cup she was holding began to rattle in its saucer. Sarah jumped up to take it from her unresisting fingers.

Her mother didn't even seem to notice. "I'm sure you must be mourning poor Mr. Vaughn. I didn't even know him, and I feel his loss terribly. You must let us know when his funeral is held so we can attend."

Sarah opened her mouth to beg her mother to stop when she saw the glitter in Mrs. Hawkes's legendary eyes. In another second the glitter became a flood and the tears spilled down her cheeks as she covered her mouth to stifle a cry.

"I'm so sorry," Sarah said, but Mrs. Hawkes didn't hear her because she was sobbing now, great wrenching sounds that shook her shoulders and shuddered through her body.

Sarah and her mother each produced handkerchiefs and Mrs. Hawkes used them both to swab uselessly at the flood of tears. Sarah's mother slipped away and returned in a few moments with a snifter of brandy that she pressed into Mrs. Hawkes's trembling hands. She sipped it gratefully.

After what seemed an age, she quieted and sank back in her chair, exhausted by her grief.

"I'm so sorry," Sarah said again.

"And so am I," her mother added. "I had no intention of . . . Well, I knew you must have been fond of Mr. Vaughn, but I had no idea . . ."

Sarah had the uncomfortable feeling her mother had a very good idea of just how fond Mrs. Hawkes was of Parnell Vaughn, or had at least suspected.

"That's all right," Mrs. Hawkes said, still dabbing at her tears. "I just . . . It was all so terrible. I gave him the quail you see, as a gift."

"Quail?" her mother asked in a whisper.

"A brass figurine," Sarah explained softly.

Her mother frowned in confusion. "But what . . . ?"

"The killer used it to, uh, kill Mr. Vaughn," Sarah said, glancing at Mrs. Hawkes in dismay.

Fortunately, she didn't appear to have heard. "I haven't allowed myself to grieve for him, you see."

"When we called on you, I had the impression you weren't grieving at all," Sarah said.

Mrs. Hawkes winced. "You have no idea how much it cost me to conceal my true feelings."

"If we just saw your true feelings, then you are an even better actress than I had imagined," Sarah said. "Please accept my apologies for putting you through that."

"Yes, well, you couldn't have known. The love scenes Parnell and I played onstage were nothing compared to the ones we played in private. Oh, I hope I haven't shocked you," she added.

"We had heard . . . rumors," Sarah admitted.

"Rumors." She dismissed them with a wave of her hand.

"We were lovers, but I'm sure everyone believed Parnell was only taking advantage of my feelings for him. People can be so narrow-minded. Why shouldn't a man be attracted to a woman a few years older than himself?"

"Why not indeed," her mother said, earning a surprised glance from Sarah, who decided not to offer an opinion.

"Mrs. Hawkes," Sarah said, "you must believe me when I assure you my husband had nothing to do with Mr. Vaughn's death. That's why I tricked you into meeting with me again. I can't help thinking you can help us figure out who really killed him."

"You'll forgive me if I'm not as sure of your husband's innocence as you, Mrs. Malloy. I've known a lot of men in my life, and I have learned to trust none of them."

"None of them?" her mother said gently. "Not even Mr. Vaughn?"

Mrs. Hawkes smiled sadly. "Not completely, I'm afraid. He said he loved me, but he was an actor. My heart believed him, but my head couldn't quite."

"Even if you doubt my husband's innocence, you should at least be willing to help us, if only to prove he did it," Sarah tried.

"You make a compelling argument, Mrs. Malloy," Mrs. Hawkes said. "And I do long to see the killer punished."

"Then tell me what you know. Were you in the theater that day?"

"Of course. We had a matinee. It was early, but I like to arrive at the theater early."

"So you could spend time with Mr. Vaughn," Sarah said, earning a shocked glance from her mother.

Mrs. Hawkes smiled sadly. "He was a magnificent lover."

Sarah decided to ignore that. "Did you see anyone else?"

"Of course I did."

"Who?"

"Baxter, of course." She turned to Sarah's mother. "My husband." She turned back to Sarah. "I suppose Parnell had arrived, too. He'd told me about his meeting with Mr. Malloy, but I hadn't seen him yet. I think Armistead was there. Yes, yes, he passed me in the hallway. And that little baggage, Eliza. She was always skulking around. Sometimes I imagined she watched Parnell and me through the keyhole."

"I'm sure she was jealous," Sarah tried.

"Not that she had any right to be."

Sarah feigned surprise. "I thought she and Mr. Vaughn were engaged."

Mrs. Hawkes gave a dismissive laugh. "Engaged? Hardly. He could barely stand the sight of her."

Sarah knew that to be a gross exaggeration, but Mrs. Hawkes probably had her own reasons for believing it. "Who else did you see that day?"

"Who else, hmmm, let me see. Oh yes, I'd almost forgotten, Wylie came by."

"Wylie?"

"Wylie Dinsmore. He's an agent and a . . . an old friend."

"And he came to see you?"

"Oh yes. I told you, we're old friends, and of course he's trying to get me to join the Syndicate."

"Is he?" Sarah asked. "Is that what agents do?"

"Hardly, but as I said, Wylie was an old friend and he probably thought he knew what was best for me. Someone might even have asked him to convince me to join because he would have more influence with me because of our . . . history."

"How long was he with you that day?"

"Not long. I . . ." Her expression darkened at the memory of whatever had occurred. She shook her head.

"What is it?" Sarah asked.

"Nothing, I'm sure."

"Plainly, you don't think it's nothing," her mother said. "Could this Mr. Dinsmore have been angry with Mr. Parnell?"

"No, of course not. It's just, well, I'm afraid I was indiscreet. I was feeling rather gay that day and when Wylie asked why, I told him I was in love."

"With Mr. Vaughn?" her mother asked.

"I don't . . . I can't remember exactly. I can't believe I said his name, but perhaps . . ."

"Perhaps you said something that helped him identify Mr. Vaughn," Sarah guessed.

"I can't remember. But what difference would that make? Wylie wouldn't care. Not after all these years. And even if he did, why would he kill Parnell? He'd have nothing to gain by it."

"After all these years?" her mother echoed. "Were you and Mr. Dinsmore lovers at one time?" her mother asked.

Mrs. Hawkes seemed a bit embarrassed, although Sarah couldn't imagine why until she said, "Yes, and, well, really, it was just a time or two lately. For old time's sake, you understand. He's such a dear man. But he couldn't possibly have taken it seriously."

"But if he did, he might see Mr. Vaughn as a rival for your affections," Sarah said.

"Hardly. Wylie never really had my affections at all, if the truth were known."

Poor Wylie. "Did he know that?"

"Of course he did, and as I said, I made it clear to him that day that . . ." The words died in her throat and her eyes grew wide with horror.

"That day you made it clear you were in love with someone else," her mother said.

"And he may well have guessed it was Mr. Vaughn," Sarah said.

Mrs. Hawkes shook her head decisively. "But he wouldn't have killed Parnell. What good would that do him?"

None at all, but Sarah knew from experience that people had been killed for far less provocation.

Frank had already heard Maeve's report on her visit to Eliza Grimes by the time Sarah got home from her mother's. She and Gino had been regaling him with their theories since they'd all returned to the house.

"You won't believe what my mother was able to find out from Mrs. Hawkes," Sarah told them in the brief moments before the children descended to welcome her home.

Watching Sarah lift Catherine up for a kiss, Frank could hardly get his breath. How could their love for this child have caused someone to die?

Frank's mother tried to herd the children back to the nursery, but Brian was eager to tell Sarah about his day at school. His small fingers flew as he signed the words he wanted to say to her. She signed back, making Frank's heart swell with love and pride and gratitude and emotions he couldn't even name. No killer was going to cast a pall over his family, not when they'd worked so hard to create it.

In the end, they let the children stay with them until they'd all eaten supper. Finally, Mrs. Malloy took them back upstairs to bed, leaving the four of them free to share the information they'd gathered that day. They brought Sarah up to date on what they'd learned from Eliza and Wylie Dinsmore and then they heard her report.

"I knew Eliza was lying," Maeve said when Sarah had amazed them with her tale of Adelia Hawkes's confessions and Wylie Dinsmore's visit to the theater on the day Vaughn was murdered. "She said she heard someone running, but she claimed she didn't know who it was."

"Do you think it was Dinsmore?" Frank asked. "That would explain why he didn't mention to me that he was at the theater that day."

"I'm not sure, but I think *she* knows who it was."

"Why wouldn't she tell you, though?" Sarah asked.

"Maybe she doesn't want to get them in trouble," Maeve said.

"Is Eliza the kind of girl who would worry about getting other people in trouble?" Frank asked.

Maeve grinned at that. "You're right. She'd have a better reason than that. Maybe she wants to blackmail him."

"Or her," Gino said. "We can't be sure who it was."

"We certainly can't," Sarah said. "Mrs. Hawkes said she saw Mr. Winters, Eliza, Mr. Dinsmore, and her own husband at the theater that day. Any of them could have killed Mr. Vaughn, and all of them had reasons to be angry with him."

"And no telling who else was there," Gino said. "Who would know for sure?"

"Not the doorman, if he's gone from his post as often as we've observed," Sarah said.

"What about Gino's girls?" Maeve asked with a wicked grin. "That Verena seemed eager to throw suspicion on Eliza."

"But she might well be right about Eliza and Mr. Vaughn not really being engaged, if what Mrs. Hawkes said is true," Sarah said.

"Why would Vaughn let Eliza go around telling people if they weren't engaged, though?" Gino asked. "Verena claimed it was just because he didn't want to get into an argument with her, but I can't believe that."

"You're right," Sarah said. "It seems more likely he'd tolerate it if it helped him hide his real relationship with Mrs. Hawkes."

"If he really had a relationship with Mrs. Hawkes," Maeve said. "We're just taking her word for it that they were both in love."

Frank nodded. "You're right. Maybe Vaughn was really in love with her or maybe he was just pretending so he could keep his role as leading man."

"And maybe Mrs. Hawkes was in love with him or maybe she's just saying that now so we won't suspect her of killing Mr. Vaughn," Sarah said.

"That's a lot of possibilities," Gino said with a sigh.

"And no real way of figuring out which one is true," Maeve said.

"So maybe Mrs. Hawkes and Vaughn were in love or at least thought the other one was, and Wylie Dinsmore was jealous, so he killed Vaughn," Frank said.

"We only have Mrs. Hawkes's word that Dinsmore might have been jealous, though," Gino said.

"Dinsmore did seem to confirm that, at least," Frank reminded them. "He admitted he's still in love with her, at any rate."

"But could he really have done it?" Sarah asked. "Remember the blood. He didn't have a dressing room or clothes to change into at the theater."

"If he was wearing a dark suit, the blood wouldn't show very much," Maeve said.

"And he could wash his face and hands in a washroom," Gino said.

"So Dinsmore could have done it. What about her husband, though?" Maeve asked. "He didn't mind her fooling around with her other leading men, but what if he thought she was in love with Vaughn? She wasn't exactly keeping it a secret if she told Dinsmore."

"Good point, Maeve," Frank said. "And if Baxter Hawkes and Wylie Dinsmore had a reason to be jealous, so did Eliza Grimes."

"But why would she kill Vaughn?" Maeve asked. "Wouldn't she be more likely to kill Mrs. Hawkes?"

"Logically, yes," Sarah said, "but if he told her they weren't really engaged and he'd only been pretending they were to cover his real feelings for Mrs. Hawkes, she would have been furious."

"And we know Vaughn was killed by someone who was furious," Frank reminded them.

"What about your pal Winters?" Gino asked. "Could he have been furious at Vaughn, too?"

"Over Eliza?" Maeve guessed. "He could've been mad about the way Vaughn was treating her, I guess."

"Or about Vaughn getting the leading role or even something else we don't know about," Frank added.

Gino shook his head. "It doesn't look like we've made much progress."

"Oh, I think we have," Maeve said with a grin. "We now know about even more people who might've killed Vaughn than we did when we started."

"That's what I mean," Gino said. "So what do we do next?"

"We haven't talked to Baxter Hawkes yet," Frank said. "I'd like to find out if he suspected his wife was in love with Vaughn."

"And someone needs to press Eliza on what she saw or heard that day," Maeve said. "I'm sure she didn't tell me everything she knows."

"And we need to ask Dinsmore why he didn't mention being at the theater that day," Gino said.

"It would probably be helpful to know where *everyone* was and what they were doing when Mr. Vaughn was killed," Sarah said.

Frank sighed. "If only we could count on them to tell us the truth."

· · ·

THE NEXT MORNING, MALLOY AND GINO WERE TO MEET at their office and then try to find Baxter Hawkes and Wylie Dinsmore. They were saving Eliza Grimes for later.

That gave Sarah and Maeve time to visit the clinic. They took the elevated train and arrived just in time to admire the latest arrival, a baby boy whose mother had found the clinic just the day before because the workmen had finally hung up the sign. Then they made their way to Serafina's room.

"I knew she was a girl," Serafina told them as Sarah cradled the tiny body and cooed to her. "The whole time I was carrying her."

Sarah nodded, which was probably what Serafina expected. She remembered that Serafina's clients typically believed in her powers. "She's beautiful. Have you chosen a name for her yet?"

"Yes, she is Lilla Nicolette Straface. Nicolette is for Nicola, of course." Serafina teared up a bit at the memory of her lost love, but she lifted her chin, refusing to give way.

"Lilla is a lovely name," Sarah said to help distract her from her sad memories.

"Yes. One of the spirits I contacted—she was the daughter of one of my clients—was named Lilla. It means 'lily.' When I saw her, I thought she was so beautiful, like a flower."

"And you're giving her your last name?"

"I call myself Madame Serafina, and in Italy women keep their names when they marry. I will be a widow if anyone asks someday."

"You said you were going to hire a servant who will pretend the child is hers?"

"Yes. She is my cousin. I sent for her from Italy, and she arrived last week. It will be good to have some family with me at last."

Lilla began to fuss, so Sarah handed her back to her mother. Serafina sat in the rocking chair they had provided each mother. Maeve carried in a chair for Sarah, then slipped out again, probably to check on the workmen's finishing touches.

"I hope you're enjoying your stay here. You're our first patient, so I'm anxious to hear what you think."

"I am so glad I came. Everyone has been very kind, and the midwives have taken good care of us. They showed me how to feed Lilla and dress her. I didn't know anything about babies."

"And you're feeling all right?"

"I'm not ready to leave yet, but yes, I'm well. We did not have time to speak of you before. Tell me, are you still helping Mr. Malloy be a policeman?"

Sarah laughed at the memory. "He's not a policeman anymore. A lot has happened since the last time we saw you."

Sarah told her an abbreviated version of their story and explained how Malloy had been forced to leave the New York City Police and had started his own detective agency.

"And do you still help him?" Serafina asked.

"Oh yes, more than ever now."

The rocking of the chair had put Lilla to sleep, and Serafina leaned her head back and closed her eyes, but if Sarah thought she was going to follow suit, she was mistaken. "I see Mr. Malloy in a dark place. I think you have some troubles, Mrs. Brandt."

"I'm Mrs. Malloy now," Sarah said with some amusement. She didn't really believe in Serafina's supernatural powers.

"Yes, Mrs. *Malloy*. And I am Sarah now, like you. You are having some troubles, too. It involves Mr. Malloy and . . . and a child." She opened her eyes. "Is someone dead?"

"It's nothing for you to worry about," Sarah tried.

"I am not worried. I can help you. You need to know who killed this man."

Someone must have shown her a newspaper or told her about Malloy being arrested. "Really, I don't think—"

"Tell me what it is, Mrs. Malloy."

Sarah sighed. She started to say it was nothing, but of course that was a lie. It was very serious indeed, and while she didn't for a moment think Madame Serafina could help her, she didn't see the harm in telling her the story.

When she was finished, Serafina—Sarah—nodded wisely. "If you bring these people to me, I can call on this Mr. Vaughn to tell us who killed him."

"I couldn't ask you to do that. You've just had a baby."

"I am strong now, and I can spare you one hour after all you have done for me. Remember this. You will need me."

Sarah wished she really believed that Madame Serafina could tell her who had killed Parnell Vaughn. She only hoped someone could.

WYLIE DINSMORE'S OFFICE WAS LOCKED UP TIGHT ON this Saturday, but Frank figured Baxter Hawkes might be at the theater since there was both a matinee and an evening performance that day. The doorman was at his post, but his chin rested on his chest and he was snoring loudly. Frank and Gino tiptoed past him.

"Where do you think Hawkes would be?" Gino asked when they had turned the corner in the corridor and were out of the guard's line of sight.

"He probably doesn't have a dressing room, but I'm pretty sure I saw offices in the front lobby. I'll check there and you can wander around back here to see if anyone wants to talk to you."

"And if I see Hawkes, I'll come and find you."

Frank left Gino and found his way to the auditorium by retracing the path he and Sarah had taken last week. The enormous room was dark and eerily silent, lit only by a single light at the back of the stage. Above him, the lavish plaster ornamentation loomed, casting ominous shadows. He resisted an unreasonable urge to run and hurried down the carpeted aisle to the back and gratefully passed through the doors into the spacious and well-lit lobby. Just as he'd suspected, several doors he hadn't paid much attention to before led off to a suite of offices. One stood open and Frank entered, ready to do battle with a secretary if necessary.

It wasn't necessary. The desk in the outer office was empty, with all papers neatly stacked and the typewriter covered. It was Saturday, after all. Or maybe even the office staff kept unusual hours and wouldn't be in until later. The door to the inner office was closed, so Frank rapped on it with authority, which experience had taught him often brought immediate results.

"Who is it?" a man called with a notable lack of hospitality.

Frank opened the door and stepped inside. Baxter Hawkes's expression of annoyance quickly changed to anger. "What are you doing here?"

"I need to ask you a few questions."

"No, you don't. You don't need to be here at all. If you've upset Adelia—"

"I haven't even seen her."

"Good, and if you leave now, you won't."

"I didn't come here to see your wife. I said I have some questions for you."

"I should send for the police."

"Feel free, but while we're waiting, I'd like some answers from you."

"I can't think of a single reason why I should speak to you at all, Mr. Malloy."

"Let me give you one, then. I'm trying to find out who killed Parnell Vaughn, and the sooner I do, the sooner you'll have seen the last of me."

"I thought the police arrested you because *you* killed him," Hawkes said with a scowl.

"The police have been wrong before, Mr. Hawkes."

Hawkes gave a long-suffering sigh and said, "All right, you can have a few minutes if you promise to leave afterward and not bother Mrs. Hawkes."

Frank took the lone empty chair that stood against the wall and moved it so he could look straight across the desk at Hawkes. When he was seated, he said, "Do you know your wife was in love with Parnell Vaughn?"

"*What*?" Hawkes nearly shouted, jumping to his feet and scurrying over to shut the office door. "How dare you say a thing like that?" His face had gone scarlet and his eyes glinted with fury.

"I didn't say it. Your wife did."

"My wife? You said you hadn't seen my wife."

"She didn't say it to me. She told *my* wife. She was quite upset about Vaughn's death, too, which made my wife believe her."

"That's ridiculous."

"Mr. Hawkes," Frank said with exaggerated patience, "we know the stories about how Mrs. Hawkes requires her leading men to, uh, visit her prior to performances."

If Hawkes's face had been scarlet before, it was now nearly purple. "How dare you!"

"It's common knowledge, I understand, and I'm also told that you don't mind. In fact, I'm told that you are the one who informs the actors of their extra duties."

"What goes on backstage in this theater is none of your concern, Mr. Malloy."

"Ordinarily, that would be true, but when a man is murdered and I'm falsely accused of killing him, it becomes my concern. Now, what I want to know is if you knew of your wife's feelings for Mr. Vaughn."

"Of course not, because she had no feelings for him. She looked upon him as nothing more than a theater prop who could walk and talk and make her look good onstage."

"Do you really believe that?" Frank asked in amazement.

"Of course I do, because it's true. Adelia has needs that I am no longer able to meet. She has chosen to accept the attentions of various young men through the years, but they mean nothing to her."

"So you don't consider her behavior adultery?"

"Of course not. Those young men were no threat to my marriage, and they helped enhance Adelia's performances."

"And she didn't tell you she was in love with Vaughn and planning to leave you?"

"Of course not, and if someone told you that, they were lying. Adelia often became fond of the young men, but she would forget about them as soon as they were gone. She would never leave me for one of them."

"How can you be so sure?"

The color in Hawkes's face had returned to normal, and now he leaned back in his chair and smiled benevolently at Frank. "Because I know my wife, Mr. Malloy. Adelia is no longer young. In fact, she's even older than most people think. No one else would cast a woman of her age as the romantic lead in a play, and she knows it. As long as I am in charge of this company, however, she will continue to play whatever role she likes and to be cast opposite ever-younger leading men. If she left me, those roles would be closed to her."

"And another manager wouldn't be likely to force the young men to, uh, attend to her needs, either."

Hawkes stiffened in outrage. "I assure you, I have never had to force them. When they understand that their role depends on Adelia's goodwill, they are only too happy to *attend* her."

"Was Vaughn as happy as the others?"

"I understand he was suitably enthusiastic."

"Even though he was engaged to another woman?"

"Mr. Malloy, you are obviously still bound by the puritanical conventions that restrict so many people in this country and prevent them from enjoying all that life has to offer."

"If that means I don't want another man *attending* to my wife's *needs*, then I'm happy to be a Puritan. But you haven't answered my question. Didn't you feel the least bit guilty about requiring Vaughn to have relations with your wife while also knowing he was planning to marry another woman?"

"Why should I feel guilty? It was his choice, and he certainly never mentioned any reservations to me."

Of course he wouldn't, if he wanted to keep his job. "Do you think Vaughn felt any guilt over being unfaithful to Eliza Grimes?"

"I have no idea. I don't concern myself with the private lives of my actors."

"Where were you when Parnell Vaughn was killed?"

"How should I know? I have no idea when he was killed."

"Shortly before I found his body and Eliza started screaming. I know you were in the theater because you came immediately."

"If that's true, I was here, in my office, when he was killed. I always arrive early to check the gate from the previous day."

"What gate?"

"The 'gate' means how many tickets were sold. I need to know if the play is losing popularity or gaining so I can judge when it's time to leave the city and go on tour."

"Are you planning to leave anytime soon?"

"I wasn't until Vaughn died. Now I'm waiting to see if the scandal brings people out or keeps them away."

"I'd expect it to bring them out."

"So would I, but we aren't getting much coverage in the newspapers."

"Finding the killer would probably get you some," Frank said without irony. "Then you'd have the trial and there would be a lot of publicity around that."

Hawkes scowled again. "I suppose that's your way of convincing me I should help you."

"You can't blame me for trying, and you seem like a man willing to do just about anything to succeed, Mr. Hawkes."

Hawkes didn't seem as insulted as Frank had intended him to be. In fact, he looked almost smug. "You're correct, Mr. Malloy. I am willing to do whatever is necessary, but killing Parnell Vaughn was not necessary."

"Then who do you think could have done it?"

"I have no idea, and now I must inform you that your time is up. I've told you everything I know, and I have work to do."

8

GINO WALKED SLOWLY DOWN THE HALLWAY, LISTENING
for sounds that would indicate any of the dressing rooms
were occupied. He wasn't sure if he should seek out someone or avoid being seen. He didn't want to be thrown out
again, but there was no use wasting this opportunity to talk
to somebody while he was here.

He was almost opposite the washroom door when it
opened and Eliza Grimes stepped out. They'd never met, but
he recognized her from seeing the play with Mr. Malloy the
other night. She stopped abruptly and looked up and down
the corridor. Seeing they were alone, she stiffened in alarm.

"Who are you?"

Gino smiled his reporter-seeking-a-story smile. "I'm
Dave Shook, a reporter for the *World*. I'm doing a story

about Parnell Vaughn's murder. Aren't you Mr. Vaughn's fiancée, Miss Grimes?"

Eliza did not smile back. "I already talked to that girl who said she was with the *World*. I forget her name."

"Mazie?" Gino guessed, proud that he'd remembered the fake name Maeve was using.

"Yes, that's her. Didn't she tell you?"

"I haven't seen her," he lied. "But my story is going to be published first. Mazie's too new to get the right attention."

Eliza frowned and looked him up and down. "How do I know you're a real reporter?"

Gino pushed back his hat and scratched his head. "That's a new one. Why would anybody pretend to be a reporter if they weren't?"

Eliza had no answer for that. "How did you know who I was?"

"They told me you were the prettiest girl in the play, so when I saw you . . ." He shrugged and gave her his best besotted grin.

That seemed to win her over. "I suppose I could talk to you for a few minutes, but then I have to get prepared for the matinee."

"A few minutes would be grand. Where can we talk?"

"My dressing room is right over there." She pointed at the door that had her name on it. No star, Gino noticed, but she also wasn't sharing a dressing room the way Verena did with the other girls. The room was, he noted, directly across the hall from Vaughn's.

Gino quickly opened the door for her to precede him and

closed it behind them. The room was small and crowded with a rack of costumes and a dressing table covered with jars and bottles and brushes and other implements he could not identify. A few photographs of Eliza in various poses wearing various costumes hung haphazardly on the wall. A slipper chair stood before the dressing table and a straight-backed chair sat against the wall. Some articles of clothing had been draped over it, but she pushed them onto the floor and gestured for him to sit down while she turned the slipper chair to face him.

He pulled out his notebook and a pencil. "I heard you were the one who found Mr. Vaughn's body."

She winced at that, although Gino wasn't sure how offended she really was at his choice of words. "I . . . I found a man coming out of his room. He had blood on his hands."

"I guess that would be . . ." Gino flipped through his notebook, pretending to search for the name. "Frank Malloy. Is he the one who found Mr. Vaughn, then?"

"That's what he said. I don't know. I just know that when I saw him coming out of Nelly's dressing room with blood on his hands, I knew something terrible had happened. I had to see for myself."

"So you saw Mr. Vaughn's body?"

"Yes, he . . ." She pressed her fingers to her lips for a moment as her eyes filled with tears. Fortunately, Maeve had warned him, so he watched in admiration as Eliza summoned her grief. He'd never seen anyone weep so artistically. "I'm sorry," she said, pulling a handkerchief from her sleeve and dabbing at her tears. "It was so horrible."

"I'm sure it was. Did you see anyone else at the theater that day? Somebody who might've been the killer?"

"I told you, that Malloy fellow was the one I saw."

"But if he didn't do it . . ."

"What makes you think he didn't?"

Gino feigned confusion. "I thought you said he found the body. That means someone else killed Mr. Vaughn."

"I don't know. He was the only one I saw."

"Are you sure? There must have been a lot of people at the theater that day, just like today. When you have a matinee, everyone comes in, don't they?"

"Not everyone. Not all the time."

"Why not?"

"Sometimes Mrs. Hawkes doesn't do the matinees. Like today. She's not performing today or tomorrow's matinee." Passing along this information had cheered her enormously, and she seemed to have forgotten she was supposed to be crying.

"She isn't?"

"No. The stars sometimes skip the matinees, but that's fine. I'm her understudy, so I get to perform the lead role when she's gone."

"I guess that's a good opportunity for you."

"Of course it is. The maid's role is too small to really get noticed."

"Have you gotten noticed for taking her place?"

Eliza seemed offended by the question. "It takes time to get noticed, but anyone can see I'm much more suited for the role than she is."

"Oh, I can see that. I was surprised when I saw the play. I thought she was Mr. Vaughn's mother at first."

"You should put that in your story for the newspaper," Eliza suggested.

"I definitely will," Gino said, scribbling some notes. "Was Mrs. Hawkes going to perform that day?"

"Yes, but they canceled the matinee after they found poor Nelly. We didn't do the show that night, either. Everyone was too upset. Mr. Hawkes was in a rage over it, too. He said we couldn't afford to miss two performances. All he cares about is the money."

Gino supposed someone had to care about it. "So who did you say you saw at the theater that day besides Mrs. Hawkes?"

"I didn't say I'd seen her."

"But you did, didn't you?"

Eliza shrugged. "I guess. She was already here when I arrived. Her door was open and some man was in with her. They were laughing."

Gino perked up at that. "Some man? Do you know who he was?"

"Mr. Dinsmore. He's an agent."

Aha! So she'd seen Dinsmore. "Did you hear what they were talking about?"

"No, but he was probably trying to convince her to join the Syndicate. He came by every now and then to do that. Mr. Hawkes was never going to let her agree, but I think she liked teasing Mr. Dinsmore."

"Did you see when he left?"

"I didn't see anything. I went to my dressing room and waited until it was time for Mr. Malloy to meet with Nelly.

He was supposed to give Nelly some money, and I wanted to make sure he did."

"Why was he going to give Vaughn money?" Gino asked with renewed interest.

"It's a long story, but he wanted Nelly to sign some legal papers. He'd offered to pay Nelly to do it, but Nelly said he didn't want the money, so I had to make sure he took it."

Well, now, Eliza had changed her story once again. She'd been claiming that Vaughn had decided not to sign the papers and that's why Mr. Malloy had killed him. She'd probably made that story up on the spot to make Mr. Malloy look guilty, but why would she do that?

"Maybe you heard something," Gino tried. "Whoever killed Vaughn must have been very angry. Maybe you heard him arguing with someone."

"I told you, I didn't see anything," she insisted.

"I said *hear*. This place isn't all that well built. If somebody was shouting across the hall, you could probably hear them."

"Nelly didn't shout, and he never argued. If somebody got mean, he'd just walk away."

"Even from his own dressing room?"

"Even from his own *bedroom*," she said with a degree of certainty that convinced him she'd know.

"So you don't think he was arguing with the person who killed him?"

Eliza narrowed her eyes. "What does all this have to do with the newspaper article?"

"I'm trying to find out what happened so we can write about it in the newspaper before the cops find out. My job is to make them look like fools. That's what sells newspapers."

"Oh." Eliza blinked in surprise, and Gino had to admit he was a little surprised himself at how well he'd answered her question. "That's what the girl said, too. That other reporter, Mazie."

Maybe he wasn't as clever as he thought. "So anything you can tell me that would help . . ." He gave her his best smile and waited, having learned from Mr. Malloy that most people can't stand silence and they'll usually start talking if you just wait long enough.

"Like I said, I didn't *see* anything," she said at last.

"But maybe you heard something," he prodded, remembering what Maeve had told him about their earlier conversation.

"I heard Mr. Dinsmore leaving Mrs. Hawkes's dressing room."

"When was this?"

"Not long after I arrived. I'd just started brushing out my hair."

"What happened after he left?"

"Oh, he didn't leave."

"He didn't?"

"No, he . . . he went to talk to Nelly."

Gino almost dropped his notebook. "Are you sure?"

"Of course I'm sure. I wouldn't say it if I wasn't."

"If you didn't see it, how do you know?" he asked, letting his skepticism show.

"I heard Nelly say hello to him and invite him in."

"And then what?"

"And then nothing. I told you, I was getting ready. I fixed my hair, and then it was time for that Malloy fellow to come, so I went to Nelly's dressing room and that's when I saw Malloy with his hands all bloody."

Still no mention of hearing someone running. "And you didn't hear anything? An argument maybe?"

"No, I told you."

Should he ask her outright? No, he didn't want to let her know he and Maeve were working together on this after he'd already told her they weren't. "Why didn't you tell this to the police?"

"I did. I told them Malloy was in there."

"But you said he killed Vaughn. You never mentioned that Dinsmore saw Vaughn first."

"Why should I? Mr. Dinsmore wouldn't kill Nelly. He didn't have any reason."

"Mr. Malloy didn't have any reason, either."

"How do you know?" Eliza asked, instantly suspicious.

Gino wanted to bite his tongue. What was he thinking to defend Mr. Malloy? "You said he was just going to pay Vaughn and get his signature. Why kill him instead?"

"Because Nelly changed his mind. He wasn't going to sign the papers. I told you."

Poor Eliza, she couldn't manage to keep her lies straight. Someone should have written a script for her to memorize. But at least she'd confirmed that Dinsmore had been with Vaughn. And Dinsmore did have a reason to be angry with Vaughn, even if Eliza didn't know it. Could he be the killer? If Vaughn really was in love with Mrs. Hawkes and she with him and Dinsmore felt this was some kind of threat to him, then . . . But would that be enough to drive a man to murder?

"Why are you frowning?" Eliza asked, reminding Gino he'd been thinking when he should have been paying attention to her.

"I was just trying to figure out a reason this Dinsmore might have killed Vaughn."

"There isn't one. Malloy did it. That's what you should write in your newspaper. Now, get out of here. I'm playing the lead today and I have to get ready."

Gino didn't want to leave. He wanted to stay here and get the truth out of Eliza, but for whatever reason, she wasn't going to tell the truth just yet. Gino had to agree with Maeve that Eliza was hiding something. Maybe Maeve should try again. Or Mrs. Malloy. But Wylie Dinsmore was looking very suspicious, even if Gino didn't think he had a very good reason to kill Vaughn.

Gino stood up and allowed her to shoo him out. She slammed the door in his face, leaving him staring at the little sign with her name painted on it while he tried to decide what to do next.

"Who are you and what are you doing here?" a man demanded.

Gino managed not to sigh in frustration. Why was everyone always so suspicious? He turned and greeted his challenger with what he hoped was a friendly smile. "Good afternoon, Mr. Winters."

"How do you know my name, and why are you outside Miss Grimes's dressing room?"

"I know your name because I've seen the play. I saw it the first night you were promoted to leading man, as a matter of fact. You're very good."

Gino's praise left Winters in a quandary. Should he acknowledge the compliment or hold on to his outrage that Gino had been gazing longingly at Eliza's door? Gino could see the inner struggle played out on his face, and he waited patiently for Winters's final decision.

"Thank you," he said at last, although he sounded a bit grudging.

"I was just chatting with Miss Grimes about the recent murder," Gino continued before Winters could work himself back up. "She was engaged to the man who was killed, you know."

"Of course I know. Everyone knew. It was a terrible thing, which is why we're being cautious about strangers being in the theater."

"That must make it hard to sell tickets," Gino observed.

Winters scowled. "Backstage, I mean. We obviously can't keep strangers from coming to see the play."

"So you think it was a stranger who killed Mr. Vaughn?"

"Of course it was. No one here had any reason to harm Parnell."

"Not even the man whose fiancée he stole?" Gino said guilelessly.

Winters gave him a look that should have drawn blood, but Gino never even blinked. Before he could answer, the dressing room door opened.

"What's going on out here?" Eliza demanded.

"This man was bothering you," Winters said.

"And now you're bothering me, Army. I'm trying to prepare for my performance and you're out here shouting."

"I'm terribly sorry. I was only trying to protect you."

Eliza glanced at Gino. "From *him*?"

Gino deeply resented not being considered a serious threat to her well-being.

"He accused me of killing Parnell," Winters reported in self-justification.

"He did? Why?"

Winters obviously did not want to answer that.

"Because Vaughn stole you away from him," Gino said. "That's a good reason for killing someone."

"Only in a play," Eliza scoffed.

"It happens in real life, too," Gino said.

Eliza shook her head wearily.

"If you want to know who killed Parnell, you should ask that agent, Wylie Dinsmore," Winters said.

Another vote for Dinsmore. "Why do you think he did it?"

"I didn't say he did, but he was here. You asked if any strangers were in the theater, and he was. He's not exactly a stranger, but he's not associated with the play, either."

"Why would he kill Parnell Vaughn?"

"How should I know? Maybe Vaughn refused to join the Syndicate or something."

"Don't be silly, Army," Eliza said. "Don't put that in your story. You'll get laughed out of the city," she told Gino.

"Story? What story?" Winters asked.

"He's a reporter. Didn't he tell you?"

"He acts more like a policeman."

"I guess reporters and policemen both ask a lot of questions," Gino said.

"He's harmless," Eliza said, insulting Gino almost past bearing. "Go back to your dressing room so I can have some peace and quiet." Before Winters could reply, she slammed the door shut again.

Gino turned his attention back to Winters. "Why did you say I should talk to Dinsmore?"

Winters glanced at Eliza's door with alarm and began to move away. "Because Eliza saw him here."

Gino followed him. "She told you that, I guess."

"Of course she did."

"And if Dinsmore killed Vaughn, that means you didn't."

"I didn't kill him no matter what," Winters said, still moving away from Eliza's door.

"But you had a good reason. He stole your girl and he stole your part in the play." Gino continued to follow him.

"He didn't steal my part. I didn't even try for that role."

"Because you weren't good enough?"

Actors, Gino noted, did not like to be thought not good enough. "No, you imbecile. Because the part was already cast. I joined the troupe when I found out Eliza had."

"So you could be close to her?"

Winters clearly regretted starting this discussion. "To make sure Vaughn didn't mistreat her."

"He's never been known for mistreating women," Gino said.

They'd stopped outside Winters's dressing room. "How would you know?"

Gino didn't want to explain that, so he said, "I've spoken to a lot of people who knew him."

"I don't know what he's known for, but I didn't want him mistreating Eliza, so I accepted a role in the play to keep an eye on her."

"And I suppose you weren't very happy when you found out about Vaughn and Mrs. Hawkes."

"Why would I care about that?"

"Because he was being unfaithful to Eliza."

Winters took a long moment to reply, during which he stared, virtually expressionless, into Gino's eyes, as if looking for some clue as to Gino's true intent. "I would've been glad if he was being unfaithful to Eliza," he said at last.

"Oh!" Gino said, thinking he'd figured it out. "Because she would've broken their engagement and turned to you for comfort."

"But she didn't, because Vaughn didn't care about Mrs. Hawkes."

"Mrs. Hawkes claims they were in love."

Winters smiled bitterly. "Some people thought so."

"Who?"

"What does it matter now?"

Winters stepped into his dressing room and slammed the door shut. Gino heard the key turn, but he wasn't finished with Winters. He raised his hand to knock, but then he heard someone walking purposefully down the hall. A man. Was it the guard?

Without waiting to find out, Gino headed down the hallway in the opposite direction, until he reached the end of the dressing rooms and found himself in the bowels of the theater, where all manner of materials were stored or stowed. He quickly made his way into the mess in hopes of evading discovery. Masses of enormous canvas-covered frames were stacked against the walls. Gino surmised from the painting on the one in the front that they were scenery. Various articles of furniture were stacked precariously everywhere and gilded wooden swords lay next to shepherd's staffs and old men's canes. Above him, the ceiling soared and was crisscrossed with catwalks and cables.

"What are you doing here?" someone demanded.

Gino started in surprise and turned to find a wizened old man in shabby work clothes glaring at him. One of the stagehands, no doubt. Gino scrambled for a good excuse. "I . . . I was looking for Verena and I guess I got lost," he lied.

"You got no business back here and you got no business visiting with Miss Verena neither."

"I'm sorry," Gino said with as much contrition as he could muster. "I didn't realize. If you could help me find my way out . . ." He gestured helplessly.

The old man snorted and motioned for Gino to follow him. "We had some trouble lately and Mr. Hawkes don't allow no strangers backstage anymore," he said, not even bothering to glance back at Gino.

"I heard one of the actors got himself killed."

"Then you should know better than to come sneaking around here. Same thing could happen to you."

"Do you really think so?"

This time the old man did look back with an expression of pity.

"Do you have any idea who might've killed Mr. Vaughn?" Gino tried.

"I mind my own business."

"Did you see any strangers around the theater that day?"

"I don't look for trouble and you'd be wise to do the same."

They'd reached the dressing room hallway again. "The killer would've been covered with blood. Where do you think he hid his bloody clothes?"

The old man looked at him as if he thought him insane. He probably did. "You'd best find the door and get out of here before Mr. Hawkes catches you." With that he turned and headed back to his domain.

Gino hadn't learned much, but after seeing the condition of the backstage area, he now knew that if someone had wanted to hide something in this building, it might never be found.

FRANK FOUND GINO ON A BENCH IN UNION SQUARE. "DID you get thrown out?"

"Of course. I got to see Eliza, though, and Winters, too."

"Really? What did Eliza have to say?"

"Not much except to contradict some of the things she told Maeve and to claim she saw Wylie Dinsmore going to see Vaughn."

"Really?"

"Well, she didn't actually see it. According to her, she heard Mrs. Hawkes and Dinsmore in her dressing room. The door was open and they were laughing, she said. Then she went to her own dressing room, which is right across from Vaughn's. But she says she heard Dinsmore and Vaughn talking a little later and Vaughn invited him in. She claims that's the last thing she heard."

"So Dinsmore really was at the theater, but Mrs. Hawkes didn't tell Sarah that Dinsmore went to see Vaughn."

"Maybe she didn't know. Or maybe Eliza made it all up. She apparently keeps changing her mind about everything. First she told me you were going to pay Vaughn for signing the papers and she was going to make sure he took the money. Then, just a few minutes later, she said Vaughn had decided not to sign them and that's why you killed him. I can't understand why she keeps changing her story."

"Lies are always hard to remember. Or maybe she's trying to protect somebody and isn't quite sure how to do it."

"Who would she be protecting and why? They killed her fiancé."

"As far as I can tell, Eliza is the only one who believed Vaughn was going to marry her."

"Really? Is that what Mr. Hawkes said, too?"

"He didn't seem to have an opinion one way or the other, but he doesn't believe his wife was in love with Vaughn or that Vaughn cared for her."

"He could be lying about that. Men don't like other people to know if their wives are unfaithful."

"He says he didn't care if his wife was unfaithful," Frank said wearily.

"Do you believe it?"

"I don't think so, but a lot of people have told us she's been carrying on with her leading men for years and he encouraged it, so I could be wrong."

"I asked Winters what he thought. He didn't think Vaughn had feelings for Mrs. Hawkes, but he did say that other people might've thought he did."

"Who?"

"He didn't say, and he locked me out of his dressing room before I could ask."

"Well, at least two people saw Wylie Dinsmore at the theater around the time Vaughn was killed, Mrs. Hawkes and Eliza, so we should probably talk to him again, at least."

"You're right. Let's go back to his office and see if he's there now."

"And if he's not?"

"We'll try to find out where he lives. He's probably in the City Directory, or maybe someone in the office building knows."

They strolled over to Dinsmore's office, but it was still locked and no one answered their knock. Unfortunately, the rest of the building was deserted, too, and the lone janitor had no idea where they might find Dinsmore.

"He was here this morning, but I didn't see when he left. You might check the bars."

"It's a little early in the day for that, isn't it?" Gino remarked.

"Not for Mr. Dinsmore," the janitor replied, not missing a stroke with his mop as he worked his way down the hallway.

"Should we start looking?" Gino asked when they'd moved out of earshot of the janitor.

"In bars?" Frank asked with amusement. "Do you know how many bars there are in the city?"

"I guess you're right. Where can we find a City Directory?"

They determined they should head back to their office, where they were sure to find one. While they were there, Frank took the opportunity to telephone the house, only to learn from his mother, who answered, that Sarah and Maeve hadn't returned from the clinic yet. His mother treated the telephone like it was a dangerous animal that had been brought into the house as a pet. She could go near it if absolutely necessary, but she was always extremely wary that it might well cause her great harm.

They found an address in the directory for Dinsmore that proved to be one of the bachelor hotels where people could rent a small apartment that had many of the amenities of a hotel. The clerk in the lobby told them Mr. Dinsmore wasn't at home, however. He usually went to his office on Saturday and then attended plays in the afternoon and evening. He was not expected home until very late that night.

"If we knew what plays he was attending, we could find him," Gino said.

"But we don't, and there are far too many for us to go searching for him. We'll come back tomorrow morning."

"But if he's going to be out late tonight—"

"He won't be leaving the house early tomorrow. With any luck, he'll be hungover, too. Angry, hungover people often blurt out things they'd never say ordinarily."

By THE TIME FRANK AND GINO GOT BACK TO THE HOUSE, Sarah and Maeve had taken the children out to the park for the afternoon. Gino decided to head home to have supper with his parents for once.

When the Malloy family had eaten their own supper and put the children to bed, the adults settled down in the parlor, and Frank brought Sarah and Maeve up to date on what he and Gino had learned that day. His mother sat quietly, knitting and apparently ignoring all of them.

"Do you think we'll ever know for sure how Mr. Vaughn really felt about Mrs. Hawkes?" Sarah asked.

"I doubt it," Frank said.

"What is wrong with that Eliza?" Maeve asked. "A child could lie better than she does."

His mother looked up from her knitting. "Not everybody has made a study of it."

Sarah covered a smile, and Frank had to bite his own lip.

But far from insulted, Maeve said, "I suppose you're right. And she probably doesn't realize we're all comparing stories, either."

"No, she doesn't," Frank said quickly. "I told Gino I think she might be trying to protect somebody."

"Maybe she's trying to protect herself," his mother said.

The other three of them looked at her in surprise.

"It makes sense," she continued a little defensively. "If she killed him, she wouldn't know who else might've heard or seen something. That's why she's trying to make you think this agent or whatever he is was the killer."

"That's very true, Mother Malloy," Sarah said. "And if Vaughn told Eliza that he wasn't really going to marry her, she would have been furious."

"But how will we ever find out?" Maeve asked.

"We'll start with Wylie Dinsmore," Frank said. "If Eliza

was telling the truth, he was the last person to see Vaughn alive. If he didn't kill Vaughn himself, he can at least tell us what they talked about and if he saw anyone else who might've been the killer."

"And if he is the killer, do you think he'll just tell you?" his mother asked.

"Probably not, but he's not an actor and I can usually tell if somebody is lying, so we might at least find out why he went to see Vaughn."

THE NEXT MORNING, SARAH TOOK MAEVE AND CATHErine to church and Frank's mother took Brian to mass, and Frank met Gino outside of Wylie Dinsmore's apartment building. A different clerk was on duty today, and he didn't recognize Frank and Gino from their previous visit.

"We'd like to see Mr. Dinsmore."

The clerk glanced over at the pigeonholed cabinet behind him. "He isn't in."

Frank and Gino exchanged a surprised glance, then Frank turned back to the clerk. "Has he already gone out this morning?"

"I'm sorry, did you have an appointment or something?" the clerk asked, a little confused.

"Yes, we did," Frank lied. "He said he'd be home."

"Oh well, then, he'll probably be along soon. It's just that he hasn't come home yet."

"What do you mean, 'he hasn't come home *yet*'?"

The clerk blinked in alarm at Frank's tone. "He, well, he didn't come home yet from last night."

"Are you saying he went out last night and hasn't come back?"

"No, he, uh, he left yesterday *morning*, like he usually does, and he just . . . He's not back yet."

"Is it usual for him to be out all night?"

"Uh, no, not at all. I mean, he keeps late hours, but he never—"

"And you're sure he's not in his apartment?"

The clerk glanced back at the cabinet. "Positive. Both of his keys are here. He leaves his key when he goes out and—"

"Thanks," Frank muttered, and grabbed Gino by the arm as he headed out to the street.

"What's wrong?" Gino asked, nearly running to keep up.

"We think Dinsmore knows something about Vaughn's murder and now he's missing."

"Do you think he's missing? I thought he just didn't come home last night."

"Maybe he's got himself a lady friend, but maybe he killed Vaughn and now he's left town."

"Oh!" Gino nearly tripped trying to keep up with Frank. "Where are we going?" he said when he'd regained his footing.

"Back to Union Square. I want to check his office."

"You think he's there?"

"Probably not, but if he left town, he might have packed up some things."

"Wouldn't it be easier to check his apartment?"

"Of course it would, but do you think that clerk is going to let us search his apartment?"

Gino had no more questions after that. The walk to

Union Square didn't take them long since they were moving so quickly and traffic was light on a Sunday morning.

The office building was deserted. Frank pounded on Dinsmore's door and called his name, but they heard nothing in response. After taking a quick look around to make sure no one was watching, Frank raised his foot and kicked the door. The flimsy wood gave with a sickening, splintering sound and needed only a small additional shove to open completely.

The outer office was just as neat and unoccupied as it had been when Frank was here the last time. The door to the inner office was closed.

"It stinks in here," Gino said.

It did, which was why Frank wasn't a bit surprised when they opened the door and found Wylie Dinsmore's corpse still seated behind the desk.

9

Since it was Sunday, Frank telephoned Titus Wesley. The coroner had proved his worth on another of Frank's cases when Doc Haynes wasn't available, and Doc Haynes usually wasn't available on Sundays. Frank made sure Wesley was on his way before he sent Gino for the police. He didn't want anyone finding a reason to accuse him of killing Dinsmore.

The roundsman whom Gino had found dozing in a doorway had taken one look at Dinsmore's body sitting upright in the chair and run out to vomit even though Dinsmore didn't actually look too bad, all things considered. His eyes were bloodshot and his skin a ghastly shade of gray, but it was the smell that got to you. His bowels had loosened when he died, and the room had been closed up for at least a day. They'd opened the windows, but still. Gino had chosen to wait for Frank downstairs in the main lobby.

Wesley was already at work when Detective O'Connor arrived. He looked like he hadn't slept much the night before, and he was definitely annoyed at being called out on a Sunday morning. Frank had requested him especially.

"Malloy, I should've known you were involved in this."

"You should thank me," Frank said cheerfully. "I'm going to let you take credit for solving this case."

"I'm not interested in solving *this* case."

"Not even when I tell you that it's connected with Parnell Vaughn's murder?"

"Why? Just because it's in the same neighborhood?"

"No, because I found out yesterday that this gentleman"—Frank gestured toward the dead man—"was with Parnell Vaughn right before he died."

"Are you saying he killed Vaughn and then, what, killed himself in remorse?"

"Not unless you can strangle yourself from behind. I think he was the last one to see Vaughn before the killer, though, and the killer was afraid he saw something."

"And what if you're the something he saw, Malloy?" O'Connor said.

"I'm not, so I'm not worried. And you don't have to worry, either, because I'm going to find the real killer and when I do, I'll telephone you to arrest him. Or her."

O'Connor feigned amazement. "You think a female could've killed Vaughn and now this fellow?"

"I don't know about Vaughn, whoever that is," Wesley called from where he was still examining the body, "but a woman could have killed this gentleman."

"How did he die?" Frank asked. By unspoken mutual

consent, he and O'Connor stayed where they were by the window.

"He was sitting in this chair, just as you see him, and the killer was behind him. The killer slipped a length of some kind of fabric around his throat and tightened it until he was dead."

O'Connor made a rude noise. "Why didn't this fellow . . ." He turned to Frank. "What's his name?"

"Dinsmore."

"Why didn't Dinsmore just fight him off or jump up out of his seat or something?"

"Because he was tied up." Wesley pointed at Dinsmore's wrists, which bore slight bruising visible beneath the edges of his sleeves. "Somebody had tied his wrists to the arms of the chair."

"His legs, too?" O'Connor asked, interested now.

"Not that I can see. Just his hands, I think."

"Then he still could've jumped up."

"Probably not. Being strangled like that, it would only be about ten seconds before he lost consciousness. By the time he'd struggled to get his hands free and realized he couldn't and needed to try something else, it would've been too late."

"So what was he strangled with?" O'Connor asked, looking around the office.

"Like I said, judging from the marks on his neck, a piece of light fabric. Silk, maybe. A rope or cord would have left one clean mark, but this is different. See how it's wavy and unclear?"

O'Connor was not interested in examining the mark more closely. "If you say so. But he's not still tied to the chair, is he?"

"No. That looks like it might have been cloth as well and something soft. A rope would have cut into the skin when he struggled, instead of just bruising. You see, I knew his hands were tied the minute I examined his neck. If he'd had the use of them, he would have been clawing at the garrote around his neck, but there are no scratch marks at all."

"So you do think a woman could have done this?" Frank asked in an effort to convince O'Connor.

"Don't be an idiot," O'Connor said. "No female would be strong enough to strangle a man. Or tie him up, for that matter. Look here, are you a coroner?" he asked Wesley.

"Of course he is. That's why I called him," Frank said.

"You can take the body, then. How long do you think he's been dead?"

"At least a day. I'll know more when I do the autopsy, but rigor mortis is almost gone. I'd guess yesterday morning or late on Friday night."

O'Connor grunted and turned to Frank. "I guess you'll have an alibi."

"Probably, but don't look so glum. This will be a nice scandal when it all comes out. Lots of newspaper stories. I'll be sure they get your name right."

"I still can't believe he's dead," Maeve said. "I was sure he killed Vaughn."

Frank and Gino had gotten home in time for Sunday dinner, so they hadn't had a chance to discuss Dinsmore's death until the children returned to the nursery. Then Sarah had gathered Malloy, Gino, and Maeve in the parlor.

"Maybe he did kill Vaughn," Gino said, "and somebody killed him in revenge."

"Don't say that," Sarah begged. "This case is complicated enough as it is."

"At least we know Dinsmore knew something," Malloy said. "Something worth killing him for."

"But what good does that do us since he can't tell us what it is?" Gino asked.

"If Dinsmore knew something, maybe somebody else did, too," Frank said.

"But we'll never figure out what it is until we figure out who else knows it," Sarah said to focus their attention on the real problem. "First of all, I think it would help to figure out who *could* have killed both men."

"You mean who doesn't have an alibi?" Maeve asked. "Do we even know for sure when Dinsmore died?"

"Sometime on Saturday morning, most likely. The clerk at his apartment said he never came home on Saturday night, but he apparently spent Friday night at home and went to his office on Saturday morning," Malloy said.

Gino nodded. "The clerk told us he usually goes to his office on Saturday morning and then attends plays in the afternoon and evening."

"So the killer came to the office, which means he probably knew Dinsmore's usual schedule," Malloy said.

"Or she," Maeve said.

"So the killer, whoever it was," Sarah said, "came to see Dinsmore at a time and place where he—or she—knew they would most likely be alone. And then what?"

She waited while Malloy and Gino considered the question.

"Then the killer tied him to the chair," Gino said finally.

"How did he do that?" Sarah asked.

"With some kind of fabric," Malloy said. "Wesley thinks it might've been silk—"

"No, I mean how did the killer get him to just sit there while he was tied to the chair?"

Plainly, the men hadn't thought about it at all.

"He must have held a gun on him," Maeve guessed.

"If he had a gun, why didn't he just shoot Dinsmore?" Gino asked.

"Because of the noise," Maeve said. "There were other people in the building. Someone would've heard and come to investigate or something."

"All right, so the killer held a gun on him," Sarah said, "but how do you hold a gun on someone and also tie him up? Tying someone up requires two hands, even if the person isn't resisting, and holding a gun requires at least one hand, so . . ."

"So there were *two* people," Maeve said triumphantly. "One to hold the gun and one to do the tying up."

"I think there would have to be," Sarah said.

"And how convenient that we have two couples involved in all this," Gino said.

"Do you think two people killed Vaughn, though?" Maeve asked.

"Oh no," Malloy said. "Whoever killed Vaughn did it in a fury, and if a second person had been there, they probably would've stopped the killer. But Dinsmore's murder was carefully planned."

"But why . . . Oh, I see!" Maeve said. "Because Vaughn's killer had to recruit a helper, and the second person helped kill Dinsmore to protect the killer."

"If two people killed Dinsmore, then yes, that must be why," Sarah said.

"So who do we think would have worked together? Eliza and Winters?" Gino guessed.

"If she killed Vaughn, I think he'd protect her," Maeve said. "I doubt if she would have killed to protect him, though."

"I think you're right," Malloy said. "And Mr. Hawkes would protect his wife. Would she protect him?"

"It's possible," Sarah said. "Married people can develop strong loyalties, especially if it works to their mutual benefit."

"And it would certainly work to their mutual benefit to stay out of prison," Maeve said.

"What about other combinations?" Gino asked.

"You mean like Winters and Mrs. Hawkes? Or Eliza and Mr. Hawkes?" Sarah asked.

"Or Eliza and Adelia," Maeve suggested. "Or even Winters and Hawkes."

"None of those sound very likely to me," Malloy said.

"But you never know," Sarah warned them. "We've seen stranger couples working together. And don't forget, we might have missed someone. Now the question is, how do we figure it out?"

"I'd like to start by breaking the news of Dinsmore's death to everybody so we can see their reactions," Malloy said.

"That would be Eliza, Winters, and Mr. and Mrs. Hawkes, of course," Maeve said. "Or do you think your precious Verena might have done it?" she added to Gino.

Gino pretended to consider. "I suppose she could have, although I don't know what reason she would've had. It wouldn't hurt to ask her, though. Maybe I'll take her out to supper this evening."

Maeve's scowl told him how little she liked this suggestion.

Sarah managed not to smile at her annoyance. "I just realized there's a matinee this afternoon, so we could catch everyone at the theater afterward."

"Not Mrs. Hawkes," Gino said. "Eliza told me she's not doing the matinee again today."

"Again?" Sarah asked.

"She didn't perform in the matinee yesterday, either. Eliza said she'd asked her to do the performance instead."

"That seems strange," Sarah said. "I'd think Saturday and Sunday matinees would have large audiences. Wouldn't they want to see the star?"

"I think audiences always want to see the star," Maeve said.

"That just reminded me," Malloy said. "When I talked to Hawkes yesterday, he told me not to bother his wife. I got the impression he thought she was at the theater."

"Is it possible he didn't know she wasn't going to perform?" Sarah asked.

"I don't know, but he definitely thought she was there."

"Maybe she was off murdering Dinsmore," Gino said.

"Alone?" Maeve scoffed. "Maybe she convinced him to hold the gun on himself while she tied him up."

"I wouldn't put anything past her," Gino replied with a grin.

"Well, if she's not performing today, do you think she's at home, then?" Sarah asked. "Alone?"

"What a perfect opportunity to break the news to her," Maeve said.

"I was thinking the same thing." Sarah turned to Malloy. "You and I could call on her to tell her of her dear friend's death."

"We need to go to the theater, too," he said.

"Maeve and I can do that," Gino said. "They all still think we're reporters. We can pretend we heard about Dinsmore being murdered, and I remembered Eliza and Winters had told me about him."

"They must be wondering when they're going to see a story in the *World* about them," Maeve said with a smirk.

"There'll be plenty of stories about them when we find the killer," Malloy said.

THE CLERK AT MRS. HAWKES'S HOTEL DIDN'T WANT TO disturb her, but Malloy slipped him a generous tip and an assurance that they had news Mrs. Hawkes would want to hear immediately. He telephoned up to her room, and she agreed to see them, although she made them wait in the lobby almost half an hour before telling them they could come up.

This time when she opened the door to her suite, she was elegantly dressed and wearing her full stage makeup. Her hair, Sarah noted, was as perfectly and intricately coiffed as it had been each time she had seen her, and for the first time, Sarah realized it must be a wig.

"I can't say I'm delighted to see you, but your message was too provocative to ignore." She ushered them into the parlor and offered them seats. She'd ordered tea and pastries, which had already arrived.

Sarah waited until Mrs. Hawkes had served them before she said, "I'm sorry to say that we have some bad news for you."

"I can't imagine how it could be worse than poor, dear Parnell's death, but I suppose it must be serious, or you wouldn't have come to see me in person."

"It's Mr. Dinsmore," Sarah said, not discouraged by Mrs. Hawkes's attitude. "I'm afraid, well, he's been murdered."

Mrs. Hawkes simply stared at Sarah for a long moment. "Wylie?" she said finally.

"Yes, he's dead. My husband found his body this morning."

"Wylie's dead?" she said as if still struggling to comprehend Sarah's words.

"Yes. I'm sorry. I know you were very good friends."

Mrs. Hawkes made a faint, mewling sound and her eyes grew moist. "How horrible. And you say he was murdered?"

"That's right."

"But when? How? Who would want to hurt poor, dear Wylie?"

Apparently, anyone who died became "poor" and "dear" to Adelia Hawkes.

"We have no idea," Malloy said, "but I assure you we'll find out."

"This is horrible. It seems all the men I care about are dying. Who would do such a thing to me?"

Sarah had to bite her tongue to keep from pointing out that the killer probably wasn't considering her feelings at all. "We remembered that you said Mr. Dinsmore had paid you a visit at the theater shortly before Mr. Vaughn was killed," Sarah said.

"Yes. Yes, he did. I think I told you that he had guessed I was in love. It's like they say, 'Love and a cough cannot be hid.'"

"Yes, well, he apparently went to see Mr. Vaughn after he left you."

"Why would he do that?"

Malloy smiled his wolfish smile. "We were hoping you could tell us."

Her grief forgotten, she managed to look completely befuddled. "How could I know that?"

"We thought Dinsmore might have said something to you," he said. "Or maybe what you were talking about involved Vaughn in some way."

"Absolutely not."

Sarah frowned with what she hoped looked like confusion. "But didn't you say you had confessed to Mr. Dinsmore that you were in love?"

Mrs. Hawkes blinked in surprise. "I . . . Yes, I suppose I did."

"And that he may have guessed Mr. Vaughn was the object of your affections."

"Oh well, I can't be sure of that, of course."

"You seemed sure of it when you told me about it the other day."

"Well, I'm not sure of it now, and even if I was, why would Wylie go to see poor, dear Parnell?"

"Perhaps he wanted to see if Mr. Vaughn returned your feelings," Sarah said.

"Why should he care about that?"

"Didn't you say that you and Mr. Dinsmore were lovers?"

Mrs. Hawkes stiffened in apparent outrage. "Where did you get an idea like that?"

"From you. You said you had been lovers in the past and that you . . . How did you phrase it? That you had resumed your relationship a time or two lately for old time's sake."

"I didn't . . . I mean . . . I think you misunderstood."

"Perhaps I did," Sarah said without much conviction. "In any case, we do know that Mr. Dinsmore went to see Mr. Vaughn in his dressing room after he left you."

"How could you possibly know that?"

"Miss Grimes told us. She heard them."

Mrs. Hawkes needed a moment to absorb this information. "Miss Grimes?"

"Yes. I think her dressing room must be near his."

"Just opposite," Mrs. Hawkes said faintly. "But if she heard that, she must also know what they discussed."

"She claims she does not, which is why we were hoping

you might know. Perhaps he was trying to recruit Mr. Vaughn for the Syndicate. Would they have paid him to do that, do you think?"

"What are you talking about?"

Sarah turned to Malloy to signal him to join the conversation.

"Dinsmore told me the Syndicate was paying him to recruit you," he said.

"Paying him? That's impossible."

"Why would it be impossible?" Malloy asked. "You'd be very valuable to them."

"He . . . He wouldn't have taken money to . . ." For the first time today Mrs. Hawkes looked genuinely upset.

"Is that why he visited you that day?" Sarah said. "To ask you again if you'd consider joining the Syndicate?"

"He . . . Yes, he mentioned it," she said absently as she obviously thought about something else entirely. What could it be? "But of course I refused. Baxter would never hear of it. Poor, dear Wylie. I shall miss him."

Sarah cast about for something that might shock her hostess back to attention. "Miss Grimes said she heard you and Mr. Dinsmore laughing."

This had the desired effect. Mrs. Hawkes's eyes widened. "How would she know that?"

"She said your door was open."

"Of course it was open. I don't entertain men in my dressing room with the door closed."

Sarah knew that was not true, but she didn't say so. "She heard you when she was walking past."

"That little snoop. I told Baxter she was trouble. He thought she'd be loyal because she was in love with Parnell. It's so difficult to keep actors in our company. The Syndicate promises them the moon to steal them away. That's probably what Wylie was doing with Parnell. He probably promised him more money and better roles."

"He was already the leading man," Malloy said. "How could he get better roles?"

"He could play Hamlet or something. Who knows what Wylie dangled before him?"

"But if Mr. Vaughn was in love with you, I'm sure nothing could lure him away," Sarah tried.

Mrs. Hawkes lifted her chin defiantly. "You're right, of course. That's probably what made Wylie so angry. Parnell must have told him he'd never leave me. That would have made Wylie furious, so that's why he killed Parnell."

"So you think Dinsmore killed Vaughn?" Malloy asked.

"Of course. He must have."

"Then who killed Dinsmore?" Malloy asked.

"How should I know? He was an agent. I'm sure many people resented him. Some even hated him."

"Why?"

"For not finding them parts. For not sending them on auditions. Actors can be very petty."

"So you think Mr. Dinsmore killed Mr. Vaughn and a few days later, purely by coincidence, someone else killed Mr. Dinsmore?" Sarah asked.

"Of course. Why not? Things like that happen every day," Mrs. Hawkes said. "Now I must ask you to leave. I'm really quite distraught to hear about poor, dear Wylie's death and I need to rest."

"That Eliza isn't very good, is she?" Maeve remarked as she and Gino waited for the audience to disperse at the end of the play. They'd come into the theater with the crowds after intermission, when no one bothered checking tickets, and found some empty seats. There were quite a few to choose from. Gino had balked at first, afraid they'd be caught and thrown out, but of course no one cared. Who wanted to come in at the middle of a play?

"I thought Eliza was better than the fellow who took Winters's old role," Gino said. "Verena was good, though."

Maeve did not let her annoyance show. She hoped. "Which one was she again?"

"You know which one, the maid. Eliza plays the maid when Mrs. Hawkes is there. Should we go out to the office and find Mr. Hawkes?"

"We should probably tell the actors first. Mr. Hawkes is likely to chase us off when we tell him."

"You're right, and maybe we can get Eliza and Winters together and see how they act with each other." The last of the audience had filed past them, leaving the way clear for them to walk toward the front of the theater. No one paid them any attention when they entered the backstage area. They knew their way pretty well by now.

Maeve stopped at Eliza's dressing room and knocked.

"Come in," she called brightly.

Maeve opened the door, but Eliza's anticipatory smile

faded when she saw who her visitors were. "What do you want?"

Gino closed the door behind them. "We have some news for you."

"That's rich. I'm still waiting to see the story you wrote about me."

"We came to tell you Mr. Dinsmore is dead," Maeve said.

"What?"

"Wylie Dinsmore," Gino said. "The agent. The one you told us visited Parnell Vaughn right before he was killed."

"That's . . . impossible," she said faintly.

"I'm afraid it's very possible. I saw his body myself," Gino said.

"What happened to him? How did he die?"

Someone else knocked on the door and before anyone could respond, the door opened and Armistead Winters stopped abruptly at the sight of Maeve and Gino.

"You're like bad pennies, aren't you?" he said angrily. "What are you doing here? Darling, are they bothering you?"

"Of course they're bothering me. They just told me Mr. Dinsmore is dead."

"Wylie Dinsmore?" Winters said. "But . . . Why would you come here to tell her that?"

"Dinsmore was with Parnell Vaughn just before he died," Maeve said.

"You told me that yourself," Gino reminded him.

"Well, yes, but . . ." Winters looked at Eliza where she still sat at the dressing table, her makeup half-removed. "Why should we care if he's dead?"

"Are you saying you don't care?" Gino asked with interest.

"Well, of course we *care*," Winters said, trying to act insulted. "I just meant . . . I mean . . . Why would you make a special trip here for that? We hardly knew him."

"And you still haven't told me what happened to him," Eliza said.

"Oh, he was murdered," Maeve said quite casually.

"*Murdered*?" they both cried in unison.

"Who murdered him?" Eliza asked in alarm.

"We don't know yet," Gino said. "We thought you might have some ideas."

"Us?" Winters said. "Why would we know?"

"He spent a lot of time here at the theater, didn't he?" Gino said.

"No, he didn't," Eliza said. "And when he was here, he just wanted to see Mrs. Hawkes. She was all he cared about."

"Was he in love with her?" Maeve asked.

"*In love*?" Eliza echoed scornfully. "Of course not. They're old!"

Maeve decided not to explain that old people can be in love, too. "I believe Mr. Dinsmore had been in love with her for a long time."

"That's disgusting," Eliza said.

"Well, not disgusting," Winters quickly corrected her, "but surprising, at least."

"We just thought it was odd that the last person to see Parnell Vaughn alive was killed just a few days later," Gino said.

"And it is odd," Winters agreed quickly. "Isn't it, Eliza?"

"Of course it is. I've never known anybody who got

murdered before and now I know two people. This is frightening."

"I'm sure it is," Maeve said. "Especially when you realize Mr. Dinsmore must have been killed because he knew something about Mr. Vaughn's murder."

Eliza's eyes nearly popped out at that. "Do you think so?"

"Of course I do. What other reason could there be?"

"So if either of you know something, you'd better say before it's too late," Gino said.

"What do you mean, '*too late*'?" Winters asked, angry again.

"Just what he said," Maeve said. "Once you've told what you know, you won't be in danger anymore."

"We aren't in danger now, are we, Eliza?" Winters said.

"Of course not." Did she hesitate just a moment before responding?

"You see? You're getting her all upset for nothing. Now I have to ask you to leave us alone."

"Wait," Eliza said. "How did he die? Mr. Dinsmore, I mean."

"He was strangled," Gino said.

For some reason, that seemed a relief. "Oh. I see. Thank you. And yes, please leave us alone now. It's been a very difficult day."

"WHY DO YOU THINK SHE WAS SO RELIEVED TO HEAR DINSmore was strangled?" Maeve asked Gino when they'd been ushered back out into the hall.

"I have no idea, but it seemed to surprise her."

"So that means she didn't kill him."

"Or that she's a good actress. The problem with this case is that everybody is a good actress."

"Or actor." Maeve wanted to be fair. "Winters didn't seem surprised at all, though. What do you think that means?"

"I wish I knew. Let's find Mr. Hawkes now. Maybe we'll get an honest reaction out of him, at least."

They didn't have to look far. A well-dressed man had just emerged from the same door they'd used to enter the backstage area and was heading right for them. He was the same man who had thrown them out before, so Gino was pretty sure who he was.

"Mr. Hawkes," Gino said before he could ask them who they were and what they were doing there and order them to leave, which seemed to be the usual order of things here. "I'm Gino Donatelli and this is my associate, Miss Smith. We work for Frank Malloy." He'd decided they would get more cooperation if he knew who they really were.

"You better not be bothering any of my cast," Hawkes said, although he seemed more alarmed than angry.

"We just came to tell you the news about Mr. Dinsmore," Gino said.

"Dinsmore? What's he done now?"

"He's dead."

Hawkes looked confused. "Dead? Do you mean *Wylie* Dinsmore? Are you sure?"

"Very sure," Gino said.

"I . . . Thank you for letting me know," he said, and turned and practically ran back the way he had come.

"That was an odd reaction," Maeve said.

"It certainly was. He didn't even ask how Dinsmore had died."

"Neither did Winters."

"Eliza did, though. In fact, she insisted on knowing. Maybe that means she isn't the killer."

Maeve sighed dramatically. "I was so hoping she was. I don't like her at all."

"Mr. Malloy always warns me not to let my personal feelings affect the investigation."

"I'm not letting them affect anything. I just don't like her."

Gino couldn't help grinning at that. "I suppose we should tell the other girls about Dinsmore, just in case."

"In case of what? Do you think one of them killed Vaughn and Dinsmore?"

"It's possible."

"I think it's possible you just want to see that Verena again."

"She did warn you about Eliza."

"She didn't tell me anything I didn't already know. Anybody can see Eliza can't be trusted."

"Not *anybody*. Winters can't see it."

"You're right. He's convinced me he'd protect Eliza no matter what."

"Even if it meant killing Dinsmore?" Gino asked.

"That's hard to say. I think it's at least possible, but we already thought that, so it doesn't really help."

"Well, I'm hoping Winters is the killer, because I don't like him, and I think he's an idiot for following Eliza around after she jilted him."

"Love is a wonderful thing," Maeve said with a wicked grin.

"Davy!" a woman called in delight.

Gino turned and smiled to see Verena bearing down on them. She had changed into her street clothes and removed her makeup.

"What are you doing here?" she asked.

"We came to let people know that Mr. Dinsmore died," he said.

"Dinsmore? The agent?" she asked.

"Yes, I hope he wasn't a friend of yours."

"I know him, of course. We all do. We have to go see the agents whenever we're looking for work. He was always help-ful to me, but I wouldn't call him a friend. How did he die?"

"He was murdered," Maeve said baldly.

Verena was suitably horrified. "Murdered? Who would want to murder him?"

"That's what we would like to know," Gino said, giving Maeve a scowl that she completely ignored. "Say, we were wondering if you were in the theater when Vaughn was killed."

Verena blinked at the sudden change of subject. "I was here when Eliza started screaming."

"What about earlier? Did you see anybody?"

"Sure. I saw Angie and Sally."

"Of course, because you share a dressing room," Gino said. "Did you see Mr. Dinsmore?"

"No. Why would he be here?"

"Visiting Mrs. Hawkes, we hear."

"Oh yes, he did come by occasionally. He kept trying to

convince her to join the Syndicate. She wouldn't even talk about it with Mr. Hawkes anymore."

"Did you see—"

"Wait," Maeve interrupted. "Did you say Mr. Hawkes used to talk to her about it?"

"Yes. He was tired of trying to make money on his own. Nobody even wants to go on tour with her anymore because you never know from one day to the next where you'll be playing or even if you'll be playing."

"You mean *Mr. Hawkes* wanted her to join the Syndicate?" Gino asked.

"Of course he did."

"But she claims *he's* the one who doesn't want to," Maeve said.

Verena shrugged. "I don't know why she'd claim that, but she's the one holding out. Have you seen the size of our crowds? We've been playing here too long. It's time the show went on tour, but he hasn't said a word to us about it. I think he knows we'll all quit and find something with the Syndicate if we possibly can. Nobody wants to take a chance of being stranded out West when they run out of money."

Gino glanced at Maeve and saw she shared his amazement at this information. "So you didn't see Dinsmore at the theater the day Vaughn died?"

"I don't think so."

"Did you hear anything strange that day?" Maeve tried. "Somebody running? Or did you see somebody carrying a bundle of clothes?"

Verena looked at her like she thought Maeve was crazy. "People are always carrying things around."

"And you didn't hear anybody running?" Gino tried once more.

Verena shook her head, still mystified by their ridiculous questions. "When are you going to write a story about us?"

"Soon," Gino said. "We just need to figure out who killed Vaughn first."

Verena sniffed in derision. "So that means I'll never see a story."

10

Sᴀʀᴀʜ ᴀɴᴅ Mᴀʟʟᴏʏ ʜᴀᴅ ʙᴇᴇɴ ʜᴏᴍᴇ ᴏɴʟʏ ʟᴏɴɢ ᴇɴᴏᴜɢʜ to change out of their street clothes when their maid Hattie informed them that Mrs. Ellsworth had come to call. Malloy chose to remain in their bedroom suite while Sarah went down to greet their nosy neighbor.

"I'm sorry to drop in like this," Mrs. Ellsworth said. The older lady didn't seem a bit sorry, and Sarah supposed she was merely consumed with curiosity over the comings and goings she had witnessed over the past few days. Mrs. Ellsworth was notorious for knowing everything that happened on Bank Street. "I saw Mr. Malloy's name in the newspaper, so naturally, I was concerned."

Sarah asked Hattie to bring them some tea while she and Mrs. Ellsworth settled themselves in the parlor. Sarah told her what had happened as briefly as she could.

"I remember Mr. Vaughn very well, of course," Mrs. Ellsworth said when Sarah was finished. "Who could forget all that trouble with little Catherine? Do you have any idea who could have killed the poor gentleman?"

"We have a few people we suspect, but so far, no, we don't know anything for certain, and this morning we discovered that someone else has been killed."

"Oh my, how dreadful," Mrs. Ellsworth said, although her expression belied her spoken dismay. She looked almost delighted. "Who is it?"

"A Mr. Dinsmore. He's a theatrical agent."

"I've always wondered what theatrical agents do. So much about the theater is a mystery to me, I'm afraid."

"You should ask Mrs. Malloy," Sarah said with a sly grin. "She seems to know all about it."

"It's those magazines she reads," Mrs. Ellsworth said. "I confess, I've found an article or two very interesting. She shares them with me when she finds something she thinks I'll enjoy."

So that was why Sarah had never seen magazines like that lying around. Mrs. Malloy gave them to the gossip-loving Mrs. Ellsworth when she finished with them. "Have you by any chance ever read anything about Adelia Hawkes?"

"Mrs. Hawkes?" she asked, and seemed to consider. "She's quite famous, you know, so naturally, one sees things written about her. She's one of the greatest actresses of our time."

"I was more interested in her private life," Sarah said.

"Oh my, you can't think she had anything to do with Mr. Vaughn's death, can you?"

"We think someone close to him is the killer," Sarah said, "so the more we know about those people, the more likely we are to find him or her."

"I see, and of course I'd like to help in any way I can. Let me think. My memory isn't what it was, you know. I've had so much to think about lately, what with Nelson and . . . Did I tell you I broke a needle yesterday? That's a sure sign of a wedding."

"I thought Nelson and Theda had already set a date." Nelson was Mrs. Ellsworth's only child.

"They have, of course. In November because 'Married in veils of November mist, Fortune your wedding ring has kissed.' But I'm just saying, a broken needle is a sure sign of a wedding, so that proves it."

Sarah wasn't sure what it proved exactly, but she loved Mrs. Ellsworth and never mocked her superstitions, no matter how silly they sounded, so she just nodded. "Mrs. Hawkes?" she prodded.

"Oh yes. She's married to her manager, isn't she? Mr. Hawkes does everything for her. They are devoted to each other."

"I thought actors and actresses were notorious for their infidelities," Sarah tried. "Isn't there even a whiff of scandal about them?"

Mrs. Ellsworth brightened at this. "Oh, I know what you mean, and one doesn't like to spread rumors, but I did read an article in which Mrs. Hawkes admitted to falling a little in love with her leading men. She said it in jest, I think. After all, she's had dozens of them through the years, but I can certainly understand how that could happen. Perhaps *love* is too strong a word. She probably meant *infatuation* or something like that. But I saw her in a play once, and I really believed she and the young man were violently in love. How could you pretend that, night after night, without at least becoming fond of the other person?"

"I see what you mean. I've never thought about it, but I can see how it could happen. That's probably why actors and actresses have a reputation for infidelity."

"I know men feel differently about these things. They're not as sentimental, but women . . ." Mrs. Ellsworth shook her head. "We women are more romantic. We fall in love far too easily, I think, and many women have lived to regret it."

Sarah wasn't about to tell Mrs. Ellsworth what she was really thinking, which was how could a woman have relations with a man day after day without becoming fond of him? Mrs. Hawkes had certainly seemed distraught about Vaughn's death when she'd wept at Sarah's mother's house. On the other hand, she'd seemed totally unaffected when Sarah and Malloy had first visited her at her hotel. Which reaction reflected her true feelings?

"Yes, many women have lived to regret falling in love with the wrong man," Sarah said. "I wonder if Mrs. Hawkes is one of them."

"It's late for her to be repenting of her decision," Mrs. Ellsworth said. "She must be at least fifty."

"Really? I hadn't thought about her age except that Malloy claimed she was at least fifteen years older than Mr. Vaughn."

"And how old was he?"

"I'm not sure exactly, but probably early thirties, so I guess that would put her in her midforties at least."

"Does she dye her hair?" Mrs. Ellsworth asked with more interest than was really seemly.

"I . . . I don't think I can say," Sarah said, realizing it was true. "I think I've only seen her wearing a wig."

"How interesting. She even wears a wig when she's not on the stage?"

Sarah tried to remember every time she'd seen Mrs. Hawkes. "Not always. I saw her wearing a turban once."

"A turban?" Mrs. Ellsworth echoed in delight. "Like a maharaja?"

"I'm sure hers was much more elegant and fashionable than a maharaja's. I think it was some kind of silk, wound up very artistically, and it had a peacock feather on it. It was very striking."

"Oh dear, I wonder if she knows it's bad luck to wear a peacock feather onstage. It's the eye, you know."

"The eye?"

"Yes, the peacock feather has an eye on it, or at least it looks like an eye. People think it's the evil eye, so they don't wear peacock feathers on the stage."

In addition to never mocking her, Sarah never bothered to dispute any of Mrs. Ellsworth's superstitions either. "She wasn't wearing it on the stage, so she probably knows about the superstition."

"I certainly hope so. Now, about this turban. Could you see any of her hair?"

"No, not a bit, now that you ask me. It's starting to seem that she keeps her real hair completely covered all the time."

Mrs. Ellsworth patted her own salt-and-pepper coiffeur. "None of us would show our gray hair if we could avoid it. Some women dye their hair, of course, but it always looks awful."

"And I think Mrs. Hawkes would avoid looking awful at all costs."

"I'm sure you're correct. Actresses must be particularly sensitive to losing their looks. Not like the rest of us, who can just grow old gracefully."

"I'm sure you're right. It seems Mrs. Hawkes has resisted joining the Theatrical Syndicate because she isn't ready to grow old gracefully, at least not yet."

"Oh yes, I've read about that Syndicate," Mrs. Ellsworth said. "I thought everyone would have joined it by now."

"Mrs. Hawkes says her husband won't allow her to join, although he says she doesn't want to because she wouldn't be able to play younger roles anymore."

"That's very possible, I guess, but does it help you figure out who killed poor Mr. Vaughn?"

"Not at all, I'm afraid," Sarah said with a sad smile. "We just keep going round and round. A lot of people have a reason to be annoyed with Mr. Vaughn, but none of them seem to have a reason to be furious enough to have killed him."

"At least you know it was a man who killed him."

"What makes you say that?" Sarah asked in surprise.

"You said he was beaten to death."

"Not with bare hands, though. He was beaten with a . . ."

"Is something wrong?" Mrs. Ellsworth asked in alarm when Sarah stopped midsentence.

"No, I just realized something."

"What did you realize?"

"Mr. Vaughn was beaten with a quail."

"A *quail*?" Mrs. Ellsworth echoed with understandable confusion.

"Not a real quail. A brass figurine. Part of a set, actually. A little family of three quail in graduated sizes. The killer grabbed the largest one and used it to, uh, beat Mr. Vaughn on the head."

"How ghastly. And you believe a woman could have done it?"

"Mr. Vaughn was apparently a very mild-mannered man not given to violence, and if the killer surprised him, he was probably stunned after the first blow, in any case."

"I see. The killer would have the advantage of surprise, so physical strength wouldn't matter so much. But why did you look so odd a moment ago?"

"Because I just remembered that Mrs. Hawkes knew the killer had used a quail. She was lamenting the fact that she had given the figurines to him as a gift."

"You knew, too. Why would it be odd for her to know?"

"Oh, someone might have told her, I guess, but *we* only know because Malloy was accused of the crime, so he had to find out as much as he could about it. I haven't heard anyone else mention it, now that I think of it."

"But surely, a woman of Mrs. Hawkes's refinement couldn't have done such a horrible thing."

Was Mrs. Hawkes refined? Sarah didn't think so. "You're probably right. It's just curious, that's all."

"I'm sure there's a logical explanation. Perhaps the killer

himself mentioned it to her. He would know what he used, of course. If she could tell you how she knew it was the figurine, you could probably identify the killer."

Sarah thought she might be right.

Gino and Maeve arrived back in time for supper, and Maeve decided she couldn't let Mrs. Malloy put the children to bed by herself another night, so they had to wait until the children were safely tucked in before they could discuss what they had learned that day.

When the adults were gathered in the parlor, Sarah started by describing their visit with Mrs. Hawkes.

"So she lied," Maeve said.

"Yes, but we don't know what she lied about," Sarah said, not bothering to hide her frustration. "She plainly told my mother and me that she was still intimate with Mr. Dinsmore 'for old time's sake,' but now she claims we misunderstood her. She also told us Dinsmore may have guessed she was in love with Mr. Vaughn, but now she's not sure any longer. But one thing is certain, she led Mother and me to believe that she was afraid Wylie Dinsmore had killed Mr. Vaughn, and today she tried to convince Malloy and me that he did it because Mr. Vaughn refused to join the Syndicate."

"Then who does she think killed Dinsmore?" Gino asked.

"Someone else entirely," Malloy said. "Someone not connected to her in any way, apparently."

"So somebody just went to his office yesterday and killed him? For no reason?" Gino asked.

"Or at least for a reason that doesn't involve Adelia Hawkes," Maeve said. "How convenient that would be, if Dinsmore killed Vaughn and some stranger killed Dinsmore."

"Which is why we don't believe it for a minute," Malloy said, his annoyance evident. "She did seem surprised when we told her the Syndicate was paying Dinsmore to recruit her."

"Surprised and offended," Sarah said. "I think she considered it a betrayal of sorts."

"She should've been flattered that anyone was willing to go to so much trouble to get her," Maeve said.

"And to pay for it," Gino added.

"She also still claims she didn't know Dinsmore went to see Vaughn after he left her," Malloy said.

"So let me make sure I understand," Gino said. "Dinsmore didn't know for sure that Vaughn was the one Mrs. Hawkes was in love with but he went to see Vaughn and beat him to death just in case?"

They all let that sink in for a minute. Then Malloy said, "What did the two of you find out?"

"Eliza seemed surprised that Dinsmore was dead," Gino said. "And Winters claimed they hardly knew him."

"You saw them both?" Malloy asked.

"Yes, and together, too," Maeve said. "It's possible they could've killed Dinsmore together. If Eliza killed Vaughn, Winters would try to protect her by helping her kill Dinsmore."

"If they killed him, they must have thought he saw something," Malloy said.

"But we have no idea if they killed anyone at all," Sarah reminded them. "Did you ask Eliza about hearing someone running?"

"She still claims she didn't hear anything except Dinsmore and Vaughn talking," Gino said. "She was pretty upset about Dinsmore getting killed, though, and she wanted to know how he died. Winters didn't even ask."

"And what did she say when you told her he was strangled?" Malloy asked.

"That's the really funny part," Maeve said. "She seemed relieved."

"*Relieved?*" Sarah asked.

"Yes, and we couldn't figure out why she would be."

"Maybe because it was different from the way Vaughn died," Malloy said.

"Why would she be relieved at that?" Sarah asked.

No one had any ideas.

"Who else did you see?" Malloy asked finally.

"Hawkes, but his reaction was even stranger," Gino said.

"And he didn't even ask how Dinsmore died," Maeve said. "He just asked if we were sure and then ran off."

"*Ran* off?" Malloy said.

"Well, he was walking pretty fast," Gino allowed. "So we didn't have time to ask him any questions."

"He probably wouldn't have answered you anyway," Malloy said.

"So you think that Winters would have helped Eliza kill Dinsmore," Sarah said, "but you don't think they did. Is that right?"

"Yes," Maeve said. "Eliza was too surprised about Dinsmore's death."

"So that probably lets Winters off, too," Gino said.

"Unless he killed them both all by himself," Malloy said. "Maybe he knocked Dinsmore unconscious or drugged him or something. We could find out something when Wesley does the autopsy."

"But until we do, we need to stick to what we know," Sarah warned.

"Which still isn't enough," Maeve said. "Maybe we should take Madame Serafina up on her offer."

"Madame Serafina, the fortune-teller?" Gino asked in surprise.

"She's a medium," Sarah said.

"Yes, that's the one. What made you think of her?" he asked Maeve.

"She just had a baby at our new clinic."

"She did? The clinic's open?"

"Yes, it's open."

"And Madame Serafina had a baby there," Gino marveled. "Is she married to that DiLoreto fellow?"

"No, he died," Sarah said. "It's a very sad story, but Serafina—or rather Sarah, she's changed her name—is still seeing clients. She just needed a private place to have her baby."

"And what offer did she make you?" Malloy asked with a frown.

"She said she would do a séance to find out who killed Mr. Vaughn," Sarah said.

"Which is the best prospect we've got, as far as I can see," Maeve said.

Since they all knew Maeve didn't believe in Madame Serafina's powers, this made them all frown.

"We can figure this out," Malloy said. "We just need to trace everyone's movements the day Vaughn died."

"And how can we do that when everyone is lying to us?" Gino asked.

"Not everyone is lying," Maeve said, perking up. "The innocent people don't need to, so we need to figure out where everyone says they were and who else they saw, and then we'll know who's lying." She jumped up and went to the writing desk that sat by the front window. She returned with paper and a pencil and laid the paper down on the small table beside her chair. "Who shall we start with?"

"Mrs. Hawkes," Sarah said. "She said she got there early and—"

"Wait a minute, when did she say she got there early?" Malloy asked.

"When she was at my mother's house. She got there early because she wanted to have, uh, time with Mr. Vaughn before the performance. Remember, I told you she said she'd seen all of the people we thought might be the killer and also that she had a visit from Mr. Dinsmore."

"Yes, I remember all that, but I also just remembered that the first time we visited her at the hotel, she said she'd just arrived at the theater when her husband was comforting Eliza after she saw Vaughn's body."

"That's interesting," Maeve said.

"It's more than interesting," Sarah said. "She lied on purpose. Not only was she there, but she'd seen all those people, so they'd probably have seen her, too."

"So the question is, why did she lie?" Maeve said.

"Because she didn't want you to know she was there when he was murdered," Mrs. Malloy said, surprising them all. They'd forgotten she was there, silently knitting in the corner.

"I think you're right, Mother Malloy," Sarah said. "So the real question is, why was her first instinct to lie about being there at all if she's innocent?"

"To avoid being involved," Maeve guessed. "She might've suspected Dinsmore was the killer and she didn't want people to know he'd been with her right before."

"Or maybe she's the killer," Gino said. "Of course she'd claim she wasn't even in the building when it happened."

"Why admit later that she was, though?" Maeve asked.

"Because," Sarah said, "she remembered other people had seen her, so she couldn't keep lying about it."

"And that would explain why she's trying to convince us now that Dinsmore did it," Malloy said.

"And if Dinsmore saw something or knew something, she would have to kill him, too," Maeve said.

"But she would need help, so naturally, she would ask her husband," Gino said.

"I don't know," Sarah said, trying to make sense of it.

"What don't you know?" Malloy asked.

"I don't know if Mr. Hawkes would have helped her do a thing like that." She turned to her husband. "Would you help me kill someone?"

Malloy grinned wickedly. "I'm a little busy tonight, but we could do it tomorrow."

Even Sarah had to laugh at that, although she noticed that her mother-in-law did not so much as smile.

"But seriously, do you think a husband would do something like that for his wife? Kill someone he's known for years just to protect her?"

"Look at what he's already been doing for her, though," Malloy argued. "He's managing her career, taking care of her appearances all over the country, and arranging for young men to *meet her needs*. He's compromised on his business decisions by staying out of the Syndicate, so she can indulge her vanity by playing roles far too young for her, and he's relinquished any claim he might have to his pride or dignity in service to her desires. Why wouldn't he kill for her as well?"

"Verena told us the play isn't doing very well, too," Gino said. "She said they should have left on tour by now, but Hawkes is afraid the cast will quit rather than take a chance on touring with them."

Maeve brandished her pencil. "You've convinced me he would kill for her. So where was Mr. Hawkes when Vaughn was killed?"

"Somewhere in the theater, probably," Malloy said, "because he came running when Eliza started screaming after I found the body."

"But it doesn't matter if he didn't kill Vaughn," Gino reminded them.

"Let's keep him on Maeve's list," Sarah said. "So he was in the theater. Could he have gotten himself cleaned up enough to be seen again so quickly?"

"Only if he had clothes to change into," Malloy said.

"His black suit might hide some of the blood, but he'd need a clean shirt at least."

"But he's not an actor, and he doesn't have a dressing room," Maeve said.

"So he couldn't have easily changed, even if he found a shirt to wear," Sarah said. "Who else?"

"Eliza," Maeve said. "I don't like her."

Sarah shook her head. "Malloy always says—"

"I know, not to let your personal feelings influence your judgment," Maeve said. "But she's definitely a suspect. She said she was in her dressing room."

"And she said she saw Mrs. Hawkes with Mr. Dinsmore," Sarah said. "Then she heard Mr. Dinsmore greet Mr. Vaughn and apparently go into his dressing room."

"And now she claims she didn't hear anything else, but the first time we talked to her she said she heard someone running," Maeve said.

"When did she hear it, though?" Gino asked.

"We don't know," Sarah said. "Presumably after Mr. Dinsmore went into Mr. Vaughn's dressing room."

"So if Dinsmore killed him, she could have heard him running away afterward," Malloy said. "But if Dinsmore didn't kill him, he would have just left and the real killer would have gone in."

"And Mr. Vaughn and the real killer would have talked about whatever made the killer angry enough to kill him," Maeve said. "And the person Eliza heard running was the killer."

"Unless," Gino said with a sly grin, "Eliza is the killer and the person she heard running was herself."

"How could she hear herself running?" Maeve asked.

"She couldn't, but maybe she was afraid someone else heard her, so she said that just in case," Gino said.

"She wouldn't have had far to run, though," Malloy reminded them. "Her dressing room was just across the hall from Vaughn's."

"But she would've needed to wash off the blood," Sarah said. "So maybe she ran to the washroom."

"That's possible. Mrs. Hawkes would have had to go there, too," Maeve said.

"What about Mr. Hawkes? And let's not forget Winters," Gino said.

"Winters probably has extra shirts in his dressing room," Malloy said. "And you're right, they both would have had to wash off the blood."

"Mr. Hawkes could have gone to the public washrooms in the lobby near his office," Sarah said.

"So all of them could have done it," Gino said.

"But what about Dinsmore?" Malloy said. "Could they all have killed him?"

"They were all at the theater that afternoon for the matinee," Sarah said, "but that wasn't until three o'clock. Any of them would have had time to see Mr. Dinsmore at his office that morning."

"And don't forget, Mrs. Hawkes didn't perform that afternoon," Gino said. "Eliza played the lead at the Saturday and Sunday matinees."

"That's right," Malloy said. "But I don't think Mr. Hawkes knew his wife wasn't going to perform when I saw him in his office on Saturday. He kept telling me not to upset her, and then I found out later from Gino that she wasn't even there."

"I suppose if you'd killed a man in the morning, you might not want to perform in a play the same afternoon," Maeve mused.

"But if she and her husband had killed a man together," Sarah said, "wouldn't he know she was too upset to perform?"

"And what about Eliza and Winters?" Gino asked. "If they killed Dinsmore that morning, wouldn't they be too upset to perform?"

"You'd think so," Sarah said, "and yet they did. In fact, Eliza played the lead."

"They both played the leads," Gino said. "That's very cold-blooded."

"I did say I didn't think Eliza was very good that day," Maeve reminded him.

"But maybe they were just very relieved because they knew with Dinsmore dead, they'd never be caught," Sarah said.

"So how is your list coming?" Gino asked Maeve with a sly grin.

She gave him a dirty look. "We need to find out where everyone was on Saturday morning, too."

"Assuming they'll even speak to us again," Sarah said. "And tell us the truth if they do."

"Maybe someone saw something at Dinsmore's office building," Malloy said. "The janitor said he saw Dinsmore that day. Maybe he saw his visitors, too."

"That's right. We didn't think to ask him because we

didn't know Dinsmore was dead then," Gino said. "I can do that tomorrow."

"Then go see Verena at the boardinghouse," Malloy said. "Ask her if Eliza went out that Saturday morning."

"How will we check on the Hawkeses?" Sarah asked.

"I can see if the clerk who was working that morning remembers. Those fellows seem to be very cooperative if you tip them well," Malloy said.

"No one will be at the theater tomorrow," Mrs. Malloy said from her corner. "It's Monday and the theaters are dark."

"Thank you for reminding us, Mother Malloy," Sarah said as everyone bit back their smiles.

"Now all we have to do is figure out how to get everyone down to Waverly Place to see Madame Serafina for a séance," Maeve said sarcastically.

"Actors are very superstitious," Mrs. Malloy said. "That shouldn't be any problem at all."

SARAH WAS ALREADY IN BED WHEN FRANK CAME OUT OF the bathroom. She wasn't asleep yet, though. She was sitting up in their elaborate four-poster bed, looking like a goddess in her lacy nightdress with her honey-colored hair in a long braid and her arms bare. Sometimes he had to pinch himself to make sure this was all real. How had an Irish cop ended up married to the daughter of one of the oldest families in the city and living in a luxurious home with millions of dollars in his account?

Maybe he should pinch himself twice.

"I've been thinking," Sarah said as he climbed into bed beside her.

"I can make you forget what you've been thinking," he tried.

"In a minute. I thought of something when I was telling Mrs. Ellsworth about the case."

"I hope it doesn't involve a lucky rabbit's foot or a four-leaf clover."

She ignored his provocation, so he knew she was serious. "Mrs. Hawkes told Mother and me that she had given Mr. Vaughn the quail figurines as a gift."

"That's . . . interesting."

"Yes, she claimed she felt awful because her gift had been used to kill him."

"That seems like a normal reaction."

"But," she said, her blue eyes sparkling, "how did she know he'd been beaten with the quail?"

"Oh, I see what you mean. Someone told her, I guess."

"I'd like to know who, though, because I don't think anyone else has mentioned it."

"Anyone we've questioned, you mean?"

"Yes. I know she's the only one whom I've talked to who did. Did anyone you talked to without me mention it?"

"No. We should ask Gino and Maeve, too."

"And then we should ask Mrs. Hawkes how she knew it was the quail figurine."

"Who told her, you mean?"

"Yes, because I think her answer might be interesting. The killer would know, of course, and the police, and we knew because our lawyer told us after he read the police report. But was everyone at the theater talking about it? Did someone see it in the dressing room and tell other people? Or . . ."

"Or is the killer the only one at the theater who knows? You're right, her answer could be interesting, but don't get your hopes up. Her husband probably saw it in the dressing room and mentioned it to her."

"But if they're the killers . . ."

"If they're the killers, we'll find out. Did you think of anything else when you were talking to Mrs. Ellsworth?"

"Only that your mother constantly amazes me. She apparently shares her magazines with Mrs. Ellsworth when she's finished with them. They both know a lot more about theater gossip than I ever would have guessed."

"You're surprised Mrs. Ellsworth likes gossip?" he asked with mock amazement.

"Of course not, but I thought she was only interested in her neighbors. She did provide a useful piece of information, though."

"And what's that?"

"She said she read an article about Mrs. Hawkes in which she claimed she always falls a little bit in love with her leading men."

"If it was in a magazine, Mrs. Hawkes was probably just being dramatic. You know how actors are."

"No, I don't, because I don't read nearly enough of those magazines, obviously, and you may be right that she was being dramatic or outrageous or whatever in order to seem more interesting than ordinary people. On the other hand, she might have been telling the truth. Mrs. Ellsworth remarked that it must be easy to fall in love with someone when you're pretending to be in love with them night after night in a play."

"She could be right."

"And we know that Mrs. Hawkes and Mr. Vaughn were doing far more than pretending to be lovers onstage."

"That they were," Frank said, thinking he'd like to end this discussion and start doing far more himself.

"So, what if Mrs. Hawkes had fallen in love with Parnell Vaughn? Really fallen in love. Maybe she always imagined she was with the others, but this time, she really did care for him. This time, she needed to believe that his passion for her was real and not something commanded by her husband to keep her happy and performing at her peak."

"That would make her the least likely one to kill him, then."

"Actually, that would make her *more* likely to kill him, because how likely was it that he would fall in love with a woman so much older than he? If she loved him and she found out he was only pretending . . ."

"I see what you mean. But how would she find out? Vaughn wasn't going to tell her because he'd lose his job."

Sarah smiled slyly. "Maybe someone else told her."

"Who? Eliza? Mrs. Hawkes isn't going to believe her. She's just jealous. And who else would know?"

"I know, it doesn't make sense, but it would certainly give Mrs. Hawkes a reason to kill him."

"Didn't she say she was feeling especially happy that day?" Frank reminded her. "She said Dinsmore noticed and she told him she was in love."

"Which supports my theory that she really was."

"Then if she killed Vaughn, that means something would have happened in just a few minutes to make her hate him. What could it have been?"

"I don't know." She sighed. "If only Mr. Vaughn could tell us. Or Mr. Dinsmore, for that matter."

"Maybe we really do need Madame Serafina. Now turn out the light and kiss me good night."

"Good night?"

"Well, kiss me."

11

Gino made a late start on Monday morning. Actors, as he had learned, were not early risers. He found Mr. Malloy on the southwest corner of Union Square, where they had arranged to meet before setting out on their various quests.

"So you know what to ask?" Mr. Malloy said.

"Yes. Find out if the janitor saw anybody going into Dinsmore's office, and ask Verena if Eliza went out on Saturday morning."

"While you're at it, ask her if she knows what the killer used on Vaughn."

"You mean the quail?"

"Yes, but don't tell her what it was. Find out if she knows, and if she does, find out who told her about it."

"Why is that important?"

"Last night, Sarah told me Mrs. Hawkes mentioned that she'd given Vaughn the quail statues as a gift."

Gino flinched. "That would be a hard thing to find out."

"Yes, but how did she know it was used to kill him?"

"Oh, you think only the killer would know."

"Maybe, although anybody could have seen it or heard the police talking or something. It might not mean anything, but just ask her."

Gino took his leave, agreeing to meet at the Malloys' house when he was finished.

Union Square and the streets around it were busy with the usual New York City traffic and pedestrians but with the added glamour of young actors and actresses parading about on their day off in their flashy garments. Ordinary people stopped to look, and the performers preened and strutted. Many of the pedestrians, like Gino, found their way to the office building where Wylie Dinsmore had died. The other agents who had offices there were busy with those seeking parts in city productions and touring companies. Gino noticed someone had nailed a board across Dinsmore's door to keep the curious out.

"He ain't here," the janitor informed Gino, pausing in his broom-pushing. Luckily, he was the same man Gino and Mr. Malloy had seen two days ago, an older fellow in a threadbare uniform. His thinning hair was gray and his face crinkled up into a series of fine lines.

"I know. He's dead," Gino said.

"Is that a fact? Nobody told me, but then, why would I need to know? How'd he die?"

"Murdered."

"You don't say?" The janitor gave the broken door an appreciative stare. "I suppose somebody broke the door down and done him in."

"No, I broke the door down to find him," Gino said, stretching the truth just a bit. "He never came home on Saturday night, so we were looking for him."

"You mean he was killed in there and somebody just locked up the door and left him?"

"So it seems."

The janitor considered this amazing piece of information. "That don't seem right."

"Did you know Mr. Dinsmore well?"

"I been working here for seventeen years, and he was already here when I come."

"Did you like him?"

"Couldn't say that. These agents, they'll cut your heart out for a ten percent commission. He was always there with a tip at Christmas, though."

"Do you remember, I was here on Saturday with another man? We asked if you'd seen Mr. Dinsmore."

He looked at Gino more closely. "I suppose so. Is that when you kicked in the door? I didn't hear nothing."

"No, we came back yesterday and that's when we kicked in the door. But we figure he was already dead when we saw you on Saturday."

The man eyed the boarded-up door with alarm. "You don't mean it."

"Yes, you said you saw him come in that day but didn't see him leave."

"I suppose I did."

"Did you see anybody go into his office?"

The janitor scratched his head. "Not into his office, I don't think."

"Did you see anybody on this floor, then?"

"I saw a lot of people. Those actors, they stream in and out of here every day. They see whatever agents are in their offices. Looking for parts, I guess. It's a funny way to make a living, if you ask me. Pretending to be somebody else."

Gino pulled a silver dollar from his pocket and casually flipped it. "I'd be very grateful for any information you have. Do you remember who you saw that morning?"

The janitor scratched his head again, eyeing the silver dollar with longing. "Like I said, a lot of folks come in and out."

"A couple maybe," Gino said. "A man and a woman together?"

"Don't see too many couples. Two girls might come in together, or two or three men, but I don't hardly ever see no couples." He shrugged.

"So you didn't see any couples that day?"

"Not that I remember."

"Or anybody going into Dinsmore's office?"

"A woman, maybe."

"A woman? What did she look like?"

He watched the silver dollar hungrily. "I didn't see her real good. You know, maybe you should ask Mr. Tuttle. His office is right next to Mr. Dinsmore's. Maybe he saw something."

Gino flipped him the dollar, even though he hadn't been much help. Maybe he'd think of something later. "Here's my card if you remember anything else."

Tuttle's office was indeed right next to Dinsmore's, although it was halfway down the hall. Unless Tuttle had been leaning out his office door, he was unlikely to have seen anyone coming or going from Dinsmore's office. Still, it didn't hurt to ask.

A young man was in with Tuttle, so Gino took a seat in the unoccupied outer office and waited. The theater posters on the walls did little to brighten up the place. The chairs were mismatched and worn. The bare wooden floor was scuffed, and the walls hadn't been painted in a good while. When the young man left, Gino went on in without waiting for an invitation.

Tuttle was a lanky man of middle age with raven hair worn a bit too long and a lavish mustache waxed into curls on the ends. His plaid suit made Gino's eyes swim. "You're new," Tuttle said, "but I think I have a part for you." Tuttle began to shuffle through some papers on his desk, so Gino quickly pulled out a business card and introduced himself.

"I've been hired to investigate Mr. Dinsmore's death," he said. It was close to the truth, at any rate.

Tuttle's professional smile vanished. "Poor old Dinsmore. Terrible thing and right next door. Can't imagine how it happened."

"A disappointed actor, maybe," Gino said with a small smile.

Tuttle wasn't amused. "Actors are temperamental, all right, but I never heard of one killing an agent."

So much for Mrs. Hawkes's theory.

"Do you know if he had any enemies?"

"Dinsmore? I don't know that he had any *friends*, but I

doubt he ever did anything to make somebody mad enough to kill him, if that's what you mean."

"What about the Syndicate?"

Tuttle frowned. "The Syndicate? You think somebody in the Syndicate killed him?"

"Somebody suggested it, yes," Gino hedged.

"They're crazy, then. Why would the Syndicate want to kill an agent?"

"I don't know, but we do know he was working for them."

"What do you mean, 'working for them'?"

"He'd been hired to convince Mrs. Adelia Hawkes to join."

Tuttle's puzzled expression exploded into laughter. "Who told you a thing like that?"

Now Gino was the one who was puzzled. "He did."

"That's the most ridiculous thing I've ever heard. Oh, I know they'd like to have Adelia join them. She just gives the new actors the idea they can make it on their own, so sometimes they get a few rebels, but she's not worth enough to pay somebody to bring her in. Just between us, her best days are behind her, and she's a fool for not joining."

"Why would Dinsmore say the Syndicate was paying him to bring her in, then?"

"I have no idea. Pulling your leg, I guess. Or did he tell Mrs. Hawkes that? Maybe he was trying to impress her or something so she'd let him put her in a play. Who knows?"

Gino definitely didn't. He needed to find out more about the Syndicate, but not from Tuttle.

"Can you tell me who you saw in the building on Saturday morning? That's when we figure he was killed."

"A lot of actors, naturally. Not as many as this morning because the ones who are working have matinees, so they come on other days."

"Actors come even when they're in a play?"

"Yeah. Sometimes they're afraid the play will close and sometimes they're just looking for a bigger part. They also like to remind me they're still around in case something comes up."

"Did you see any couples in the building that morning?"

"Couples? I don't think so. Actors know better than to show up with a lady friend. Nobody wants a couple in the company."

"Really?" Gino asked, thinking of Vaughn and Eliza. "Why not?"

"Because when they get into a fight somewhere out in Missouri and one of them wants to go back home, then what do you do?"

"So you wouldn't cast a couple together in a play?"

"No. I'm not saying it doesn't happen, but most agents wouldn't do it."

"So you wouldn't see a couple in the building."

"They might come in together, but they'd see the agents alone."

"Did you see anybody from Adelia Hawkes's play that day?"

"I don't know who's in it."

Gino gave him all the names, even Verena and Sally and Angie. "I've seen all of them from time to time, but not recently. They must be pretty happy working for Hawkes," he added sourly.

Or else they didn't show their faces because they were working outside the Syndicate. Gino tried one last time. "Did you see any women come in alone?"

"Unless they came in here, I didn't see them, and I'm thinking whoever killed Dinsmore wasn't making the rounds. I'm sorry, but I was busy with my own work that day. I don't have any idea who saw Dinsmore."

Tuttle wasn't going to be any help. "If I wanted to talk to somebody in the Syndicate, who should I see?"

Tuttle gave him a name and address, but he said, "You're not going to find your killer there, son. The Syndicate just doesn't care that much about us."

F RANK FOUND THE CLERK AT THE MARQUIS HOTEL doz-ing behind the counter. He hit the silver desk bell at least a dozen times and took great delight in seeing the young man jolt awake and jump to his feet.

"So sorry, sir. What can I do for you?" he asked with remarkable poise in spite of his embarrassment. He looked to be about twelve and was trying to grow a mustache with little success.

"I need to speak to whoever was working on Saturday morning."

The young man blinked several times, obviously not quite awake yet. "I see. Saturday morning?"

Frank slipped a silver dollar across the counter and the young man made it vanish with the skill of a magician.

"Saturday morning, you say. Well, I was working that morning."

"I'd like to know if Mr. and Mrs. Hawkes went out at all."

The young man frowned, obviously torn between his duty and the knowledge that Frank probably had more silver dollars in his pocket. "We aren't allowed to discuss our guests."

"I don't want you to discuss them. I don't want to know anything personal. I just need to know if either or both of them went out on Saturday morning."

"They have a matinee on Saturdays," he said.

"I know, but that isn't until later in the afternoon."

"I'm trying to remember. I think . . ." He looked up hopefully.

Frank laid another dollar on the counter.

The clerk snatched it up. "They both went out."

"Together?"

"Uh, no, not together."

Frank pulled another dollar from his pocket but this time he merely held it up where the young man could see it and waited.

"Mrs. Hawkes went out first."

"What time?"

"Not very early. Between nine and ten, I think."

"You're not sure?"

"I don't keep track. It's really none of my business when guests come and go."

"All right. When did Mr. Hawkes go out?"

"Not long after. Maybe a half hour or so."

"I don't suppose they told you where they were going."

"Our guests don't usually confide that information."

Frank was sure they didn't. The chance that one of them

had mentioned to the desk clerk that they were going out to murder someone was painfully slight under any circumstances. "And how long were they gone?"

"I don't think Mr. Hawkes returned until late that night. As I said—"

"Yes, I know, he had a matinee."

"And an evening performance. He doesn't come back in between."

"And Mrs. Hawkes?"

"She usually performs on Saturday afternoons, but she returned around noon, I think."

"And did she go out again?"

"Not while I was on duty, but she also usually performs on Saturday nights, so she may have gone out again later."

Frank laid the last dollar on the counter and thanked the young man for his assistance.

"Does that mean anything? That they went out, I mean?" he asked.

"Probably not," Frank lied. "And I know you won't mention this to Mr. and Mrs. Hawkes because they won't be pleased that you're sharing information about them with strangers."

"Oh no, sir, I won't say a word."

Frank was pretty sure he wouldn't. He just wished he knew if the information really did mean anything.

GINO WAS WONDERING IF HE'D WAITED TOO LATE TO CALL on Verena. She and her friends might already be out, showing themselves up and down Broadway on this lovely afternoon. If so, he'd have to go in search of them, he supposed. But Sally answered the door and called Verena down, to his relief. Both girls were dressed in their finery, so he figured he had arrived just in time.

"Davy!" Verena cried, obviously delighted to see him. "Don't tell me you need more information for your story."

Gino gave her his best smile. "I was hoping you'd like to go for a walk and get something to eat."

She glanced over at Sally. "I won't be joining you girls today. I'll be stepping out with Mr. Shook."

He waited while she got her hat and gloves, and they set out. He let her chatter about her friends and the play and waited while she stopped to exchange pleasantries with other performers they passed. She introduced him each time, but he noticed she didn't say he was a reporter, just a friend. Finally, they stopped at a café she recommended and ordered their lunch.

Gino had decided to wait to confess his deception until they'd ordered, figuring she wouldn't run out until she'd eaten, at least. "Verena, I'm not really a reporter."

She didn't seem too shocked. "That's good. You'd be terrible at it."

"What?" He was genuinely stung.

"I knew there was something not quite right about you. You didn't ask the right questions. And that girl, is she a reporter?"

"No, we're both detectives."

"With the police?" she asked in alarm.

"No, private investigators. We're trying to find out who killed Mr. Vaughn."

Oddly, she seemed quite pleased by this information. "What about that Irish fellow? He seems a likely prospect."

"He's not. We work for him."

"Oh." She considered this for a moment. "Oh! Now I see. You're trying to find out who killed Parnell so that Irish fellow doesn't get blamed."

"That's it exactly. And you've been very helpful so far."

"I have?" Now she seemed even more pleased.

"Yes, and I need you to keep being helpful, if you would."

"I'd be happy to. This is the most interesting thing that's ever happened to me, but I think I've already told you everything I know. I have no idea who killed Parnell."

"The day he died, you said you were in the theater."

"That's right."

"Did you hear anybody running?"

"I don't think so. I wasn't really paying much attention. Our dressing room is noisy with three girls in it."

Gino nodded to encourage her. "What about this past Saturday morning. Did any of you go out? I know everyone went to the theater for the matinee, but did anyone go out earlier?"

"We usually sleep late on Saturdays because we have two shows."

"When you woke up, was anybody already gone?"

She frowned in concentration. "Wait, I think Eliza . . . Yes, I remember. I don't know when she left, but she came back right before we had to leave for the theater. I remember because she was wearing this long silk scarf."

"Was that unusual?"

"Of course it was unusual. None of us can afford silk. She had it wrapped around her neck and hanging down."

"So it was new?"

"She'd never worn it before, at least not that I ever saw. She was showing it off, too, and she claimed it was just like the ones Mrs. Hawkes ties up into a turban when she's tired of wearing her wigs."

"Wigs?"

"She always wears a wig. Her own hair . . . Well, we all laugh about it when she can't hear us. We don't know if it all fell out or if she just cut it off short so she can wear the wigs, but nobody ever sees it and you can tell there isn't much of it under the wigs."

"And she wears a turban sometimes?"

"Yes, real fancy. We don't know how she does it, but she wraps up a long silk scarf somehow so that it covers all her hair."

"Did Eliza say where she got the scarf?"

"She said it was a gift. She was very mysterious, but none of us cared enough to make her say from who. She was full of herself that day. She said she was going to play the lead that day and Sunday, too. Of course that made me happy, because I got to play her part and—"

"Who do you think gave her the scarf?" Gino asked to get her back on the right track.

"I thought it must be Armistead. He's the only one who cares enough about her to give her something so fine." Verena leaned forward eagerly. "Do you want me to find out for sure?"

Did he? No, because he couldn't trust her to be discreet. If Eliza was the killer, she might decide Verena was asking too many questions and . . . Dear heaven, Dinsmore had been strangled with some kind of fabric and now Eliza shows up on Saturday with a silk scarf.

"Davy, do you?" she prodded when he didn't reply.

"Uh, I should probably also tell you that my name isn't Davy."

She blinked in surprise. "It's not? What is it?"

"Gino. Gino Donatelli." He pulled out a business card and handed it to her.

"I knew you were Italian," she said, pronouncing it "eye-talian." "I told the other girls, but we didn't care because you're so handsome."

Gino wasn't sure if he was flattered or not. "Anyway, don't say anything to Eliza yet. She . . . If she knows someone is interested in the scarf, she might get rid of it."

"I hope she gives it to me, then. It's very pretty. We saw this dancer a couple years ago. Her name was Isadora something or other. She draped herself with lots of scarves. I think that's what Eliza was trying to do, but it didn't look as good on her as it did on the dancer."

Gino was only half listening. Luckily, the waiter brought their food, so that distracted Verena for a few moments while he tried to remember what else he was going to ask her. Finally, he remembered.

"Do you know how Vaughn was killed?"

"Somebody hit him over the head."

"How do you know that?"

"Everybody knows it."

"But how? Who told you the first time?"

"I don't remember. We were all standing in the hallway. This was after we heard Eliza scream and they took that Irishman away. Mr. Hawkes and the guard did, I mean. The rest of us—the cast and crew—were just standing there. Somebody from the crew looked into Parnell's dressing room, even though Mr. Hawkes had closed the door and told us not to go in. He said Parnell's head was all bloody."

"What did the killer hit him with?"

"I . . ." Verena frowned. "I don't know. I don't think anybody said. We just knew he'd been hit on the head. I was in a play once where the victim was hit with a candlestick. Do you think that was it?"

"Did he have a candlestick in his dressing room?"

"I don't think so, but maybe the killer brought it with him. Or a cane. He could've been hit with a cane."

Plainly, she had no idea what the real weapon had been.

How soon could he get away from her and find Mr. Malloy? He'd want to know about the scarf and the fact that Verena didn't know what had killed Vaughn. But Gino couldn't afford to offend her since he might need more information from her later. So he had to at least finish his meal and walk Verena back home before he made his escape. The next hour was torture.

WITH NOTHING ASSIGNED TO THEM FOR THAT MORNING, Sarah and Maeve went down to the clinic again. Maeve delivered an ultimatum to the workmen, who suddenly discovered they were completely finished and accepted the final payment before disappearing.

Sarah visited all of the new mothers who were still in residence. The clinic had been operational for only ten days, but they'd already delivered a dozen babies. Most of the women had returned to their homes but a few had no homes to which they could return and the midwives were helping them plan for their futures. Sarah saved Serafina and Baby Lilla for last.

Lilla had filled out well and appeared to be thriving. Serafina had dressed her in a long, white cambric infant slip that trailed over Serafina's lap and onto the floor as she sat in the rocker. The slip was trimmed with lace and ruffles and had mother-of-pearl buttons and was of far finer quality than the plain, cotton slips the clinic provided for free to the needier mothers. Serafina herself wore a fashionable gown and seemed radiant with happiness.

"You're both looking well," Sarah said, sitting on the neatly made bed.

"The midwives say we are ready to go home whenever I want to go."

"How soon do you think that will be?"

"I would leave today, but I must plan. I think I will arrive home with my luggage this afternoon so my neighbors see me return. Then I will sneak out the back door and return here to be with Lilla. Tomorrow, I will sneak back, and my cousin will arrive openly with Lilla."

Sarah wasn't sure the plan would fool anyone who was paying close attention, but perhaps no one would be. Serafina's clients would want to believe the best of her because they valued her services, so they would simply choose not to inquire too closely about the new baby in the house. "Do you have other servants?"

"I have a maid to help with the housework and a butler who also helps me with my readings."

Sarah knew that meant he helped make the eerie sounds and perform the other effects that accompanied Serafina's séances, but she didn't say so. "And they know about Lilla?"

"They have known all along. They will keep my secrets, because they are very happy working for me."

Sarah took a turn holding Lilla and admiring how beautiful she was while trying to make her smile. She even succeeded once or twice. When Serafina had taken the baby back again, she said, "Have you found out who killed that actor yet?"

"Not yet, but I think we're getting closer. Maeve keeps saying we should ask you to do a séance."

"Maeve says this?" Serafina asked with amusement. "I think she is joking. She does not believe."

"I'm sure she's joking, but my mother-in-law says actors are very superstitious and we should try it."

"You would have to bring them to my house, of course. I wonder what excuse we could use."

Sarah had no intention of bringing murder suspects to Serafina's house, but there was no harm in making conversation. "Why do people usually come?"

"You know that as well as I," Serafina said, reminding Sarah she had attended a séance herself. "They want to speak with the dead. But more than that, they want to be assured the dead rest in peace."

"I'm guessing that murder victims do not rest in peace," Sarah said.

"No, they do not. They are also interested in seeing their killers punished."

"I'm sure they are, although I'm not sure how we would identify the killer if we don't know who it is."

"You do not trust the spirits, Mrs. Malloy," Serafina said with a small smile. "They would tell us."

"Serafina—I mean Sarah—I've seen what happens behind the wall at your house. I know you control the spirits."

Serafina shook her head. "I control the sounds in order to set the mood, but the spirits still speak for themselves. I think if you bring your people, the ones you suspect, I can frighten the killer into confessing."

Perhaps she could, but . . . "I couldn't expose you to that kind of danger."

"I would be in no danger."

"Two people are already dead."

"Two? Has someone else died?"

"I forgot, you didn't know. Yes, a Mr. Dinsmore. He died on Saturday. He was a theatrical agent who . . . I think I mentioned him the other day. He was Mrs. Hawkes's lover years ago, and apparently, they were still occasionally, uh, renewing their affections."

"And why was he killed?"

"We're not sure, but he was at the theater that day. In fact, he visited Mr. Vaughn just before he was killed, so he may have seen the killer or have had some knowledge that would have identified the killer. In any case, the killer probably thought he was a danger."

"And how did he die?"

"He was strangled. In his office, not at the theater."

"So a man did it."

"That's what you'd think, because a woman wouldn't be strong enough to strangle a man, but he had been tied to a chair and—"

"Tied how?"

"His hands were tied to the arms of the chair. Then someone wrapped something around his neck from behind."

"So a woman could have done it."

"Yes, but how did she get him tied up? No man is going to just sit quietly while a woman . . . or a man either, for that matter . . . ties him up. So we think there must have been two people involved."

"But only one who killed Mr. Vaughn."

"Yes. That seems very clear."

"And the second murder, with two people, is confusing. Why would a second person help?"

"For love, we think."

"People do strange things for love. I have learned this from my clients."

"I don't suppose any of them have killed people."

Serafina smiled again. "You would be surprised. But usually, it is like the first killing. A person becomes angry and loses control. This second killing is very different, though."

"Yes, it required some planning and a lot of nerve."

"And yet, I think the killer is now feeling sad."

"I'd like to think so."

"I am sure of it. These are not evil people who enjoy killing. I think the nerve it took to kill this agent cannot last.

The person will be sorry, but they cannot find anyone to forgive them."

"But all they have to do is keep their secret, and they will never be punished."

"Perhaps they do not want to keep their secret," Serafina said. "That is what I know from my clients. If they have done evil, they want to be forgiven by the person they offended. If that person is dead, they must come to me."

"I can't imagine this killer would confess in front of other people, though."

"Again, you could be surprised. If you cannot find out any other way, you can always come to me."

"I'll certainly keep that in mind," Sarah said, although she had no intention of doing it.

GINO FOUND THE ADDRESS TUTTLE HAD GIVEN HIM. Like most of the businesses related to the theater, it wasn't far from Union Square. The elevator operator took him up to Mr. Frohman's office, where he encountered a rather formidable gentleman who guarded Mr. Frohman and served as his secretary.

Gino presented his card and asked to see Mr. Frohman.

"You don't have an appointment," the secretary said. He looked down at Gino although he wasn't very much taller. His suit and shirt were impeccable and his hair had been pomaded into complete submission.

"No, I don't, but I wanted to talk to him about . . . about some murders that happened recently."

"Murders? Who has been murdered that Mr. Frohman would know?"

"Mr. Parnell Vaughn, an actor, and Mr. Wylie Dinsmore, an agent."

"We read about Mr. Vaughn. Terrible thing. Right in the theater, but of course it's not one of our theaters. But we haven't heard about Mr. Dinsmore."

"He was only found yesterday. I expect it will be in the newspapers today."

"And you say he was murdered?"

"Yes, strangled in his office."

"Horrible. I don't know what this world is coming to."

"So could I speak with Mr. Frohman?"

"Why on earth would you need to speak to Mr. Frohman?"

"Because the Syndicate has been implicated in these murders."

"Implicated? In what way?" He was outraged.

Gino could've bitten his tongue. He'd overplayed his hand. "Well, not implicated exactly, but Mr. Vaughn was appearing in a play with Mrs. Adelia Hawkes."

"Yes, of course, but Mrs. Hawkes has steadfastly refused to join the Theatrical Syndicate, so how could this possibly involve us?"

Gino glanced longingly at the door to the inner office where Mr. Frohman probably sat, if he was even in today. "Because Mr. Dinsmore admitted that he had been hired by the Syndicate to convince Mrs. Hawkes to join, and when he was murdered, we naturally thought—"

"What did you say?" the secretary demanded, still outraged. "About Mr. Dinsmore being hired by the Syndicate?"

"He admitted it himself," Gino said, figuring the Syndicate management would naturally be upset at having been exposed.

But the secretary wasn't upset. He was confused. "I don't know why he would say a thing like that, because the Syndicate would never . . . Why should we? We don't have to recruit actors. We . . . Excuse me a moment."

Without so much as a backward glance, he disappeared into the inner office, closing the door behind him.

After a few long minutes, the secretary returned and said, "Mr. Frohman will see you."

He held the door for Gino and closed it behind him.

"Come in, young man, and sit down. I hear you've been accusing the Syndicate of all sorts of mysterious machinations."

Gino sat down in one of the leather chairs placed in front of an impressive desk that was covered with papers and booklets of all sorts. Mr. Frohman was a pleasant-looking man, clean-shaven and completely bald. He sat behind his desk with his legs crossed, eyeing Gino as if he were quite possibly mad.

"I don't know how much your secretary told you . . ."

"He told me Parnell Vaughn was dead, which I knew, and that Wylie Dinsmore was dead, which I didn't. He also said Wylie claimed the Syndicate was paying him to recruit Adelia Hawkes. Who told you such a tale?"

"My associate, Frank Malloy, but Mr. Dinsmore had told him so himself."

"That is an outrageous claim, and I have no idea why Mr. Dinsmore would say such a thing, but let me assure you, the Syndicate has never paid a . . . a *bounty* to anyone for recruiting any actor or actress. We do not need to coerce or recruit people. They come to us of their own free will. I'll admit that Adelia was somewhat of a thorn in our sides. She is a great actress and beloved by many. Have you seen her Lady Macbeth? No? Well, in any case, her refusal to join the Syndicate has been a disappointment, but not so much of a disappointment that we would pay someone to change her mind."

This didn't make any sense at all. "Could somebody else in your organization have paid him without you knowing?"

"Absolutely not. My partners are in complete agreement with me, at least where Adelia is concerned. When we organized the Syndicate back in '96, we had several important actors resist joining. They wanted artistic freedom and some other silly things that actors think are important until they realized they can earn a lot more money if they give up a little of that freedom. It didn't take long for all of them to change their minds. All of them except Adelia, but I'm sure Baxter will eventually convince her to see some sense."

"Baxter? You mean her husband, Baxter Hawkes?"

"Yes, he's not a fool, and he's already lost a fortune by catering to her whims. He'll change her mind eventually."

12

Frank and Gino met at their office. Frank had been there for a while, having finished his one errand much more quickly than Gino, who had done three interviews so far today.

Frank started by telling him that both Adelia and Baxter Hawkes had gone out separately on Saturday morning and Adelia had returned, still alone, at midday, while Baxter had not returned until much later.

"And don't forget she didn't perform in the matinee that day," Gino said. "Verena told me that Eliza went out on Saturday, too. She wasn't sure when Eliza left, but she didn't get back until it was almost time to leave for the theater. Verena told me two strange things she noticed that day. First, Eliza was wearing a long silk scarf that Verena had never seen before."

"Why is that strange?"

"Because Verena said the girls can't afford to buy things like that for themselves. Eliza said it was a gift. Verena thought maybe Winters gave it to her, but would he be able to afford things like that if the girls can't?"

"The male actors probably earn more than the actresses do," Frank said. "Men always make more than women."

"That's true, and he'd just gotten the lead role after Vaughn died, so maybe he got a raise."

"He probably did and decided to spend some of it on Eliza. So what was the second thing Verena told you?" Frank asked, hoping it was more important than a scarf.

"That Eliza told them she was playing the lead for the Saturday and Sunday matinees."

"Was that unusual?"

"Apparently. Nobody seemed to know about it except Eliza, and remember Mr. Hawkes didn't seem to know his wife wasn't at the theater on Saturday. Wouldn't he know if something like that happened?"

"I don't know. Maybe."

"Remember, we were wondering if Mrs. Hawkes didn't appear that afternoon because she was upset after killing Dinsmore."

Frank did remember. "But when did she arrange for Eliza to take her place? And she must have arranged it herself because her husband didn't know about it."

"She and Eliza were both out that morning. Do you suppose they met somewhere?"

"Are you thinking they met at Dinsmore's office?"

Gino's eyes widened. "I didn't think of that! We know

two people had to work together to kill Dinsmore. We never thought Eliza and Mrs. Hawkes might have been the two, though."

"But why would they? If one of them killed Vaughn, why would the other help her conceal it by killing Dinsmore?"

"Maybe Dinsmore killed Vaughn and they both loved him, so they decided to work together to get revenge," Gino said.

"You're too romantic, Gino. Why wouldn't they just tell the police Dinsmore was the killer? And don't forget, Eliza tried to blame it on me, so plainly, she didn't know who really did it."

"Maybe she was trying to protect Dinsmore."

"To protect him so she and Mrs. Hawkes could kill him?"

Gino sighed in defeat. "I guess you're right. That doesn't even make sense. But there's still the scarf."

"What scarf?"

"The new silk scarf that Eliza had on Saturday."

"What about it?"

"A *silk* scarf. Didn't Wesley say Dinsmore was strangled with some kind of fabric? And Verena said she'd never seen Eliza wear it before that day."

Suddenly, Frank felt energized again. "Yes, he did, and we should probably pay him a visit to see if he found out anything else in the autopsy."

TITUS WESLEY WAS ONE OF DOZENS OF MEN IN THE CITY who claimed to be coroners and one of only a few who was truly qualified. Frank had found him by chance during one of his previous cases. Wesley welcomed him and Gino to his rather grim storefront office that smelled of carbolic and death.

"I've just finished with him," Wesley said happily. He always seemed to enjoy his job. "Nobody has claimed the body yet, so you can take a look if you like."

Frank had no desire to look at the dead man. "Just tell me what you found."

"He was in good health for a man of his age and probably would have lived a long time if someone hadn't choked him to death. As I said, he was strangled from behind. His hands were tied to the chair with material similar to what was used to choke him, and he struggled against his bonds as he died. I think I mentioned that he would have lost consciousness after about ten seconds. That doesn't sound like a long time unless you're choking to death. I imagine it seems very long when you realize you're helpless to stop your killer. At any rate, his wrists were bruised across the top but not cut, the way you'd expect if he was tied with rope or twine or something rough and had struggled against that."

"Could he have been tied up with silk?" Gino asked.

Frank shot him a look, which he ignored.

"Silk," Wesley mused. "Yes, I think I mentioned that as a possibility, although it's a bit high-class for most killers, in my experience. Silk is surprisingly strong."

"Were there any other injuries?"

"None that I found. Like I said, if his hands had been free, he would have been clawing at whatever was around his neck, but his hands weren't free."

"No head injuries?"

"None. Why do you ask?"

"We thought maybe the killer knocked him unconscious so he could tie him up," Gino said.

Wesley considered this. "If he was unconscious, why not just strangle him, then? It would've taken quite an effort to get an unconscious man into the chair just to tie his hands before you choked him. And we know from the bruises on his wrists that he was conscious when he was strangled."

"Which also means it was unlikely he was drugged," Frank said.

"Yes, for all the same reasons. If you were going to drug him, why not just poison him? And if he's unconscious from the drugs, why not just strangle him then?"

"But," Gino said, refusing to be discouraged, "you think he could've been strangled with a silk scarf."

"A silk scarf, yes. I think that would have worked perfectly. And two more for his wrists, although those would have had to be smaller. Or, I should say, narrower and shorter than a scarf. I think it would be hard to tie a bulky scarf tightly enough to hold a grown man's wrists when he's obviously going to be struggling with the superhuman strength of the dying."

"Which means," Frank said with a growing sense of horror, "the killer carefully planned every detail of what he was going to do and brought everything with him."

"Or her," Gino said with more than a little satisfaction.

"I guess so. You'd hardly expect to find silk scarves lying around an office. And the killer also had the presence of mind to take them away," Wesley said. "Probably because they could be linked to him. Or her," he added with a grin at Gino.

"One of our suspects was seen wearing a silk scarf that day," Gino said.

"But we can't figure out how the killer got Dinsmore to sit still while tying him up," Frank said. "Do you have any ideas?"

"Held a gun on him, maybe," Wesley said.

"We thought of that, but it would take two killers, then," Gino pointed out. "Because how does one person hold a gun on someone and tie him up at the same time?"

"Oh, I see what you mean. And that means the killer or killers brought a gun along, too. So why not just shoot him?"

"Too many people around," Frank said.

"But if you have a gun and are worried about someone hearing, why not just wait until a time and place where it won't matter," Wesley said.

"Like a dark alley?" Gino said. "If the killer is a female, that might be difficult."

"There aren't many places in the city where you could fire a gun without attracting a lot of attention, either," Frank said.

"You're right," Wesley said. "This murder is getting too complicated for me. Should I let you know if someone wants to claim the body?"

"I guess so," Frank said. "I think we already know everything we need, though." He paid Wesley for his services just in case the police didn't bother because they didn't seem very interested in solving Dinsmore's murder.

"Where to now?" Gino asked when they were on the street again.

"Home, I guess. Sarah and Maeve should be back by now. We'll tell them what we know so far and see if they can make any more sense of it than we did."

Sarah and Maeve listened patiently to Gino and Malloy recount the visits they had made that day. Mrs. Malloy and the children had not yet returned home from school, so the house was quiet.

"What did Eliza's scarf look like?" Sarah asked.

"I don't know," Gino said. "I didn't think to ask."

"Mrs. Hawkes was wearing a turban the first night we met her. Remember, Malloy? When she came into Mr. Vaughn's dressing room to find out what was keeping him."

"That's right. I remember. She had her head all wrapped up and some kind of feather stuck in it."

"A peacock feather," Sarah said. "And the turban was a length of blue-patterned silk wrapped very skillfully around her head. There must have been yards of it."

"Verena says she doesn't have any hair," Gino said.

"What do you mean, 'she doesn't have any hair'?" Maeve asked, thoroughly shocked.

"She said Mrs. Hawkes always wears a wig or some kind of turban, but she never shows her real hair," Gino said with far too much glee. "The girls said she either keeps it cut very short or it all fell out. Whichever it is, there's not much underneath the wigs."

"How interesting," Sarah said. "When I was talking to

Mrs. Ellsworth, I mentioned the age difference between Mrs. Hawkes and Mr. Vaughn. She asked me if Mrs. Hawkes dyes her hair, and I told her about the wigs. We decided her hair is probably gray or nearly so, and she's too vain to let people see it."

"That makes sense," Maeve said. "I suppose people can't see your wrinkles very well from the stage, either. That's probably why she's still managing to have leading men who are so much younger."

"But it wasn't Mrs. Hawkes who had the silk scarf on Saturday," Malloy reminded them. "It was Eliza. Where did she get it?"

"And if she'd just strangled a man with it, why was she wearing it and bragging about it?" Maeve said. "Is she really that cold-blooded?"

"She's an actress," Gino said. "Who knows?"

"Or maybe," Sarah said, "Mrs. Hawkes is the killer because she was the one who was too upset to perform that day."

"And she must have seen Eliza at some point to tell her she was playing the lead that day," Maeve said.

"And Eliza told Verena the scarf was a gift," Gino said. "What if Mrs. Hawkes was the one who gave it to her?"

"But did she give it to her before or after Dinsmore was killed?" Malloy said.

"So we really need to speak to all these people again and ask them these new questions," Sarah said. "But how many times can we sneak back into the theater? And I can't imagine Mrs. Hawkes will ever admit us to her hotel suite again."

"Verena would help," Gino said. "I, uh, I told her I'm a detective."

"I'm sure she was very impressed," Maeve said snidely.

"She was. I told her you were one, too," he said, undaunted.

"Good," Malloy said. "That means she doesn't have to be tricked into doing anything. Do you think she'll help Maeve get into the boardinghouse to question Eliza again?"

"Or at least to find out if the scarf is the same one Mrs. Hawkes was wearing," Maeve said.

"That would be nice," Sarah said, "but if Mrs. Hawkes wears the turbans with any regularity, I'm sure she has more than one. We just need to find out if Mrs. Hawkes gave one to her."

"So I'll need to speak with Eliza, if I can, because we need to know who gave her the scarf and when, and we need to know when Mrs. Hawkes told her she'd be playing the lead for the two matinees," Maeve said.

"If she'll tell you," Gino said.

"And if she won't, who will?" Sarah asked. "I'm sure Mrs. Hawkes won't be confiding in us anymore."

"What about Mr. Hawkes?" Malloy said.

"What about him?"

"From what Gino found out from that agent and the fellow from the Syndicate and even from Verena, Baxter Hawkes is going broke from not joining the Syndicate."

"What does that have to do with the two murders?" Sarah asked.

"Maybe nothing. But Adelia blames him for not allowing her to join when she's really the one resisting," Malloy said. "I'm wondering how I'd feel if my wife was being so unreasonable and causing us financial ruin."

"I'm sure you'll never have to find out," Sarah said with a grin.

"I certainly hope not," Malloy said with a grin of his own. "But Hawkes also had to stand by while his wife had affair after affair with her leading men. He must be very annoyed with Adelia by now."

"Annoyed enough to help us?" Sarah asked doubtfully. "He might have been the one who helped her kill Mr. Dinsmore."

"But if he's not, I'm just thinking I'd like to talk to him one more time. Maybe I can appeal to his better nature."

"Or to his frustration with his impossible wife," Maeve said.

"Where will you find him?" Sarah asked.

"Probably at the theater tomorrow. I'll have to wait until he gets there in the evening."

"And I'll see if I can convince Verena to get Maeve in to see Eliza tomorrow. I'll probably have to take Verena to lunch again," Gino said with an innocent grin. He should have been an actor.

"I'll be so grateful," Maeve replied, not even bothering to pretend she was.

"IS THAT ALL YOU WANT ME TO DO?" VERENA ASKED THE next day as they waited for their food in the small café around the corner from the boardinghouse.

"I don't think Eliza will talk to me, and she might not talk to Maeve, but maybe if she's caught off guard, she'll answer a few questions at least."

"I could ask her the questions. What do you want to know?"

"I don't want you to get involved. It could be dangerous."

Verena didn't seem to mind that at all. Her eyes sparkled with anticipation. "Dangerous? How?"

"Parnell Vaughn and Wylie Dinsmore are both dead. That's how dangerous."

The sparkle in her eyes died instantly. "Oh. But surely you don't think Eliza killed them."

"Somebody did. Somebody who was in the theater that day. And she certainly had good reasons to be angry with Vaughn, at least."

"I think you're being silly, but I'll get this Maeve girl in to see her, if that's all you want."

"Oh, I just thought of something. What did the scarf look like? The one Eliza was wearing on Saturday?"

"That's easy enough. It was blue and it had tiny little peacocks on it. Does that help?"

"I don't know. Mrs. Malloy saw Mrs. Hawkes wearing one as a turban, so we were wondering if it was the same one."

"Not likely. Eliza wouldn't dare take anything from Mrs. Hawkes."

"But didn't Eliza say it was a gift?"

"A gift from Mrs. Hawkes?" she scoffed. "Mrs. Hawkes would never give Eliza Grimes so much as the time of day, much less something so nice. Except it wasn't quite as nice as I thought at first."

"What do you mean?"

"I mean Eliza tried to tie it up into a turban like the ones Mrs. Hawkes wears, but she couldn't get it to stay. I was helping her, and that's when I noticed it was torn on one end."

"Torn how?"

"Well, maybe not torn, but there wasn't a hem on one end. It was ragged and fraying."

"Maybe that's why Mrs. Hawkes gave it to her," Gino suggested. "Or maybe she threw it away and Eliza found it."

"I doubt she'd throw away something so nice because the hem was out. She could've got the wardrobe people to fix it for her. But I guarantee Mrs. Hawkes didn't *give* it to Eliza."

"Why is that?"

"You should know. She hated her."

"Because of Vaughn, you mean."

"Not exactly. Some people might've thought so, because Mrs. Hawkes was in love with him and Eliza kept saying they were engaged, but that wasn't it. She knew Parnell wasn't going to marry Eliza. No, she hated Eliza because she was young and she had her whole career ahead of her, and Mrs. Hawkes was old and everybody was laughing at her behind her back for trying to pretend she could still fool people."

"Then I guess she hated you and Sally and Angie, too."

"Maybe, but we didn't take her role when she wanted a rest."

"That's another thing," Gino said. "Eliza played the lead at both matinees this weekend. Wasn't that unusual?"

"Yes, it was, unless Mrs. Hawkes was sick, but she wasn't sick. She did the Saturday night show just fine."

"Why did Eliza take her part those two afternoons, then?"

"I don't know. Everybody was surprised. She didn't tell

anybody but Eliza, I guess. Mr. Hawkes was bellowing like a bull when he found out, too. You should be asking Mrs. Hawkes these questions."

"I know, but we're afraid she won't answer them. We might have to ask her something eventually, but we want to get as much information as possible before then, in case she refuses to see us."

"It must be interesting being a detective."

"It's like being an actor sometimes, I guess. Like when I pretended to be a reporter."

Verena made a face. "You didn't fool me. But I could fool people, because I'm a real actress. Do you think I could be a detective?"

"They, uh, they don't have lady detectives."

"That girl Mazie is one. You said so yourself."

"Not really. Her real name is Maeve and she's Mr. Malloy's nanny."

Verena's eyes were sparkling again. "Is she? And he trusts her to pretend to be a detective?"

"And a reporter and whatever else she decides, I guess."

"She's better at it than you are," Verena said. "But don't worry, I'm sure you're a fine detective."

MAEVE WASN'T TOO HAPPY TO BE DEPENDING ON VERENA for help, but she dutifully knocked on the door of the boardinghouse. Verena answered it, and Maeve almost groaned. The girl was plainly having the time of her life assisting in this little charade, even though she was actually doing little more than opening a door for Maeve.

"She's in the parlor," Verena whispered. "We're putting a puzzle together."

"Remember, she thinks my name is Mazie."

Verena was insulted. "Of course!"

Maeve followed her into the parlor, a threadbare room with worn horsehair furniture that would be as comfortable as sitting on a hairbrush. Some old theater posters hung on the walls, but their original colors had faded to mere smudges. Eliza sat at a small card table holding a puzzle piece as she searched for a place it might fit. Hearing them enter, she looked up and immediately frowned.

"There she is, the world's worst reporter," she said.

Maeve simply smiled, not the least insulted for not doing a job she didn't even have. "I just need a little more information."

"Verena, the next time this girl knocks on the door, push her back down the front steps."

"That's no way to act," Maeve said cheerfully. "I'm going to make you famous." That part might actually be true. She plopped herself down in the chair Verena must have been using, across the table from Eliza. She noticed the puzzle was a street scene in some exotic foreign city where people like Eliza and Verena and Maeve would never go. She pulled out her notebook and pencil. "Do you know how Mr. Vaughn was killed?"

"I don't think I want to talk about this," Eliza hedged.

"I don't need any details, at least not if it makes you uncomfortable," Maeve hastily assured her. "I just . . . Nobody has told me exactly how he died."

"Someone hit him on the head."

Maeve scribbled in her notebook. "With what?"

"What do you mean, 'with what'?"

"Do you think they hit him with a fist?" Maeve asked innocently.

"Of course not."

"Maybe it was a candlestick," Verena said, earning a black look from Maeve, which she ignored. "I was in a play once where they used a candlestick to kill someone."

"Do you think it was a candlestick?" Maeve asked with mock eagerness.

"What would a candlestick be doing in Nelly's dressing room?" Eliza asked in disgust. "The theater has electricity."

"Oh," Maeve said with mock disappointment. "What could it have been, then?"

"How should I know?"

"Didn't anyone tell you?"

"No, and I didn't ask. Some things . . . Well, it's just too painful to think about," she said primly.

Maeve tried to judge if Eliza looked to be in pain, but in Maeve's opinion, she just looked annoyed. Could she really not know about the brass quail? If she'd killed Vaughn, maybe she was pretending not to know, but if she hadn't killed him, then she also hadn't even asked how her fiancé had died. How interesting.

"You're Mrs. Hawkes's understudy, aren't you?"

"Yes, I am." Eliza smiled now that they were talking about something that concerned her.

"How often do you substitute for her?"

Her smile faded a bit. "A . . . Once a week, usually."

"You played her part on both Saturday and Sunday, didn't you?"

"For the matinees, yes." Her smile was completely gone now.

"Was that what you usually did?"

"No, I . . . Mrs. Hawkes wasn't . . . She was tired."

"But she performed on Saturday night," Verena said.

"She just wanted to rest," Eliza said, a little belligerently. "It's hard doing three shows in two days like that."

"So she asked you to take her place for the matinees," Maeve clarified.

"That's right. Actually," she added with a touch of pride, "she asked me to take all the matinees from now on."

"All of them?"

"Yes. I told you, she's tired. She's pretty old, you know. So she asked me to take them so she can get more rest."

"When did she ask you?" Maeve asked.

Eliza blinked. "What?"

"When did she ask you to take the matinees?"

"I . . . The night before. Friday night, after the show."

Maeve frowned, pretending to be confused. "Then why didn't Mr. Hawkes know about the change?"

"What do you mean?"

"I mean he had no idea his wife wasn't going to perform on Saturday. I wonder why she didn't tell him if she'd made arrangements with you the night before."

"I don't know. You'll have to ask her about that."

Maeve flipped some pages in her notebook, pretending to look for something. "Mrs. Hawkes said she didn't tell you until Saturday, shortly before the performance," she lied.

Eliza frowned, but she recovered quickly. "Oh, that's right, she told me right before the show."

"When did you see her?"

"At the theater. She, uh, she told me and then she went home."

"But she wasn't at the theater that afternoon."

Eliza frowned again. "I'm sure she was."

"She wasn't. You must have seen her someplace else. Did you see her someplace else?"

Eliza jumped to her feet, suddenly furious. "Get out of here. I'm done talking to you. None of this has anything to do with Nelly's murder."

"Yes, it does," Maeve said calmly, making no move to get out. "And it has something to do with Wylie Dinsmore's death, too. Did you know he was strangled with a silk scarf?"

All the color drained from Eliza's face. "A scarf? But you said he was just strangled."

"Does it matter that the killer used a scarf?" Maeve asked with interest.

"No, I . . . I don't have to listen to this." Then she ran from the room and they could hear her feet clattering on the stairs.

"I don't think Gino will be pleased," Verena said. "She didn't answer any of your questions."

Maeve, however, was perfectly satisfied. "Watch for the scarf. She might try to get rid of it."

"Can I keep it if I find it?"

Maeve smiled magnanimously. "Suit yourself."

Frank waited until an hour and a half before the evening performance was to begin. He tried the front doors of the theater, figuring he might not get by a guard at the alley entrance, on the off chance the guard was even on duty. Or awake. Luckily, he found one of the front doors already unlocked in anticipation of the attendees to come.

The silence of the lobby seemed odd for such a public space, and for a moment he wondered if he'd actually find Hawkes in his office. But hadn't the man said he always came in early to check the gate from the day before? Frank hadn't realized the significance of that until he'd learned the Hawkeses hadn't been doing particularly well financially for the past few years. He went to the office door and stepped inside.

Once again the desk in the outer office was unoccupied, and Frank wondered if anyone ever sat there. The door to the inner office was ajar and a voice called out, "Who's there?"

Frank went in and Baxter Hawkes cursed when he saw who it was. "I thought I was finished with you."

"Not yet. I'm still trying to figure out who killed Parnell Vaughn and now I'm also trying to figure out who killed Wylie Dinsmore."

"Dinsmore?" he echoed, trying to act surprised. He was no actor, however. "Why would you be concerned about that?"

"Then you do know he was murdered."

"It was in the newspaper, and of course everyone was talking about it."

"Dinsmore is an old friend, I guess."

"I've known him since I started in this business, yes."

"Did your wife introduce you?"

Hawkes had begun to sweat, although the weather was

quite cool today and the office was comfortable. "Why would you think that?"

"Mrs. Hawkes told my wife that she and Dinsmore were lovers back before she met you."

"That's a lie. She'd never say a thing like that."

"Why?" Frank asked with genuine curiosity. Just to let Hawkes know he wasn't leaving soon, he took a seat in the single empty chair in front of Hawkes's desk.

"What do you mean? She'd never say it because it wasn't true."

"Not only did she say it, she said they were, uh, occasionally lovers even lately. I believe she said it was for old time's sake."

"That's ridiculous."

"Why? Because she already had a lover? One who was much younger and better-looking?"

"I won't have you talking about my wife that way, Malloy."

"I'm only repeating what you told me yourself. I also know that Dinsmore was at the theater the day Parnell Vaughn was murdered."

"How do you know that?"

"Once again, your wife told mine, and then Dinsmore confirmed it. He was visiting Mrs. Hawkes that day, it seems."

"I doubt that," Hawkes tried, but he didn't seem very certain.

"He claims he was trying to convince her to join the Syndicate. He said the Syndicate had hired him to bring her into the fold."

"He said that?" Hawkes said in genuine surprise.

"Yes, he did," Frank said, intrigued by Hawkes's reaction. "But I happen to know the Syndicate wasn't paying him. In fact, they said they weren't all that interested in having her join."

"That's . . . That's not true," he said weakly. "They . . . they would kill to have Adelia Hawkes."

"Would they really?" Frank said in mock surprise.

"Oh, I don't mean *kill*. Not *murder*! But they . . . Adelia could make them a fortune."

"Mr. Frohman said her best days are behind her."

"No, he didn't! He knows better than that!" Hawkes insisted.

"Oh, he'd be happy to welcome her, but not happy enough to pay Dinsmore to recruit her. Why do you think Dinsmore made that claim if it wasn't true?"

"I . . . How should I know why Dinsmore did anything? Oh, I knew he was still in love with Adelia. He'd known her before I did, but she'd never cared for him that way. She made no secret of it. That's why she married me and not him."

"He was still carrying a torch for her after all these years, I guess."

"Adelia is a remarkable woman," Hawkes said, unwittingly echoing Dinsmore's assessment.

"So maybe he was just trying to convince her to join the Syndicate out of the goodness of his heart. Because it would be in her best interest."

"Yes, that's probably it," Hawkes agreed quickly. Too quickly.

"Mr. Hawkes, I know your wife blamed you for not letting her join the Syndicate. She claimed you'd convinced her she could do much better without it, but that's not true, is it?"

"I think I already explained that my wife insists on playing the leading roles, even though those tend to be much younger women."

"Yes, you explained that no one else would allow her to take those roles or to take advantage of her younger leading men," Frank said baldly.

Hawkes flinched a bit, but he didn't fly into a rage as Frank had half expected. "That is correct. She knows if we join the Syndicate, she will be relegated to more mature roles. She could do them brilliantly, of course. Her Lady Mac—Well, her lead in the Scottish play is magnificent. But she won't hear of it."

Frank blinked, realizing his mother had been right about theater people not saying *Macbeth* in a theater for fear of bad luck. But he didn't let it distract him. "Even though you encouraged her to join the Syndicate. And you did, didn't you?"

Hawkes slumped in his chair as if the weight of the world had settled upon him. "Of course I did. We're losing money every night here. You've attended the play, so you've seen the crowds. They get smaller each night, and I don't dare go on tour. I'm still in debt from the last one."

"So you tried to convince your wife to join the Syndicate, and when she refused, you . . ."

"I hired Wylie Dinsmore to convince her."

13

THE NEXT DAY WAS WEDNESDAY, EXACTLY ONE WEEK since Parnell Vaughn had died. Sarah hugged Catherine extra hard before sending her off to school that morning.

Sarah blinked at tears as she watched Mother Malloy and the children disappear down Bank Street. She should be happy that their way was now clear to adopt Catherine and become a real family, but how could they take joy in the prospect when a man was dead and people believed Malloy had killed him? Why couldn't they figure out who had killed Mr. Vaughn?

Gino arrived at the house midmorning so he could hear what Malloy had discovered last night at the theater and they could discuss their theories of who the killer might be. Again. They should be closer to figuring it out than they were. As many people as they had questioned and as many questions as they had asked, they should at least have a solid theory. Instead the killer was still as elusive as a shadow dancing on a wall.

Maeve joined them as they gathered around the table in the breakfast room and drank the coffee their cook, Velvet, had made fresh for them.

"I don't have much news to tell you," Malloy said to Gino. He'd already shared his news with Sarah and Maeve the night before. "Hawkes confirmed that his wife and Dinsmore were lovers back before he married her, but he didn't seem to know they'd renewed their acquaintance recently."

"That's probably not something either of them would have mentioned to him," Gino said.

"Probably not, so he wouldn't have been jealous," Malloy said. "The only thing new that Hawkes told me is that he's the one who paid Dinsmore to recruit Mrs. Hawkes for the Syndicate."

"What?" Gino yelped.

"It makes perfect sense," Sarah said, "when you realize the play is losing money and Mr. Hawkes is in debt."

"Which I guess is something else new that he told me," Malloy admitted. "He can't even afford to take the play on tour. The Syndicate is really his only hope."

"Do you think Mrs. Hawkes knows this?" Gino asked.

"We wondered that, too," Maeve said.

"She can't know," Malloy said. "Why wouldn't she agree to join the Syndicate if she understands they'll go bankrupt if they don't?"

"So maybe Mr. Hawkes hasn't told her how bad it really is," Sarah said, "or else she's chosen to ignore his warnings.

He must be desperate if he hired one of his wife's old lovers to convince her, though."

"I can promise you he's desperate," Malloy said. "But I can't see where all this has any bearing on Vaughn's murder, or Dinsmore's either, for that matter."

"Except that with Dinsmore dead, Hawkes loses a chance to persuade his wife to join the Syndicate," Gino said.

"On the other hand," Maeve said, "if Vaughn died, the play might fold and that could force Mrs. Hawkes to join."

"I can't imagine whoever beat poor Mr. Vaughn to death was thinking about closing the play or anything else so coolly logical," Sarah said.

"Which probably means Hawkes didn't kill Vaughn," Malloy said. "At least not because he wanted the play to fold."

"But he might've killed him out of jealousy or he might've helped his wife kill Dinsmore if she'd killed Vaughn," Maeve said. "He'd want to protect her at all costs."

"So we can believe Mrs. Hawkes might have killed Vaughn and her husband helped her kill Dinsmore," Malloy said. "But if he killed Vaughn, would he have asked her to help him kill Dinsmore?"

"That doesn't seem likely," Sarah said. "How could any man assume his wife would cheerfully help him murder an old friend?"

"He knows her better than we do," Maeve said. "Maybe he knew perfectly well that she'd help."

"That's frightening," Sarah said while they all considered just how frightening it was.

Malloy brought them back to the issue at hand. "What about Eliza and Winters?"

"I can't imagine Winters getting angry enough to kill Vaughn," Maeve said. "For such a handsome man, he's awfully dull. You can see that Eliza still doesn't think much of him, and I can see why."

This pleased Gino, although Maeve pretended not to notice. Sarah said, "The question is, would he help kill Dinsmore to save Eliza?"

"He might if he thought it would win her devotion," Maeve said. "He wouldn't like it, though, and I think it would play on his conscience."

"And if he did help her, she should be showing more devotion," Gino said.

"And I'm certain Eliza wouldn't help Winters kill Dinsmore because she doesn't care a fig for him," Maeve said.

"So we think either of the women could have killed Vaughn, and we're fairly sure the men would be willing to help kill Dinsmore, but not the other way around. Is that right?"

"Yes, but why couldn't the two women have worked together?" Maeve asked. "I'm sure there's something funny going on between them, at least."

"Why do you say that?" Malloy asked.

"Because of the scarf. Mrs. Frank thinks it's the same one Mrs. Hawkes was wearing as a turban the night you first met her."

"Yes, blue with small peacocks printed on it," Sarah said. "That explains why she wore a peacock feather with it, even though Mrs. Ellsworth assures me it's bad luck to wear one on the stage."

"But she wasn't wearing it on the stage," Maeve said.

"As I pointed out to Mrs. Ellsworth. At any rate, it was Mrs. Hawkes's scarf, and on the day Mr. Dinsmore was murdered—"

"By being strangled with a length of fabric," Gino reminded them.

"—Eliza returns home to her boardinghouse with the scarf. How did she get it?"

"Maybe Mrs. Hawkes gave it to her," Malloy said.

"Except Mrs. Hawkes hated Eliza," Gino said. "Verena claims Mrs. Hawkes wouldn't give Eliza the time of day, much less an expensive silk scarf."

"So maybe Eliza stole it," Sarah said.

"How would she get away with stealing it, though?" Maeve asked. "Everyone would know who it belonged to, so she'd never be able to wear it."

"Or maybe Eliza found it," Sarah said.

"But how would something like that get lost?" Gino asked.

"And if she found it because Mrs. Hawkes had lost it someplace," Maeve said, "it would be the same as if she stole it. She'd know who it belonged to and would either need to return it or hide it, since everyone else would know who it belonged to, too."

"Maybe she found it in the trash," Sarah suggested.

"Verena thought that was what happened because the scarf was torn on one end," Gino said.

"It was?" Sarah cried. "You didn't say that before."

"That's because I only found out from Verena yesterday. She said Eliza tried to tie it up into a turban like Mrs. Hawkes did, but she couldn't get it to stay, and that's when

Verena noticed the scarf was ragged on one end, like the hem was out or torn off or something."

"What are you thinking, Sarah?" Malloy asked.

The tiny hairs on the back of her neck were prickling. "Didn't Mr. Wesley tell you Mr. Dinsmore's wrists had been tied with strips of cloth?"

"He didn't say *strips* but yes, that's probably what it was."

"They might have been cut or torn from the end of the scarf."

"Of course!" Maeve said.

"I should've thought of that right off," Gino said. "When Verena told me, I said maybe Mrs. Hawkes had thrown it away because it was torn, but she said the costume people could have easily fixed it."

"But maybe she didn't want the costume people or anyone else to see it," Malloy mused. "Maybe she did try to get rid of it somehow and Eliza found it and claimed it."

"Or maybe Eliza found it somewhere and used it to kill Dinsmore but didn't see any reason not to wear it afterward," Maeve said.

"You really don't like her, do you?" Gino marveled.

They heard the doorbell echoing through the house and waited while their maid Hattie answered. In a few minutes Mrs. Ellsworth came in carrying a plate over which she had draped a napkin.

"I saw Mr. Donatelli arrive, so I thought he might enjoy some of the carrot cake I made yesterday," she announced happily. "Nelson and I will never eat it all before it gets stale."

Hattie took the plate from her unresisting hands. "I'll

just put this on some plates," she said, and disappeared into the kitchen while Frank pulled out a chair for their neighbor.

"How fortunate. We were just discussing the case we're working on," Sarah said with a smile. Mrs. Ellsworth would have known that's what they were doing if Gino was here. "I'm sure you're interested to know who the killer is."

"Of course I am," she said happily. "So you've solved it?"

"No, but we think we have some new information," Sarah said. She quickly explained about the scarf while the others somehow managed to hide their amusement.

Malloy, however, could not resist a little teasing. "Did you know actors won't say the name *Macbeth* in a theater?"

"Of course they won't," Mrs. Ellsworth said in all seriousness. "It's terribly bad luck, although I believe they have a little ritual they do to break the spell if someone says it accidentally. Something about going outside and turning around three times, I think."

"Oh, like throwing a pinch of spilled salt over your shoulder," Maeve said. She had honed the art of seeming completely sincere when discussing superstitions with Mrs. Ellsworth.

"Exactly. Actors are more superstitious than most people, although I'm not sure why. Perhaps because an actor's life is rather uncertain even in the best of times. I believe I told you about the peacock feather, didn't I, Mrs. Frank?"

"Yes, you did."

"And the ghost light?"

"Uh, no," Sarah said.

"Ghost light?" Maeve echoed. "What is that?"

"Oh, actors are terrified of ghosts. I'm not sure why

theaters should be more prone to hauntings than any other building, but actors seem to think they are. They always leave a light on when the theater is empty to keep the ghosts away."

"What kind of a light?" Malloy asked with a level of interest that surprised Sarah.

"I don't know. I suppose they use electricity now, if they can, but in the past—"

"No, I mean where is this ghost light?"

"Oh, I see. On the stage. At the back, if I remember correctly. I read this fascinating article about—"

"I saw that light," Malloy told them. "The first time I questioned Hawkes. I walked through the auditorium and it was completely dark except for one light on the stage."

"They wouldn't want to take any chances, I'm sure, especially since there really was a murder in the theater," Mrs. Ellsworth said with some satisfaction.

Hattie arrived with the cake, which she had divided into five pieces, and served it to them along with a new pot of coffee. They chatted amiably about the children and Nelson Ellsworth's upcoming wedding while they enjoyed the cake, but Malloy contributed nothing to the conversation. He sat silently, eating the delicious cake absently while he considered something that obviously had nothing to do with what they were now discussing.

Sarah wanted to ask him, but maybe he didn't want to reveal his thoughts with Mrs. Ellsworth there. She was just a neighbor, after all. But he proved Sarah wrong.

"Mrs. Ellsworth, do you think actors might participate in a séance?"

"A séance? You mean like that lovely Italian girl used to do? What was her name?"

"Madame Serafina," Sarah supplied.

"Oh yes, she was really quite gifted, if I recall. She helped me find my dear husband's watch. I wonder if she is still giving readings."

"She is. And she just had a baby," Sarah said, remembering too late that this was supposed to be a secret. "Which is how I happened to see her."

"Did you deliver it?" Mrs. Ellsworth asked, delighted.

"Yes, I did. It was rather unexpected and I was visiting and, well, she had a little girl. Lilla Nicolette." Sarah didn't mention her last name was Straface because that would distract Mrs. Ellsworth, who would undoubtedly want to know what had happened to Mr. DiLoreto.

"And," Malloy said as if sensing Sarah's need to distract Mrs. Ellsworth from the subject of babies, "she offered to do a séance to help us figure out who killed Parnell Vaughn."

"She did help you once before, didn't she?"

"Yes, but that time it wasn't the spirits who told us who the killer was," Malloy said with just a hint of a grin.

"I think you underestimate the spirits, Mr. Malloy," Mrs. Ellsworth replied with a grin of her own. "And to answer your question, I think you could easily frighten a bunch of superstitious actors into having a séance."

"ARE YOU SERIOUS?" SARAH ASKED HIM WHEN MRS. Ellsworth had finally gone. "Do you really want to stage a séance?"

Frank loved the way her eyes sparkled when she was annoyed with him. He would have kissed her if Gino and Maeve weren't looking on with such avid interest. "It worked the last time."

"Yes, but the killer was involved with Serafina and the séance and . . . And you know perfectly well Serafina staged that whole thing to frighten the killer into a confession."

"Which is what we'll do, too. We'll need to meet with her first so she knows everything we know and so she can set everything up." They both knew from experience that a successful séance usually included sounds and even lighting effects that were not produced supernaturally.

Sarah gave him a black look. "All right, maybe Serafina really could frighten the killer into confessing, but how do you propose to get everyone to attend a séance in the first place? I can't imagine the killer would ever agree and the rest of them won't have a reason to attend."

"Then we'll have to give them a reason," Frank said.

"How will we do that?" Sarah asked.

"I bet Madame Serafina would have an idea," Gino said.

Serafina did have an idea. No, she wanted to be called Sarah now, although Sarah found it difficult to remember.

Sarah and Malloy had decided to go to Waverly Place to consult with her right after lunch, leaving Gino to check in at their office to see if any paying clients had turned up looking for help and Maeve to tend to the children when they got home from school.

Serafina's maid had tried to turn them away, claiming Madame Serafina was on holiday, but when Sarah explained who they were, they were admitted to Serafina's private quarters where she was spending some time playing with Lilla.

She was very happy to see Malloy, and he paid the new baby the appropriate amount of attention, admiring her beauty and saying how much she looked like Serafina. Sarah inquired after her health and gave the baby a quick check.

When all the pleasantries had been dealt with, Serafina said, "You have decided to have a séance."

"How did you guess?" Sarah asked jokingly.

"I did not guess. The spirits told me. You want to frighten the killer into confessing."

"Without giving him—or her—a reason to hurt anyone else," Sarah cautioned, remembering the near disaster the last time they had set a trap for a killer.

"Do not worry, although I do not know why this person killed, so I cannot be sure they will not kill again. We will be careful, though. Who is it you suspect?"

Malloy summarized the four people they suspected and the reasons why. Sarah explained about the scarf and why they thought it was important.

"You do not know how this Eliza got the scarf?"

"No, we don't," Sarah said. "But we did learn one thing that might be very helpful. Actors are notoriously superstitious."

"They are also afraid of ghosts," Malloy said. "They actually leave a light burning when the theater is empty to scare them away."

Serafina was nodding, obviously intrigued. "Yes, that is

very helpful. We must give them a real ghost, then. If they think this Mr. Vaughn is haunting them, all of them will be anxious to send him back to the spirit world."

"Are you suggesting that we have someone pretend to be a ghost?" Sarah asked in alarm.

"Oh no, nothing like that. If a real person pretends to be a ghost, he may be discovered and the whole plot will be ruined. No, we need someone to pretend to have seen Mr. Vaughn's ghost. Do you think Maeve could do this?"

Maeve would be very gratified that Serafina had suggested her, but . . . "I'm afraid too many people at the theater know Maeve works for us, so they're not likely to believe her."

"I see. Is there someone else?"

"What about that Verena girl of Gino's?" Malloy said to Sarah.

"Officer Donatelli has a lady friend?" Serafina asked in amusement.

"He's not *Officer* Donatelli anymore," Malloy said. "He works for me now. I'm a private investigator."

"I know. Mrs. Malloy told me all about your success."

"And Verena Rose, the young lady, is one of the actresses in the play. We don't believe she's involved in the murders and she's been very helpful," Sarah said.

"And she might be a little sweet on Gino, so she's also very eager to please him," Malloy said.

"If she is an actress, she could be very convincing, too. I will need to speak with her and make some plans. She will be very upset after seeing Mr. Vaughn's ghost, and she must know me and suggest that I can help."

"But won't the killer be too smart to come to a séance if

Vaughn is going to tell everyone who killed him?" Malloy asked.

"That will not be the purpose of the séance," Serafina told him sweetly, "because we do not yet know who killed him. Instead he will want to be freed from this earth, and his friends will gather to help him go. Only someone who is not his friend would refuse."

Sarah saw it now. "So the killer will be afraid not to attend because other people will wonder why he or she didn't want to help Mr. Vaughn."

"Even if they do not believe in the spirits," Serafina said, "they will want to please their friends."

"Verena has a matinee today and a show tonight, too," Sarah said. "Well, they all do, but she probably won't be able to meet with you until tomorrow."

"That will be fine. I am not seeing clients yet." She smiled fondly at the baby lying in the cradle beside her. "I am too busy seeing my baby, so any time is good."

"We'll be glad to pay you for the séance, too," Malloy said.

But Serafina waved away his offer with a flick of her wrist. "That is not necessary. I am a wealthy woman now. You both helped me and Nicola when we needed it. I will never forget what you did."

"BE SURE TO TELL MAEVE," GINO SAID WHEN MR. MALloy met him at their office and told him he was to attend the play that night and take Verena to a late supper afterward.

"She already knows," Mr. Malloy said. "And she's not speaking to me."

"Because she's jealous?" Gino asked hopefully.

"No, because there's nothing for her to do. Nothing for any of us to do yet."

"Maybe we can help with the séance. Don't you have to make sounds and knock on things?"

"Madame Serafina has a staff to do that for her. All you have to do is convince Verena to pretend to see Vaughn's ghost and get everyone else to go to the séance."

"I'm sure she'll be thrilled to help. And she should be pretty good about seeing the ghost. I've seen her in the play twice now, and she's a great actress."

"Be sure to tell her you think so. Women love compliments," Mr. Malloy advised.

Gino enjoyed seeing the play again that evening. He had technically seen it only one and a half times before, since he and Maeve had sneaked in at intermission once. But Verena was still just as convincing as the ne'er-do-well brother's gold-digging fiancée. Mrs. Hawkes wasn't quite as good as he'd remembered from the first time he saw the play, though. She looked older under the harsh lights, and she moved stiffly, as if she'd hurt herself and was concealing it. Gino had never seen her perform with Parnell Vaughn, but Armistead Winters didn't seem to inspire her very much, and Gino couldn't help wondering if he was diddling her the way Vaughn had been. Watching them pretend to be in love was a little embarrassing, if the truth were told, and the many empty seats said others may have felt the same.

Gino had learned he should send a message in with the doorman so Verena would know he was waiting for her and needed to see her alone. Otherwise, her friends might try to join them since the crowd of stage-door johnnies waiting for an available actress was sparse tonight.

Verena hurried out to meet him in the alley and squealed happily at the bouquet of flowers he had brought. "Actresses always love getting flowers."

"Is there a superstition about them?" Gino asked in jest.

"Why, yes, there is," she said to his surprise. "No actor will accept flowers before a performance, because we haven't earned them yet. That's why people bring flowers up to the stage at the end of a play."

"I never saw them do that," Gino said as she took his arm and they started toward the street.

"That's because you've never been to a good play," she said with a grin.

"I thought *you* were very good," he said, remembering his instructions.

"That's because I am," she replied happily.

They decided to eat at the Chinese restaurant a few blocks away. Other theatergoers had preceded them, so they had to wait a bit for a table. When they'd finally been seated and placed their order, Gino leaned over the tiny tabletop so he could keep his voice low and said, "We're going to need your help again."

As he'd expected, her eyes widened and she actually laughed out loud. "I knew it! What do you need me to do? I hope I don't have to seduce Mr. Hawkes."

Gino almost choked at that. "Oh no. All you have to do is see a ghost."

. . .

The next day, at midmorning, Gino fetched Verena at the boardinghouse. He brought her flowers again, so the other girls would believe he was here for reasons of romance and not business. The way Verena clung to his arm as they walked away made Gino wonder if Verena was starting to believe that, too.

"Is this woman a real medium?" she asked as they walked to the Third Avenue elevated train station at 18th Street.

"There's no such thing as a real medium," Gino said.

"Who told you that?" she asked in amazement.

"I just . . . know."

She gave an unladylike snort. "You need to at least pretend or she'll be insulted."

"I don't think she'll be insulted by anything I do."

Verena's eyes narrowed as she studied him. "How well do you know her?"

"Not very. I, uh, worked on a case she was involved in a few years ago."

"What kind of case?"

"Somebody got killed at one of her séances," Gino said before thinking maybe that was not the best way to ensure Verena's cooperation.

But instead of being shocked, she looked delighted. "I can't wait to meet her!"

Gino had forgotten just how lovely Madame Serafina Straface was. He found himself a little breathless when she took his hand and greeted him like an old friend.

"Mr. Malloy tells me you work as a private investigator now," she said.

"That's right. I, uh, I work for him in his agency."

"And this must be Miss Rose." She held out her hand and Verena took it tentatively.

Gino couldn't blame her for her hesitation. Serafina looked positively exotic. Besides being beautiful, with large, dark eyes that seemed to see into a person's soul, she wore a purple robe made of shiny fabric that made her look like some sort of saint.

"Please, sit down," she said. They were in a small parlor furnished with a sofa and a few stuffed chairs. Serafina probably used it for her personal living room. The other rooms, he knew from previous visits, were used as a waiting area for clients and the large parlor was the séance room. "Has Mr. Donatelli told you what we would like you to do?"

"Sort of, I guess," Verena said. She didn't look nearly as excited as she had on the way down, but he could see her making a visible effort to get her confidence back. She already knew Serafina wasn't a real medium, even though she might look like one at the moment. "You want me to pretend to see a ghost."

"Yes, the ghost of Mr. Vaughn. You will tell me about the theater and we will decide where you will see him. We will also plan what he will say to you, or rather what you will tell people he said to you. You are an actress, so you can do this."

"Oh yes," Verena said eagerly.

"This plan will take some time. Tonight you will see the ghost after the play is over. You will be very upset and you will make everyone else upset, too."

Verena was smiling now. "I can do that."

"Good. Tomorrow night and Saturday, you will perform as usual, but you will be afraid to go back to the place you saw the ghost. You will tell everyone you know a medium and you have arranged for me to contact Mr. Vaughn's spirit and find out how to remove it from the theater. You will tell them they must come with you to the séance so Mr. Vaughn can leave the theater and rest in peace."

"When will we have the séance?" Verena asked.

"I think we will have it on Sunday. Is it true you actors do not go to church?"

"That's true. It can't be early, though."

"I think we will set it for eleven o'clock. Will that do?"

"Yes, I think that would be perfect."

"Good. We will practice before you leave so you know what to do and what to say when you see the ghost. Is this something you can do?"

"Of course!" Verena said.

"Then on Sunday, you will bring everyone here for the séance."

"What will I have to do for that? I've never been to a séance."

"You will come that morning and we will talk. You will tell me what everyone has said and if anyone has refused to come. Then I will tell you what you should do. I think you will only have to be here and react to whatever happens, though."

"That should be easy enough."

"But you cannot tell anyone of our plan. Not anyone at all. No one will keep a secret like this."

"Gino already warned me. I can tell them about it afterward, though, can't I? When the killer is caught?"

Serafina smiled. "I think that will be a very good idea."

"WHAT IS SHE GOING TO DO?" MAEVE ASKED THAT AFTERnoon when Gino arrived at the Malloy house to report on the visit with Serafina. Sarah noted that Maeve seemed more than a little jealous that Verena was getting the spotlight.

"She's going to see a ghost at the theater tonight, and tomorrow night she's going to tell everyone she's scheduled a séance with an old friend of hers so Vaughn can be released. I think that's what Serafina called it. His soul is stuck here for some reason, haunting the theater."

"Verena will talk about the ghost on Friday and Saturday and hopefully get everyone thoroughly frightened. Then, on Sunday, they will hold the séance," Sarah said. "Malloy and I will be observing from peepholes like we did the time we helped Serafina."

"Why can't I observe, too?" Maeve said. "Or at least be there?"

"Do you know how many people will be in the house even without you?" Sarah asked.

"I could watch the baby," Maeve said. "Does Serafina have a nursemaid?"

"Yes, she does. Her cousin just came over from Italy. In fact, she's letting people think the cousin is the baby's mother."

"Maybe I could—"

"Everyone knows you, Maeve," Gino reminded her. "If they see you or me there, they'll know something isn't right."

"What about Mr. and Mrs. Malloy, though?" she argued. "Everyone knows them, too."

"Yes, but we'll be hidden, and there isn't room to hide anyone else," Malloy said, ending the argument.

"All right, but you have to make it up to me."

"To both of us," Gino said.

"We'll think of something," Malloy said with a grin. "Maybe I'll let you tell O'Connor who the killer is. That should make him like you, too."

"I don't know why you're complaining," Maeve said to Gino. "You get to be at the theater tonight."

"Somebody has to see what happens and watch everybody's reactions and cover for Verena if she messes up," Gino said. "She isn't trained for that."

Maeve's glare told him she didn't think he was either, but she said, "What do we do if the people we suspect don't want to come to the séance?"

"Verena might have to see the ghost again, but Serafina thinks once will be enough."

"Serafina told me that people who have hurt another person want to be forgiven," Sarah said, remembering. "That's why they try to contact people who are dead."

"Not everyone is sorry for hurting another person," Maeve said.

"Let's hope this killer is," Sarah said. "A guilty conscience would be very helpful in getting them to confess."

14

THAT NIGHT GINO WAS IN HIS CUSTOMARY SPOT IN THE alley beside the theater after the show. He'd come bearing flowers again, and he was giving his message for Verena to the guard so he could pass it along to her when they heard a bloodcurdling scream.

The two other stage-door johnnies took off running in the opposite direction, but Gino followed the guard back into the building. He didn't even have to pretend to be alarmed. The screaming continued as Gino and the guard ran down the hallway. By the time they reached the main corridor where the dressing rooms were, the rest of the cast and most of the crew had already converged around the source of the caterwauling.

"Stop it!" some man was shouting.

"Slap her!" a woman suggested.

Gino wasn't fast enough, and the man—who Gino realized was Mr. Hawkes—did just that. The screaming stopped instantly, and after a second or two of complete silence, Verena began to sob.

By then, Gino had managed to push himself through the crowded hallway to where Verena was slumped on the floor. "Verena, what's going on?" He turned to Mr. Hawkes, who was absently rubbing his palm as if he were the one injured. "What did you hit her for?"

"She was hysterical," he said defensively.

Gino turned his attention back to Verena. "Why were you screaming? Did somebody attack you?"

Verena looked up from where she'd collapsed after her knees gave way from her terror. She was still sobbing and holding a hand to her stinging cheek. "Thank heaven you're here," she cried, reaching for him.

He dropped the flowers and took her hand, helping her to her feet. "What happened?"

"It was Parnell," she told him, completely horrified. "I *saw* him!"

Even Gino gasped.

But Mr. Hawkes, at least, was determined to be sensible. "That's impossible. Parnell is dead."

"But he was there! I saw him!" she cried, her voice trembling as she pointed an unsteady finger at Vaughn's dressing room. It still bore his name, Gino noticed, and the little star below it. Actors probably had a superstition about dead actors' dressing rooms.

"What were you doing in there anyway?" someone asked.

"I heard my name," Verena said wildly. "I was just coming down the hall and someone called my name! I thought . . ." She looked around until she found Armistead Winters among the onlookers. "I thought Armistead must have finally moved in there. The door was ajar, so I pushed it open and—" Her voice broke on a sob.

"Was it him?" Angie demanded. She'd also worked her way through the crowd to Verena's side, and she slipped her arm around Verena's waist. "Was it Parnell?"

"As plain as day! He was . . . He looked so sad! He said, 'Help me, Verena. I can't get home.'"

More gasps and now murmurs as people expressed horror or disbelief or simply amazement.

"What did he mean by that?" someone else asked.

"Just what he said, I'm sure! He said he couldn't get home and begged me to help him. Then I started screaming and he faded away." She shuddered and began to sob again. This time Gino put his arms around her and let her weep against his chest.

"There now, don't cry," he said, assuming his role of manly protector. "It was just your imagination. There's no such thing as ghosts."

Verena's head jerked up and her sobbing ceased as anger replaced her terror. "No such thing?" she demanded.

"Well, no," he said with a little less certainty. "I mean, you can't believe that—"

"I *saw* him! With my own eyes. He was just as clear as you are now!"

"But he's dead," Gino said quite reasonably.

"I know that, and so does he," she argued right back. "But he said he can't get home. Don't you know what that means?"

"I, uh, no, but—"

"It means his soul is stuck here," she said, every bit of her horror visible on her lovely face. "Right *here*, in this theater."

More gasps, but now Eliza was pushing her way to Verena. "If it was really Nelly, why didn't he call for *me*?" she demanded. "I'm his fiancée. I'm the woman he loved!"

Did someone snicker? More than one someone, or Gino's ears were deceiving him. Eliza, however, chose not to notice.

"How should I know why he called me instead of you? I didn't ask him to, I'll tell you that. I've never been so scared in my whole entire life!" She shuddered again and Angie put her arm around her once more.

"There now, don't get yourself all worked up again."

"But what are we going to do?" This was Sally, who had also managed to reach them.

"We're going to go to our dressing rooms and change clothes and go home," Mr. Hawkes said with the voice of reason. "Just like we always do."

"But there's a ghost in the theater," Sally said.

"We don't know that," Hawkes said. His reason was slipping just a bit.

"*I* know it!" Verena said, her voice verging on hysteria again. "Maybe the rest of you aren't scared, but I am!"

"But there's no such thing as ghosts," Gino tried again. This time Verena literally pushed him away and turned to her friends, who started murmuring all the comforting things women said to each other when someone was upset.

This gave him the opportunity to look around to see how

the rest of the cast and crew were reacting. Everyone looked worried, but when he found Mrs. Hawkes at the edge of the crowd, her face was as white as if she'd seen the ghost herself.

"Verena," someone called, silencing the murmured words of comfort. Gino needed a second to realize Mrs. Hawkes had said the name.

Verena looked up and found her. The crowd parted so Mrs. Hawkes could approach. Even in a hallway she commanded the stage. When she reached Verena, she took her hand. "How did he look?"

"He . . . Like he always did. I knew him right away, and for a minute, I didn't remember he was dead. I mean, you never expect to see a ghost, do you? And he didn't look like a ghost, not the way you think a ghost would look. He just looked like himself. Except he was so sad, and when he said he couldn't get home, I remembered that he was dead and then I was so scared . . ."

She was sobbing again, and Mrs. Hawkes patted her shoulder. "There now, it's over and you're all right."

Verena's head snapped up and the sob caught in her throat. "Over? Do you really think it's over? You don't think he's stuck here and will keep haunting the place?"

"Haunting?" Sally echoed. "Is that what he said? That he's going to *haunt the theater*?"

Now Eliza's face was white, too, and Mrs. Hawkes looked as if she might faint.

"Stop this," Mr. Hawkes shouted. "You're all being ridiculous."

"Ridiculous?" his wife shouted back. "Is that what you think? She saw Parnell! He spoke to her. That's not ridiculous. That's terrifying!"

She swayed and Armistead Winters caught her. "Are you all right, Mrs. Hawkes?"

"Doesn't anyone have any smelling salts?" Angie wailed.

"I'll get some," a woman from the crew said, and hurried off.

"This has gotten out of hand," Mr. Hawkes said in another effort to assert his authority. "Miss Rose thought she saw something, but it was probably just another actor playing a trick on her."

"It wasn't a trick," Verena cried.

"Or she was imagining things," he said less magnanimously. "We've all been upset since Parnell's death, but there's no reason to believe he's haunting us."

"*Us?* What do you mean *us?* I thought he was just haunting the theater," one of the crew said.

"He's not haunting anything, because he's dead," Mr. Hawkes said, apparently unaware of how faulty his logic was. "Now, everyone, get back to your business. It's been a long day and we're all tired and want to get home."

"Oh, Army," Eliza said, her eyes fluttering, "where are those smelling salts?"

For a moment Armistead Winters was torn between continuing to support his employer, Mrs. Hawkes, and going to comfort his intended, Miss Grimes. Luckily for him, Mr. Hawkes shouldered him out of the way and took possession of Mrs. Hawkes and her grief, leaving Winters free to turn his attentions to Eliza.

"He's still here," Mrs. Hawkes said to her husband as he led her to her dressing room. "I knew it. I felt it."

Mr. Hawkes muttered something Gino didn't catch and then practically shoved her into her dressing room and slammed the door behind them.

Winters tried to comfort Eliza but she was too interested in pretending to be upset to tolerate comfort at the moment. She'd let Verena steal the scene from her, and she wasn't doing a good enough job of stealing it back, and that annoyed her.

Eliza clutched Winters's arm and gazed up at him, wide-eyed. "Oh, Army, what shall we do?"

Maeve was right. She really wasn't a very good actress.

"What shall we do about what?" Winters asked, trying to nudge her along to her dressing room.

Verena's friends were ushering her away as well, and some of the crew members were going with them while Verena lamented her bad luck at being the one to see the ghost of Parnell Vaughn.

"Verena," Gino called after her, "I'll wait for you."

She cast him a black look. "Don't bother. I'm too upset to go out tonight, especially with somebody who doesn't believe me."

"I believe you," he called after her, but that only earned him black looks from everyone else.

"I think you ruined your chances with her, son," the guard said as they watched everyone else drift away, back to whatever they had been doing when Verena screamed.

"You might be right. I guess I should've pretended to believe her about the ghost."

The guard made a strange motion that might have been a shiver. "I believe her. There's been too many strange things happening around here."

"Like what?" Gino asked with real interest. Could the theater really be haunted?

"I don't know. Nothing I can put my finger on, but I can feel it. Mr. Vaughn's spirit won't rest until his killer is punished."

"It would help if he'd told Verena who that killer is," Gino tried.

The guard shook his head at such nonsense. "Don't make fun of the dead, mister."

Gino watched him walk away, then bent to pick up the flowers he'd dropped. They were a bit worse for wear, but his mother would be thrilled to receive them. Too bad he wasn't going to see Maeve this evening, although she'd realize he'd bought them for Verena and he didn't want to know what she'd say if he tried to give them to her.

THE NEXT MORNING, SARAH AND MALLOY ACCOMPANIED Gino down to Waverly Place to Madame Serafina's house, leaving a disgruntled Maeve behind. To their relief, Verena was already there when they arrived. That meant she was still going along with the plan.

"You're out early," Sarah observed when they joined Serafina and Verena in the private parlor. Verena didn't even look tired.

"I was so excited, I could hardly sleep last night," Verena

said. "I kept thinking of all the things I could say or do to convince people I really did see Parnell's ghost."

"I think most people believe you already," Gino said, taking a seat on the sofa beside her. "You almost had me convinced."

Verena preened under his admiring gaze. "Eliza's nose was out of joint. She wouldn't even talk to me."

"Is she jealous of a ghost?" Sarah asked in amusement.

"She's jealous of the attention," Verena said.

"She couldn't understand why Vaughn appeared to Verena and not her," Gino said.

"Did anyone act as if they do not believe you?" Serafina asked.

Verena wrinkled her nose as she considered the question. "Mr. Hawkes . . . Well, you heard him last night, Gino. He kept trying to say I imagined it, but I don't think he convinced anybody."

"I don't either," Gino said, "and by the end, he didn't sound so sure himself."

"He took me aside before I left last night and told me not to say another word about seeing Parnell."

"Did he threaten you?" Malloy asked.

"I think he thought so," Verena said, "but he doesn't scare me. Nobody will join the company now, so he can't fire anyone unless he wants to close the play."

"What about Mrs. Hawkes?" Sarah asked.

"She definitely believed me. She was scolding her husband because he didn't."

"And that leaves Winters," Malloy said.

"I couldn't tell if he believed me or not," Verena said, glancing at Gino.

"I couldn't tell either, but he'll follow Eliza in whatever she thinks," he said.

"And do you think Eliza really believes?" Serafina asked.

Verena and Gino exchanged a glance. "She didn't seem frightened," Gino said.

"She was angry, like I said, but I couldn't tell. I don't think it matters, though. She'll want to be at the séance if we're going to contact Parnell. She'll want to make sure he speaks to her first this time," Verena added with a grin.

"Are you sure about what you are to do now?" Serafina asked.

"Yes. I'll tell everyone that I came to see you today because you're an old friend. We grew up together, and when I told you what happened, you offered to do a séance for free to help release Parnell's spirit. But what if nobody wants to come with me?"

"Your friends will come, will they not?"

"Angie and Sally? I don't think anything could keep them away, but I thought we especially needed Mr. and Mrs. Hawkes and Eliza and Armistead."

"This is true. I think Eliza will come because of what you said. She must be the one to speak with Mr. Vaughn first. Mr. Winters, I think, will come with her even if she does not want it."

"Oh, because he'd be jealous," Verena said.

"Yes, he will."

"But what about Mrs. Hawkes?"

Serafina considered for a moment. "If she does not tell you she would like to attend, you should go to her and ask for her help. Tell her you're afraid and would feel much better if she went with you."

"Oh, that's a good idea," Verena said. "I know she'd like to see Vaughn again, too. I could tell from the way she was asking me about him last night. I don't care what anybody else says, she was in love with him. You could tell by the way she looked at him, if nothing else. Did you know she hasn't even made Armistead come to her dressing room? Not once!"

That was very interesting information. Sarah saw her own surprise mirrored on everyone else's face except Serafina's. She just looked confused.

"We'll explain later," Sarah told her. "What else does Verena need to do?"

"Yes, what else? Should I see the ghost again tonight?" she asked hopefully.

"Not tonight. We will see. If everyone is willing to come to the séance, you will not need to see him again. You will be too afraid to go to his dressing room, too. But you will be sure the people we want to come know that they are welcome."

"I will. I remember what you said about how to invite them without seeming to."

"Good. Only if someone is refusing will you need to see the ghost again."

"Will I really see him at the séance?" Verena asked.

Serafina smiled sweetly. "I never know what the spirits might do."

. . .

THE REST OF FRIDAY AND ALL DAY SATURDAY PASSED agonizingly slowly. Sarah visited the clinic and helped deliver another baby. Frank and Gino spent some time at their office talking to potential clients. Maeve pouted and took the children to the park and pouted some more.

On Saturday night, Gino waited in the alley outside the theater with a bouquet of flowers so Verena could tell him how their plan was progressing while they pretended to have an argument and Verena sent him off in disgrace. No one could suspect that Gino was influencing her in any way after the performance she gave that night. He reported back that everyone they wanted to be there had promised to be present. Angie had begged off at the last minute, too afraid to really hear a voice from beyond the grave, but Sally would be there to support Verena.

Frank and Sarah arrived at Waverly Place early on Sunday morning and entered the house from the rear alley so no one would see them. Serafina was spending time with her baby, nursing her so she'd sleep through the séance. Serafina's new assistant, Jock Kingston, welcomed them. He was a distinguished-looking fellow of middle years with dark hair graying at the temples and an erect carriage that was either that of a military man or a well-trained butler. He explained to them what Serafina had planned.

The séance room, as they both knew from helping Serafina before, had a false wall that created a small room between it and the outside wall of the house where Serafina's assistant could create special sounds to augment Serafina's readings. Mr. Kingston took them there to show them the gramophone with the collection of wax cylinders on which were recorded various sounds.

"Madame tells me you also understand the purpose of this door," Kingston said, indicating a panel on the false wall.

"Yes," Frank said, remembering it well. "It leads to the cabinet in the séance room. Serafina can show everyone it's empty before she turns out the lights, but you can enter the room through the cabinet if necessary."

"We do not think it will be necessary today."

"Yes, they all know what Mr. Parnell looked like, so it would be difficult to fool them," Sarah said.

Mr. Kingston smiled. "You would be surprised."

Then he took them back to the kitchen, which also shared a wall with the séance room. He lifted a very ugly picture of a cow off the wall to reveal two holes stuffed with cotton wool. "Madame said you have observed from here before."

"Yes, we have," Frank said, trying not to remember they'd almost been too late to stop the murderer the last time.

Sarah reached out and clasped his hand, so he knew she was remembering, too. He gave her fingers a reassuring squeeze. Luckily, they had no reason to think this killer would strike again, especially not today.

When Kingston had finished refreshing their memories about the procedures, he left them alone in the private parlor to wait. After what seemed an eternity, they heard the doorbell that meant the others were beginning to arrive.

Kingston opened the door to the parlor. "Madame has suggested you come upstairs before I admit them."

He sent them up the back staircase with directions to go to the bedroom at the very front of the house. When they opened the door, they found Serafina already inside, sitting in a comfortable chair. She put her fingers to her lips to indicate they should be quiet and pointed to a grate on the floor. Through it they could faintly hear Kingston greeting the first arrivals, but after a few moments, their voices grew louder. Frank realized the visitors had been escorted into the room at the front of the house that served as the reception room, the room directly beneath them. Clients would gather there while they waited for everyone to arrive, and naturally, they would chat. Frank could see how easy it would be for Serafina to eavesdrop on their conversations and know what they were most concerned about and even who they hoped to contact.

From the voices, Frank realized that Verena had arrived with Eliza and Winters and another woman, most likely Sally. The four of them had probably come down together on the elevated train. The voice Frank didn't recognize, Sally's voice, was almost shrill with excitement, but Eliza wasn't saying anything.

"Are you all right, my dear?" Winters asked. "Maybe I could ask that man for something. Tea or coffee, perhaps?"

"I'm fine," Eliza snapped. "I just want to get this over with."

"We all do," Winters said.

"Not *all* of us," Sally said. "I've never been to a séance before. Do you think we'll see Parnell? I'd love to see a real ghost."

"That's because you never saw one," Verena said. "Madame Serafina says spirits hardly ever manifest at a séance, though."

"What does *manifest* mean?" Sally asked in alarm.

"Let you see them, like Parnell did for me the other night," Verena said. "That's why I had to go see Madame Serafina right away. I knew this was very serious and we needed to take care of it as soon as possible."

"I don't know why we needed to come all the way down here," Eliza said. "You saw the ghost at the theater. Isn't that where we should be for this?"

"Madame Serafina says that's not where his spirit is, though. That's only where his energy was trapped." Verena was doing a great job of sounding knowledgeable, in spite of her limited experience. Or maybe she was just acting.

"None of this matters, of course," Winters said, "because we're just humoring Verena, darling. This is important to her."

"You mean you don't really believe I saw Parnell?" Verena asked. She sounded suitably offended.

"I'm sure you thought you did," Winters said in the placating voice Frank realized he always used with Eliza.

"We'd just better get back in time for the matinee," Eliza said before Verena could respond to Winters's condescension. "You know I need time to prepare when I'm playing the lead."

"Are you playing the lead *again*?" Sally asked. "You play it so often now that I almost forget Mrs. Hawkes is even in the show."

"Don't be silly, Verena," Eliza said. "I only play the matinees."

"Yes, three performances a week, and Mrs. Hawkes

never used to miss a single one unless she was too sick to get out of bed. How did you get her to agree to that?"

The doorbell distracted Eliza from whatever she might have replied. They all fell silent while Kingston went to answer the door.

The voices sounded like Mr. and Mrs. Hawkes, and soon the others greeted them as they came into the reception room.

"Who else is coming?" Mrs. Hawkes asked. Did her voice sound odd? Frank glanced at Sarah, who was frowning. Plainly, she thought so, too.

"This is all of us," Verena said. "Some of the crew wanted to come. They wanted Parnell to find some peace, too, but I told them it would be too many people."

"Quite right," Mr. Hawkes said. "No sense having even more people waste their time." He simply sounded like himself, an overbearing blowhard.

"Eliza," Verena said as if she hadn't heard Hawkes's jibe, "I see you got that scarf mended."

"What do you mean?" Eliza said with alarm.

"I mean it's very pretty, but the hem was out when I was helping you figure out how to tie it into a turban."

"Yes, it's fine now," Eliza said sharply.

Was Eliza wearing Mrs. Hawkes's scarf as a turban? And if so, why hadn't Mrs. Hawkes said anything about it?

"Maybe you should ask Mrs. Hawkes to show you how to tie it," Verena continued. "We never did figure it out."

"The wardrobe mistress can show her," Mrs. Hawkes said. "It's very simple."

So Mrs. Hawkes did see Eliza's scarf and didn't think anything of it. Didn't she recognize it as hers? Or had she actually given it to Eliza after all? Or maybe it wasn't really hers to begin with. At least Frank now knew Eliza wasn't wearing it as a turban, although he couldn't imagine why that mattered.

"How long do we have to wait?" Mrs. Hawkes said. "Does this Madame Serafina know we have a matinee?"

"I thought Eliza was playing the lead today," Winters said.

"Of course she is," Mrs. Hawkes snapped. "The rest of you have to perform, though. I'm only thinking of the good of the troupe."

"We have hours yet," Mr. Hawkes said as if trying to calm her.

Serafina rose from her chair and signaled to Frank and Sarah that she was going downstairs.

Frank nodded and watched her go before turning his attention back to the grate and the voices coming through it.

Someone was coughing.

"Are you all right, Adelia?" Hawkes asked.

"Of course I'm all right. It's just, the air in here is so dry. I don't know why I let you convince me to come."

"It was *your* idea," Hawkes said. "You wanted to put *poor, dear* Parnell to rest." Was he mocking her?

"Oh, I suppose you'd be happy to let him keep roaming the theater forever."

"He's not roaming the theater."

"He was roaming one of the dressing rooms," Verena reminded him.

"We just have your word for that," Hawkes said. "Really, this whole thing is a farce, and if this woman tries to finagle any money out of us—"

"Good morning, everyone," Serafina said cheerfully. "Verena, it is so nice to see you again, and I am glad you brought your friends today."

"Thank you for having us, Madame. I don't know what we would have done without your help."

"I am glad to do this for you. What good is it to have a talent if you cannot use it for your friends? Would you introduce me to them, please?"

Verena did so, although Frank noticed she didn't mention any relationship between Eliza and Winters.

"Ah yes," Serafina said when the introductions were complete, and Frank could picture her holding out her hand as if she was giving a blessing. "Mr. Winters, you are the one who took Mr. Vaughn's place in the play."

"I took his role, yes," Winters said uncertainly. "Someone had to, of course, or the play would have had to close."

"I do not think Mr. Vaughn bears you any ill will, although I am sure he will tell us if he does. And Mrs. Hawkes," she continued, "you were very close to Mr. Vaughn. A good friend to him, I think."

"Yes, of course. I was a very good friend to him," she confirmed nervously.

Frank glanced at Sarah, who rolled her eyes.

"We will go into the séance room in a moment, but since you are all new to this—"

"My wife is not new to it," Mr. Hawkes said.

"You have attended a séance before?" Serafina asked.

"Yes, I . . . Once or twice," Adelia admitted.

"Were you able to make contact?"

"I, uh, no, not really."

"Perhaps we will have better luck today. Now I will explain to the rest of you what will happen. We will sit around a table, and we will join hands, but not in the usual way. Each person will grasp the wrist of the person to his left, so each person's left hand will be holding the right wrist of the person next to him or her. I will show you how when we go inside. Then I will turn out the light and close the door so the room will be completely dark."

"Dark?" Eliza cried. "No one said it would be dark."

"There is nothing to fear," Serafina said. "We will all be holding each other's hands and you will not be alone."

"But Verena said there would be spirits," Eliza said.

"They only speak to us. They speak through my spirit guide. His name is Yellow Feather."

"Yellow Feather?" Winters scoffed. "Like an Indian?"

"Yes, he is an Arapaho."

This was a surprise. Yellow Feather had apparently joined an Indian tribe since they'd last attended a séance with Serafina.

"He lived hundreds of years ago, and he died heroically in battle. Now he is my spirit guide. I must warn you that sometimes the spirits are not cooperative, so it is possible Mr. Vaughn will not come to us, but I will try. For Verena's sake, I will try. Please, follow me."

Frank and Sarah could hear the footsteps as they left the room, and then Hawkes's voice speaking softly, probably to his wife. "I bet Yellow Feather would cooperate pretty well if we paid her enough."

As soon as the footsteps died away, Frank motioned to Sarah and she followed him out of the room and down the back stairs to the kitchen. Kingston had just come in. He nodded to the space where the picture of the cow had been, then moved on to the small room behind the false wall where he would do his spiritual machinations.

Frank pulled the cotton wool out of one of the holes and put his ear to it while Sarah did the same to the other one. The room would be pitch-dark, so there was no use looking through the opening. He could hear Serafina instructing them to clasp each other's hands the way she had shown them, then getting up and closing the door. Someone coughed again, and Mrs. Hawkes apologized.

"Would you like some water?" Serafina asked.

"No, thank you. I'm fine."

Serafina gave them a chance to settle down and when the silence had gone on for just a few seconds too long, she said, "Yellow Feather, are you there? I have some seekers. We need to find a spirit. He is their friend. His name is Parnell Vaughn."

"The spirits have no names," a deep voice replied, and Frank could hear the gasps of surprise.

"Please, everyone," Serafina said, "I need for you all to think of Mr. Vaughn. Picture him in your minds. Summon him with your thoughts. Yellow Feather, we seek a spirit. Is he near?"

"Not a spirit," the deep voice replied. "It is a bird. A bird. A bird."

"What kind of a bird?"

"Kwaa, Kwaa!"

Frank jumped at the cry and noticed Sarah had, too. She shrugged at his questioning look. She had no idea what it was either.

"Yellow Feather, what kind of bird is it?"

"A strange bird. Small and round. It waddles on the ground."

"Kwaa, Kwaa!"

"A quail," someone said. Who was it? Mrs. Hawkes, he thought.

"Yellow Feather, why is it here?"

Because it had killed Vaughn, but of course no one said that.

"It hurts. It hurts." This was a new voice, and the group gasped again in surprise.

"Who is that?" Serafina called. "Who is there?"

"Parnell."

"Parnell Vaughn, is that you?" Serafina asked.

"Yes. Yes."

"We hear you, Parnell," Serafina said. "Verena saw you. You asked for her help."

"I cannot escape. Help me."

"We will help you, Parnell. What can we do?"

"Find. My. Killer."

"Who is it, Parnell? Tell us who it is."

The only answer was a choking sound.

"What is it?" Serafina cried. "Who is there?"

"Dins . . ." the strangled voice gasped. "Dinsmore."

"Why is *he* here?" Was that Eliza?

"Dinsmore," the new voice said. "I saw."

"What did you see?" Serafina asked.

"Parnell's . . . killer."

15

Sarah could see Malloy was as surprised as she. Serafina was being quite bold, and the group fairly exploded with questions.

"Who is it?"

"Who?"

"What did you see?"

The questions came so quickly, Sarah couldn't tell who was asking what.

"Dinsmore, who are you?" Serafina asked.

"A . . . friend."

"And you know who killed Parnell?"

"Yes, but . . ." The voice faded into choking sounds as if the speaker were being strangled.

Very effective, Sarah thought.

"Who is it?" Verena called. "Tell us, Mr. Dinsmore! Tell us!"

"A scarf! So jealous!" Dinsmore's voice shouted. Sarah understood now. Serafina was simply throwing out the clues they had to see if someone would react.

Something niggled at Sarah's memory. Jealousy, yes. Eliza was jealous of everything. She wanted pretty things, like the scarf. She wanted Vaughn for herself. But mostly she wanted to be the star of the show, and somehow she'd gotten Mrs. Hawkes to give her a scarf and to let her play all the matinees, even though Mrs. Hawkes hated her and had never been generous with those things before.

When had it started? When had Adelia Hawkes suddenly become so generous with Eliza Grimes? Of course! It was the day Wylie Dinsmore died.

Sarah quickly stuffed the cotton wool back in the hole and motioned for Malloy to do the same. Then she grabbed his hand and pulled him to the other side of the kitchen.

"Eliza is blackmailing Mrs. Hawkes," she whispered. "That's why Mrs. Hawkes gave her the scarf and is letting her play the lead in the matinees. Eliza must know that Mrs. Hawkes is the killer."

"But how would she know?"

"She must have seen or heard something the day Mr. Vaughn was killed."

"That certainly makes sense, but what about Dinsmore? How would she know about that?"

"I don't know, but it was the day Mr. Dinsmore was killed that Eliza got the scarf and announced that she would be playing the lead in the matinees."

"So you think she confronted Mrs. Hawkes and then helped her kill Dinsmore? Mrs. Hawkes couldn't have killed him alone."

"I don't know who else was involved, but Mrs. Hawkes must be at least, or Eliza couldn't be blackmailing her."

"Should we stop the séance?"

"No, let's help." She took his hand and led him to the curtain that covered the entrance to the secret room.

Kingston looked up in surprise when they joined him in the narrow space.

"Parnell," Serafina was calling. "Are you there? Can you hear me?"

"Too far . . . too far . . ." Parnell said. Serafina was doing all the voices herself, so Kingston only had to handle the other sounds.

"Yellow Feather, help me," Serafina said.

Sarah couldn't tell Malloy what to say without possibly being overheard, so she pitched her voice as low as she could and cried, "The scarf! The scarf!"

"Who's there?" Serafina called. "What scarf?"

"Dinsmore," Sarah said. "Peacock scarf! She strangled me!"

"Who? Who strangled you?" Serafina asked.

"I saw her," Sarah said. "I saw her kill Parnell."

"I knew it!" Verena cried. "It was Eliza, wasn't it?"

"Eliza?" Winters shouted. "What is it? What's wrong?"

Sarah saw her own alarm register on Malloy's face and without a word, they both turned and ran. Malloy was faster, but she was close behind, through the kitchen, down the hall to the door. He threw it open and barreled into the séance room with her in his wake.

The scene was eerily familiar, with the group around the circular table, frozen in their little tableau and blinking in the sudden brightness when Sarah pushed the button to turn on the electric light. The tableau was wrong, though, terribly wrong, because one chair was empty and another person had slumped in her chair and was slowly sliding to the floor.

"Adelia!" Hawkes cried, jumping to his feet, and that's when Sarah saw her. She'd tried to escape, but there was nowhere to go and nowhere to hide, so she'd merely backed up to the wall behind Eliza's chair where she cowered, her famous eyes wide and wild with a murderous rage.

"Eliza!" Winters had managed to catch her before she fell, but he could barely support her limp body. The scarf had been pulled tight around her throat, and Sarah rushed over and yanked it loose.

Almost instantly, Eliza drew a ragged breath and then another and her eyes flew open. "What happened?"

"Mrs. Hawkes tried to strangle you," Malloy said, fixing Adelia with the glare that had cowed too many murderers in the past.

"How dare you?" Adelia tried, pulling herself up to her full, leading-lady height and returning his glare with one of her own.

"Darling, are you all right?" Winters was saying as Sarah continued to unwind the scarf from Eliza's neck.

"I . . . I think so," she said.

"What happened?" Verena asked from where she still sat

at the table. Like the others she was looking around, taking in the empty chair between Mr. Hawkes and herself and the spot where Adelia now stood. "How did she get up? She never let go of my hand."

"She probably was never holding your hand in the first place," Sarah said.

"She has attended a séance before," Serafina said. "Her husband told us."

"Could she have known the trick for keeping your hands free?" Sarah asked.

"She knows all the tricks," Hawkes said. "She made a point of learning all about it for a role she played several years ago."

"Tell me," Serafina said to Verena and to Mr. Hawkes, who had been sitting on the other side of Adelia. "After I turned out the lights, did Mrs. Hawkes release your hand for a moment?"

Hawkes merely turned his furious gaze to his wife, but Verena said, "Yes, she did! When she started coughing."

"And then," Sarah said, "she would have guided the two of you to join your hands in the dark. You thought you were holding her hands, but she was completely free."

"Eliza let go of my hand," Sally said, "but not until just before these people burst in."

"Yes," Winters said. "She let go of mine, too. That's why I asked her if something was wrong. But why would Mrs. Hawkes . . . ?"

"Do you want to tell them?" Malloy asked her. "Or do you want me to?"

Adelia lifted her chin even higher. "I have no idea what you're talking about."

"All right," Malloy said. "The day Vaughn was killed, Wylie Dinsmore had stopped by the theater to visit his old friend Mrs. Hawkes. Her husband had paid him to convince her to join the Theatrical Syndicate because the Hawkeses were nearly bankrupt."

"*What?*" Adelia cried. "That's ridiculous!"

"But true all the same," Malloy said. "You can ask your husband if you don't believe me. After Dinsmore visited Mrs. Hawkes, he went to see Parnell Vaughn. We don't know what they talked about, but Mrs. Hawkes went to Vaughn's dressing room right afterward and picked up one of the quail figurines she'd given him as a gift and beat him to death with it."

"Oh, a *quail*!" Sally said in delight. "Like Yellow Feather said. I couldn't imagine what that had to do with anything." She didn't seem to notice the disapproving frowns from the others.

"What did Vaughn tell you, Mrs. Hawkes?" Malloy asked. "Did Dinsmore have another play for him? Was he going to leave you?"

"Yes." Everyone turned to Hawkes. His face was nearly purple with rage. "Yes, he was. Dinsmore had told me he was going to lure Vaughn away. She'd fallen in love with Vaughn, and it was our last hope of convincing Adelia she had to join the Syndicate."

"He was going to leave me!" Adelia cried. "After all I'd done for him! After all we'd meant to each other."

"*You* didn't mean anything to *him*," Eliza said, but Winters shushed her.

"I guess poor Dinsmore must have seen Adelia going to Vaughn's dressing room as he left," Malloy continued. "Or maybe she just couldn't take a chance that he would tell someone she had a reason for being furious with Vaughn. Whatever her excuse, she decided she had to kill Dinsmore, too, so she begged her husband to help her—"

"What?" Hawkes nearly shouted. "I didn't help her. There was no reason to kill Wylie. He would never have betrayed her, no matter what she'd done."

"But she couldn't be sure," Malloy said. "So who helped you kill Dinsmore, Mrs. Hawkes? Was it Eliza?"

Eliza made a squeak of protest. "I never killed anybody!"

"Then how did you blackmail Mrs. Hawkes? And we know she couldn't have killed Dinsmore by herself."

Adelia's scornful laugh sent chills down Sarah's back. "You think I needed help to control a worm like Wylie Dinsmore? All I had to do was suggest a little experiment where I tied his hands and took advantage of him, and he was as meek as a kitten while I trussed him up."

"So you cut off strips from your silk scarf and tied his hands and then used the rest of the scarf to choke him to death," Malloy said.

Eliza made another squeak, this time of horror. "You gave *me* the scarf you used to kill Mr. Dinsmore with?"

"Yes, she did," Sarah said. "And we know you were blackmailing Mrs. Hawkes. I think you must have seen something the day that Mr. Vaughn was killed. You said once that you'd heard someone running down the hall, but later you denied that. I think you realized it was Mrs. Hawkes running away from killing Mr. Vaughn. She could have gone to her dressing room and changed her clothes and hidden her bloody ones. When did you decide you could blackmail her with what you knew?"

"I never . . ." she tried, but stopped when she saw the disapproving frowns. "I didn't even know she'd killed Mr. Dinsmore." She looked up at Sarah. "You told me he was strangled, so I thought it must have been a *man* who killed him."

At least until Maeve told her he'd been strangled with a scarf, Sarah thought. "When did you tell Mrs. Hawkes you knew she'd killed Mr. Vaughn?"

Eliza winced. "I didn't actually . . . I waited outside her building for her to come home that Saturday morning, and she invited me to her suite. I told her I knew she'd been in Nelly's dressing room right before he died, so she . . ." Eliza glanced in horror at the scarf Sarah still held. "She gave me the scarf and told me I could play all the matinees for her. I knew no one was going to arrest Adelia Hawkes for murder just because I thought I heard her running down the hall, so what was the harm in asking for a favor?"

"And what was the harm in insisting an innocent man had killed Mr. Vaughn instead?" Sarah asked, suddenly furious at this silly, selfish girl.

"I wouldn't have . . . I mean, nobody really thought Mr. Malloy had . . ." she stammered.

"The police thought it because you said so. They arrested him and put him in jail," Sarah said.

"But he got out!" she argued.

"And you got to play the lead in the matinees and you got to wear a lovely scarf that happened to have killed a man," Sarah said, "while you continued to lie, and just now you almost paid the ultimate price for your lies."

Eliza's hand flew to her throat, where bruises were already forming. "Why did she try to kill me? I wouldn't have told anyone."

For a moment Sarah wished Adelia Hawkes had been just a little more successful.

"Baxter, you aren't going to let them arrest me, are you?" Adelia said. "Adelia Hawkes can't go to prison. And just think what the publicity will do for us. Everyone will want to see me if I'm rumored to be a murderess."

Sarah sighed. Adelia was right, of course, and if she paid her bail and the appropriate bribes, she could walk free, just as Malloy could have.

"It's too late, Adelia," Hawkes said wearily. "You've ruined me, and I can't help you anymore."

"Brian wants to know why he can't have cake," Catherine reported to Sarah as she was checking the preparations for the party in the dining room.

The two children had been signing surreptitiously to each other for the past few minutes, and this was apparently the plan they had concocted to get an early taste of the beautiful confections their cook, Velvet, and their neighbor, Mrs. Ellsworth, had created.

"You know why," Sarah said. "The cakes are for the party later."

"But there's so many cakes. Why can't we have a little bit now?"

"Because they're for the celebration. You don't want to ruin the celebration, do you?"

Catherine took a moment to consider her next argument. "But Brian and me are the reasons for the celebration, so we should be able to—"

"Brian and *I*," Sarah corrected her.

"Brian and *I*," she repeated obediently. "We should get extra cake because we're getting 'dopted."

Sarah reached out and lovingly stroked Catherine's silky brown hair. Not willing to be ignored, Brian skillfully inserted himself between them, and Sarah managed to collect them both into a hug. She loved them so much, she thought her heart would burst. She'd considered both of them her children for a long time now, and later today they would become her children legally and forever.

"What's all this?" Malloy asked as he entered the dining room.

"The children are trying to convince me they need to sample the cake."

Brian made the sign for *cake* and smiled his sweetest smile.

"Come in here, you two," Velvet called from the doorway. "I got some special cake just for you."

Catherine delightedly signed the message to Brian, and they scampered off to the kitchen to be spoiled by their doting friend.

"Don't let them get their clothes dirty," Sarah called after them. "We're leaving for court soon." She blinked at a suspicious moistness in her eyes, and when she looked up, she saw Malloy was still staring lovingly at the doorway, too.

"I just wish Mr. Vaughn didn't have to die," she said.

"He didn't have to die, at least not for us to adopt Catherine. That wasn't our fault, Sarah. It was just a nasty coincidence."

How many times had he reassured her about this in the weeks since Parnell Vaughn's death? "I do know that. I just can't help thinking that if he were alive, I would have invited him to the celebration today."

"And he probably wouldn't have come," Malloy said. "Catherine meant nothing to him, but she means everything to a lot of other people, and they'll all be here today."

"You're right." Then she remembered something. "Did you see the story about Mrs. Hawkes in the newspaper this morning?"

"Yes." The newspapers had been increasing their sales by featuring regular updates on the scandalous murder and upcoming trial. One newspaper had even mentioned Malloy's efforts to get Mr. Vaughn to sign away his rights to Catherine, but fortunately, that story hadn't piqued much interest because it wasn't very salacious and had nothing to do with the murders, so it had been quickly dropped. "I can't believe she's still performing."

"And drawing bigger crowds than she has in years. I guess they need the money, and as long as she is out on bail, I suppose there's no reason not to take advantage of her notoriety."

"I can't help thinking she might get acquitted," Malloy

said. "But at least they'll really bring her to trial. They can't just ignore it after all this publicity."

"A jury might believe she hadn't meant to kill Mr. Vaughn, but she planned Mr. Dinsmore's death out so carefully that they couldn't possibly think she hadn't meant that one."

"And Eliza will testify about how she almost strangled her. She can't explain that away, either."

"I couldn't believe it when Verena told us someone has written a play about the murders and Eliza is going to play Mrs. Hawkes in it."

Malloy gave her a pitying look. "Eliza was blackmailing a killer to help her career. I don't think there's anything she wouldn't do."

"Maybe not. How much longer do you think Gino will keep seeing Verena?"

Malloy grinned at that. "Until Maeve can't pretend it doesn't bother her anymore."

The doorbell rang.

"That's probably my parents," Sarah said. They were stopping by to fetch the Malloy family in their carriage to take them all to the courthouse to finalize Malloy and Sarah's adoption of Catherine and Sarah's adoption of Malloy's son, Brian. She turned to Malloy and took his hand. "This is your last chance to change your mind."

He squeezed her fingers. "Never," he said. "Let's go make ourselves a family."

Author's Note

REGULAR READERS OF THE GASLIGHT MYSTERIES WILL recognize several characters in this book who have appeared in previous Gaslight Mysteries. Serafina Straface made her debut in *Murder on Waverly Place* and Parnell Vaughn in *Murder in Chelsea*. My thanks to real-life attorney/Gaslight fan Bill Jonson, who wrote me a thoughtful letter explaining why Frank and Sarah could not legally adopt Catherine. The information he shared with me gave me the idea for this book, which is one reason I love hearing from fans! If I made any legal errors, they are a result of my inadvertent misinterpretation of his advice.

Union Square was the original heart of the theater district in New York City, eventually spreading to Broadway. In 1896, Charles Frohman and five other theatrical managers and booking agents met and organized all the theaters that they owned or represented into a national chain, marking the beginning of the Theatrical Syndicate. The Syndicate operated until 1910, when competition from the Shubert brothers, who started collecting actors instead of theaters, gave smaller theaters the motivation to organize themselves, ending the Syndicate's hold on American theater.

Although some of the more prominent actors of the day tried to resist the Syndicate in the beginning, most were eventually forced to join. Minnie Maddern Fiske was practically the lone holdout. She continued to remain independent, which meant that she, like Adelia Hawkes, found herself performing in church halls and skating rinks. Her refusal to join the Syndicate cost her a fortune in income, and she died penniless. I have based the character of Adelia Hawkes on Mrs. Fiske, although Mrs. Fiske never committed a murder and I have no reason to believe her reasons for refusing to join the Syndicate had anything to do with vanity or that she abused her leading men the way Adelia Hawkes did. I apologize to Mrs. Fiske in case anyone thinks she was the least bit like Mrs. Hawkes.

I hope you enjoyed *Murder on Union Square*. Please let me know how you liked this book. You can contact me through my website, victoriathompson.com, or follow me on Facebook at facebook.com/Victoria.Thompson.Author or on Twitter @gaslightvt.

PEOPLE OF DARKNESS

"Hillerman transcends the mystery genre."

—*Washingon Post Book World*

"Hillerman's mysteries are unique in American crime fiction."

—*Los Angeles Times*

"Hillerman knows the value of suspense. He packs his scenes with tantalizing details, his detectives with intelligent persistency and his story with an understated sense of urgency."

—*People*

Continued . . .

Books by TONY HILLERMAN

FICTION

Coyote Waits
Talking God
A Thief of Time
Skinwalkers
The Ghostway
The Dark Wind
People of Darkness
Listening Woman
Dance Hall of the Dead
The Fly on the Wall
The Blessing Way
The Boy Who Made Dragonfly
(for children)

NONFICTION

The Great Taos Bank Robbery
Rio Grande
New Mexico
The Spell of New Mexico
Indian Country

TONY HILLERMAN

PEOPLE OF DARKNESS

HarperPaperbacks
A Division of HarperCollinsPublishers

HarperPaperbacks   *A Division of* HarperCollins*Publishers*
10 East 53rd Street, New York, N.Y. 10022

A hardcover edition of this book was published in 1980 by
Harper & Row, Publishers, Inc.

Cover illustration by Peter Thorpe

First HarperPaperbacks printing: January, 1991

Printed in the United States of America

HarperPaperbacks and colophon are trademarks
of HarperCollins*Publishers*

10 9 8 7 6 5 4 3 2 1

≫ 1 ≪

It was a job which required waiting for cultures to grow, for toxins to develop, for antibodies to form, for reagents to react. And while she waited, the bacteriologist would roll her wheelchair to the windows and look down upon the world. The world below was the parking lot of the Cancer Research and Treatment Center, the neighbor of the bacteriologist's Communicable Disease Laboratory on the University of New Mexico North Campus. It was a crowded lot, and a competitive one, and somewhere in the second year of watching it, the bacteriologist found herself familiar with its patterns. She knew when the meter maids made their rounds, and how long it usually took the tow truck to arrive, and what sort of violation provoked this ultimate punishment, and which vehicles tended to park illegally. She even knew of a romance which seemed to have flared between the female owner of a Datsun and the male owner of the blue Mercedes convertible that parked in the space reserved for one of the lofty administrators. Somewhere in that same second year she had started bringing her binoculars to the lab. She had finally left them there. They were in her hands now—focused upon a dirty green pickup truck which was nosing its way hesitatingly into a space guarded by a sign that read:

RESERVED FOR ASSOCIATE DIRECTOR
VIOLATORS WILL BE TOWED AT OWNERS
EXPENSE

The bacteriologist had learned long ago that cancer patients tended to be scofflaws. They were dying and they knew it. In the face of that, other considerations became less important. But habits of civilized behavior still generally prevailed. It was rare to see such open defiance as the pickup was now demonstrating.

The defiant one was male, an Indian. Through the binoculars he didn't look defiant. He looked stolid and sick. He climbed laboriously from the cab. The bacteriologist noticed a suitcase on the passenger's seat and felt a sudden mild thrill of admiration. He was checking himself in, abandoning his truck forever to the mercies of the law. The nose thumbed at fate. But the Indian left the suitcase behind.

He was a large man, with the heavy torso and slender hips the bacteriologist had learned to identify with Navajos. He wore jeans and—despite the August heat—a denim jacket. He walked slowly toward the patients' entrance—a sick man's walk.

He'll check himself in, the bacteriologist thought, and then he'll come back and get the suitcase, and move the truck.

Now there was another vehicle showing equally blatant illegality. It was a Chevrolet, silver-gray and new, which rolled past the green pickup and came to rest in the space reserved for the CRTC director. The driver's door opened and a slender man emerged, dressed in white, a straw hat pushed back on his head. The man stood for a moment, apparently looking at the pickup truck. Then he walked around his car and opened the door on the passenger's side. He leaned in, apparently working on something on the front seat. Finally he lifted out a grocery sack with its top folded down. He placed it on the bed of the pickup, among the boards and boxes against the cab. That done, he looked around him, studying the parking lot, the sidewalks, staring finally directly toward the bacteriologist. He was very blond, she saw. Almost an albino. Within a minute he was back in the gray Chevy, driving slowly away.

It was almost noon when the bacteriologist determined that the life form that had reproduced itself in her petri dish was not a food-poisoning salmonella but harmless nonpathogenic *Escherichia coli*. She made the required notes, completed the report, and pushed her chair back to the window. A tow truck had arrived. The bacteriologist focused her binoculars. The driver's helper was completing the attachment of the towing bar to the rear of the green pickup. He waved his left hand and squatted beside the pickup wheel, watching something. The sound of the tow truck winch was lost to distance and insulated glass. But the bacteriologist could see the rear of the pickup begin to rise.

Abruptly, all vision was lost in a dazzle of light. The sound came a second later—a cannon-shot boom. The glass on the bacteriologist's window was pressed inward to its tolerance and just beyond; it cracked, then flexed violently outward, where its shards joined those of a hundred other windows raining down on the empty sidewalks below.

>2<

The rain converted itself abruptly into a flurry of popcorn snow. It rattled off Jim Chee's uniform hat, bounced down the collar of his uniform jacket, and made him shiver. It was the third day of November by the First National Bank of Grants calendar back on Chee's desk, and the very beginning of the Season When the Thunder Sleeps by the less rigid traditional calendar of the Dinee. By either calendar it was too early for this sort of weather—even at this mile-and-a-half altitude on the slope of Mount Taylor. Howard Morgan had predicted possible snow flurries on his Channel 7 weathercast, but Chee hadn't believed it. He'd left his winter coat back at the police station.

He glanced at his vehicle—a white Chevrolet with the seal of the Navajo Nation and the legend NAVAJO TRIBAL POLICE blazoned on its door. He could retire to the car and turn on the heater. He could seek shelter at the entryway of the residence of Benjamin J. Vines, and perhaps ring the bell a few more times in the hope of attracting someone. The bell made an odd singing sound which he could hear echoing pleasantly through the heavy door. While it had attracted no response at all, Chee was tempted to ring it again just to hear it. The third alternative was to turn up the collar of his jacket to ward off the sleet and continue satisfying his curiosity about this house. It had been designed, so he'd heard, by Frank Lloyd Wright, and was reputed to be the most expensive home in New Mexico. Chee's curiosity about it, as about all things in the white man's world, was intense. It was all the more intense at the moment because he might very soon enter that strange world. By December 10, less than five weeks away, he had to decide whether he would accept an appointment to the FBI, and a place in the world of singing doorbells.

He pulled his jacket collar around his neck, and folded down his hat brim, and continued his inspection. Chee was standing beside a semidetached triple garage. Like the house itself, it was built of native granite, linked to the structure by a low, curving wall of the same material. Just behind the wall, in a grassy plot no more than fifteen feet long, two small markers of black marble held Chee's attention. Gravestones. He leaned over the wall. The name chiseled into the one just to the right of where Chee stood was DILLON CHARLEY. Under it, the legend read:

He Didn't Remember When He Was Born
Died December 11, 1953
A Good Indian

Chee grinned. Was the sardonic double meaning intended? Was Vines, or whoever had ordered this legend carved, familiar with General Sheridan's dictum that the only good Indian was a dead Indian?

The stone to Chee's left read:

MRS. BENJAMIN J. VINES (ALICE)
Born April 13, 1909
Died June 4, 1949
A Faithful Woman

Faithful to B. J. Vines? It seemed an odd thing to put on a tombstone, but then everything about the white man's burial customs seemed odd to Chee. The Navajos lacked this sentimentality about corpses. Death robbed the body of its value. Even its identity was lost with the departing *chindi*. What the ghost left behind was something to be disposed of with a minimum risk of contamination to the living. The names of the dead were left unspoken, certainly not carved in stone.

Chee glanced again at the Charley tombstone. The name tugged at memory. There were no Charleys in Chee's clan—the Slow Talking Dinee—and none among the other clans that occupied the Rough Rock country of his family. But here on the east margin of the reservation—among the Salt Dinee, and the Many Goats Dinee, and the Mud Clan, and the Standing Rock Clan—the name seemed fairly common. And somebody named Charley had done something recently which he should be able to remember.

"Does it seem an unusual place for a graveyard?" The voice came from behind him. A woman, perhaps in her mid fifties, with a thin, handsome, unsmiling face. She was wearing a coat of some expensive fur over jeans. A navy knit cap covered her ears. "It's one of B.J.'s little eccentricities, burying people by the garage. Are you Sergeant Chee?"

"Jim Chee," Chee said. The woman was looking at him, frowning critically, making no offer to shake his hand.

"You're younger than I expected," she said. "They told me you were an authority on your religion. Could that be right?"

"I'm learning to be a *yataalii,*" Chee said. He used the Navajo word because no English word really expressed it. The anthropologists called them shamans, and most people around the reservation called them singers, or medicine men, and none of these expressions really fit the role he would play for his people if he ever finished learning to play it. "Are you Mrs. Vines?" he asked.

"Of course," the woman said. "Rosemary Vines." She glanced at the tombstone. "The second Mrs. Vines. But let's get out of this sleet."

The house had puzzled Chee. Its front wall was a sweeping, virtually windowless curve, suggesting a natural formation of stone. But inside the massive entry doors and through the entry foyer the puzzle solved itself. The front was actually the back. The ceiling rose in a soaring curve toward a great wall of glass. Beyond the wall, the mountain slope fell away. Now the view was obscured by clouds and gusts of sleet, but on the usual day Chee knew the glass overlooked immense space—across the Laguna and Acoma Indian reservations to the south and east, southward across the forty-mile sea of cooled lava called the malpais toward the Zuni Mountains, and eastward across the Cañoncito Reservation to the great blue hump of the Sandia Mountains behind Albuquerque. The room was almost as spectacular as the view. A fireplace dominated the native-stone interior wall to Chee's left, with the pelt of a polar bear on the carpet by the hearth. On the wall to his right, a hundred glassy eyes stared from trophy heads. Chee stared back: water buffalo, impala, wildebeest, ibex, oryx, elk, mule deer, and a dozen species he couldn't name.

"It takes some getting used to," Mrs. Vines said. "But at least he keeps all the fierce-looking ones in his trophy room. These are the ones that couldn't bite back."

"I had heard he was a famous hunter," Chee said. "Didn't he win the Weatherby Trophy?"

"Twice," Rosemary Vines said. "In 1962 and 1971.

≫ 9 ≪

Those were bad years for anything with fang, fur, or feathers." She draped the mink over the back of a sofa. Under it she wore a man's plaid shirt. She was a trim woman, one who took care of her body. But there was a tension about her. It showed in her face, in the way she held herself, in the taut muscles along her narrow jaw. Her hands twisted together at her belt line.

"I'll have a drink," Mrs. Vines said. "Join me?"

"No, thank you," Chee said.

"Coffee?"

"If it's no trouble."

Mrs. Vines spoke into the grillwork beside the fireplace. "Maria." The grille buzzed in response.

"Bring a Scotch and some coffee."

She turned back to Chee. "You're an experienced investigator. That's right, isn't it?" she asked. "And you're stationed at Crownpoint and you know everything about the Navajo religion."

"I was transferred to Crownpoint this year," Chee said, "and I know something about the customs of my people." This was not the time to tell this arrogant white woman that the Navajos had no religion in the white man's meaning of the term (in fact, had no word in their language for religion). First he would find out what she wanted with him.

"Sit down," Rosemary Vines said. She gestured toward a huge blue sofa and seated herself in a chair of stainless-steel tubing and polished leather.

"Do you also understand witchcraft?" She

perched at the edge of the chair, smiling, tense, her hands twisting now in her lap. "That business about Navajo Wolves, or skinwalkers, or whatever you call them. Do you know all about that?"

"Something," Chee said.

"I'll want to hire you, then," Rosemary Vines said. "You have some accrued annual leave coming. . . ." An elderly woman—a Pueblo Indian, but Chee wasn't sure which Pueblo—came in with a tray. Mrs. Vines took her glass—from its color, more Scotch than water—and Chee accepted his coffee. The Indian woman examined him from the corner of her eye with shy curiosity. "You have thirty days' leave time," Mrs. Vines continued. "That should be more than enough."

For what? Chee thought. But he didn't say it. His mother had taught him one learns through the ear and not the tongue.

"We had a burglary here," Mrs. Vines said. "Someone broke in, they got into B.J.'s quarters and stole a box of his keepsakes. I want to hire you to get it back. B.J.'s at a hospital in Houston. I want it back before he gets home. I'll pay you five hundred dollars now and twenty-five hundred dollars when you return the box. If you don't get it back, you don't get the twenty-five hundred dollars. That's fair enough."

"You can have the sheriff do it for you for free," Chee said. "What does the sheriff say about it?"

"Gordo Sena," Mrs. Vines said. "B.J. has no use

for Sena. Nor do I. B.J. wouldn't want him involved in any way. Besides, what good would it do? They'd send out some ignorant deputy. He'd ask a lot of questions and look around and then he'd go away and that would be the end of it." She sipped Scotch. "There's absolutely nothing for the police to go on."

"I'm police," Chee said.

"It will be simple enough for you," Mrs. Vines said. "The People of Darkness stole the box. You find them and get it back."

Chee felt swallowed by the sofa, engulfed in velvety royal-blue comfort. He considered what Mrs. Vines had said, seeking some sense in it. Her eyes were studying him. One of her hands held the glass. The ice moved in the trembling liquid. The other hand fidgeted on the denim of her jean leg. Sleet rattled and scratched at the plate-glass window. Beyond the glass, night was coming.

"The People of Darkness," Chee said.

"Yes," said Rosemary Vines. "It must have been them. Did I tell you nothing was taken except the box? Look around you." She gestured at the room. "They didn't take the silver, or the paintings, or anything else. Just the box. They came to get it. And they took it."

The silver service was on the sideboard—a great urn and a dozen goblets on a massive tray. Worth a lot, Chee thought. And behind it, on the wall, a perfect little Navajo *yei* rug which on the reservation would bring two thousand dollars from the greediest of traders.

Chee resisted an impulse to ask Mrs. Vines what she meant by "People of Darkness." He'd never heard of them. But it would be smarter to simply let her talk.

She talked, perched on the edge of the chair, sipping occasionally. She said that when she had come to this place—the house then still under construction—the foreman of the B. J. Vines ranch had been a Navajo named Dillon Charley—the man now buried next to Vines' first wife by the garage. Vines and Charley had been friends, Rosemary Vines said. "The old man had organized himself some sort of church," Mrs. Vines said. "B.J. was interested in it. Or seemed to be. He claimed he wasn't; said he was just humoring the old man. But he was interested. I'd hear the two of them talking about it. And I know B.J. contributed money. And when you Navajo Police were arresting them, B.J. helped get them out of jail."

"Arresting them?" Chee asked. Understanding dawned. "Was it for using peyote?" If it was, Dillon Charley's cult was part of the Native American Church. It had flourished on the Checkerboard Reservation after World War II, and had been outlawed by the Tribal Council because of its use of the psychedelic drug in its ritual; but the federal court had thrown the tribal law out on grounds that it violated freedom of religion.

"Peyote. Yes. That was it," Rosemary Vines said. "Drug abuse." Her voice was scornful. "B.J. is never discriminating in his interests. Anyway, B.J. gave them some sort of thing out of that precious box of his. He and Dillon Charley had the box out several times. And whatever it was seemed to be very important to their religion. And now they've stolen it."

"What was in the box?" Chee asked.

Mrs. Vines took a drink. "Just keepsakes," she said.

"Like what?" Chee asked. "Anything valuable? What was it these people wanted?"

"I've never seen the inside of that goddamned box," Rosemary Vines said. She laughed. "B.J. has his little secrets. He has his private side, just as I have." Her tone said this was a source of an old resentment. "B.J. called it his keepsake box, and he said nothing in it was worth anything to anyone but him." She laughed again. "Obviously wrong about that."

"Do you have any idea what he gave Dillon Charley out of the box? Any idea at all?"

She looked over the glass at him, her expression wry. "Would moles make any sense?"

Now Chee laughed. This conversation, more and more, reminded him of his very favorite tale from the white culture: *Alice in Wonderland.*

"No," he said. "Moles wouldn't make any sense to me."

"What's your word for moles?"

"Dine'etse-tle," Chee said. He pronounced the series of gutturals.

She nodded. "That's what Dillon Charley called it," she said. "I asked him what B.J. had given him and that's what he said. We had a Navajo maid then—that was back when Navajos would work for B.J.—and I asked her what the word meant, and she said 'moles.'"

"That's right," Chee said. Technically, when broken into its parts, it meant more than that. *"Dinee"* was the word for "people." The expression literally meant "people of darkness."

"Why do you call Dillon Charley's church the 'People of Darkness'?" he asked her.

"That's what B.J. called them. Or something like that. It's been so many years, it's hard to remember."

But you do remember, Chee thought. He said, "There's another possible motive for taking that box. This is a legendary place." He motioned around the room. "B. J. Vines is a legendary person. So maybe there's a legend about his keepsake box. Maybe there's a rumor that he keeps it full of gold, or diamonds, or thousand-dollar bills. So somebody who came to take it wouldn't be interested in paintings, or silver, or Navajo rugs. Was it locked? Would they have to carry it out and break it open before they could find out what was in it?"

"It was always locked," Rosemary Vines said. "You'd have thought B.J. kept the crown jewels in it. But B.J. said it was just mementos, odds and ends to remember. I don't think he was lying." She smiled her taut, humorless smile. "B.J. is very big about saving keepsakes. He saves everything. If he can't frame it, he stuffs it." The humorless smile became a humorless chuckle. "You'd think he was afraid of losing his memory."

"But an outsider . . ."

"An outsider wouldn't have known where B.J. kept it," Mrs. Vines said. Her voice was impatient. "Dillon Charley knew. I can only presume that Dillon told his son." She rose, a graceful motion. "Come along and I'll show you."

Chee followed her. "One more point," he said. "Your husband knows all about this People of Darkness business. Wouldn't he rather go after the box himself?"

"I said he was at a hospital," Mrs. Vines said. "He had a stroke last summer. Away hunting in Alaska. They flew him back. He's partly paralyzed on his left side. They're fitting him with a device in Houston so he can get around better, but I don't want him chasing after burglars."

"No," Chee agreed.

She paused at an open doorway which led off the hall, motioning Chee past her. "He's the kind who would, crutches and all," she said. "He'd try to go after them in an iron lung. That's why I want the box back right away. I want it back when he gets home. I don't want him worrying about it."

The room that Rosemary Vines called "B.J.'s office" was down a carpeted hallway. It was large, with a beamed ceiling, a stone fireplace flanked by windows that looked across the mountain slope, and a great glass-surfaced desk. Three of the walls were covered with the heads of cats, each snarling in terminal rage. Chee's glance took in three lions, two lionesses, four tigers, and a variety of panthers, leopards, pumas, cheetahs, and predator cats which Chee could not identify. In all, forty or fifty, he guessed. The light reflected from hundreds of bared teeth.

"The burglar came through that window beside the fireplace and he went directly to the place where B.J. kept the box and he took it. He didn't disturb anything else," Rosemary Vines said. "He knew where it was." She looked at Chee. "Would you?"

Chee examined the room. Rosemary Vines had said her husband collected mementos. He did indeed. The room was cluttered with them. The west wall, the only one free of Vines' array of trophy predators, was a gallery of photographs and framed certificates. Vines beside a dead tiger. Vines at the controls of a speedboat. Vines holding a trophy. Vines dwarfed by the wheel of one of those immense ore trucks at the Red Deuce Mine. Vines' broad, gray-bearded face beaming under a pith helmet. His narrower, younger, black-bearded face peering out the cockpit window of a plane. Chee glanced away from the gallery of Vineses. Two glass-fronted cabinets, one crowded with trophies and cups, the other with carved and sculpted items of wood and stone. Shelves, a table, every flat surface carrying its burden of the artifacts of memory. Mrs. Vines was watching him, her face amused. "All those *objets d'art* are his sculpture," she said. She gestured toward the gallery of photographs. "And as you can see, my husband has a problem with his ego."

"Would it have been in the desk?" Chee asked.

"Wrong," Mrs. Vines said. She walked to the fireplace wall and lifted down the head of the smallest tiger. Behind it, a metal panel swung slightly open, one corner bent.

"They knew where to look, and they knew they had to bring something to pry this door open, and that's exactly what they did," Mrs. Vines said. "Didn't even bother to shut the panel, or hang the head back up."

Chee inspected the panel. It was mounted on heavy hinges and secured with a lock that looked expensive. Whoever had opened it had jammed something like a crowbar between panel and frame and pried until the lock gave. The door was thick and surprisingly heavy on its hinges, but it hadn't been strong enough to withstand the leverage. Chee was mildly surprised. The door looked stronger than it was.

"How big was the box?" Chee asked.

"Just about the size of that empty space," Mrs.

Vines said. "B.J. had it made. It had the knob of a combination lock in the front of it. What I want you to do is find those people, and tell them unless they give it back—and everything that was inside of it— I'll make damn sure they go to prison for it." She moved to the doorway and motioned Chee out ahead of her. "You might also tell them B.J. will put a spell on them if he gets home and finds that box gone."

"What?" Chee said.

Mrs. Vines laughed. "The Navajos around here think he's a witch," she said.

"I had the impression that he got along well with the Dinee," Chee said.

"That was a long time ago. Dillon Charley died and that was the end of getting along with Navajos. Within a year or two nearly every one of them who was working here had quit. We haven't had one of your people on the payroll for years. Maria is an Acoma. Most of the hired hands are Lagunas or Acomas."

"What happened?"

"I honestly don't know," Mrs. Vines said. "I'm sure it was something B.J. did, but God knows what. I asked Maria, and she said the Navajos think B.J. is bad luck."

"And you haven't reported this burglary to the sheriff?"

"Gordo Sena would do absolutely nothing for us," Mrs. Vines said. "B.J. got him beaten for reelection once, many years ago, and tried it a couple of times since. Sena's not an honest man, and I don't want him involved with this in any way whatsoever."

"I'm going to have to report it," Chee said. "I have to get along with the sheriff. We're in the same line of work."

"Go ahead," Mrs. Vines said. "If he sends someone out, I'll tell him we're not signing a complaint and not pressing charges and it was all a mistake."

Chee retrieved his hat from the sofa. It was damp.

"The man you want to find is old Dillon Charley's son. He took over the church. His name's Emerson Charley and he lives around Grants somewhere. He used to come around here some after his father died and get into arguments with B.J."

"About what?"

"I think he wanted whatever was in the box," Mrs. Vines said. "I heard him say something about having their luck locked up in it. Something like that. I remember hearing old Dillon saying about the same thing. He was laughing about it, but Emerson wasn't laughing."

Chee revolved his hat in his hands, looking thoughtful.

"Two more questions," he said. "How would Emerson Charley have known about the safe?"

"That's easy," Rosemary Vines said. "Dillon knew about it. Dillon was in here with B.J. a lot. I'm sure Dillon told his boy about it. After all, Emerson was going to keep Dillon's crazy cult going. What's the other question?"

"How did Dillon Charley die?"

"How?" Mrs. Vines looked puzzled. Then she laughed. "Oh," she said. "I see what you're thinking. Nothing mysterious. He died of cancer." She laughed again. "That's the reason for that strange line on the tombstone about him being a good Indian. He'd been sick and he came back from Albuquerque one day and told B.J. that the doctor told him he couldn't be cured. He told B.J. the doctor told him he was going to be a good Indian in a couple of months." Rosemary Vines grimaced. "Laughing at his own death—that's the sort of weird thing that impressed B.J. He put it on the tombstone." She handed him an envelope.

"I'm going to have to talk to my office about this," Chee said. "And give it some thought. I'll let you know in a couple of days. Maybe I'll return this."

"Your superiors will approve," Mrs. Vines said. "I already checked on that."

"I'll call you," Chee said.

The old woman from Acoma opened the front door for Chee and held it against the gusting wind. He nodded to her as he stepped into the darkness.

"Tenga cuidado," the old woman said.

It occurred to Chee as he started the cold engine that she couldn't speak Navajo, and he wouldn't understand her Keresan language, and that it would have been more logical of her to say "Be careful" in English instead of Spanish, which he might not understand. Then it occurred to him that perhaps Mrs. Vines did not speak Spanish, and that the warning might not have anything to do with the weather.

≫ **3** ≪

By the time Chee had made his cautious way down the mountain and into Grants, the storm had moved away to the east. It left behind an air mass which was windless, arid, and twenty degrees below freezing. It also left a half-inch layer of snow as light and dry as feathers. Chee detoured past the Valencia County Office Building on the chance that the tricky road conditions would have the Sheriff's Department working late. The light was on. He pulled into the parking lot.

Except for the east, the clouds were gone now and the night sky, swept clean of dust, was ablaze with starlight. Chee stood for a moment, enjoying it. He hunted out the autumn constellations—the formations that rose from the south as the earth tilted to end summer and begin the Season When the Thunder Sleeps. Chee knew them not by the names the Greeks and Romans had given them, but from his grandfather. Now he picked out the Spider Woman (named Aquarius by the Romans), low on the southern horizon, and the mischievous Blue Flint Boys, whom the Greeks called the Pleiades, just above the blackness of the storm against the northeast sky. Almost directly overhead was Born of Water, the philosophical member of the Hero Twins. Over his right shoulder, surrounded by stars of lesser magnitude, soared the Blue Heron. According to the Origin Myth as told in Chee's clan, it had been the Heron whom First Man had sent back into the flooding underworld to rescue the forgotten witchcraft bundle and thus bring evil into the surface world. Chee felt the cold seeping under his collar and through his pant legs. He hurried into the warmth of the county building.

The third door down the hall bore the legend LAWRENCE SENA, SHERIFF. VALENCIA COUNTY. WALK IN. The capitalized LAW, Chee had heard, represented Sena's effort to replace "Gordo" with a less insulting nickname. It hadn't worked. Chee turned the doorknob, hoping that Sena had left a deputy handling the overtime. He had met the sheriff only once, making a courtesy call after his transfer to Crownpoint. Sena had impressed him as being hard, smart, and abrasive—like Mrs. Vines, moved beyond the need for tact by access to power. Perhaps it was the product of having too much money, Chee thought. Uranium. Vines had found it, and had sold his leases for a fortune and an interest in the huge open pit mine called the Red Deuce. The Sena family's fortune was the accident of scratch-

ing a living on a worn-out ranch which happened
to have radioactive ore twenty feet below the cactus
roots. Ah, well, Chee thought, such a rich man
would be at home on a night like this.

Sheriff Sena was standing in a glassed-in cubicle
which insulated the department's radio operator
from the world. He was listening while a middle-
aged woman wearing headphones argued with
someone about dispatching a wrecker somewhere.
A long moment passed before he noticed Chee.

"Yeah," he said. "What can I do for you, Sergeant?"

"I want to report a burglary," Chee said.

Sheriff Sena registered the mildest form of surprise by lifting his heavy black eyebrows a fraction
of a millimeter. His black eyes rested on Chee's
face, bland and neutral, waiting for an explanation.

"Somebody got into B.J. Vines' house and stole
his lockbox," Chee said. "Nothing very valuable.
Just keepsakes."

Sena's eyes were watchful. "Well," he said finally.
"That's interesting." He moved past Chee out of the
cubicle. "Come on in to my desk and I'll get my pencil."

The sheriff's office was a room even smaller than
the radio cubicle—barely large enough for a desk
with a swivel chair on one side of it and a wooden
kitchen chair on the other.

Sena eased his bulk into the swivel and looked up

at Chee. "I guess Vines broke his telephone," Sena said. "Is that why he didn't report it himself?"

"Vines is away," Chee said. "His wife told me she didn't report it because she didn't see how the police could solve it."

Sena pulled open the top desk drawer and extracted a pencil and a pad. "Couldn't solve it," he said. "She say why?"

"Nothing to go on," Chee said.

"Have a seat," Sena said, indicating the chair. The years and the weather had engraved Sena's round face with a thousand expressive lines. They expressed skepticism.

"She didn't say anything about old B.J. not having any use for me?"

Chee smiled. "I think she mentioned something about you two not being friendly. I don't remember exactly how she put it."

"How come she told you about the burglary? You a friend of the Vineses?"

"She wants to hire me to get the box back," Chee said.

"Oh," Sena said. The eyebrows rose again, asking why.

"She thinks an Indian did it. A Navajo. That it's got something to do with religion, or witchcraft. Something like that."

Sena thought about it. "Just the lockbox, that right? Nothing else missing?"

"That's what she told me."

"Most likely somebody figured he kept his money in it," Sena said.

"Probably," Chee said.

"But she don't think it's that simple," Sena said. It was a statement, not a question, and Chee didn't answer it.

He was looking at a framed photograph on the wall behind the sheriff. It seemed to be a disaster scene, twisted steel wreckage in the foreground, a burned-out truck on its side, two men in khaki uniforms looking at something outside the frame, a police car and an ambulance of 1950 vintage. The scene of an explosion, apparently. A small white card stuck in the corner of the frame bore six typed names—all apparently Navajo. Victims, perhaps. The picture was grainy black-and-white, and glass and card were dusty. Sena inserted the pencil eraser between his teeth, leaned back in the swivel chair, and stared at Chee. The sheriff moved his jaw and the pencil waved slowly up and down, an antenna seeking logic. Sena removed it. "What else did she say?"

Chee described the hiding place for the box and how it had been pried open. "Nothing else was missing," he said. "Lots of valuable stuff in the house—right in plain view. Silver. Rugs. Paintings. Worth a lot of money."

"I imagine so," Sena said. "Vines has got more money than Saudi Arabia. What'd she say about religion?"

Chee told him, outlining briefly Mrs. Vines' account of her husband's interest in the church of Dillon Charley, her speculation that something in the box was important to the cult, and that only Charley had known where the box was kept.

"Dillon Charley's a long time dead," Sena said.

"Mrs. Vines said he had a son. She figured he'd told his son about it years ago, and the son decided to come and get it."

Sena sat immobile, studying Chee. "That what she figured?"

"That's what she told me."

"The son's name is Emerson Charley," Sena said. "That ring a bell?"

"Faintly," Chee said. "But I can't place him."

"Remember that killing they had in Albuquerque in August? Somebody put a bomb in a pickup and it killed a couple of fellows in a tow truck trying to haul the pickup away. That was Emerson Charley's pickup."

Chee recalled having read about it. It was a puzzling case. "I remember it," Chee said. "Understand they think the bomb was intended for one of the big shots at the hospital. Divorce settlement or argument or something, from what I heard."

"That's what the Albuquerque police seem to think," Sena said. His tone was skeptical.

"Anyway, Mrs. Vines figures Emerson got the box. She wants me to get it back from him."

"Emerson didn't get the box," Sena said. He reinserted the pencil and chewed on it. His eyes were on Chee, but his attention was far away. He sighed, shook his head, scratched his left sideburn with a thick forefinger. "Emerson's in the hospital," Sena said. "BCMC in Albuquerque. If he's not dead, that is. Last I heard, he was in bad shape."

"I thought he didn't get hurt," Chee said.

"He was already hurt," Sena said. "He'd gone to the hospital to check into that Cancer Research and Treatment Center the university has there. The son of a bitch is dying of cancer." He focused on Chee again, and emitted a snort of ironic laughter. "The APD and the FBI between 'em couldn't figure out why anyone would blow up a Navajo when he's already dying."

"Can you?" Chee asked.

The pencil waved, up and down, up and down. "No," said Sena, "I can't. Not a thing. Did Mrs. Vines say anything to you about some people they used to call the People of Darkness?"

Sena made the question sound casual.

"She mentioned it," Chee said.

"What did she say?" The sheriff's voice, despite his efforts, was tense.

"Not much," Chee said. He repeated what Rosemary Vines had told him about her husband's interest in Dillon Charley's church, about his contributing money, helping members when they were arrested, and giving Charley something "lucky" from the box—perhaps a talisman, Chee guessed.

Halfway through it, Sena stifled a yawn. But his eyes weren't sleepy. "Like she said herself, it was all pretty vague," Chee concluded.

Sena yawned again. "Well, I'll send somebody out tomorrow or so and get all the details. No use wasting your time." Sena examined the pencil top. "You weren't figuring on taking that job, were you?"

"Hadn't really decided," Chee said. "Probably not."

"That'd be the best," Sena said. "It was like I was telling you that day you first came in here and introduced yourself—that first week you replaced old Henry Becenti. Like I was telling you then, this jurisdiction business can be a real problem if you ain't careful with it."

"I guess so," Chee said. As far as he could remember, jurisdiction hadn't been discussed during that brief meeting. He was sure it hadn't been.

"I don't know if you ever worked out here on the Checkerboard Reservation before," Sena said. "You're driving along and one minute you're on the Navajo reservation and the next minute you're in Valencia County jurisdiction and usually there's no way in God's world to know the difference. It can be a real problem."

"I bet," Chee said. The Navajo Police lived with jurisdiction problems. Even on the Big Reservation, which sprawled larger than all New England across the borders of New Mexico, Arizona, and Utah, jurisdiction was always a question. The serious felony brought in the FBI. If the suspect was non-Navajo, other questions were raised. Or the crime might lap into the territory of New Mexico State Police, Utah or Arizona Highway Patrol, or involve the Law and Order Division of the Bureau of Indian Affairs. Or even a Hopi constable, or Southern Ute Tribal Police, or an officer of the Jicarilla Apache tribe, or any of a dozen county sheriffs of the three states. But here on the southwestern fringe of the reservation, checkerboarding complicated the problem. In the 1880s, the government deeded every other square mile in a sixty-mile-wide strip to the Atlantic and Pacific Railroad to subsidize extension of its trunk line westward. The A&P had become the Santa Fe generations ago, and the Navajo Nation had gradually bought back part of this looted portion of its Dinetah, its homeland, but in many places this checkerboard pattern of ownership persisted.

"Tell you the truth, Becenti and I had us some trouble when he first took over the Crownpoint station. The Tribal Council had just passed itself a law outlawing peyote, and they were cracking down on the church. You old enough to remember that?"

"I knew about it," Chee said.

"Old Henry got pretty carried away with that," Sena said. "He got so interested in rounding up the peyoteheads that he'd forget where the reservation boundary was and he'd get over into my territory. So I had my boys arrest some of his boys and one thing and another, and finally we got together here and worked out a way so we wouldn't interfere in one another's business." Sena's eyes were intent on Chee's face, making sure he'd understood the lesson.

"I'd think enforcing that peyote ban would have been Lieutenant Becenti's business," Chee said.

"Normally," Sena said, "yes. This time, though, we were looking into another crime and Henry was messing us up." Sena wiped away the disagreement with a wave of his hand. "The point is we learned how to coordinate. Like I'd call Henry when something Navajo came up and find out where he was on it. And Henry'd call me when he had something that was crossing the Checkerboard lines and ask me if we was touchy about it. And if we was touchy, he'd stay over on the reservation and let it alone."

Sena replaced the pencil between his teeth and sat back in the chair. The pencil pointed directly at Chee's nose. Sena's eyes asked Chee if he had received the warning.

"Sounds sensible," Chee said.

"Yeah," Sena said. "It's sensible." He pushed back the swivel chair and pushed himself out of it. "Been a long day," he said. "Get a little dustin' of snow and the goddamn Texans coming through on I-40 ain't never seen it before and we got 'em slid off the road all the way from Gallup to Albuquerque." Sena moved around the desk, agile for such a bulky man, showing Chee out.

"I think you was smart deciding not to take that

job," he said. "We'll just solve that little burglary for Mrs. Vines ourself. Just show her how to do it. She say anything about Dillon Charley? Anything at all?"

Again it seemed to Chee that the question was deliberately casual.

"Just what I told you," Chee said.

"You know, they got old Dillon Charley buried up there. Right by the house. That always seemed awful funny to me."

Chee said nothing. Sena's hand gripped his arm.

"She say anything about why they did that?"

"No," Chee said. "All she said was something about the old man joking about it when the doctor told him he was dying."

"About that burglary. You think she was telling all she knew?"

"People usually don't," Chee said.

Sena eyed him thoughtfully. "Yes," he said. "That's always been my experience." He released Chee's elbow. "You be careful, now," he said.

≫ 4 ≪

Jimmy Chee sat with his boot heels propped on the edge of his wastebasket and his fingers locked behind his head and his eyes on Officer Trixie Dodge. Officer Dodge was, as she had already told him, trying to get some work done.

"Come on, Trixie," Chee said. "Think about it. What could be in the box? Why is old lady Vines so hot to get it back? Why is old Gordo Sena so uptight about it?"

Officer Dodge was sorting through legal papers in her in box, transferring them into a cardboard folder. The papers were to be delivered this morning to the Bureau of Indian Affairs office in Gallup. Officer Dodge was running late. "How the hell would I know?" Trixie said.

"And you never heard of anything called the People of Darkness?"

"Nope," Trixie said. "I've heard of moles. I've heard of the peyote church. In fact, I've got a cousin who's into that." Officer Dodge put the last of the papers into the folder and headed for the door. "And I've heard of people with moles, but I never heard of people who call themselves moles."

"Maybe it had something to do with an amulet, or a fetish—something like that," Chee said.

"Of a mole?" Officer Dodge's voice was incredulous. "What kind of a Navajo would use a mole for an amulet?" Officer Dodge left for Gallup without waiting for an answer.

What kind of a Navajo would use a mole for an amulet? It was a fair enough question. Chee sat, feet on wastebasket, hands locked behind head, thinking about it. It wouldn't be a traditional, old-fashioned Navajo, probably, except under unusual circumstances. More likely one of those Eastern Navajos whose clans had mixed more Pueblo Indian ritualism and Christianity into their culture. The Navajo used representations of the predator Holy People for his amulets. The mole was a predator in the Navajo mythology, but he was much less powerful and much less popular than his more glamorous cousins—the bear, the badger, the eagle, the mountain lion, and so forth. In Chee's own medicine pouch, suspended from a thong inside his trousers, was the figure of a badger. It was about the size of Chee's thumb and carved from soapstone, a gift from his father. In the mythology of the Slow Talking Dinee, Hosteen Badger was a formidable figure. Hosteen Mole played a trivial role. Why use the mole? He was the predator of the nadir, downward, one of the six sacred directions. He was the symbol of the dark underground, with access to those strange dark subsurface worlds through which the Dinee rose in their evolution toward human status. But compared to the bear, the eagle, or even the horned frog, he had little power and no prominence in ceremonials. Why pick the mole? The only explanation Chee could think of was the obvious one. The oil well drilled toward the nadir, into the mole's domain.

Chee unlocked his hands and put his feet squarely on the floor beneath his desk. He should get some reports finished. But halfway through the first one he found himself thinking of the nervous Rosemary Vines offering three thousand dollars for a box of keepsakes and the intense, probing questions of Gordo Sena. An arrogant woman presumed he could be bought, and an autocratic man presumed he could be bluffed. What was it that made this little burglary so important to them?

Chee picked up the Albuquerque telephone book. He found the number and placed a call to the Bernalillo County Medical Center. Two transfers later, he was talking to a nurse in the Cancer Research and Treatment Center.

"I'm sorry," she said. "The patient can't have any visitors."

"We're investigating a crime," Chee said. "Mr. Charley is the only one who can provide some information we need. It would be two or three quick questions."

"Mr. Charley is not conscious," she said. "He's under sedation. He's in very critical condition."

"It would only take a few seconds. I could come and wait for him to regain consciousness," Chee said.

"I'm afraid that won't happen," the nurse said. "He's dying."

Chee thought about that. It made the question he was going to ask sound absurd.

"Can the hospital confirm that Emerson Charley didn't leave the hospital last Tuesday?"

"We can confirm that Mr. Charley hasn't left his room for a month. He's being fed intravenously. He's too weak to move." The tone was disapproving.

"Well, then," Chee said, "I'll need the name of his next of kin."

He got it from the records office, and jotted it on his note pad. Tomas Charley, Rural Route 2, Grants. No telephone. A son, grandson of Dillon Charley. What would Tomas know of something that had happened about the time he was born? Probably not much. Perhaps nothing.

Then who would know?

One question, at least, Chee could find an answer for. What had caused the trouble between Sheriff Sena and Henry Becenti? He would locate Becenti and ask him. And then Chee would decide whether he would collect Mrs. Vines' three thousand dollars.

> 5 <

"**S**ome of it's easy to remember," Henry Becenti said. "Hard not to. Six people killed. But hell. It was way back in '47 or '48. That's a long time ago."

"I can just remember hearing somebody talking about it," Chee said. "But it was long before my time."

"It was a little independent outfit," Becenti recalled. "Trying to do some drilling back in there northeast of Mount Taylor, and they had an explosion that wiped out the whole crew. That's how old Gordo and I got in trouble with each other."

"Just an accident?"

"Yeah," Becenti said. "You know anything about oil drilling? Well, this one was a dry hole. No oil. So they was going to shoot it. Perforate the casing." Becenti glanced at Chee to see if he understood. "They lower a tube of nitroglycerin down the well to the level where it looks best and they shoot it off. Idea is to shatter the rocks down there and get the oil running into the hole. Anyway, this time the

> 38 <

nitro went off on the floor of the rig. Wiped everybody out. Little pieces of 'em scattered all over."

A look of distaste crossed Becenti's face. He shook his head, shaking off the vividness of the memory. They were sitting on a shelf of stone that jutted from the slope above Henry Becenti's place. They were there because Chee's arrival had coincided with a visit from Becenti's mother-in-law to Becenti's wife. Changing Woman had taught the original Navajo clans that while the groom should join his bride's family, the mother-in-law and son-in-law should scrupulously avoid all contact. In forty years, Old Woman Nez and Henry Becenti had never broken that taboo. Becenti had built his house at his in-laws' place, but away from the hogan of his bride's parents. When Old Woman Nez came to call, Becenti arranged to be elsewhere. This high ridge, which looked across the great valley of Ambrosia Lakes, was a favored retreat.

"If it was an accident, what was bothering Sena?" Chee asked.

"Sena's older brother was one of them," Becenti said. "He was one of the drillers. I think he was what they call the 'tool pusher.' And Sena got sort of crazy about it."

Becenti shook a cigaret out of his pack, offered it to Chee, and then selected one for himself and struck a kitchen match to it. He sat smoking, looking at Mount Taylor, thirty miles to the east. The sun had dropped behind the horizon, but the top of the mountain, rising a mile above the valley floor, still caught the direct light. Tsoodzil, the Navajos called it, the Turquoise Mountain. It was one of the four sacred peaks which First Man had built to guard Dinetah. He had built it on a blue blanket of earth carried up from the underworld, and decorated it with turquoise and blue flint. And then he had pinned it to the earth with a magic knife, and assigned Turquoise Girl to live there and Big Snake to guard her until the Fourth World ended. Now it appeared the magic knife had slipped. The sacred mountain seemed to float in the sky, cut off from the solid earth by the ground haze.

Beautiful, Chee thought. And on the other side of the mountain was the home of B. J. Vines, who had a wife who decided the theft of a keepsake box was very, very important and probably involved witchcraft, or something akin to it. The smoke from Becenti's cigaret reached Chee's nostrils.

"The first couple of days we thought we had twelve people killed," Becenti said. "Wasn't no way of telling. Lot of people around there now, but then there wasn't nobody for miles. The only ones we could find that heard the explosion were a long ways off. They hadn't gone to see about it. Sometimes the crew stayed out on the rig for several days, so nobody got to wondering about it until the weekend. Somebody got nervous. Gordo was a deputy then. He went out to see about it."

Becenti inhaled a lungful of cigaret and exhaled

slowly. The smoke made shapes in the motionless air. Seen in profile, his face was ageless. But his eyes had spent more than forty years looking at drunks, at knife fighters, at victims, at what happened when pickup trucks hit culverts at eighty. They were old eyes.

"The blast was on a Friday, I think it was. Gordo got out there Monday. The birds had been there, and the coyotes. Hauling bits and pieces off." He glanced at Chee, making sure he understood the implications. "Anyway, like I said, his brother worked out there. Gordo couldn't find him. Or couldn't find enough to know whether it was his brother or not. And then one of the men that we thought was killed showed up in Grants. It turned out there was a crew of six roustabouts working out there and we had 'em all down as dead and they was all alive."

Becenti's old eyes looked away from the mountain and made contact with Chee's. "They'd been warned not to go to work," he said.

"It was an accident," Chee said slowly. "Who knew it was going to happen?"

"Their foreman was a peyote chief. He'd had services the night before and he had a vision," Becenti said. "God talked to him and God told him something bad was going to happen out at the well."

"And he warned his crew?"

"That's right," Becenti said. "And when Sena found out about it he just about went crazy. Sena didn't believe in visions. He figured there was some funny business and somebody had killed his brother."

"Hard to blame him," Chee said.

"Anyway, Sena had three of the crew locked up at Grants and was looking for the peyote chief. I was, too—for illegal use of a narcotic on the reservation. One of our people found him first and we had him in custody when a deputy sheriff got there to arrest him." Becenti's wrinkled face folded itself into a grin. "Big damned argument over who was gonna get him. Whether it was reservation land or county jurisdiction where he lived, and where the oil well was. Looked like we was going to have another Indian war there for a while. But the well wasn't on Navajo land, so I let Sena have him."

Becenti inhaled a puff of cigaret smoke, breathed it out, and looked at the mountain. Its slopes were rosy now with the sunset. Chee said nothing. In Navajo fashion, when Becenti knew what he wanted to say next he would say it. There was no reason to hurry.

"Nothing ever came of it," Becenti said. "Not as far as Sena was concerned. The peyote preacher stuck to his story, and there wasn't any reason in the world to believe anyone would have blown up those men on purpose, and so finally Sena turned him loose. But something came of it for us. The Council wanted the peyote church stopped. So we was trying to arrest anyone with peyote. But word got around about the preacher saving those lives, and the congregation kept growing."

"And you kept arresting them?"

"Trying to," Becenti said. "They kept moving the services around. First one place and then another. Sort of went underground." Becenti laughed again. "Got real secret. The leaders took to wearing mole amulets and they called themselves the People of Darkness." Becenti used the same Navajo word that Mrs. Vines had remembered.

"The peyote chief was a Navajo named Dillon Charley?"

"That's right," Becenti said. "He was the peyote chief. He was the one who had the vision."

"Did B. J. Vines have anything to do with that oil well?"

"No," Becenti said. "He didn't come into this country until after all that happened." Becenti slammed his fist into his palm. "By God, though," he said. "Vines and Charley got connected later on. Charley worked for him. After that explosion Sena hated Charley and pretty soon Sena was hating Vines, too." He glanced at Chee. "How much you know about Vines?"

"Just what I've heard," Chee said. "Came in here a poor boy at the very beginning of the uranium discoveries. Made the big uranium find on Section 17 and sold his leases to Anaconda for ten million dollars and a percentage royalty on the ore, and now he gets a little richer every time they drive an ore truck out of the Red Deuce Mine. Got more money than the U.S. government, big-game hunter, flies an airplane, so forth."

"That's about it," Becenti said. "Except early on he and Sena had their troubles. Sena was sheriff by then, and Vines ran some Anglo against him and spent a lot of money and be damned if he didn't beat Sena. And Sena came back two years later and beat the Anglo. Sena's been sheriff of Valencia ever since, and he never did forgive Vines."

"How did Charley get involved with Vines?" Chee asked.

"Politics. He started working with Vines against Sena—getting out the Navajo vote, and the Lagunas and Acomas. On Vines' payroll, probably. Later on he worked out there at Vines' ranch. Died years ago."

"What happened to the People of Darkness?"

"Haven't heard of them for years," Becenti said. "But the church is still operating. You remember the courts ruled that peyote was a sacrament and they had a right to dope themselves up with it. Charley's son—I think his name was Emerson—he was the preacher after Dillon died. And Emerson's boy, he's a peyote chief since Emerson's sick."

"Tomas Charley?"

Becenti nodded. "He's a crazy little son of a bitch," Becenti said. "All them Charleys was crazy and this youngest one is the worst. His mother's a Laguna. From what I hear, he's into one of the Laguna kiva societies, and he's the peyote chief in the Native American Church around here, and he does some curing for the People on top of it all."

"How'd that happen?" Chee asked.

"One of the boy's paternal uncles is a *yataalii,*" Becenti said. "Pretty good old fellow. He taught Tomas the Blessing Way and the kid does it now and then. But most people would rather get someone else."

"Why do you say he's crazy?"

Becenti laughed and shrugged. "Chewed too goddamn many peyote buttons," he said. "Got his brains curdled. Sees visions. Thinks he's talking to God. Silly little bastard." Becenti paused, searching for an illustration. "He come in the office last year and said Jesus had told him there was going to be a terrible drought and we should warn everybody to stock up on food. And then this fall he was in telling us that some witch was making his daddy sick. His daddy, that's Emerson Charley."

"Well, it's been dry as hell," Chee said, "and his daddy is dying."

"It's always dry," Becenti said. "And his daddy's got cancer. That's what I heard. I didn't know he was dying." Becenti thought about it. "Anyway, he didn't get witched. I think cancer runs in that family, like craziness. I think that's what the grandfather died of, too."

"Dillon Charley? Yeah. That's what Mrs. Vines said."

Becenti looked uneasy. He was old enough to

have the traditions of the People worn deep into the grain, and one of the traditions was not to speak the name of the dead. The ghost might overhear and be summoned to the speaker.

"Did you know Vines had Dillon Charley buried up at his house?" Chee asked.

"I heard that," Becenti said. "White men sure got some weird customs."

Especially their burial customs, Chee thought. He'd spent years among the whites, first at boarding school, then through enough years at the University of New Mexico to win a degree in anthropology, but he still couldn't fathom the attitude of whites toward the corpse.

"You have any idea why Vines would want to bury Dillon Charley?" Chee asked.

Becenti made a wry face. "Hell, no."

"This Tomas Charley," Chee said. "You said he was crazy. Would he be crazy enough to get into Vines' house and steal a lockbox with keepsakes in it?"

Becenti extracted the cigaret from between his lips and looked at Chee. "Did something like that happen?" he asked. "Why would he want to steal something like that? Vines and his woman are both big hunters. I understand either one of them would just as soon shoot somebody as not."

"I heard that Tomas' grandfather thought Vines

kept the luck of the Darkness People in that box," Chee said. "Maybe Tomas heard about that."

Becenti nodded. "Okay, then. I'd say yes. That kid would be about crazy enough to break in to steal himself some luck."

>> 6 <<

The spike on his desk the next morning held three pink "While You Were Out" slips. One told him to call Captain Leaphorn at the Chinle substation. The other two, one left over from yesterday, and one received just before he'd got to work, told him to call B. J. Vines. He put those aside and called the Chinle station. Leaphorn's business involved identifying a middle-aged Navajo killed in a truck-pedestrian accident. The captain wanted him to send someone to Thoreau to check with a family there. Chee added it to the afternoon assignment of Officer Dodge. Then he picked up the "Call B. J. Vines" slips, leaned back in his chair and considered them. Both were initialed "T.D." Trixie Dodge was at her desk across the room. He glanced at her. She looked grim this morning. Trixie, he suspected, should have written "Call Mrs. B. J. Vines." Vines wouldn't be back for weeks.

"Hey, Trixie," he said. "You put down 'Call Vines' here. Wasn't the call from Mrs. Vines?"

Trixie didn't look up. "Vines," she said.

"*Mr.* Vines?" Chee insisted.

"It was a man. He said his name was B. J. Vines. He asked for you and then he asked you to call him at that number." Trixie's voice was patient.

Chee dialed the number. It rang once.

"Yes." The voice was male.

"This is Jim Chee of the Navajo Tribal Police. I have a note to call B. J. Vines."

"Oh, good," the voice said. "I'm Vines. I'd like to talk to you about that little theft we had. Could you come out?"

"When?"

"Well," the voice said, "the sooner the better. I understand my wife talked to you about it and . . ." The voice paused and interjected a nervous laugh. "Well, there's some misunderstandings that need to be cleared up." The tone was ironic now. "There tends to be when Rosemary gets involved."

"Okay," Chee said. "I'll be out there after lunch."

"Good," Vines said. "Thanks."

Chee marked the Thoreau assignment off Dodge's assignment sheet. It was on his way. He'd handle it himself.

≫ 7 ≪

The Pueblo woman answered the doorbell and showed Chee into the predator room without a sign she'd ever seen him before. There was a man behind the glass-topped desk now—a small man with a round face made rounder by the great bush of iron-gray beard that surrounded it. The man pulled himself to his feet. "Ben Vines," he said, offering a small, hard hand. "Have a seat." Chee sat. So did Vines. The room was brighter now than it had been when he had seen it with Mrs. Vines. Autumn sunlight streamed in, reflecting from the glass eyeballs and ivory teeth of the cats. The sunlight made the room less hostile. The lioness above Vines' left shoulder seemed to be smiling. So did Vines.

"I understand my wife told you we had a break-in, and she hired you to solve the crime," Vines said.

"She asked me," Chee said.

"This is embarrassing," Vines said. What Chee could see of his face through its frame of hair didn't look embarrassed. His alert black eyes were studying Chee. "I have a feeling there really isn't a crime to be solved."

"No?"

"No," Vines said. He laughed. "My wife is not a very predictable woman at times. She's a very nervous woman. Sometimes things get confused."

"Having someone break into your wall safe can make you nervous," Chee said.

"How nervous it makes you depends on who broke into it," Vines said. He shifted his weight, glanced out the window and then back at Chee. "Do you know where the safe is?"

"It's behind that head," Chee said, nodding to the appropriate cat.

Vines got to his feet again and maneuvered himself laboriously to the wall. He balanced carefully and lifted the mounted head off its hook, dumping it on the carpet. The safe door eased itself open on well-oiled hinges. The space behind it was dark and empty. Vines looked at it, his expression thoughtful. He extracted a pack of cigarets from the side pocket of his jacket, shook one out and lit it. At his feet, the cat's head smiled benignly at the ceiling.

"Rosemary and I weren't young when we married," Vines said. "We'd enjoyed lives of our own and we were going to continue to be private persons as well as man and wife. We kept our old friends and our old memories. Both of us. Separate."

Vines had been talking to the safe. Now he glanced around at Chee. A trickle of tobacco smoke leaked through his lips. It made its way through his mustache like gray fog. Chee could see now that the left side of Vines' face was affected. The corner of his mouth and the muscles around his left eye drooped. "This safe operates with a key and a combination. Rosemary doesn't have either one of them. I have a toolbox in the stables. There's a prying bar in it." Vines pushed the safe door closed. "You'll notice that this wall safe is like a lot of wall safes. It has a limited purpose and it's not built like a bank vault. It's not designed to do more than slow down a safe-cracker. You can take a pry bar and jam it in the door fitting, and it gives you enough leverage to spring the lock. Take a look."

Chee looked. He noticed, as he'd noticed the first time he'd examined it, that the safe door did seem to have been pried open. Whatever had been used had left marks, and the door had been slightly bent. Once again, that seemed odd. The door was heavy. Unless it was poor metal, it would take tremendous strength to bend it even with the leverage of a wrecking bar. Chee looked for a trademark and found none.

"I think you should get your money back on that door," he said.

Vines laughed. "I'm afraid the warranty's run out. As a matter of fact, I had the safe made and installed, and I guess they didn't use the most expensive material."

"Who did it for you?"

"I don't remember," Vines said. "Some outfit in Albuquerque. I had it done when I built this place, and that was thirty years ago." He pushed the door shut. "The point I was making was that Rosemary doesn't have a key to the wall safe, but she does have a key to the tool locker. The pry bar was gone. I found it in her closet."

"Oh," Chee said.

Vines shrugged. He produced a wry face. "So I want to apologize for all this. And I'd like to pay you for your trouble." He produced a check. "You made two trips out here. Would two hundred dollars be fair?"

Chee glanced from Vines to the sly smile of the tiger. He thought of the bent metal of the door and the empty space behind the door, and of what Mrs. Vines had told him. Among other things, she had told him that B. J. Vines was away at a hospital. But two hundred dollars was too much to be offered. Vines was watching him. Vines had told him, in effect, that the crime was family business, and thus no crime at all, and no concern of Chee's. To ask a question now would be impertinent.

"Did Mrs. Vines have the box?" Chee asked.

Vines considered this impertinence, his mild eyes on Chee's face. He sighed. "I don't know," he said. "Maybe she had it. Maybe she disposed of it. The point is it doesn't matter. I think she told you there wasn't much in it. There wasn't. Mementos. Things that reminded me of the past. Nothing of value. Not even to me any longer."

Vines held the check toward Chee, dangling it between his fingers.

"I understand you reported it to the sheriff," he said. "Of course you'd have to do that. Old Gordo came out yesterday to ask about it. I wondered how much you told him."

"Just what Mrs. Vines told me."

Vines took three careful steps toward Chee and put the check in Chee's shirt pocket.

"This isn't necessary," Chee said. "I'm not even sure it's allowed."

"Take it," Vines said. "Rosemary and I will both feel better. If it's against policy, tear it up. I wonder if you noticed that our sheriff is very interested in my business?" Vines made his laborious way back to his chair.

"I noticed," Chee said.

"Did he ask a lot of questions?"

"Yep," Chee said. Vines waited for more. He realized gradually that it wouldn't be forthcoming.

"Gordo asked me a lot of questions about the People of Darkness," Vines said. "I got the impression that you'd told him Rosemary thought one of the Charley boys had taken the box."

"That's right," Chee said.

Vines waited again. He sighed. "I've had a lot of trouble with Gordo Sena," he said. "Years ago. I thought it was over with." Vines put out his cigaret and walked to the window. Past him, Chee could see an expanse of Mount Taylor's east slope. At this altitude it was the zone of transition from ponderosa pine into fir, spruce, and aspen. The ground under the aspens was yellow with fallen leaves. The slanting sunlight created a golden glow a little like fire.

"It was early in the 1950s," Vines said. "I'd found that uranium deposit that the Red Deuce is mining now, and I was building this place, and I hired a Navajo named Dillon Charley as a sort of foreman to look after things. I didn't know it, but Gordo had a thing about Charley, and about a bunch of other Indians in a church old Dillon was running." Vines glanced back at Chee, the window light giving his gray beard a translucent frosting. "It was the peyote church. It was against tribal law in those days."

"I know about it," Chee said.

"Well, Sena was dogging them. He was picking them up, and beating them up. I got involved in it. Hired a lawyer over in Grants to take care of bonding them out and to bitch to the Justice Department about rights violations, and finally I put up some money behind a candidate and we got Sena beat for reelection for one term. For several years there, it was hairy between Sena and me. Things had settled down for the last few years. I'm wondering if he wants to stir it up again. That's why I wanted to know what kind of questions he was asking you."

"He asked why your wife wanted to hire me,"

Chee said. He gave Vines a quick résumé of Sena's questions.

"What do you think of that oil well business?" Vines asked. "Did Sena tell you about that? About why he hated old Dillon Charley?"

"He didn't talk about it," Chee said. "But I understand he thinks it's funny Dillon Charley got that advance warning."

"You don't believe in visions?" Through the bristling whiskers Vines' expression seemed to be amused. Chee couldn't be sure.

"It depends," Chee said. "But I don't believe in crimes without motives. No one can find one for this explosion, I guess."

"Well, there are some theories."

"Like what?"

"You know Sena's, I guess. He doesn't seem to have any ideas about a motive, but he appears to think that Dillon Charley was tied up in some sort of conspiracy. And then there's another theory that Gordo did it himself."

"Why?"

"The way the story goes, the older brother was the apple of everybody's eye—including his mother's. Gordo is supposed to have known that the old lady was leaving the ranch to Robert. So he blows up the oil well."

"How'd he handle it?"

Vines shrugged. "I don't know," he said. "I heard it was a nitroglycerin explosion, some sort of charge they lower down into the shaft of oil wells to shake things up, but it went off too early. I guess you could set that stuff off by shooting into it with a rifle. It was all before my time."

"How does the Sena-did-it theory explain Dillon Charley's vision?"

"That's easy," Vines said. "Dillon finds out somehow that Sena was planning something funny. So he arranges to have his peyote vision at the church service, and he tells his crew to stay away from the well. Sena blows the place up, but he finds out that Dillon must have known something. So he tries to drive him away with the harassment."

"Could be," Chee said.

"I think Gordo would like to know if Dillon Charley told me anything," Vines said. "Did his questions lead that way?"

"More or less," Chee said. "Did Dillon Charley tell you anything?"

Vines smiled. "Did Gordo tell you to ask me that?"

"You brought it up," Chee said. "I'll change the question. What do you think happened out at that oil well?"

"I understand nitro is touchy stuff. In those days those accidents happened. I think they had another case like that in the state a few years earlier."

"Do you think it was an accident? Do you think Dillon Charley was just nervous about having the nitro at the well?"·

Vines swiveled his chair to give himself a view out the window. Chee could see only his profile.

"I think Gordo Sena murdered his brother," Vines said.

8

Colton Wolf was running a little behind schedule. He had prepared *oeufs en gelée* for his breakfast. He meticulously followed the recipe in *Gourmet* and that took time. The aspic required twelve minutes at a rolling boil, and preparing the purée of peas for the garnish took longer still, and then another hour was required to allow the eggs to cool properly in their molds of aspic. It was midmorning when he folded away the breakfast linen and cleared the silver and china from the Formica top of his trailer's eating surface. He had planned to work two hours on the model Baldwin steam engine he was building. Now he cut that to eighty minutes, working most of the time with his jeweler's glass in his eye and getting much of the fitting done on the piston assembly. The alarm dinged at 11:35 A.M. Colton pulled the covers over his lathe and drill and put his metal working tools carefully back in their proper places in his toolbox and the toolbox back in his lock cabinet. The cabinet also held his collection of steam engines, all of which actually operated—blowing whistles, driving belts, and turning wheels—and all of which had been made by Colton himself. The engines sat among the tools of his trade—two rifles, the chambers and trigger assembly sections of three pistols, an assortment of barrels to be screwed into these assemblies, an array of silencers, three small boxes trailing insulated wires, which were bomb detonaters, a candy box which held plastic explosive (Colton kept eight sticks of dynamite and his dynamite caps safely cool in the refrigerator), and a row of cans of shaving cream and spray deodorant. Except for the rifles and their telescopic sights, he had manufactured much of this paraphernalia himself—partly because if it wasn't purchased it couldn't be traced and partly because some of it couldn't be bought. The shaving cream and deodorant cans were Colton's way of getting his tools through the x-ray stations at airport loading gates. One could fit the parts of one of Colton's pistols plus its silencer into two cans, screw the tops back on, and show an airport inspection nothing more questionable than Burma Shave. The bomb detonators were also the products of Colton's skill. He'd learned the principle from a former Special Services soldier he'd met in Idaho's Point-of-the-Mountain prison. It involved two batteries and a little ball of mercury which closed the electrical connection when the box moved.

Colton locked it all away, and went to make his mail check.

It wasn't that Colton Wolf expected any mail. It was part of the routine by which he lived. In whatever town he parked his trailer, Colton immediately rented a post office box. He rented it in the name of whatever commercial-sounding noun came to mind. Then he mailed a note to Boxholder at a post office box number in El Paso, Texas, in which he reported his new address. That was Colton's link to the man who provided him with his assignments. It was his only link with the world. In Colton Wolf's mind, and sometimes in his dreams, it was the flaw through which the world would someday catch him and kill him. Colton wished there were another way to do business. There wasn't. So he minimized the risk as much as he could. Minimizing risks was very much a part of Colton Wolf's life.

He drove his GMC pickup slowly past the branch post office, inspecting parked cars. Nothing looked suspicious. He parked at the Safeway lot and strolled the block and a half to the post office, taking inventory of what he saw. Two women and a man were in the lobby. The clerks behind the counter were familiar faces. Colton walked to the wall of post office boxes. Through the glass of box 1191 he could see an envelope. He ignored it and inspected box 960. It was empty. Colton walked out through the lobby, memorizing the customers. He went back to the Safeway, bought a small filet, a half pound of mushrooms, a pound of white grapes, a half pint of cream, and an ounce of black pepper. He put the groceries in the truck, climbed in himself, and tuned in a country western music station on the radio. He let twenty minutes pass while he listened. Then he walked back to the post office. Five customers were in the lobby now and none matched the previous three. Colton walked directly to box 1191 and removed the envelope. A smaller envelope lay under it. He slipped both into his jacket pocket and returned to the truck. No one followed him, and no one followed him a few minutes later as he drove back up the freeway ramp. Colton Wolf had survived another contact with the world.

The smaller envelope was addressed simply to his box number. It contained a slip of paper on which a series of numerals was penciled. Properly sorted out, they gave Colton a telephone number to call and the time of 2:10 P.M. to call it. He had put the slip in his shirt pocket. The second envelope bore the return address of Webster Investigations and a Los Angeles street number. Colton had known that it would, since no one else knew his box number, but even so he had felt his stomach tighten as he put the envelope on the seat beside him. When he got home he would open it. Meanwhile he would try not to think about it.

In the trailer, he put away the groceries and plugged in the coffeepot. Then he sat in his recliner, dried his palms on his trouser legs, slit open the envelope, and removed the contents. Two typewritten pages were folded around an expense statement. Wolf put the statement aside.

Dear Mr. Wolf:

First the bad news, which is that the lead I had run across in Anaheim didn't pay off. The woman was far too young to be your mother. I found her birth certificate in the county courthouse before I made arrangements with the detective in Anaheim, so I saved you that money.

The good news is that I located a truckdriver who worked at the Mayflower agency in Bakersfield in the early 1960s and he remembers working with Buddy Shaw. He found an address where Shaw lived in San Francisco. It's old, but it will give us a place to start tracking him down. . . .

Wolf finished the first page, laid it carefully on the arm of the recliner, and read through the second page. That done, he read both pages again, very slowly. Then he glanced at the itemized statement. It covered a month, charging Wolf for five days of time and an assortment of expenses which added up to a little more than eleven hundred dollars. He sat then with his slender, long-fingered hands resting in his lap, and thought.

His face, too, was slender, and his body and his bones, but a sinewy tension about him gave his thinness the look of a honed blade. His hair was thin, the shade of old straw, and his eyebrows and lashes were almost invisible against pale, freckled skin. His eyes were a faint blue-green—about the tint of old ice. Colton Wolf looked bleached, drained of pigment, antiseptic, neat, emotionless.

In fact, at the moment his emotions were mixed. At one level of his intelligence, Colton was encouraged. The detective would find Buddy Shaw. Shaw would still be living with Colton's mother. Or Shaw would know where to find her. And then there would be the reunion. At another level, Colton believed none of that. Webster was screwing him. The private detective had been screwing him for four expensive years. There were no trips, no hotel bills, no long-distance calls, no trace of Buddy Shaw. Webster had had no more success than the first private detective Colton had hired. Webster simply sat in his office in Encino and once a month dreamed up a letter and fabricated an itemized bill. The first detective had gone to the house Colton and his mother and Buddy Shaw had occupied in Bakersfield. He had found it occupied by transients who knew absolutely nothing helpful. Absolutely nothing about a man and a woman and a child who had lived there nineteen years before. Colton had destroyed that report, tearing it savagely into shreds. But he still remembered what it said. It said the house was now occupied by a Mexican woman. The realtor who handled the place kept records back only five years. During that time there had been three other occupants. None had left forwarding addresses. There was no record in the county courthouse of a marriage between a man named Buddy Shaw, or any other Shaw, and a woman named Linda Betty Fry. Mayflower Van Lines records showed that a Buddy Shaw had been employed at their warehouse for eleven months nineteen years earlier. He had been fired for drunkenness. Police records showed an E. W. Shaw, a.k.a. Buddy Shaw, three times. He had been booked once for drunk and disorderly, had done thirty days for aggravated assault, and had been arrested for assault with a deadly weapon. No disposition of that was recorded. Relative to the woman herself there was hardly a trace. Just the booking sheet on Shaw, showing a woman identified as Linda Betty Maddox, brought in with him on the disorderly charge.

Colton remembered the letter in detail. He especially remembered the final paragraph:

Unless you can provide more information relative to this woman, there's no hope of finding her. Can you tell us her age, where she was born, something about her family, mother, father, brothers, sisters, where she was educated, where she was married, or any information about her past? Without such information to develop leads, there is simply no hope of finding her.

No hope of finding her. He had been living in Oklahoma City then, using the name Fry. He had driven to Bakersfield. Two hard days and nights on the highway. In Nevada, he'd decided his name probably wasn't Fry. Maybe it was Maddox, but it wasn't Fry. He remembered Fry faintly—a round, dark, pock-marked face, a round belly, a sullen, unhappy mouth. They had lived with him in San Jose and Colton had been Colton Fry in school there. He'd assumed Fry was his father. Perhaps it was someone named Maddox. Colton could remember no one by that name. Somewhere west of Las Vegas, he'd decided to choose a neutral name for himself. He'd use it only until he could find his mother. She'd tell him his real name. She'd tell him about his father, and his grandparents. And about the family home. It would be in a small town, Colton thought, and there'd be a graveyard with tombstones for the family. When he found her, she'd tell him who he was. Until then, he'd pick a last name. Something simple. He picked Wolf.

The coffee was perking now on the butane burner. Through the aluminum walls of the trailer came the sound of a truck's air horn blaring on the freeway. Colton was not conscious of either sound. He was remembering arriving in Bakersfield, the drive to the old neighborhood. The Mexican woman who came to the door spoke no English, but her daughter had talked to him. She knew nothing of a thin, blue-eyed blond woman named Linda Betty, nor of a burly man named Buddy Shaw. He could see the girl now, nervous at his questioning. And he could see the cracked concrete steps as he left the porch—no more broken now than they had been when he was eleven and had sat on them those nights when Buddy Shaw and his mother were drunk, had sat waiting for Shaw to go to sleep so that he could slip in.

Colton had stood beside his pickup, looking back at the house. The sparse grass he remembered was no longer there, the glass in one window was replaced by plywood. But otherwise it looked much the same. The last time he had seen it was the day after his twelfth birthday—the last time he had come home. The boy he knew at school had said he couldn't stay at his house any longer and he had walked home to see if Buddy Shaw had sobered up, and if Buddy Shaw would let him return. He had found the house empty. He had peered through the windows and seen the kitchen stripped of his mother's pans, and the bathroom stripped of her toiletries. But in the room where he slept, his things were still scattered. The bedclothing was gone from the cot, but the blue jacket his mother had got for him somewhere was still hanging on its peg. And his books were there. And his cap. He had broken a window and gone inside, cutting his hand in his panic. There had been nothing except the old furniture that had been there when they moved in and his own spare clothing.

Colton Wolf stirred uneasily in the recliner. All the desolation of that discovery came back to him again—the sense of loss and confusion and rejection, and with it the bleak, hopeless loneliness. Where could she be? How could he find her? Why had she gone? On the burner, the percolator gave a final cough and fell silent, its duty done. Colton Wolf ignored the sound, if he heard it. He was considering the same questions he'd considered for nineteen years.

A few minutes after one-thirty, he pushed himself out of the recliner and poured a cup of coffee. He took it to the truck, to sip as he drove. At a pay booth beside Central Avenue he made the call. He dialed the El Paso, Texas, area code, and the prefix number, and then waited while the second hand of his watch swept toward 2:10. Then he completed the dialing. He dropped in the coins and heard the number ring just a moment before the second hand swept past his deadline.

It was answered instantly. "This is Boxholder," the voice said. That address had become something of a joke between them. A joke and a code.

"Okay," Colton said. "Boxholder here, too."

"We have another opportunity in New Mexico," the voice said. "One thing led to another, I guess."

"Same client?" Colton asked.

Silence. "We never talk about clients," Boxholder said. "Remember?"

"Sorry," Colton said.

"Conditions are a lot the same, though. The subject won't be on guard. And there's a hurry."

"How much hurry?" Colton asked. Hurry bothered him. And his voice showed it.

"Nothing specific," Boxholder said. "Just the quicker the better. Every day increases the risk. So forth."

"I don't like to rush things," Colton said. "Things go wrong."

"You don't have to handle it," Boxholder said. "Maybe you'd better not. But I know you wanted to clean up that original business, and that kept you in Albuquerque anyway, and . . ."

"I think I'll have the other business finished in twenty-four hours or so," Colton said. "Maybe tonight."

"Well, that's all we're committed to. After that's done we've kept the original contract." Boxholder chuckled. "Took a little longer than anybody figured, but what the hell?" Silence. "I thought maybe you'd like to show these folks how good you usually are."

Colton grimaced. Boxholder assumed the thought of a dissatisfied customer would bother him. That was correct. Boxholder assumed he took intense pride in his work. That was also correct. "Okay," he said. "Tell me about it."

Boxholder told him. Then, as they always did, they arranged the time and telephone number for Colton's report.

Colton used up three hours. He walked. He dropped the letter he had written to Webster Investigations into a mailbox. It contained his check for $1,087.50 and a note suggesting that Webster run personal ads in West Coast newspapers asking Linda Betty Shaw/Fry/Maddox to contact him. He walked some more. He sat on the bench at a bus stop. The bus stop was near a school crossing and he studied the homeward-bound students. They seemed to be junior-high age and younger, and most of them walked in little clusters and bunches, talking. Once a single kid came along, all by herself. Colton guessed the single was somebody who had just moved to the neighborhood. If you did that, you couldn't make friends, because everybody already had them. When he was eight they had lived in San Diego in this one apartment almost a year and he had made a friend there. And then when he was fourteen and had been in Taylorville long enough, he had made a friend or two. But that was different. In reform school nobody knew anybody at first and everybody was looking for connections. Taylorville had been a pretty good place, all in all, and he'd been glad enough to go back for his second stretch. They kept the gays off of you in Taylorville. Not like in Folsom, where he'd done his armed robbery time.

Finally it was late enough. He called the University of New Mexico Hospital and asked for Mrs. Myers on the terminal ward. As always, her voice was placid. "I'm afraid it's all over," she said. "He's been in a coma all day and his heart finally quit."

"Well, you just have to be philosophical about it."

"That's right," Mrs. Myers said. "But it's always a blow."

"Well," Colton said. He found himself searching for something else to say—a way to extend the conversation. But there was no reason for that. He was finished with Mrs. Myers. This would be the last of more than two months of intermittent conversations, all carefully planned, all carefully executed. First he had learned the name of the nurse who ran the middle shift on the cancer ward. He had got that from hospital information by pretending he wanted to send her a thank-you card. And then, on his first call to learn the patient's condition, he had said, "By the way, are you Mrs. Myers? He's told me how kind you've been to him. I want to thank you for that." That had set the tone. Colton rarely talked to anyone, but he knew how to do it well. He watched television, and he listened carefully to conversations in airports and restaurants and the waiting lines for movies—the places where people talked to each other. Once in a while he practiced, with cabdrivers or the call girls he took to motels twice a month. But he rarely talked to the same person more than once or twice, except for Boxholder. After all this time, he found himself imagining how Mrs. Myers looked and what she was like—just as he wondered about

Boxholder. He had been tempted to go to the ward some evening and take a look at her. But that involved a risk. Colton did not take risks. "Well," he said again. "Thank you very much," and he hung up.

≫ 9 ≪

Colton left the trailer just as the ten o'clock news was beginning on Channel 7. He was wearing charcoal slacks, a black pullover, and his crepe-soled shoes. He preferred going bareheaded, but tonight he pulled a navy-blue stocking cap over his straw-colored hair. He took with him a canvas flight bag in which he had put a folding shovel, a green blanket, a white cotton coat with the legend STRONG-THORNE MORTUARY printed on the back, and a New Mexico automobile license plate. He had driven past the Albuquerque airport after telephoning and had collected the plate from a car left in the low-rate parking lot where long-term travelers parked their cars. Then he'd replaced the plate he would use with one switched from another car. If the theft was reported, the police would have the wrong number.

He drove back to the airport now, left his pickup in the upper lot, and rented a Chevrolet station wagon from Hertz, using a driver's license and credit card that identified him as Charles Minton, with a Dallas post office box address. Then he took Interstate 25 south and turned the wagon westward at the Rio Bravo exit. He drove slowly, counting the tenths of miles on the odometer. Near the river, he turned off the pavement onto a narrow dirt road. He got out of the wagon there, taped down the switch to keep the courtesy light off when the door was opened, and replaced the Hertz license with the stolen plates. It was after 11:00 P.M. now, a cloudless night lit by a partial moon. The dirt road crossed a cattle guard, curved across a culvert, and branched. Colton angled left. The road became two tire tracks winding through the cottonwood of the Rio Grande's silted flood plain. The tracks crossed an irrigation drain on a rattling plank bridge and dropped abruptly downward. A hundred jolting yards beyond the drain levee, Colton stopped. His headlights illuminated the stripped body of an old Ford sedan, rusty and riddled with bullet holes. Beyond it was the ruins of another car, also the target of years of hunters. Trash was everywhere—a rotting mattress, the corpse of a refrigerator, cans, bottles, boxes, papers, rags, tattered roofing paper, brush. Colton flicked off headlights and engine and rolled down the windows on both sides of the car. He sat without moving for perhaps ten minutes. He heard the ticking of the cooling engine, and the occasional sound of diesels moving on the interstate far up the valley. It was a windless night and he heard nothing else. Satisfied, he removed the shovel from the bag and climbed out of the wagon.

He pulled the mattress aside and dug where it had been, piling the earth carefully. Even in the dark, it was easy going in the loamy soil. He wanted a hole about six feet long and at least four feet deep.

≫ **10** ≪

Colton reached the University of New Mexico parking lot a little before 2 A.M. He had scouted it before, but two weeks had passed. If anything had changed, Colton wanted to know it early. He replaced his windbreaker with the mortuary coat. The woman at the desk didn't look up and the hall to the elevators was empty. The second-floor hall was also deserted. So far, fine. But down the hall Colton could see a paper sign taped to the door of the morphology laboratory. It read: MORPHOLOGY LABORATORY MOVED TO STATE LABORATORY BUILDING. He stared at the sign, dismayed. He moved quickly around the corner. The wide door that opened into the morgue was still shielded with a sheet of plywood to protect it from the bumps of metal body carts. He tried the knob. Locked. He had expected it to be locked. Would they have moved the morgue along with the autopsy laboratory? Even if they did, the hospital would need a place to hold bodies overnight. From his trouser cuff he extracted a thin steel blade which he had stitched into place. It proved as quick as a key. He swung the door shut behind him and found the switch in the darkness. Three body carts were lined against the wall. All were empty. Beyond them the stainless-steel door of the walk-in refrigerator stood closed. Colton swung it open. Two carts were parked inside, each bearing a sheet-shrouded figure. Colton read the tag on the nearest one. It identified the victim as Randy A. Johnson, 23 years old, Roswell, New Mexico. Dead on arrival. Head and neck injuries. Motorcycle accident. Colton checked the next tag. It said: EMERSON CHARLEY. AUTOPSY. HOLD FOR CRTC. "CRTC" would mean Cancer Research and Treatment Center. Colton folded back the sheet. He had seen the face before only at a distance. It was gaunt now, drawn with the effects of a lingering death. But he recognized it. This time nothing would go wrong. He replaced the sheet.

In the hall, he stood a moment, listening. A faint thumping came from the hospital laundry. All else was quiet. Colton glanced at his watch. Five after three. He decided not to wait. The odds, he decided, wouldn't improve.

It was fourteen after three when he parked the station wagon beside the loading dock. The dock door stood partly open, as he had left it, and he could still hear a thumping from the laundry. He left the station wagon's tailgate open. It was thirty-five steps from the doorway of the dock to the morgue door. He picked the lock again and slipped in.

There were two red plastic sacks of clothing on the floor beside the carts. He put the nearest one under the sheet beside the corpse and wheeled the cart out of the refrigerator. At the door of the morgue he paused again, listening. Thirty-five steps, and then perhaps sixty seconds on the dock while he lifted the body into the station wagon. The hall was absolutely silent. The cart rolled down it, trailing the slight sound of rubber tires on tile. On the dock, Colton pushed the cart out of sight of the doorway. He extracted the clothing sack and tossed it into the back of the wagon.

"Come on, friend," he said, and he tucked the sheet around the body and lifted it in his arms. It was stiff with rigor mortis. Surprisingly light. "Here we go now," Colton said. He slid the body into the station wagon and covered it with the green blanket.

The period of high risk was almost over now. He closed the tailgate, rolled the body cart back into the hallway. The station wagon's engine started instantly. As he did the left turn out of the service drive, he glanced in the rear-view mirror. The dock was deserted. No one had seen him. It had gone perfectly. Absolutely no tracks had been left.

Colton tuned in a country western station on his way back to the grave. He felt happier than he had for months. Happy for the first time since he had called Boxholder and told him of the failure. The memory was vivid. Two hours sitting in the airport, waiting for the time to call the El Paso number. Dreading it. He had never failed before. From the very first—torching the nightclub in Denver seven years before—he had always reported only success. Not just success but perfection. The job done. No witnesses. No evidence. No tracks. Perfection. And always Boxholder's voice, warm and friendly, congratulating him. This time there had been no congratulations. First there had been only silence, and then Boxholder's voice was cold.

"Give me the number you're calling from. Wait right there. I'll call the client and call you back. Be there."

"Tell him I won't accept the fee," Colton had said. "Tell him I'll finish the job."

"You just wait," Boxholder said.

Colton had waited. It was more than four hours before the telephone rang.

"Your man was checking into the hospital," Boxholder said. "He's in now. We're to just keep an eye on things and when he dies, you get rid of the body. Get it right away and get rid of it."

"My God," Colton said. "I baby-sit this guy until he dies?"

"Not long," Boxholder said. "He's got a kind of cancer that works fast."

"Then why . . ." Colton let the question trail off.

"Maybe it doesn't work fast enough," Boxholder said. "Do you care?"

"No," Colton said. "I guess not."

But it seemed curious then, and it seemed curious now, this business of getting rid of the body. Curious, but well done. The grave filled. The rotting mattress pulled across it and the trash scattered over the mattress. No one would ever find the body of Emerson Charley. Reporting time was noon tomorrow. Colton anticipated it happily. Boxholder would be pleased.

≫ 11 ≪

Jim Chee had rolled the two-hundred-dollar check from Ben Vines and the five one-hundred-dollar bills from the envelope Mrs. Vines had handed him into a tight cylinder. It was not much larger than a cigaret. Each night he dropped the tube into one of the boots beside his bed. Each morning, after he'd said his brief prayer of greeting to the dawning day, he shook the tube out of the boot and considered what to do with it. And each morning he finally stuck the tube back into his shirt pocket, thereby signaling that the matter remained undecided. On the fourth morning, Chee noticed that the edge of the check was frayed. He unrolled the tube, put check and cash side by side on his table, and stared at them.

Two hundred dollars was too much to be offered for the little trouble he'd been involved in. Worse, why would Mrs. Vines offer him three thousand dollars to recover a box she had stolen herself? For those as inconceivably rich as the Vineses the money would be relatively meaningless. But his uncle had warned him against that kind of thinking.

"Don't think a man don't care about one goat because he's got a thousand of 'em," Hosteen Nakai would say. "He's got a thousand because he cares more about goats than he cares about his relatives." In other words, don't expect the rich to be generous.

And what would his uncle advise him to do about this particular money? Chee grinned, thinking about it. There'd be no advice—not directly. There'd be a hundred questions: Which one was lying? What motivated the large payments? Why did the Checkerboard Navajos think Vines was a witch? Or did they? How was the Charley outfit mixed into this affair? And when Chee could offer no answers, Hosteen Nakai would smile at him and remind him of what he had told Chee a long time ago. He'd told Chee he had to understand white people.

Chee used his two forefingers to tap the stack of currency into a neat pile. Mrs. Vines had lied to him, at least a little. He picked up the check and looked at B. J. Vines' bold signature. Vines' story had been almost purely lies. Chee folded the check and slid it into the credit card pocket of his billfold. He put the currency in the cash compartment. He would talk to Tomas Charley and see what he could learn.

Talking to Tomas Charley meant finding him. Becenti had remembered only that he lived somewhere beyond the eastern limits of the Checkerboard—somewhere near Mount Taylor. Chee made telephone calls. Shortly before noon he learned that Charley was employed by Kerrmac Nuclear Fuels. A quick call to the Kerrmac personnel office at Grants revealed that Charley was the driver of an ore loader, that he had the day off, that he had no telephone, the rural route address from the Grants' post office matched the one the hospital had provided—a mailbox on the road between Grants and San Mateo village.

It was probably no more than thirty miles from Crownpoint as the raven flew, but for something with wheels it was around ninety. Chee told Officer Benny Yazzie, who was holding down the office, that he wouldn't be back until evening.

While he drove, Chee worked at memorizing the Night Chant. He switched on the tape recorder and ran the cassette forward to the place where the singer awakens the spirit of Talking God in the sacred mask. On Interstate 40, he drove in the slow lane, listening carefully. Truckers, wise to the ways of this stretch of highway, roared past him, safe in the knowledge that tribal police had no jurisdiction here. Passenger cars slowed to the legal fifty-five, eyeing him nervously. Chee ignored them all. He concentrated on the voice of his uncle, strong and sure, singing the words that Changing Woman had taught at the very creation of his people.

Above the hills of evening, he stirs, he stirs.
Covered with the pollen of evening, he stirs,
  he stirs.
The Talking God stirs, he stirs amid the sunset.
Along the trail of beauty, he stirs, he stirs.
With beauty all around him, he stirs, he stirs.

The recorder was on the seat beside him. Chee silenced Hosteen Nakai's voice with a touch of the off button, concentrated a moment, then repeated the five statements, trying to reproduce cadence and notes as well as meaning. By the time he reached the Grants interchange, he was confident he had the entire sequence of mask songs fixed in his mind.

Even among a people who placed high value on memory and who honed it in their children almost from birth, Chee's talent was unusually strong. It had caused his family to think of him from a very early age as one who might become a singer. The Slow Talking Dinee had produced more famous singers than any of the other more than sixty Navajo clans. And the family of his mother had produced far more than its share. His uncle, the brother of his mother, was among the most prominent of these. He was Hosteen Frank Sam Nakai, who performed the Night Chant and the Enemy Way and key parts of several other curing ceremonials, and who sometimes taught ceremonialism at the Navajo Community College at Rough Rock. It was Hosteen Nakai who had chosen Jimmy Chee's "war name," which was Long Thinker. Thus his uncle was one of the very few who knew his real and secret identity. His uncle had named him, but when he had asked his uncle to teach him to be a singer, his uncle had at first refused.

"There is a first step which must be taken," Hosteen Nakai had said. "Nothing important can happen before that." As a first step, Jimmy Chee must study the white man and the way of the white man. When he came to understand this white man's world which surrounded the People, he must make a decision. Would he follow the white man's way or would he be a Navajo?

His uncle had driven his truck into Gallup and parked it on Railroad Avenue, where they could see the bars and watch the Navajos and the Zunis going in and out of them. Jimmy Chee remembered it very well. He remembered the woman who came out of the Turquoise Tavern and the man in the black reservation hat who followed her. They had walked unsteadily, both drunk. The woman had lost her balance and sat heavily on the dirty sidewalk, and the man had bent to help her. His hat had fallen and rolled into the gutter. Hosteen Nakai's fierce eyes had watched all this.

"They cannot decide," he said. "The way Changing Woman taught us is too hard for them, and they have lost its beauty. But they do not know the white man's way. You have to decide. It is easy, now, to be a white man. You have gone to school and there are scholarships to go more, and jobs if you learn what the white man puts his value in."

Jimmy Chee had said that he had already decided. He wanted to walk in beauty as a Navajo.

"You can't decide until you understand the white man. They have much that we don't have. To be a Navajo is to have no money," Hosteen Nakai had said. "When you are older we will talk again. If you still wish it, I will begin teaching you something. But you must study the white man's way."

Chee had studied. After Shiprock High School, he had enrolled at the University of New Mexico. He'd studied anthropology, sociology, and American literature in class. Every waking moment he studied the way white men behaved. All four subjects fascinated him. When he came home during semester breaks to his mother's place in the Chuska Mountains, Hosteen Nakai taught him the wisdom of the Dinee. Finally his uncle began teaching him the ritual songs that brought the People back from their sicknesses to walk in beauty. And Chee's memory always served him well.

On the road that leads from Grants into the back side of Ambrosia Lakes uranium fields, Chee returned the recorder to its case and concentrated on finding the home of Tomas Charley. He found it some thirty feet west of the narrow asphalt pavement. It was a two-room adobe to which someone had connected a wooden frame lean-to with a roof of red composition shingles. A 1962 Chevrolet Impala squatted on cinderblock supports in the front yard, all four of its wheels missing. Chee pulled his patrol car to a stop beside it and sat waiting. If someone was home, willing to receive a visitor, he would appear at the door. If he didn't after a polite interval of waiting, Chee would knock.

The front door opened and Chee could see someone looking at him through the screen. A child. Chee waited. No one else appeared. Chee climbed out of the carryall.

"Ya-tah," he said. "Hello."

"Hello," the child said. It was a boy, about ten or twelve.

"I'm looking for Tomas Charley," Chee said.

"He went to get my mother," the boy said.

"Where's that?"

"They won't be there," the boy said. "She's a weaver. My uncle was taking her to the rug auction."

"At Crownpoint?" Chee asked.

"Yeah," the boy said. "She's going to sell a bunch of rugs."

Chee laughed. "I'm not very lucky today," he said. "That's where I came from and now I'll have to drive right back."

"You going to see my uncle there?"

"If I can find him," Chee said. "What's he driving?"

"A 1975 Ford pickup," the boy said. "An F-150. Blue. If you see him, tell him maybe somebody wants to buy our old Chevy. Tell him a man came by right after he left, looking for him," the boy said.

"Sure," Chee said. "Anything else?"

"Maybe the man will see him there at the rug auction," the boy said. "He's a blond guy, wearing a yellow jacket. He was going to look for him there."

"Okay," Chee said. He looked at the car with more interest now. The exposed brake drums were brown with rust and the upholstery in the back seat hung down in dusty festoons. Tomas Charley's nephew was overly optimistic. No one was going to drive all the way to Crownpoint to arrange to buy that junker.

≫ **12** ≪

It was after sundown when Chee drove past the Tribal Police office. It was dark. On the other side of the village, perhaps two hundred assorted vehicles were parked at the Crownpoint elementary school, suggesting a good turnout for the November rug auction. Chee found a blue Ford 150 pickup. Parked next to it was a green-and-white Plymouth, like the one Charley's nephew had said the would-be car buyer was driving. Chee checked it quickly. It was new, with less than three thousand miles on the odometer. A folder on the dashboard suggested it had been rented from the Albuquerque airport office of Hertz.

Inside the school, the air was rich with a mélange of aromas. Chee identified the smells of cooking fry bread, floor wax, blackboard chalk, stewing mutton and red chili, of raw wool, of horses, and of humans. In the auditorium, perhaps a hundred potential buyers were wandering among the stacks of rugs on the display tables, inspecting the offerings and noting item numbers. At this hour, most of the crowd would be in the cafeteria, eating the traditional auction dinner of Navajo tacos—tortillas topped with a lethal combination of stewed mutton and chili. Chee stood just inside the auditorium entrance, methodically examining its inhabitants. He had little idea what Charley would look like—just Becenti's sketchy description. His inspection was simply a matter of habit.

"Looking for someone?"

The voice came from beside him, from a young woman in a blue turtleneck sweater. The woman was small, the sweater large, and the face atop the folds of bulky cloth was unsmiling.

"Trying to find a man named Tomas Charley," Chee said. "But I don't know what he looks like."

The woman's face was oval, framed by soft blond hair. Her eyes were large, and blue, and intent on Chee. A pretty lady, and Chee recognized the look. He had seen it often at the University of New Mexico—and most often among Anglo coeds enrolled in Native American Studies courses. The courses attracted Anglo students, largely female, enjoying racial/ethnic guilt trips. Chee had concluded early that their interest was more in Indian males than in Indian mythology. Their eyes asked if you were really any different from the blond boys they had grown up with. Chee looked now into the eyes of the woman in the bulky blue turtleneck and detected the same question. Or thought he did. There was also something else. He smiled at her. "Not knowing what he looks like makes it tougher to find him."

"Why not just go away and leave him alone?" she asked. "What are you hunting him for?"

Chee's smile evaporated. "I have a message from his nephew," he said. "Somebody wants to buy his old car and . . ."

"Oh," the young woman said. She looked embarrassed. "I guess I shouldn't jump to conclusions. I'm sorry. I don't know him."

"I'll just ask around," Chee said. Her distaste for police was another standard reaction Chee had learned to expect from the young Anglos the reservation seemed to attract. He suspected there was a federal agency somewhere assigned to teach social workers that all police were Cossacks and that Navajo police were the worst of all. "Are you with the Bureau of Indian Affairs?" he asked.

"No," she said. "I'm helping the weavers' cooperative." She gestured vaguely toward the check-in table, where two Navajo women were sorting through papers. "But I teach school here. Fifth grade. English and social studies." The hostility was gone from her eyes now. The curiosity remained.

"I'm Jim Chee." He extended his hand. "I've been assigned to the police station here. Fairly new here."

"I noticed your uniform," she said. She took his extended hand. "Mary Landon," she said. "I'm new,

too. From Wisconsin, but I taught last spring at Laguna Pueblo school."

"How do you do," Chee said. Her hand was small
and cool in his, and very quickly withdrawn.

"I have to get back to work," Mary Landon said,
and she was gone.

It took Chee about thirty minutes to establish that
Tomas Charley was present at the auction and to get
a description of the man. He might have done it
faster had there been any sense of urgency. There
wasn't. Chee was more involved in getting acquainted with the occupants of his territory. Then
Mary Landon was at his elbow again.

"That's him," she said. "Right over there. The red-
and-black mackinaw and the black felt hat."

"Thanks," Chee said. Mary Landon still wasn't
smiling.

Tomas Charley was leaning against the wall
alone. He seemed to be watching someone in the
crowd. Mary Landon said something else, but Chee
didn't hear it. He was studying Charley. He was a
small man—not over five and a half feet—and
skinny. His face was bony, with small, deep-set eyes
and a narrow forehead under the brim of his
tipped-back hat. There was an alertness about him,
a tension. The eyes shifted to Chee now, quickly
past him, and back again. Becenti had said he was
half crazy, a fanatic. The small black eyes had the
look of those who see visions. Getting Tomas Char-

ley to talk, Chee thought, would take a lot of care and a lot of luck.

As it developed, it was no trouble at all. They talked a bit about the rug auction, and about the drought. Chee leaned against the wall beside the man, guiding the conversation. The auctioneer was on the stage now, a florid white man explaining the rules in a West Texas voice. Chee talked of Sheriff Gordo Sena, of jurisdiction problems between Navajo police and white sheriffs. The first rug was auctioned for $65. Bidding on the second one stuck at $110. The auctioneer put it aside and joked with the crowd about its stinginess. He moved the offer up to $155, and sold it.

Chee talked of Mrs. Vines' job offer, of what she'd said of the burglary, of his decision not to get involved in it, and of Vines' withdrawing the offer. Tomas Charley said less and less.

"It's no business of mine," Chee said. "I don't care about the burglar." He grinned at Charley. "I know who went in Vines' house and got that box. You know who went in. And Gordo Sena never is going to know. What I'd like to know is what was in that box."

Charley said nothing. Chee waited. On the fifth rug, bidding was spirited. The auctioneer sold it for $240.

"I've got a curious mind," Chee said. "Lots of things funny about Vines. Lots of things funny about Gordo Sena. Mrs. Vines, too."

Tomas Charley glanced at him, then glanced away. He stood with his arms crossed in front of him. The fingers of his left hand, Chee noticed, tapped nervously against his right wrist.

"Why did Vines bury your grandfather there at his house?" Chee asked. "I wonder about that. And why did somebody try to kill your father? And why did Mrs. Vines want me to find Vines' old box? And then not want me to find it? And why did Gordo Sena warn me to mind my own business?"

Chee asked the last question directly to Charley. The drumming fingers stopped. Charley pursed his lips.

"I don't give a damn if you got into Vines' house and took something," Chee said. "None of my business. But what was in that box?"

"Rocks," Tomas Charley said. "Chunks of black rocks."

It occurred to Chee that he hadn't really thought about what the box might hold. But he hadn't expected this. He considered it. "No papers?" he asked. "Nothing with anything written on it?"

"Mostly rocks," Charley said.

"Nothing else?"

"Some medals," Charley said. "Stuff from the war. Stuff like that." He shrugged.

"Tell me everything that was in it."

Charley looked surprised. "Well," he said. "There's a little card glued inside the lid. Got Vines' name and address on it. Then there was three medals. One was the Purple Heart and the other two were like stars. One out of some kind of brown metal and the other one looked about the same, but it had a little silver star in the middle of it. And there was a set of wings like paratroopers wear, and a shoulder patch with an eagle head on it and silver bars like lieutenants wear in the army." Charley thought. "Photographs. A picture of a girl, and a picture of a man and woman standing by an old car, and then a whole bunch of black rocks." Charley stopped. The catalog was complete.

"Nothing else?" Chee asked. "What did you expect to find?"

Charley shrugged.

"Luck?" Chee asked.

Charley's face tightened. "Vines was a witch," he said. He didn't use the Navajo word, which meant witch, or skinwalker, or Navajo Wolf. He used a Keresan expression—the word the people of Laguna and Acoma used to mean sorcerer.

"I heard that, too," Chee said. "You think you'd find his medicine bundle?"

Charley glanced at Chee, then looked away. Time ticked past. The auctioneer began the rhythmic litany of another transaction.

"He was killing my father," Charley said. "I wanted to turn the witching around. I wanted to find something for that."

Chee didn't say any of the obvious things. He didn't say, "Your father is dying of cancer." He didn't say, "It's not witchcraft; it's something wrong with the way the cells grow." He said nothing at all. Tomas Charley was sure his father had been doomed by a witch. When that happened, the Navajo way was a ceremonial—usually the Enemy Way or the Prostitution Way. Each invoked a traditional formula which reversed the witchcraft and turned it against the witch. And each required something that the witch had used. But Tomas Charley was half Laguna. He saw Vines as the Lagunas saw sorcerers. Perhaps they had a different formula. The auctioneer completed his transaction, selling a small diamond-patterned rug to a woman using bidding card 72. Chee and Tomas Charley leaned against the wall, watching, their shoulders touching.

"Why was Vines witching your father?" Chee asked. "Do you know that?"

"Vines wasn't always a sorcerer," Charley said. "Once he was a good man, I think, and he helped my grandfather and he helped our church. He gave us our totem. He gave it to my grandfather. The mole. It is powerful, and it helps the Lord Peyote open the door for us. It helps bring us visions. Vines wanted to get it back. So he made my father sick. And then he stole my father's body."

On the stage, the auctioneer and his assistant held up a saddle blanket. "This un's a dandy," the Texan was saying. He leaned comically against its pretended weight. "Take a stout horse to carry this un.

Wove so tight you couldn't get water through it. I'm starting at eighty. Yum at eighty. Eighty. Eighty. Yum at eighty. Eighty-five. Have eighty-five. Yum at eighty-five. Ninety. Yum at ninety."

"Stole your father's body?" Chee asked. He was thinking Emerson Charley had been alive last week. Very sick but alive. How long ago was it? Five days? Six? He glanced at Charley. The thin man was staring straight ahead, every line in his face rigid. He seemed to be remembering something.

"When did Vines steal your father's body?"

"Two, three days ago," Charley said. "Out of the hospital there at Albuquerque. And he got the mole back again."

"But how did he do it? Did he just walk in and walk out with it?"

Charley shrugged. "Vines is a witch," he said. "The hospital, they call me, and they tell me my father died and what to do with the body? When I get there, Vines had already got off with it. That's all I know."

"What was the hospital's explanation?"

"They didn't know what happened. Just the body was gone. One man told me that some of the kinfolks must have got a funeral home to get it. He said the body was put where they put the bodies, and the next day it was gone. He said it must have been a funeral home got it."

"You reported it to the police?"

"Yeah," Charley said. "They didn't do nothing."

They wouldn't, Chee thought. He imagined Charley showing up at the Albuquerque police building, trying to find somebody to take the report, telling a clerk (would the clerk have been incredulous, or merely bored?) of a missing body taken by a witch. What would the crime have been? At worst, transporting a cadaver without a permit from the medical examiner. And the police would have guessed it was merely a mix-up: the body claimed by another relative, a family feud perhaps. And Tomas Charley wouldn't have raised hell and pressed for answers. He already knew two answers. One was that nobody would pay much attention to a Navajo trying to raise hell. And the other was that a witch had flown away with the body. Still, Chee felt his anger rising at this indignity.

"Those sons-a-bitches," he said. "You want me to try to find him for you?"

Charley thought about it.

"Well," he said. "I'm half Acoma and half Navajo, and I guess I'm Navajo far as bodies go. When the old man died, he died. Body don't mean nothing but trouble. But my mother, she's Acoma. She'd like to know he's buried the right way. She wouldn't want a witch to have him."

"I'll see what I can do," Chee said. "Why do you think Vines got him?"

Charley hesitated. "It's got to do with our church," he said. "I got to go way back to explain it."

Tomas Charley went back to World War II, when

his grandfather was working on the Santa Fe Railroad track crew, and had met an Indian from Oklahoma, and had been introduced to the Native American Church and Lord Peyote. His grandfather had founded a church in the Checkerboard country, and one day Lord Peyote had opened the door so his grandfather could see God. He was working then on an oil well, and God told him that something bad would happen the next day and to tell his crew not to go to work. The oil well had blown up just as God had warned and the word had spread among the Navajos and the Laguna-Acomas of this miracle, and the grandfather's congregation grew. By the next year more than two hundred people were coming to the Peyote Ways. Then one time a white man came. He was a uranium prospector named Benjamin Vines. Vines told everyone at the Peyote Way that the Lord Peyote had given him a dream of where to find uranium ore.

"All this is the way my father told me," Charley said. "He said Vines came back about a month later and told my grandfather the uranium ore was where the Lord Peyote said it would be. They had another Peyote Way and Vines had another vision. This time Lord Peyote told Vines he had now done two miracles for my grandfather's church. He had saved the men from the explosion, and he had led Vines to the ore. He said Vines was blessed, and those men he had saved were blessed, and since the blessing had come from under the ground, from an oil well and uranium ore, their totem would be the mole and their name would be the name of the moles—the People of Darkness."

"And Vines gave your grandfather a mole fetish?"

"A little later," Charley said. "They didn't have a Way for a while because the Navajo Police and the BIA cops were arresting everybody and searching people for peyote buttons, and Gordo Sena was after everybody in the church. But then they had a Way at a secret place, and Vines gave these mole fetishes to my grandfather and to the other men who Lord Peyote had saved." Charley paused. "That was before Vines got to be a witch," he explained.

"How'd that happen?" Chee asked.

"First my grandfather got sick," Charley said. "They had a sing for him, but it didn't help very long. He went into the hospital. In and out a lot. Finally he died and Vines buried him up at his ranch. He was just building that big house then. The church sort of died out then for years. Then my father got it going again. After that, Vines came around. He tried to get my father to give him the medicine bundle, the box for Lord Peyote, the mole totem, all of the sacred things. My father wouldn't give them up. After that Vines didn't come to the Peyote Way again."

That seemed to be the end of the story. Charley slumped against the wall, looking across the crowded auditorium toward the stage. The Texan had just sold a small yellow *yei* rug to number 18 for forty-five dollars and was describing a black-and-gray diamond design from Two Gray Hills as "worth three hundred dollars in any trading post on the reservation."

"Then what?" Chee prodded.

Charley didn't say anything for a moment. "Then we started hearing things."

"Like what?"

"Hearing Vines was a witch."

There was another pause. The Navajo half of Charley seemed to be ascendant, Chee thought. Navajos did not like to talk about witches.

"Tell you what," Chee said. "You don't want that old box of Vines' with the rocks in it. You let me know where to look, and we'll get it back to the owner. If anybody asks how we found it, it was an anonymous telephone call."

"It's out in the malpais," Charley said. "It was locked. I took it to a place out there where I go and pried it open. It was heavy, so I just left it there." He explained to Chee how to find it. "I got to go now," he said. "I've got to work tomorrow."

"Did the man see you about buying that old Chevy?"

Charley looked surprised. "No," he said. "Somebody want to buy that?"

"That's what your nephew said. He said to tell you a man came looking for you, and he wanted to buy that old car, and he was going to look for you here."

"Must be crazy," Charley said. And he walked away.

And I must be crazy, too, Chee thought as he watched Charley move down the aisle toward the table where an association clerk was paying off rug weavers for their sales. Rocks in a keepsake box. B. J. Vines as mystic prophet. B. J. Vines as witch. A body lost out of a hospital morgue. And Chee wasting his time in an affair that made no sense at all.

He wasted more time watching the auction, moving among the spectators idly at first and then looking for Mary Landon. She was interested in him, of that he was sure. He was equally sure that it was nothing very personal. The interest was more generic than individual. Another Navajo male, adequately scrubbed and trimmed, would have been just as interesting to the blue-eyed woman. Fair enough. At the moment, he was particularly interested in whites, and white women. The Navajo women he knew—his mother, her two sisters, who were his "little mothers," the Navajo girls he'd been involved with—did nothing to explain Rosemary Vines. And he'd never really known the white girls. Their curiosity had put him off. But Mary Landon he would study. Unfortunately, Mary Landon was nowhere to be seen.

He walked into the parking lot, savoring the cold fresh air after the stuffy heat inside. Tomas Charley was standing beside his truck, talking to a white man in a yellow windbreaker. The white man was blond. The buyer of worthless rusty Chevrolets had found his man. Chee stared at him, curious. The white man seemed to feel the eyes on him. He stared back. The same man, Chee realized, had been watching him and Charley in their long conversation against the wall. Mary Landon was still invisible.

He found her, finally, in the cafeteria kitchen helping a half-dozen other women with cleanup operations.

"The message is delivered," Chee said. "Thanks."

It was the third time he had spoken to her, and Chee had a theory about third meetings between people. The third time you were no longer strangers.

"It must have been a long message," Mary said. "I think you found something to talk about besides someone wanting to buy a car." The words were skeptical, but after she said them she smiled.

Chee found himself trying to think of something to ask her, of a reason to be in this kitchen talking to her. His mind was blank. "How about having a cup of coffee?" he heard himself saying. "The coffee shop will be open late."

The first time she had looked at him she had been inspecting a Tribal Police sergeant. Now she was looking at a man asking her out for coffee. It was a different sort of inspection. "I have to finish with these pots," she said.

"I'll do it for you," Chee said.

Chee washed dishes each evening in his mobile home—a plate, cup, knife, and fork left over from breakfast, a second plate, a cup, and cutlery from dinner, and the frying pan used to cook both meals. But never since his university days had he washed dishes socially.

"You look like you enjoy that," Mary said. "Maybe you missed your calling."

Chee tried to think of something witty. He couldn't.

In the booth at the Crownpoint Café, Chee learned a little about Mary Landon, and she learned a little about him. She had come to Laguna the previous year to replace a teacher hurt in an automobile accident. Then she had landed the Crownpoint job. She was from a little place not far from Milwaukee. She had attended the University of Wisconsin. She liked canoeing and hiking, and the outdoors in general. She didn't like pretentious people. She liked teaching Navajo children, but wasn't sure what to do about their conditioning against competitiveness. She hoped to learn Navajo, but it was hard to pronounce and so far she could speak only a few phrases. She spoke them, and Chee pretended to understand, and Mary Landon was not fooled by the pretense but appreciated it and rewarded him with a genuinely friendly look. Chee asked her about her parents, and learned her father ran a sporting goods store. He decided not to ask her about her hostility to police. This wasn't the time for that, and the attitude was common enough.

Mary Landon learned Chee was one of the Slow Talking Dinee, the clan of his mother, and was "born to" the Bitter Water Dinee, the clan of his father. She learned that Chee's father was dead, that his maternal uncle was a noted *yataalii,* and she had been around Navajo country long enough to know about the role of these shamans in the ceremonial life of the People. She learned a good deal more about his family, ranging from his two older sisters through a galaxy of cousins, uncles, and aunts, one of whom represented the Greasy Water district on the Tribal Council.

"She's my mother's sister, which makes her my 'little mother,' " Chee said. "A real tiger."

"You're not playing the game," Mary Landon said. "I told you about me. You're just telling me about your family."

The statement surprised Chee. One defined himself by his family. How else? And then it occurred to him that white people didn't. They identified themselves by what they had done as individuals. He added sugar to his coffee, thinking about it.

"That's the way we play the game. If I was introducing you to Navajos, I wouldn't say, 'This is Mary Landon, who teaches at Crownpoint,' and so forth. I'd say, 'This woman is a member of . . .'—your mother's family, and your father's family—and I'd tell about your uncles and aunts, so everyone would know just exactly where you fit in with the people around you."

"'This woman'?" Mary Landon asked. "You wouldn't tell them my name?"

"That would be rude. Now more people have English names, but among traditional Navajos it's very impolite to say someone's name in their presence. Names are just reference words, when the person's not there."

Mary Landon looked incredulous. "I think that's . . ." She stopped.

"Silly?" Chee asked. "You have to understand the system. Our real names are secret. We call them war names. Somebody very close to you in the family names you when you're little. Something that fits your personality, if possible. Not more than a half-dozen people are ever going to know it. It's used for ceremonial purposes: if a girl is having her *kinaalda*—her puberty ceremony—or if you're having a sing done for you. Then, as you grow, people give you nicknames to refer to you. Like 'Cry Baby,' and 'Hard Runner,' or maybe 'Long Hands' or 'Ugly.'" Chee laughed. "I've got an uncle on my father's side everybody calls 'Liar.'"

"How about Jim Chee? Isn't that your real name?"

"Along came the trading posts," Chee said. "Along came the white man. He had to have a name to write down when one of us pawned our jewelry to him, or got credit for groceries. The traders started formalizing the nicknames, and before long we had to have names on birth certificates, so you got family names, like mine. I've had nicknames, too. Two or three. And I'm sure you do, too."

"Me?" Mary Landon looked surprised.

"How long you been at Crownpoint? Three months? Sure. The people have a name for you by now."

"Like what?"

"Something that fits. Maybe 'Pretty Teacher.' Or 'Stubborn Girl.' " Chee shrugged. " 'Blue Eyes.' 'Blond Woman.' 'Fast Talker.' Do you want me to find out for you?"

"Sure," she said. Then, "No, wait. Maybe just forget it. How about you? What do they call you?"

"Here? I don't know. When I was at Rough Rock they used to call me . . ." He paused, and then said the word carefully in Navajo. "It means 'One Who Studies to Be a Singer.' "

"Oh," Mary Landon said. "Are you?"

"I was," Chee said. "I guess I still am, in a way. It depends."

"On what?"

"I applied for admission to the FBI. More or less to see how I'd do. Took the tests. Got interviewed by the screening panel at Albuquerque. Last week I got a letter telling me I'd been accepted. I'm supposed to report to the academy in Virginia. December tenth."

She looked at him curiously. "So you're going to be an FBI agent."

"I don't know," Chee said.

"You haven't decided?"

"What's the rush? We work on Navajo time." Even as he said it, the flippancy sounded false. December 10 wasn't Navajo time. It was four weeks away. A specific, ironclad, unbendable deadline.

"But you can't be both a Navajo medicine man and an FBI agent?"

"Not really," Chee said. He wanted to change the subject, wanted not to talk about it. As a matter of fact, you couldn't be both a Navajo and an FBI agent. You couldn't be a Navajo away from the People. "By the way," he said, "thanks for helping with Tomas Charley. I learned what I needed to know. If he told me the truth, that is."

Mary Landon studied him. Chee remembered, belatedly, what he had told her about why he wanted to find Charley.

"Do people lie a lot in your business?"

The question sounded innocent. And if it was, the answer was yes, a lot of people lie to a policeman. But Chee sensed the barb. And the answer was different.

"I'm sorry about that," he said. "I did tell his nephew I'd pass on the message about the car. But I also wanted to see him about police business."

"And you couldn't tell me that." It was more a statement than a question, and the proper answer, of course, was "No, I couldn't." But Chee sensed the hostility again (or perhaps it could now better be described as a mixture of caution and suspicion), and he was not in the mood to give the proper answer.

"I could tell you, but only if you don't mind complicated accounts of things that don't amount to much," Chee said. "Do you want to hear about it?"

She did. Chee told her about Vines, and Mrs. Vines, and the stolen keepsake box, and Sheriff Gordo Sena, and about the People of Darkness and the disappearing body, and finally about where Tomas Charley had left the box.

"And when you look at it all with a detached view," Chee said, "you see a Navajo cop simply exercising his curiosity. A crime of no particular importance. A total lack of jurisdiction."

"But it is curious," she said. "What do you think happened to Mr. Charley's father? And what are you going to do next?"

"I don't know about the body. Probably lost by the bureaucracy somehow and nobody cared enough to find it. As for me, next I'll go out in the malpais when I have some time and get the box and take a look at those rocks, and then I'll get the box back to Vines. He says he doesn't want his box back. But he must want those medals."

"What will you tell Vines?"

"I won't. I'll call the sheriff's office at Grants and tell them I got an anonymous tip on where the box had been left, and went out and found it, and for them to tell the Vineses to come and get it if they want it back."

Mary Landon raised her eyebrows and sipped her coffee.

"Okay," Chee said. "It's a lie. But how else does Vines get his box back without Charley getting in jail?"

"I can't think of a way," she said. "Something else puzzles me. How did Charley know he could trust you?"

Chee shrugged. "Because I look trustworthy?" he asked.

She laughed. "As a matter of fact, you don't," she said. "Could I go along when you go hunting the box?"

"Sure," Chee said. "We'll go tomorrow."

The apartments the Crownpoint school district provided for its teachers were a quarter mile beyond the school. The school was dark now, and the parking lot empty except for a single pickup truck. The pickup was a blue Ford 150. Charley's. Chee slowed his carryall, staring at it.

"Not here," Mary Landon said. "It's those apartments up ahead."

"I know," Chee said. "I'll get you home in just a minute."

He pulled into the parking lot, beside the pickup. "This is Charley's truck," he said. "Why would he leave it?"

The truck was locked. Frost was turning the windshield opaque. Chee walked around it, shone his flashlight into the cab, looking for anything that would answer that question. He didn't find it.

>> 13 <<

*M*alpais, translated literally from the Spanish, means "bad country." In New Mexico, it signifies specifically those great expanses of lava flow which make black patches on the map of the state. The malpais of the Checkerboard country lies just below Mount Taylor, having been produced by the same volcanic fault that, a millennium earlier, had thrust the mountain fifteen thousand feet into the sky. Now the mountain has worn down to a less spectacular eleven thousand feet and relatively modern eruptions from cracks at its base have sent successive floods of melted basalt flowing southward for forty miles to fill the long valley between Cebolleta Mesa and the Zuni Mountains. Some of this malpais was ancient, long since softened by algae, moss, rain, wind, and durable desert grasses. Elsewhere it was only a few thousand years old, still raw, black, and relatively lifeless. The track Chee was following zigzagged its way across a smoother, more ancient flow. Nonetheless, it was rough going.

"I've never been out here before," Mary Landon said. "Not out in it. It's like someone was boiling a whole oceanful of black ink, and all of a sudden it froze solid."

"Even the rodents out here tend to be black," Chee said. "Protective coloration, I guess."

"It doesn't look like there'd be anything alive."

"Lots of reptiles," Chee said. "All kinds of snakes and lizards. And quite a few mammals. Rabbits, mice, kangaroo rats, so forth."

"What do they drink?" Mary asked.

"Some of them don't. They get their water from the plants they eat. But rain and snow melt and collect in potholes," Chee said. "And now and then there's a spring. That's where we're going. Charley has a spring out here. He collects herbs, datura, stuff like that. For his ceremonials. That's where he left the box."

"How do you find it?"

"Either by the powers of deduction," Chee said, "or by asking Charley. I asked Charley and he told me to follow this track until I came to the place where the new lava flow crosses the old." Chee pointed ahead. "Like right there. And then I'd see a place where the track forks. See? Right there ahead. And the spring was maybe a hundred yards down the right fork of the track. He said there was a bunch of tamarisk sticking up out of the lava flow to mark it. See? Over there."

"So why aren't you taking the right turn?" Mary asked.

"I want to show you that new lava up close," Chee said. "We'll park there and we can walk over."

The new lava was at least a thousand years old. It looked as if it had hardened yesterday. It was as black as coal, raw and rough, still marked with the froth of its white-hot bubbling as it boiled across the landscape. They climbed from the ancient lava onto the final wave of the new and stood looking across ten miles of tumbled, ragged blackness at the blue shape of Cebolleta Mesa.

"I'm impressed," Mary said finally. "It's like looking backward a hundred million years."

"Do you know any of our legends?" Chee asked.

"I know a few," Mary said. "A Laguna girl I know told me one about the Laguna migrations. And the Corn Maidens."

"Those are Pueblo," Chee said. "If you were Navajo you'd know that you are looking at the blood of the Horned Monster."

"Oh. Black blood." Mary grinned at Chee. "You Navajos have black-hearted monsters."

"Yes, indeed. A historic spot. Right around here is where the Hero Twins started making Dinetah safe for the Dinee to live in. The Horned Monster was the first one they bagged. Born of Water distracted him, and Monster Slayer shot him with an arrow."

"He certainly bled a lot," Mary said.

"And then they cleaned the rest of them out," Chee said. He helped her down from the lava crest. "The Winged Monster, and the Water Monster. We even had one they called One Who Kicks People Over the Cliff."

"How'd they do him in?"

"His hair grew out of the cliff, keeping him from falling," Chee said. "Monster Slayer gave him a haircut."

The ancient lava flow made fairly easy walking. Eons of time had rubbed away its roughness and turned its blackness gray. It was coated with lichens, and grass grew wherever dust had accumulated in its cracks. Chee talked of Navajo mythology. Mary Landon listened. He was carrying a grocery sack which contained a thermos of coffee, two apples, and two king-sized Lottaburgers picked up in Grants. Chee hadn't been on a picnic since school days. He was happy. To their right, the morning sun reflected off the snow on the high slopes of Mount Taylor, making it glitter against the dark-blue sky.

"We call it Turquoise Mountain," Chee said. "First Man built it out of earth he brought up from the Third World, and he pinned it to the world with a magic knife to keep it from flying away. He put Turquoise Girl on top of it, to keep the Navajos safe from monsters, and he assigned Big Snake to live on the mountain for eternity, to keep Turquoise Girl safe from whatever bothers Turquoise Girls."

"Speaking of big snakes," Mary Landon said. "Am I right in remembering that they hibernate in the winter, and I therefore have absolutely nothing to worry about? Or is that hibernation business just another of your myths?"

She was climbing a great hump of lava. Just beyond it were the tamarisks and the spring. "When are you going to tell me your war name?"

"It's a good rule to stay off those humps when you're walking on lava," Chee said. "They're the tops of old bubbles, and about one in twenty thousand is thin enough so that you can fall through and . . ."

Chee's voice trailed away. Mary had stopped atop the hump and stood frozen, looking down.

"Jim," she said. "There's someone . . ."

Chee scrambled up beside her.

Just beyond the hump was a sinkhole, a circle of clear, dark water rimmed by cattails and a species of green reed. This was surrounded, in turn, by a small expanse of buffalo grass. The man wore a red-and-black mackinaw and his black hat lay beside his head. His hands were together behind his back, secured by what seemed to be an electric cord.

"I think he's dead," Mary Landon said in a very small voice.

"I'll see," Chee said. The left hand looked distorted, and coated with something dark. "I think you should wait in the truck."

"All right," Mary said.

The kneeling man was Tomas Charley. The black on his hand was blood, long dried. But when Chee placed his fingers on Charley's neck to confirm the certainty that he was dead, he found the flesh resilient and warm. He stepped quickly back from the body and studied the area around him. Tomas Charley had been dead only a matter of minutes. Chee became intensely aware that his pistol, inappropriate for a picnic with a girl, was locked in the glove box of the patrol car. Perhaps Tomas Charley had been left here hours ago and had been a long time dying. And perhaps he had been killed only moments ago, which would mean his killer must be nearby. Chee glanced at the body again. There was no sign of what had killed him. The only blood visible was from the hand. Chee grimaced. The hand had been methodically mutilated. He examined the mackinaw, looking in vain for a bullet hole. Then he noticed a place where the black hair on the back of Charley's head had been scorched. He knelt beside the body and gently parted the hair. Beneath it, the skin over the skull had been punctured, leaving a small round hole. A bullet hole, probably no larger than a .22. Turquoise Girl had not kept this half-Navajo safe from the monsters.

The sound of the car starting was close. It came from beyond the tamarisks. Chee trotted around the pool toward it, conscious that the driver was probably armed. The car, he saw when he reached the screen of brush, was a green-and-white Plymouth—

the one that had been parked beside Charley's car. It was moving away from him down the track. He couldn't see the driver. Chee turned and scrambled up the lava formation. When the Plymouth reached the place where the tracks forked, it would angle left, back toward the highway and Grants. Then Chee could see the driver. And he would need only a glimpse to confirm what he already knew. It would be the blond man in the yellow jacket.

But the Plymouth didn't angle left. It turned right and jolted slowly toward Chee's patrol car.

He could see Mary at the passenger-side window, looking at the approaching car and then at him.

He cupped his hands and shouted: "Run. Mary. Run."

She emerged from the driver's-side door, running toward the new lava flow. She was carrying his 30-30 carbine. Chee raced toward the patrol car, doing what he could to keep out of sight behind the humps and hillocks of old lava. The Plymouth stopped and the driver got out. He was a blond man wearing a yellow jacket, and he raised his right arm and aimed the pistol he held at Mary Landon. It seemed to Chee to have a remarkably long and heavy barrel. The barrel smoked, or seemed to, but Chee heard nothing. Mary was in the new lava and out of sight. Chee's plan took no thought at all. He would circle around the patrol car, find Mary in the new lava, and get the rifle. The blond man would think he was armed and wouldn't come after him. The risks were relatively light. In the first place, the chances of being hit at one hundred yards by a pistol were small, unless the man was a hell of a lot better shot than most. And in the second place, a .22 bullet at that range wouldn't be lethal. Chee ran.

The pain was sudden and intense. Chee stumbled, lost his footing, and fell to his hands and knees. The pain was in his left chest. A heart attack, he thought for one illogical moment. And then he felt blood running down his side and made a quick inspection. A bullet seemed to have struck a rib. He inspected the place with cautious fingers and grimaced with the pain. The bullet had apparently broken the bone. But he didn't seem to be hurt in any critical way. No reason to change his plans, except for a more realistic view of the blond man's marksmanship. He raised himself cautiously. He'd locate his adversary exactly, and then he'd resume his run toward the new lava, on a wider, safer circle.

The blond man was trotting directly toward him across the worn waves of gray stone, the long-barreled pistol held in front of him. Chee ducked. The blond either didn't care if the Navajo policeman was armed, or knew that he wasn't. Perhaps he had seen that Chee wasn't wearing his holster. And now he came to finish the job, as he had finished it with Tomas Charley. Chee felt panic, choked it off, and started a scrambling zigzag run. He'd worry about reaching Mary Landon and his rifle later. Now the problem was to stay alive, to put some distance between himself and the blond, to find a place to hide. He vaulted over a ridge of stone and heard the sharp snap of a bullet whipping past him. He heard no gunshot. Behind the ridge, the lava had hardened into a wide trough perhaps five feet deep. Chee sprinted down it, the rib feeling like a knife in his chest. Then he heard the booming crack of a shot, and the whine of a ricocheting bullet. And then another, and another. Those were not the blond's silent .22. It was the muzzle blast of his 30-30. The trough ended at a grassy pothole catch basin. He was back at Emerson Charley's spring. Chee stopped and looked over the rim. The blond man was moving back toward his car, keeping low in a dodging run. From the escarpment of new lava, Chee saw a puff of blue smoke and heard again the cracking boom of the 30-30. Then the blond was behind Chee's patrol car. For a moment Chee lost sight of him. Then he was visible again, getting into the Plymouth. The Plymouth backed around the patrol car with a squeal of tires on rock and then was jolting down the track, far faster than was safe for tires or springs.

About then Chee realized that his patrol car was burning. The flames came from under the rear of it, apparently fed by fuel leaking out of the gas tank. The fire mushroomed abruptly, engulfing the rear half of the vehicle. Chee watched it grimly. The tank was about half full as he remembered it—perhaps twelve gallons. There was another twenty in the auxiliary tank. When that heated up, it would go off like a bomb.

What had been Tomas Charley still knelt, forehead to grass. Chee walked past the body and picked up the sack containing the thermos of coffee and the picnic lunch. They had a long walk ahead of them. He spent another few minutes making a methodical search of the spring area for the box. Charley had said he'd left it in plain view on the rock just beside the water. There was no box now. Behind him, he heard the muffled boom of the gas tank exploding.

"Boy," Mary Landon said when he walked up. "You Navajos give exciting picnics." She laughed, but it was a shaky laugh. The fire flared up again with a *whoosh* of flame as a front tire exploded, and she raised her hand to shade her face from the heat. Her sleeve was torn and her wrist was smeared with blood from a long scratch on her forearm.

"You all right?" he asked. "Thank God you took the rifle with you."

"I knew you'd say that." Suddenly Mary Landon was furious. "Why wouldn't I take it? Because I was stupid, that would be why. I'd just seen a tied-up dead body, and the man who must have killed him coming right toward me, and you yelling at me to run, and the rifle right there in the scabbard. Why wouldn't I take it?" Her voice was fierce. "Because I'm a half-wit woman? I wouldn't have said that if you'd taken the rifle. I'd take it for granted. But no. I'm a woman, so I'm stupid."

"Sorry," Chee said.

"What's wrong with this damned rifle anyway?" Mary said. She handed it to him, which reminded Chee that his spare ammunition was in the glove box and would be exploding any minute.

"Let's back away a little," he said. As he said it, the 30-30 rounds began exploding, no louder than firecrackers.

"I'm a pretty good shot, I thought," Mary said. "I was missing him a mile."

"Sorry about that, too," Chee said. "When I'm not using it I let the rear sight down." He showed her, pushing the leaf sight up with his thumb and sliding the calibrated wedge forward to the 200-yard mark.

Mary looked from Chee's thumb to Chee's face, her glance asking: Is this man for real? She shook her head. "Why? Why would you do that?"

"Takes the strain off the spring," Chee said lamely.

Suddenly she leaned against him. He felt her shaking. "Sorry I've been so bitchy," she said, talking into his coat. "I'm not used to this."

"Me either," Chee said.

"That man back there. Was that Mr. Charley? The one you were looking for? He was dead, wasn't he? Did that blond man kill him? Do you know what's going on?"

"Yes," Chee said. "And no. It was Charley. He was dead. And I don't have any idea what the hell is going on."

While he was saying it, Mary became aware of the blood on his shirt. Childish as he knew it was, being wounded made him feel a little less foolish. If the rib hadn't hurt so much, and if he hadn't had a five-mile walk back to the highway ahead of him, it would have been almost worthwhile.

≫ 14 ≪

Colton Wolf had left tracks. Two witnesses had seen him. Close and clearly. They could identify him. They could connect him with murder and with a rented car. The car-rental connection would provide other witnesses and uncover the false identity. He gunned the Plymouth down the access acceleration lane and onto Interstate 40 west. There was no time wasted deciding what to do. He'd decided that before he'd left his trailer. This was Plan B. Plan B was what he did if the operation created the sort of disturbance that made the routine withdrawal in some way risky. There had been a Plan B and variations of Plan B for each of his previous operations. But he'd never used one before because there had never been a disturbance. Previously, the targets had died unobserved, quietly and unobtrusively. The only exception had been the old CPA in Reno. The man had suspected something. Perhaps it had been the product of a guilty conscience, perhaps the product of age and wisdom. At any rate, part of the information provided to Colton had been the detail that the target would be alert and wary. And he had been. Colton had spent an extra day scouting because of that. And the set-up had seemed perfect. The accountant's office had been on the fifth floor of a downtown bank building. At midmorning for three consecutive days the old man had emerged from his office, crossed the corridor to the men's rest room, and relieved himself. Rest rooms were ideal. And this had been the best kind. A single-stall men's room. The jimmy blade flicking the latch open. The victim startled, embarrassed, refusing to credit what his eyes were telling him—that the intruder upon his privacy was pointing a pistol at his forehead. The victim starting to blurt some banality like "This booth is occupied." The voice being stopped by the *thud* of the silenced .22. The bullet fired into the hair, where it would go undetected for a time. The body propped on the stool. The unhurried departure. But this time it had been different. The old man had sensed something when Colton had come into the room. Through the gap beside the booth door, Colton had seen a single eye peering out at him, and the screaming had started the moment the jimmy touched the latch. The man was up from the stool, pants around ankles, trying to resist. It had taken three bullets and a little more time, and then, as he was propping up the body, the door had swung open and the old man's secretary had burst in. He had shot her twice, and wedged her body in with the old man's, and walked away. It had been tense for a moment, but when he emerged from the elevator, there had been absolutely no tracks left behind. He had dumped the pistol by opening the emergency hatch and putting it on top of the elevator car. When he stepped through the doors into the bank lobby, there was no chance of connecting him with the bodies in the men's room. He had hated to lose the pistol, but it couldn't be traced. There had been absolutely no tracks.

This time there were tracks everywhere. He drove west on Interstate 40 past the Grants interchange, thinking about them. Out here tracks were easy to follow. Too few people in too much space. Had all gone smoothly, Colton would have driven back to Albuquerque, checked in the car at the airport, picked up his truck, and returned to his trailer. That was Plan A, simple and quick. Then, after a few days, he would have hitched the trailer to the truck and moved along. Somewhere warmer. Maybe Houston, or maybe somewhere in California. It didn't matter where. Until he could find his mother. Then there would be a home place. A place to settle.

But now he had to use Plan B. That took him in the other direction—to Gallup. There he would check the car into a garage for a major tune-up, leaving a Gallup number to be called when repairs were completed and telling the mechanic that there wasn't any hurry. That would mean days before the car surfaced. He'd walk to the bus station, take the next bus to Phoenix, and fly back to Albuquerque.

He drove exactly five miles above the speed limit—the margin highway patrolmen allow. There was no serious hurry. He'd bought himself some hours by burning the policeman's car and radio. He'd wounded the man, probably in the abdomen. And it would take the woman at least three hours to walk out of the lava rock and turn in the alarm. By the time any serious search could be organized, he'd be well into Arizona. Outside the circle.

A semi-trailer rig breezed past him, going perhaps fifteen miles above the limit. That would mean the trucker's CB had assured him he was safe from the state police. But Colton held the rental Plymouth at a steady sixty. He was thinking how he would erase his tracks. Not since he was a boy had Colton felt so vulnerable. He knew the Indian policeman had seen him at the auction, clearly and close up. The policeman and the woman had seen him again on the lava. The policeman and the woman had to be killed just as quickly as Colton could manage it.

➤ 15 ◄

The way Jimmy Chee was propped against the pillows, he could shift his eyes to the left and look out the window of his fifth-floor room in the Bernalillo County Medical Center and see, across Lomas Avenue, the tan book tower of the University of New Mexico library and the modern-sculpture form of the Humanities Building. If he shifted his eyes to the right, he'd see on the TV screen the has-beens and never-would-bes of *Hollywood Squares* pretending to enjoy themselves. The TV screen was silent, the sound turned off. All Chee could hear was the voice of Sheriff Gordo Sena, whose face Chee could see when he turned his eyes straight ahead. Voice and face were angry. "What I want you to do," Sena was saying, "is drop all the bullshit. Just tell me some by-God truth for once. I want to know how you knew Tom Charley had that box. And what was in it. And what happened to it. And how come that feller in the Plymouth was after him."

And what I'd like to know, Chee was thinking, is

how Gordo Sena got past the nurse. The FBI people had come earlier, while he was trying to eat his breakfast, and the nurse had peered in at him and said, "You're not ready to talk to police, are you," and that had been the end of the FBI. But thirty minutes later, Sena had simply pushed the door open, stalked in, turned off the TV volume, sat in the bedside chair, and said, "By God, we're going to get some things straightened out." It was now about thirty questions later.

"I didn't know Charley had the box," Chee said for the third time. "It was an educated guess. I told you what Mrs. Vines told me. About thinking the burglary had a religious connection. Well, the religion is peyote, and Charley is the peyote chief. One plus one is two."

"*Was,*" Sena corrected. "*Was* the peyote chief. So you just walk up to Charley and ask him if he's the burglar, and he admits it. That's what you're trying to get me to believe."

"That's what happened," Chee said. "Not quite, but just about." His ears were ringing, and his rib hurt, and the nausea that had come and gone all morning was coming again. He didn't feel like talking. He closed his eyes. Sena's glowering face went away, but not the voice. Question after question about why Charley had stolen the box, what Charley had said was in the box, what Charley had said about the Vineses. Questions that explored from every possible angle what Chee knew about the blond man in the green-and-white Plymouth.

"What kind of voice did he have?" Sena asked.

Chee opened his eyes. "Never talked to him." He'd told Sena that before. Twice, in fact.

"That's right, you didn't," Sena said. His alert eyes were studying Chee's face. Why did Sena think they had talked? Why was that so important to the sheriff?

More questions. Why had the blond man burned Chee's car? The answer seemed obvious to Chee, but he answered it. To prevent pursuit and the quick radio call that would have inevitably snared the Plymouth at a roadblock. Why did the blond man seem inclined to pursue Mary Landon? Obvious again. She and Chee had had a good look at the killer. He was trying to eliminate witnesses.

Sena hitched his chair closer to the bed. He leaned forward. "Did you find the box?"

"No," Chee said.

"Had Tomas Charley opened it? Did he tell you that?"

"He opened it," Chee said. They had already covered this.

"What was in it?"

Chee was dizzy. He wanted Sena to go away. The sheriff's avid face went slightly out of focus.

"Did he tell you that? What was in the box?"

"What I said; mostly just some rocks," Chee said. "A bunch of black rocks, and some old military stuff—medals, a paratroop badge, a shoulder patch, and a few old photographs of people. Family, Charley thought they were."

"Rocks?" Sena said.

"Mostly full of black rocks," Chee said.

Sena was silent. His hard dark eyes stared at Chee. "You got any brothers?"

"No," Chee said. "Two sisters. No brothers." The question surprised him.

"I had one," Sena said. "Older brother. His name was Robert. He was smart. Smartest kid in Grants High School. Made the valedictorian speech. First time in years it hadn't been some Anglo girl. Got a scholarship to the university here, but he didn't go at first. Our old man had heart trouble. Robert worked in the onion fields, in the oil fields, things like that. He looked after us kids. Took care of us. Kept us out of trouble. The old man died and left some social security, so Robert finally went to the university. He was studying engineering."

Sena had delivered that information in a flat staccato. Now his voice trailed off. He looked down at his hands, drew in a long breath, held it and then let it go. When he looked up again, his eyes were no longer hard. "I'm going to ask you a favor," he told Chee. "I don't do that much."

Chee nodded.

"I want to tell you how Robert died," Sena said. He described the oil well explosion and how the chief of the Navajo roustabout crew had kept his men away that day. "For a while I thought he did it. Now I just think he was in on it somehow. Knew about the plan. Knew Robert was going to be killed. That fella was Dillon Charley, Tomas' granddaddy."

Sena looked down at his hands. The muscles in his jaw were working.

"What do you want me to do?" Chee asked.

Sena didn't look up. "I want to know who killed Robert," he said. "I want to nail the sons of bitches. You talked to Mrs. Vines. You talked to Dillon Charley's grandson. There's some secret here that's got to do with being Indian, and with that peyote religion. One of them told you something. You've figured something out. You know more than you're telling. Otherwise, you wouldn't have found Vines' box so quick."

"I don't know a damned thing," Chee said. "Not about that oil well explosion. You think the Vineses had something to do with it?"

Sena shook his head. "He didn't live here then. And she didn't get here until his first wife died. I think Dillon Charley told Vines something. Anyway, it's a damned cinch Mrs. Vines knows something. Why else would she connect stealing that box with that bunch of peyote freaks?"

"I don't know," Chee said.

The room fell silent. An ambulance turned off Lomas toward the BCMC emergency room entrance, its siren abruptly growling out.

"Nothing to tell me, then?" Sena asked.

"Not that I haven't already told you," Chee said.

Sena pursed his lips, glanced at his watch. "It's a hell of a way to kill a man," he said. "Blowing 'em to pieces like that. We didn't hardly find enough of Robert to bury. And part of what we buried might not have been him. Had one of his legs with the boot still on it. Part of the torso we could recognize because his belt buckle was in it. Never found a lot of him. The coyotes and the buzzards and things had had a couple of days to carry it away." Sena's eyes were hard and bright, staring into Chee's eyes. His jaw muscles were rigid. "My mother used to go out there and look. She'd walk around in the creosote bush looking for pieces of bone." Sena produced a series of sounds that might have been a laugh. "I think she wanted to put Robert all back together again. What do you think of that?"

Chee could think of nothing to say. White people's attitude toward their dead was beyond his understanding.

"Two things," Sena said. "One I'm asking you, and one I'm telling. If you can tell me anything about that peyote bunch, or the Vineses, or anything that will help me, well, I'd appreciate that. I'd remember it. I never forget a favor. And two, I'm telling you to stay out of my jurisdiction. This whole business is mine. The burglary and the killing and everything else. It's mine. It's been mine for most of my life, and I don't want you in it. I told you that once, and you didn't pay attention to me." Sena's voice was shaking. He stopped talking for a moment, gaining control. "Now, I got a name for being hard," he continued. "I've killed a man or two in the line of duty, and there's some that says I've killed some that didn't need to be killed. However that is, I'll tell you this. You think you're unlucky that blond man run into you out there on the malpais. Fact is, you're lucky it wasn't me."

Sena got up and placed his chair neatly against the wall under the television set. He went through the door without a glance or a word.

On the television screen, a barrage of commercials replaced *Hollywood Squares* and gave way in turn to what seemed to be a soap opera. The screen was filled with the tear-wet face of a woman. Her lips moved soundlessly, and she dabbed at her eyes. Chee shifted his own eyes to the left, and stared out across the central campus of the University of New Mexico. He thought first about Gordo Sena's hatred. And then about the pattern of his questions. It had not been a debriefing—one officer collecting information from another. It had been an interrogation—the probing of a hostile witness, skillfully done. But exactly what had Sena wanted to learn?

Part of that was obvious. Part of it wasn't. Chee sorted it out in his mind. Three times, in three different ways, Sena had tried to learn if there had been any communication between him and the blond man. Why was that so important to Sena?

Was the blond man working for the sheriff? Had Sena hired the man to get the box away from Tomas Charley? There was no way to answer that question. It would seem more logical that he had been hired by Vines.

The telephone rang. Chee groaned.

"I'm Sergeant Hunt," the voice said, "with the Albuquerque Police Department. You feel like having a visitor?"

It was a soft voice, very polite.

"Why not?" Chee said.

"You're going to have to tell that nurse, then," the voice said. "She wouldn't let me in."

"I'll tell her," Chee said.

"Be right up, then," Hunt said, and hung up.

Chee pushed the button to summon someone from the nursing station. Why would the APD send a man to talk to him? It was an FBI case, or, as Sena insisted, the Valencia County sheriff's. That would depend on whether you counted the abduction, which had happened in federal jurisdiction on the reservation, or the murder, which was probably in Sena's territory, depending on where the lines fell on the checkerboard. Either way, it would be of zero interest to the Albuquerque law.

Hunt was a small man, with pale-gray eyes and a narrow, bony face.

"Looks like you forgot to dodge," Hunt said. "In case you wondered, the bullet broke up, but it looks like a .22. Probably a hollow point."

"It looked like it might have been a .22 pistol with a silencer on the barrel," Chee said. "Felt like a cannonball."

"I've got the report you gave to the state police here," Hunt said. "Sounds like you got a pretty good look at him."

"Yeah," Chee said. "Close enough." He tried to remember what he had told the state policeman. It was all hazy. They had started to walk back to the highway. Mary Landon and he. It had quickly become slow and painful. Each step produced a stabbing pain in his chest. Soon he had been dizzy. He had sat beside the track. Mary had spread her coat on the ground and made him lie down, and she had gone, running, intending to flag down some driver and get help. He had dozed and awakened and dozed again. Finally, when the sun was almost directly overhead, he had awakened to see a man in the black uniform of the New Mexico State Police bending over him. He remembered talking to the policeman, and Mary's worried face, and driving to the interstate, and being transferred to an ambulance. He remembered Mary riding with him. But that was about all he remembered. Where was Mary now?

"We'd like to get another description," Hunt said. "Have you go over it again."

"Medium-sized," Chee said. "About thirty. Probably weighed about 150. Five ten, probably less. Looked to be in good shape. Hair was very blond, medium short. Sort of prominent bone structure, as I remember. Strong chin, blue eyes, light eyebrows. No mustache. No beard. Light complexion. Pale. Ears fairly large and laid close to his skull."

Hunt had been making notes. Chee closed his eyes, seeing the face again as he had seen it at the auction, the light-blue eyes watching him. "I can't think of any more details. He looked smart, if you know what I mean by that."

Hunt had opened a manila folder. "He look anything like this?" he asked. He handed Chee a sketch done in pencil on thin white cardboard. It looked like a sketch made by a police artist. It also looked a lot like the blond man.

Chee handed it back. "Could be him," he said. "Probably is. Who is he?"

"We don't know for sure," Hunt said.

Chee's rib throbbed. He felt a sudden wave of sickness. His ears were ringing. He was not in the mood for coyness. "God damn it," he said. "Let's not play games. Who was the sketch supposed to look like? And how come it's APD business? It's a hundred miles out of your territory."

"That takes a minute to explain," Hunt said. "We have a file on old unsolved homicides in the detective division, and I'm the one who keeps track of it. You know, review it every six months or so to see if anything new fits in. Anyway, last summer we had a funny double killing. Two guys on a wrecker were going to tow an old pickup out of a reserved parking zone, and the thing blew up and killed 'em both. We got lucky and found a witness who'd been sitting at a window watching the world go by. She had seen somebody who looked like this"—Hunt tapped the sketch—"put a package in the back of the pickup before it went boom."

"Ah," Chee said. He was no longer conscious of the ache in his left side, or of the nausea. Part of the pattern that had been trying to form in his mind for hours took firm, clear shape. Hunt was looking at him expectantly, waiting for a comment. "That's interesting," Chee said.

"It is," Hunt agreed. "We never could figure it out. Obviously the bomb wasn't intended for the wrecker crew—although we finally even checked on that. You'd figure if a guy puts a bomb in a pickup, he wants to waste the pickup driver. But the driver was a poor-boy Navajo who was already on his last legs with cancer. Already dying. No motive to hurry it along. Then we checked on the guy who had the parking space reserved. Big shot doctor. Money. Wife trouble. Maybe she wanted an instant divorce. No evidence, but we figured the doctor was the target. Now it looks like we got our bomber killing another Navajo, and he's got the same last name."

"They're father and son," Chee said.

Hunt slapped his leg. "That's exactly what I hoped you'd say. That, or maybe brothers. You know for sure?"

"I know it for sure," Chee said.

"Well, now," Hunt said. "That tells us a couple of things."

Yes, Chee was thinking. It should tell us a lot. But he couldn't think of what.

"Like what?" he asked.

"Like that bomb wasn't intended for the doctor. If that hit man was aiming for Charley Junior, he must have been aiming for Charley Senior."

"Yes," Chee said. His head ached. Who would hire a professional killer to murder a man who was already dying? Why would anyone want to hurry the death of Emerson Charley? There were no apparent answers. Hunt was watching Chee, waiting for more response.

"Did Emerson Charley's body ever turn up?"

Hunt frowned. "What do you mean?"

"Tomas Charley told me that the hospital lost his daddy's body. Emerson died one night, and Tomas came to get the body the next morning, and it was gone out of the morgue."

Hunt opened his mouth, and closed it again. "I didn't know that," he said. "Be damned. Why wasn't it reported?"

"Tomas reported it to APD," Chee said.

Hunt's embarrassment showed. "You know how that'd be," he said. "Probably told some clerk at the front desk, and filled in a form, and somebody did a little calling around, and that was about it. Nobody pushing it. By then the bombing case wasn't active. And nobody up front would have a way to know the detective division was interested in a sick Navajo."

"Guess not," Chee said.

"I'll check on it. Right away." He frowned again. "How can a hospital lose a body?"

"Tomas thinks it was stolen."

"Stolen? Why? Who'd steal it? This guy?" He tapped the drawing.

Chee didn't feel like talking about the Vineses. "Tomas thinks a witch stole it," he said. "Why? Who knows?" But a reason was forming in his mind.

And, apparently, in the mind of Hunt.

"What did he die of?" Hunt asked. "They told us he had cancer."

"But maybe the guy who tried to hurry him along with the bomb found another way to hurry him along. That's what you're thinking?" Chee found himself respecting the way Hunt's mind worked, and liking the man.

"Exactly," Hunt said. "And if the body's gone, there's no autopsy. I'll check into that."

"Good," Chee said.

"I'll let you know," Hunt said. "And there's one other thing." He fished the sketch out of the folder again and looked at it. "If our man here is the same as your man, I think he's a biggie. I think the FBI's going to be very interested."

"They were here this morning," Chee said. "The nurse wouldn't let 'em in. What do they want?"

"Past several years they've had a run of professional killings done a lot the same. People shot in the head with a .22. Nobody hears a shot. And then there was a couple of cases where they had one person hit with a .22 and one bombed. A couple of hoods in the construction union in Houston and witnesses in an extortion case in Philadelphia. Anyway, mostly the little silenced pistol and a couple of times with the bomb. And both times the bombs seem to have been the kind that get set off by tilting the package. That's the kind of bomb he used here."

"Tilting the package?"

"Clever as hell," Hunt said. "It uses mercury to make the electrical connection. You just set the damn thing down and take off the safety gadget, and the next time the thing moves, or tilts, or shakes, the mercury slides and it goes off. No timer to screw you up, no wiring it up to the ignition. No fuss. No muss. If the driver doesn't see it, it goes off when the car moves. If he does see it, it goes off when he picks it up."

"Then what went wrong here?" Chee asked.

"Luck. Wrecker crew was going to haul off the truck," Hunt said. "They started to hoist the rear end. Tilt. Boom. But that was sheer bad luck. It's quite a gadget. Understand the CIA developed it."

The FBI arrived as Hunt was leaving. His name was Martin. He was young. He wore a brown suit with a vest. His mustache was trim, and his haircut would not have offended the late J. Edgar Hoover.

Being second to an Albuquerque policeman did not please him.

"The nurse told me you were asleep," he said. It was more an accusation than a statement.

"No," Chee said. "I was watching *Hollywood Squares*. I guess she didn't want to interrupt. Ever watch 'em?"

Martin denied it. He wanted to talk about what the blond man looked like. And about why anyone would want Tomas Charley killed. And about the Vines burglary. It took Chee less than five minutes to exhaust all he knew about all three subjects and ten minutes more to go over it all twice more from slightly different angles.

"You find anything in the man's car?" Chee asked. "It was a rental car, wasn't it?"

"We haven't recovered it yet," Martin said. "We think it was rented from Hertz at the Albuquerque airport." He fished a folder from his briefcase and extracted a copy of Hunt's sketch.

"Your man look like this?"

"Pretty close," Chee said.

"The Hertz people identified him as the man who rented a green-and-white Plymouth sedan. Now the car's overdue. He gave his name as McRae and an Indiana address. It doesn't check out."

Chee didn't comment. Talking to Hunt had tired him. His chest hurt. His ears were ringing. He wanted Martin to go away.

"When you get out of here, we want you to come

down to the office," Martin said. "We want you to look at mug shots and give us more details on the identification if you can."

"Mug shots? You think you have a record on him?"

"Not really," Martin said. "We think we have a ten-year accumulation of suspicions. We want you to look just in case. And we want you to spend a lot of time remembering everything you can about him. Everything."

Chee said nothing. He just closed his eyes.

"It's important," Martin said. "This guy's slick. That little pistol he used must be really silent. And he gets it in places where nobody sees anything. Apparently he scouts everything out very methodically, and then he likes to catch them alone for one quick close shot at the head. In the john is a favorite of his. We know of four found sitting on the john with the stall door closed. And a couple in telephone booths. Places like that. A quick shot and he just walks away. Never any witnesses. Not until the bombing. And now you and Miss Landon."

Chee opened his eyes. "We're the first witnesses?"

Martin was staring at him. "The first he knows about. He didn't know anyone saw him putting the bomb in Charley's truck. Medium-sized. Blond. So forth. You're the only two who actually got a look at him and who could pin him to a killing."

Chee's head ached. He closed his eyes again.

"You know," Martin said, "I think I'd be careful if I were you."

Chee had already had that thought.

>16<

When Martin left, Chee spent the next ten minutes on the telephone. He got Mary Landon's number from information, but no one answered when he called it. He remembered then that it was a school day and called the school. Miss Landon had taken the day off. He called his own office, explained the situation, and told Officer Dodge to see if she could find Mary and do what she could do to keep an eye on her. The doctor came in then—a young man with red hair and freckles. He inspected Chee's ribs, replaced the dressing, said, "Take it easy," and left. The nurse arrived, took his temperature, gave him two pills, watched while he took them, said, "This isn't a police station. You're supposed to be resting," and left. Chee rearranged himself on the pillow and gazed out across the university campus. He thought about Mary, and about the peyote religion, and B. J. Vines' keepsake box, and the ways of white men, and drifted off into an uneasy sleep. When he awoke it was late afternoon. The sun was slanting through his window and Mary sat in the bedside chair.

"Hello," she said. "How're you feeling?"

"Fine," Chee said. He did feel fine. Vastly relieved.

"Boy," she said. "You sure scared me. I thought you were dead. I waved down a truck, and he got that state policeman on his CB radio. And when we got back to you, you were just lying there." She grimaced at him. "Like dead."

Chee told her what he'd learned about the blond man. "You see the problem? There's a chance he's going to decide he needs to get rid of us."

Even as he was saying them, the words sounded melodramatic to him. In this quiet, antiseptic room, the idea of anyone wanting to kill Jim Chee and Mary Landon seemed foolish.

"Don't you think what he'd really do is just run?" Mary asked. "That's what I'd do."

"But you're not a professional gunman," Chee said.

"If that remark's a reflection on my shooting, I want to remind you that it was you who screwed up the rear sight."

"Be serious," Chee said. "This guy kills people."

The humor left Mary's face. "I know," she said. "But what can you do? It's sort of like being struck by lightning. You can't go around all the time hiding from clouds."

"But you don't stand under trees while it's raining, either," Chee said. "Why don't you take a leave and go off and visit some relatives somewhere for a while and don't tell anyone where you're going?"

Mary's expression shifted from somber to skeptical. "Is that what you're going to do?"

"I would if I could," Chee said. "But I'm a policeman. It's my business."

"No, it's not," Mary said. "You don't even have jurisdiction. That's what you told me. It's FBI business. Or maybe the sheriff's."

"Legally," Chee said. "But this sore rib sort of gives me a special interest. And besides, I'm a material witness."

"So am I," Mary said.

They argued about it, an uneasy, tentative sparring of two persons not yet sure of their relationship.

Mary changed the subject to his earlier visitors, to Sheriff Sena, to Sena's obsession with the death of his brother in the oil well explosion. The conversation was oddly strained and uncomfortable.

"When I get out of here," Chee said, "I'm going to dig into the newspaper files and learn everything I can about that oil well accident, and get some names, and see what I can find out."

"I'll go see about it," Mary said. "The university library keeps newspapers on microfilm." She got up and collected her purse. "I'll see if they have the right ones. If I hurry, I can get it done today."

≫ 17 ≪

It was 3:11 A.M. when Chee looked at his watch. He had been awake perhaps fifteen minutes, lying motionless with his eyes closed in the vain hope that sleep would return. Now he gave it up. Sleeping away the afternoon had left him out of tune with time. The nurse had given him another sleeping pill at ten o'clock but he had let it lay. His policy was to take pills only when unavoidable. Having his sleeping habits dislocated was the price he was now paying for that pill at lunch. He sat on the edge of the bed and put on the hospital slippers. Much of the soreness had gone out of his side. Only when he moved was there still pain under the heavy bandages. Through the curtain that now partitioned the room he could hear the heavy breathing of a drugged sleep. They had wheeled a man in from the post-surgery recovery room about midnight—a young Chicano sewn up after some sort of accident earlier in the evening. Chee flicked on his bed light and began to reread the newspaper. Through the curtain he heard his roommate mumble in his sleep. The man shifted his position, groaned. Chee switched off the light. Let him sleep, he thought. This is the time of night for sleeping. But Chee had never felt more wide awake. He put on his robe and walked down to the nurse's station. The nurse was a woman in her middle forties, with a round, placid face and a complexion marred by those ten thousand wrinkles the desert sun inflicts upon white people. She glanced up from her paperwork through bifocal glasses.

"Can't sleep," Chee said.

"Let's see," Bifocals said. "You're Chee?" She found his folder and glanced at it. "You had a pill at ten, but I guess I could give you another one."

"I don't like 'em," Chee said. "They make me drowsy."

Bifocals gave him a double take, detected the irony, and grinned. "Yes," she said. "That's the trouble with sleeping pills."

"A while back this hospital lost a body," Chee said. "Fellow named Emerson Charley. You hear about that?"

"Not officially," Bifocals said. "But I heard." She grinned at the memory. "There was some hell raised over it."

"How could it happen? What do you do with bodies?"

"Well, first the attending physician comes, takes care of the certification," Bifocals said. She looked thoughtful. "Then the body is tagged for identification and moved to the morgue on the second floor. It's held there until relatives get a funeral home to claim it. Or, if there's an autopsy, it's tagged for that, and it's held until the morphology laboratory does the postmortem. The way I heard about this one, it was tagged for an autopsy, but somebody came and took it."

"Tell me about it," Chee said.

"Nothing to tell. He died late in the day. The body was taken down and put in the cooler. In the morning, morphology called for it and the body was gone." Bifocals grinned. "Lots of embarrassment. Lots of red faces."

"Did somebody steal the body?"

"Had to be that," Bifocals said. "Somebody in the family, probably. Indians usually don't want an autopsy made."

Chee didn't correct her. Charley was a Navajo and most Navajos had even less distaste for autopsies than do whites. It was the Pueblo Indians who tended to resist autopsies. Their dead needed to be buried in the same cycle of the sun as their death. They had to begin on time the tightly scheduled four-day journey of the soul into eternity. But for most of the Navajo clans, death produced only a short-lived and evil ghost, and everlasting oblivion for the human consciousness. They had little sentiment for corpses.

"Could somebody just walk in and walk out with a body?" Chee asked.

"I guess they did," Bifocals said. "And with clothing, too." She chuckled. "We had two flaps out of this one. First the body was missing, and then two days later it turned out we'd given this Emerson Charley's clothing to another corpse. Whoever took him took the other man's clothing."

"How could that happen?"

"Easy enough. When a patient comes in, his clothing goes into a red plastic bag—looks sort of like a shopping bag—and it goes to the morgue with the body. Whoever got the body just picked up the wrong bag."

"But don't they keep the place locked?"

"Supposed to be. But somebody probably left it open for some funeral home. That's what I think happened. And somebody from the man's family came, found it unlocked, and just walked out with the body. The morgue's right by the laundry dock. They could go out that way and nobody would see them. And you should be back in bed."

"Okay," Chee said. "Good night."

But Chee still wasn't sleepy. At his doorway, he glanced back. Bifocals was immersed in her paperwork. He walked down the hall, around the corner, and out the door to the elevator landing. He took the stairway down to second, and paused there to get his directions. From what Bifocals said, the morgue was near the laundry loading dock. That made sense in terms of logistics. The hospital was built on a slope, a hillside that angled downward from northeast to southwest. Thus if the laundry loading dock was on a second floor, it must be on the northeast side of the hospital. Chee took a hall that led north and made a right turn eastward. As he walked down this empty, echoing corridor he could hear thumping sounds ahead. The sounds, Chee guessed, a laundry would make. On the next door, a sheet of typing paper had been stuck. A legend printed on it with a marking pen declared that the morphology laboratory had been moved to the New Mexico State Laboratory. Just around the corner, Chee found the door to the morgue. It was a wide door, protected by a plywood bumper sheet. Three body-tables-on-wheels were parked beside it. The door was locked. Chee examined the lock. He guessed he could open it with a flexible blade, but there was no way to be sure. The ceiling offered another possibility. He glanced up and down the hallway and down the connecting hall that led to the laundry dock. All deserted. The only sound was the thumping of the laundry machinery. Chee pushed one of the carts against the door and climbed stiffly atop it. He lifted the acoustical ceiling tile and stuck his head through the opening. There was about four feet of crawl space between the false ceiling and the floor above. Chee tested the aluminum-alloy gridwork that supported the ceiling tiles. It seemed sturdy but probably not strong enough to support the full weight of a man. There were, however, other means of support—electrical-cable conduits, water pipes, and the heavily insulated sheet-metal tubes through which the hot and cold air of the heating-cooling system flowed. Chee could see well enough in the darkness now to tell that getting into the morgue wouldn't be difficult even if the door was locked. One could simply climb into the false ceiling, cross the partition, lift another of the acoustical tiles, and drop into the room. He withdrew his head, and sliding the ceiling section back into place, climbed gingerly down from the body cart. At the elevator he yawned. Suddenly he felt both tired and relaxed. He had answered a question that no one had asked, and that didn't matter anyway. But now he could sleep.

≫ **18** ≪

Colton Wolf had left the car parked in the darkness about fifty yards from the laundry loading dock. He tested the dock entrance door. It was unlocked. Then he circled the hospital, checking the parking lots. He found no police cars. His plan was simple. He would use the front entrance of the hospital. He would take the stairs to the fifth-floor post-surgical wing, find room 572, and kill the Indian policeman. The next steps would depend on the circumstances—whether there was any sort of disturbance. Colton expected none. The Indian policeman would be sleeping the heavy sleep that hospitals impose upon their patients. He should present no problem. If there was a nurse on duty, Colton would evade her if he could and kill her quietly if he couldn't. And then he would walk downstairs, take the hall past the morgue, go out the laundry loading dock exit, and drive away in a common, nondescript two-year-old Chevy. He had taken the Chevy from the low-rate, long-term parking lot at the airport; the ticket on the dashboard of the one he picked showed it had already been left overnight. It might not be missed for days. But in the event it was missed, he had stopped in the parking lot of an all-night grocery store and switched license plates.

It was cold. Colton hated cold. He felt exposed and vulnerable. Overhead, as he walked across the almost empty front-entrance parking lot, the sky was a dazzle of strange stars. Unlike the soft, warm protecting darkness of his California boyhood, the night here was hostile. He could hear the soft sound of his crepe-rubber soles on the asphalt, the sound of his trouser legs rubbing, cloth on cloth. Behind him a truck moved up Lomas Avenue. Except for that, the night was silent. Colton squeezed the pistol in his coat pocket. It had a solid, reassuring feel. It was a good piece. Long-barreled and unhandy to look at, but efficient. He had made most of it himself to exactly fit his needs. The grip was walnut, roughed to eliminate the possibility of fingerprints, as was every metal surface. The barrel was threaded at both ends so that a half turn removed the silencer from its muzzle and a turn and a half detached barrel from firing chamber. Only the barrel—with its telltale ballistic tracks left on the lethal bullet—was directly incriminating. Within minutes after a job, the barrel was disposed of and a new barrel screwed into place—apparent proof that the pistol Colton carried had never been fired.

The automatic door sighed open in front of him

and closed behind him. Inside, the air was stuffy. The young woman at the reception desk was reading what looked like a textbook. She didn't glance at Colton. From somewhere out of sight down a hallway came the sound of a cart being pushed. No problems. Colton adjusted his plans. He walked past the stairwell door to the elevators. Entering a lift, he pushed the sixth-floor button. The elevator rose silently, a new machine in a new wing. Colton took out the pistol, quickly checked the round in the chamber and the cocking mechanism. Perfect. Some would have said the caliber was too small for killing humans. A .22, they would say, was for rabbits. But Colton believed in silence. With a silencer on, a .22 made no more sound than a finger makes thumping on a skull. Small but sufficient, and for Colton's purposes, it was perfect. He had studied the skull and the brain within it in the Baylor University library when he was living in Waco. He understood the skull's bone thickness, and the tissue forms behind the bone, and where a small lead pellet could be placed above the hairline so that it would kill instantly and inevitably.

Colton put his hand, with the pistol gripped in it, back into his coat pocket before the elevator stopped at the sixth floor. The door slid open. He listened. He moved to the front of the elevator, pushed the door hold button, and listened again. Nothing. No one was in the hall. He walked to the stairwell door and moved quietly downward.

The policeman's name was Jimmy Chee. The newspaper said he had suffered a bullet wound in the chest and had undergone surgery. The woman with him was named Mary Landon, a schoolteacher at Crownpoint elementary school. The woman could wait. She had not seen him as closely as had the policeman. The policeman had stared at him at the rug auction, and policemen were trained to remember faces. At the bottom of the stairs, Colton reviewed his plan.

Room 572 was a double room. At 6:00 P.M., when Colton had called to ask about Chee, the nurse had said he had no roommate. Probably he would still be alone. That would make it simpler. A roommate would probably not awaken. If he did awaken, his bed would doubtless be screened from the target's bed. Keep the killing to an absolute minimum, that was Colton's rule. The less killing, the shorter the manhunt it provoked.

Colton paused just inside the stairwell door, listening again. Here was a crucial point. With a policeman wounded under these circumstances, there was a chance a guard would be posted. This was why Colton hadn't risked arriving in an elevator. He peered through the glass panel of the stairwell door. No one visible. He slipped silently out of the stairwell to the ward door. He listened again. Nothing. Things had gone perfectly so far. Now the risk must be taken.

He pushed through the swinging doors. A nurse

was walking directly toward him. She was a medium-sized woman, perhaps forty-five, with dark hair covered by a nursing cap. Behind horn-rimmed glasses, her face registered surprise. "Yes?" she said.

"I'm Dr. Duncan," Colton Wolf said. "You have a patient named Jimmy Chee. I think we have him down for the wrong medication." He said it without hesitation, walking directly toward the nursing station, where the charts would be kept. Dealing with the nurse was the sort of contingency Colton was always prepared for. There was no guard in sight. But one might be sitting in the room with Chee.

"I think it's just a broad-spectrum antibiotic and a pain-killer," the nurse said.

"Let's take a look," Colton said. "I heard they were going to have a guard up here for one of the patients. What's the story?"

"Nobody told me anything about it," the nurse said. Behind the nursing station desk, she flipped quickly through the medication order slips. "I'm almost sure it was Achromycin and Empirin number three," she said, intent on the forms. "Who wanted it changed?"

"The surgeon," Colton said. He extracted the pistol, cocking it as it left his pocket. He raised it, muzzle a half inch from the tip of the white cap.

"Here it is," she said. "Let's see . . ."

Colton squeezed the trigger. The pistol thumped and produced a thin spurt of blue smoke. The

nurse's head fell forward onto the desktop. Colton
held her with his free left hand on her shoulder
until he was sure she wouldn't slip from the chair.
Then he felt under her ear. The pulse fluttered, and
fluttered, and died. If anyone looked in, the nurse
appeared to be asleep at her desk. Now he would
find room 572, finish the policeman, and leave.

≫ **19** ≪

Jim Chee had been in the bathroom, getting himself a pre-bed drink. Then, from the doorway, he had watched the nurse get up from her desk and walk toward the swinging doors. He had seen them open, and the man enter. The man wore a blue cotton hospital coat. He was blond, with pale skin and pale-blue eyes, and Chee recognized him instantly. The recognition was a two-staged affair. First came the thought that he had seen the blond doctor now walking toward him at the Crownpoint rug auction; a millisecond later came the gut-wrenching realization that the blond doctor was the man who had killed Tomas Charley and was no doctor at all but had come here to kill him. Chee stepped back from the doorway. He felt a desperate panic. The window! It didn't open, and it led to nothing but a lethal drop. The man was between him and the only exit from the wing. Chee forced himself to think. A weapon? There was nothing that would work against this marksman's pistol. Could he hide?

He swung himself quickly onto the bed and stood pushing the acoustical tile overhead. The space here was like that on the second floor, and here, too, the space between the false ceiling and the floor above was crisscrossed with electrical wiring, pipes, and the rectangular sheet-metal conduits that carried hot and cold air. Chee had no time to check weight-carrying capacity. He pushed the tile aside, grasped the brace that held the air-return conduit, and pulled himself painfully into the ceiling space.

The conduit was perhaps two feet wide and wrapped in a white insulation material. Chee maneuvered himself on top of it, reached frantically back, and pushed the tile into place. He found he was panting, partly from the sudden violent exertion and partly, he guessed, from fear. He controlled his breathing. Even with the tiles pushed back into place, the darkness was not absolute. He lay face down on the conduit insulation, smelling dust. He could hear the sounds buildings make at night, a ticking from somewhere in the darkness to his left, the noise of the elevator motor, and a faint hiss which might be nothing more than air passing through the metal tube under his ear. There were no voices. The conversation between the blond man and the nurse had stopped. Chee raised his head and stared down the conduit into the darkness. If he crawled along it, it would take him over the elevator foyer. But could he reach it without noise? The conduit braces supported it about six inches above the ceiling tiles, which left about two feet of space above it—enough for crawling but not enough for any rapid hands-and-knees scrambling. Chee gripped the insulation and pulled himself cautiously forward. The movement was almost soundless, but it turned the throbbing pain in his ribs to a sharp dagger thrust of agony. He suppressed his gasp by holding his breath. As he released it, he heard a metallic noise just below him.

Chee recognized the sound. It was made when the curtain that surrounded the beds was pulled along its metal track. The man who had come to kill him was standing just below. Only a quarter inch of Celotex insulation and perhaps forty-eight inches of air separated him from the blond man and his pistol. Chee lay utterly still. What would the blond man do? Would he think of the hollow ceiling as a hiding place? Chee turned his thoughts away from that. What was that blond man doing now? Chee imagined him standing, pistol ready, staring with those patient, incurious eyes at Chee's empty bed. He would look behind the bed, and in the bathroom, and behind the curtain that surrounded the bed of Chee's roommate. With that thought another came. Would the blond man mistake the Chicano for a Navajo? He might. The realization brought two contradictory emotions. Pity for the man sleeping a drugged post-surgical sleep below him struggled with a desperate hunger to stay alive.

Something bumped against metal. Then silence.

Then a creaking noise. Silence again. His rib stabbed him with pain, and his lungs cried out for air. The curtain rustled. What should he do? What could he do?

Then there was another sound. A thump. A knuckle whacked against wood? And then a sort of sigh and a rasping intake of breath. Silence again, followed finally by the whisper of soft soles on a polished floor. The room door clicked shut.

Chee took in some air as quietly as he could. Relief flooded through him. He felt himself shaking. The man had gone. Not far, perhaps. Perhaps only to check other rooms. Perhaps he would be back. But at least for the moment, death had walked away. Perhaps the blond man wouldn't come back. Perhaps Chee would live. He felt a kind of crazy joy. He would wait. He would lie there motionless forever—until morning came, until he heard the voice of a nurse below him, arriving with his morning medicine. He would take no chance at all that the blond man was waiting somewhere for him to move.

Chee waited, and listened. He heard absolutely nothing but the natural sounds of the night. Time ticked away. Perhaps three minutes. Chee became aware of an odor. It was acrid—faint but unmistakable. The smell of gun smoke. What could have caused it? He knew the answer almost instantly. The thumping sound had been a shot from the blond man's pistol.

Chee reached down from the conduit, carefully moved a ceiling tile aside, and looked down. To eyes adjusted to darkness above the ceiling, the room was comparatively bright. He could see only his bed and an expanse of floor beside it. He gripped the conduit braces and lowered himself. The blond man was gone. Chee pulled back the curtain by his roommate's bed. The man's dark head lay on the pillow, neatly, face toward the ceiling, eyes closed in the profound sleep that follows surgery. But behind the curtain the smell of smoke was stronger. Chee reached out a tentative hand. He touched the sleeping face. His forefinger rested just under the nose. His fingertip felt warm skin. But there was no breath. He moved his hand downward, letting the palm rest over the sheet against the chest, holding it there. The man's face, illuminated dimly by the city night through the window, was young and clean-shaven, a longish face with a slightly sardonic cast. Chee had been training himself away from seeing all non-Navajos as looking very much alike. This one looked mostly Spanish in blood, with a little Pueblo Indian. The chest under Chee's palm moved not at all. No lung stirred, no heartbeat. The mouth Chee saw was a dead mouth. He shifted his eyes away from it and looked for a moment out into the night. Then he walked quickly to the door and pulled it open. There was no fear now. He ran to the nurse's station and picked up the telephone beside the hand of the sleeping nurse, and dialed past the switchboard to the Albuquerque Police Department's number.

While he talked, quickly describing the deed, the man, and the pistol, and suggesting that the gunman was probably in a new green-and-white Plymouth sedan, his free hand touched the hair of the nurse, felt the cap, and found the small round hole burned in the crest of it.

"Make it two homicides," Chee said. "He also shot the fifth-floor nurse."

≫ 20 ≪

Even as he trotted down the stairs toward the laundry level something troubled Colton Wolf about the policeman's room. Why was the unused bed rumpled? Had a visitor sprawled on it? It seemed too unkempt for that. But there was something else out of tune. He had left the loading dock and was walking toward the car he was using when he realized what it was. The smell around the face of the man he had shot was an anesthetic. Natural enough. But it was too strong. It was still being exhaled. Chee had been out of surgery far too long to smell like that.

"Son of a bitch!" Colton said. He ran back to the loading dock and was through the door before his caution stopped him. How had Chee escaped? Where was he now? He would have called for help. Certainly he'd be alert. And Chee was a very smart cop—that was clear. A second try now would be too risky. There wasn't time.

He was out of the parking lot and heading westward on Lomas Avenue when he heard the first siren. But he wasn't worried. No one had seen the car. He left it three blocks from where he had stolen it, walked to his pickup, and drove slowly back to his trailer. By the time he had reached it, his new plan for killing Jimmy Chee was taking shape. It was a good plan. This time Chee wouldn't escape.

> 21 <

Chee kept the control lever of the viewer pressed halfway to the right. Above his forehead, the micro-film reels hummed. The pages of the *Grants Daily Beacon* fled past his eyes like the boxcars of a freight passing a traffic signal. They moved too fast to be read, but not too fast to tell a front page from a gro-cery ad, or to spot the sort of black banner headline that would signal the kind of story he was looking for. Half of Chee's attention focused on the moving image under his eyes. But he was aware of the silence of this huge basement room in Zimmer-man Library, of the new .38 caliber revolver that weighted his coat pocket, and of Hunt pretending to be studying beyond the glass pane of the carrel door behind him. He was also aware of the near-ness of Mary Landon.

The page that flashed below his eyes had a heavy black streak across the top. He stopped the reel and pushed the lever to the left to back it up. The head-line read:

POLLS PROJECT DEWEY LANDSLIDE

"Ha!" Mary Landon said. "Wrong disaster." She was sitting beside and a little behind him, saying nothing much. She brought to his sensitive nostrils the scent of clothing dried in sunlight, and of soap.

Chee pushed the lever to the right again and glanced up. A librarian moved down the aisle to his left, pushing a cart loaded with bound periodicals. A slender white girl with a fur-collared coat was hunting something in the microfilm files. Beyond her, movement caught Chee's eye. An elbow, covered with blue nylon, jutted out from behind one of the square white pillars. It retracted, jutted out again, retracted, jutted. Doing what? Someone scratching himself?

Chee wanted suddenly to look over his shoulder, to make sure that Hunt was still in the carrel, alert and ready. He resisted the urge. Theoretically, Hunt was tagging along as a guard. But while it hadn't exactly been spoken, it was understood that purpose number one was to get the blond man. Protecting Chee was a by-product. It sounded cold-blooded but it made sense. One protected Chee and Mary Landon by catching the blond man. There was no other way to do it. The law wanted very, very badly to catch the blond man. On the other hand, the world was full of tribal policemen.

Under his eyes, the record of June 1948 raced past and became July. The reels overhead hummed, paused, hummed again, paused again. On this pause the banner read:

WELL EXPLOSION KILLS CREW

"Here it is," Chee said.
The subhead added:

TWELVE FEARED DEAD
IN BLAST ON RIG FLOOR

"Scoot over a little," Mary said. She leaned over the projected page, pressed against him, reminding him again of sunshine and soap.

All members of an oil well drilling crew were apparently killed instantly northwest of Grants several days ago in what authorities believe to have been the premature explosion of a nitroglycerin charge.

Valencia County Sheriff Gilberto Garcia said the toll may be as high as twelve men, including ten working on the drilling crew on the east slope of Mount Taylor and two employees of the oil field supply company, who had brought in the nitro charge.

Garcia said the death toll is uncertain because the force of the blast "blew everything apart and scattered bits and pieces of people for half a mile."

"It looks like they had the nitro on the floor of the well when it went off," Garcia said. "It didn't leave much." He said the explosion probably took place Friday, which was the day the crew from Petrolab, Inc., delivered the explosive to the site. The accident was not discovered until Monday, when a deputy sheriff went to the site to investigate why men working there had not been heard from.

Garcia said the well is about 25 miles north and west of Grants near the border of the Checkerboard district of the Navajo reservation. "We haven't found anyone who heard the explosion," the sheriff said. "No one lives for miles around out there."

The sheriff said coyotes, other predators, and scavenger birds had complicated the problem of identifications. "We think we have one identification positive now, and we expect we have enough to pin down a couple of others, but we're not too optimistic about the rest."

He said payroll records named the drilling crew as Nelson Kirby, about 40, of Sherman, Texas, the crew chief; Albert Novitski, age and address unknown; Carl Lebeck, age unknown, a geologist who was logging the well; Robert Sena, 24, of Grants, and six as yet unidentified Navajos working on the well as a roustabout crew.

Also feared killed were R. J. Mackensen, about 60, and Theo Roff, about 20, both employees of Petrolab, a Farmington company which supplied the explosive.

Chee scanned the remaining paragraphs.

"Pretty much what Sena told you?" Mary asked. "The names ring any bells?"

"Just Robert Sena," Chee said. "He was Gordo's big brother."

Mary was reading over his shoulder. "Carl Lebeck," she said. "My cousin used to date a boy named Carl Lebeck. Or maybe it was Le Bow. Something like that."

"Let's see what they said when they found the Navajos were alive," Chee said.

It was on the front page of the Wednesday edition, a brief item reporting that the crew of six Navajo laborers, originally believed killed in the explosion, hadn't gone to work that day. The story included their names, which Chee copied off in his notebook. It didn't mention why they had missed work. Chee found that in the following day's paper. Again the headline stretched black across the top of the page:

ARREST MADE IN WELL BLAST

SHERIFF REPORTS NAVAJOS
GIVEN ADVANCE TIP

One of the Navajo workers who escaped last week's fatal explosion at a Valencia County oil drilling site was being questioned today about reports that he had advance knowledge the explosion would occur.

Sheriff Gilberto Garcia identified the man as Dillon Charley. He said Charley has admitted warning five other Navajo co-workers at the well not to go to work last Friday "because something bad was going to happen."

"He claims he got the warning from God in some sort of religious vision," Garcia said. He said that Charley is the "peyote chief" in the Native American cult and that the five other Navajos on the work crew were also members of the religious organization.

Members of the cult chew seed buttons from the peyote cactus as part of their rites. A narcotic in the peyote reportedly affects the nervous system, causing hallucinations in some users. Possession of the substance is illegal, and the Navajo Tribal Council has passed specific legislation banning its use or possession on the reservation.

The sheriff also revealed that Charley had been injured in what Garcia called "an attempt to resist arrest." He said Deputy Sheriff Lawrence Sena had been placed under suspension "until we can determine if undue force was used." Deputy Sena's brother, Robert Sena, was one of the men blown to bits when a nitroglycerin charge went off prematurely at the well last Friday.

"Notice that?" Chee asked. He poked his finger at the proper paragraph. "Gordo roughed up Dillon Charley. He must have *really* roughed him up to get suspended for it. Beating up a Navajo wasn't considered such a big deal in those days." He leaned back, away from the microfilm projector hood, and looked at Mary. Her expression was quizzical.

"What do you think?" he asked.

"I think you're strange," she said. "I think you're weird. You have this creepy murderer trying to shoot you, and you're down here all excited, reading about something that happened thirty years ago."

"You, too," Chee said. "How about you?"

"I'm not excited," she said.

"I mean he's trying to shoot you, too."

"I don't believe that," Mary said. "You're the one who got a good look at him. You're the one he came after." She looked away from him, leaning again into the microfilm reader. A nice profile, Chee thought. Nice. She was looking down, reading the projected type. Her eyes were very blue and the lashes curved away from them in a long, graceful sweep. Her hair fell across her cheek. Soft hair. Soft cheek.

"Another thing," Mary said without glancing up. "What's all this concern about a cop beating a

Navajo? From what I heard at Laguna, the worst cops for beating up Navajos were Navajo cops."

"We'd rather beat up Anglos," Chee said, "but we don't have jurisdiction over you folks." He watched her profile as he said it, looking for the reaction that would tell him something about her. Her jibe about Navajo police was partly serious—probably mostly serious. Navajo police, like most police, had a reputation of being toughest on their own people. Her eyes were still on the projected page. "You haven't really told me what happened up in the hospital. How you got away. And you haven't told me your secret name."

The elbow had reappeared from behind the pillar. Motionless now. Its owner must be leaning on the pillar. Reading, perhaps.

"I hid," Chee said. "Like a rabbit."

She looked at him. "Why like a rabbit? You think you should have come on like Monster Slayer?" She grabbed his wrist and raised his hand. "Me mighty redskin. Me take on gun with bare hands. Me big hero. Me dead, but me hero." She dropped his hand. "If you didn't have time to do a little ghost dance to make your hospital gown bulletproof, I think the smart thing to do was get under the bed."

"The way it worked, I guess I was hiding behind another guy. My roommate." He gave her a quick sketch of what had happened, from the furtive trip downstairs to find out how the body had been stolen from the morgue. He told it quickly, without interpretation and without speculation. Just the facts, he thought. Just the facts. And while he told them, he watched her face.

She pursed her lips into a soundless whistle and shuddered. "I'd have been terrified." She looked at him a moment, her lower lip caught between her teeth. "How did you think to climb up into the ceiling?"

"That's not the point," Chee said. "The point is I got away because I left the blond man somebody to shoot. He came into the room to shoot himself an Indian. Nobody home but a Mexican. So the Chicano gets shot instead of me."

She was frowning at him again. "So?"

"So? What do you mean, so?"

"So what," she said. "You on some guilt trip? You think you should have stayed behind? Bared your chest and said, 'Here I am. Don't shoot this other guy.' Come *on.*" Her voice was scornful. "He shot the nurse, didn't he? The only difference would have been he'd have shot both of you."

"Maybe," Chee said.

"You really are weird," Mary Landon said. "Either that, or you want me to think you are."

"Well," Chee said. "No use talking about it now. Let's see what else we can find."

They found very little. There was a lengthy story about the Native American Church, the ceremony, and what the members said about Dillon Charley's vision of warning. There was a short item in which the sheriff reported that one of the victims had been definitely identified from dental work as an employee of Petrolab. But the story seemed quickly to die away for lack of new information.

If Sena, or any of the other victims, was identified, it wasn't mentioned in the *Beacon*. Nor was there any follow-up story on the arrest of Dillon Charley. His release, whenever it happened, went without notice in the paper.

They worked through the microfilm slowly now, page by page, looking for the remainders of a story that was no longer banner headline news. Halfway through the September editions, after an hour of finding nothing, Mary had an idea.

"Hey," she said. "Newspapers do anniversary stories. You know. They start, 'A year ago today . . .' and then they rehash it all. Why don't we skip ahead a year?"

Chee stood and stretched. He pushed the lever to the left. The reels hummed with the rewinding. The young woman had left the microfilm area. The elbow was missing from the pillar. Protruding now into Chee's line of vision was the tip of a nose and a shock of hair. The hair was blond. Very blond. Chee felt his stomach muscles tighten. He released the lever and moved his right hand into his coat pocket. The hand found the pistol grip. The thumb found the hammer.

"What?" Mary said. She was staring at him.

The man emerged from behind the pillar. He

glanced at Mary. He was very blond, but he wasn't the blond man. Far too young. No resemblance at all. He moved to the microfilm file and began rummaging.

"Nothing," Chee said. "I'm just jumpy."

They found the anniversary story. It reported little new.

By the time the copying desk had made Xeroxes of the microfilmed stories for them, it was five o'clock.

"Now what?" Mary asked. "It occurs to me that Sergeant Chee of the Mounties has just wasted one afternoon, plus the afternoon of one Crownpoint schoolteacher, and isn't going to have the slightest idea of what to do next. This is a dead end. Right?"

"No," Chee said. They were climbing the stairway that spiraled upward through the four levels of the working end of the university library. An artist had used the stairwell walls to depict in paint and plaster the history of man's efforts to record his communication with his fellows. Here, below the ground floor, they climbed past pictographs and petroglyphs. The Phoenician alphabet was far overhead, and the symbolic language of computers even higher. "Maybe it doesn't lead anywhere, but I'd like to talk to some of those men who got warned away from that explosion. I'd like to find out what Dillon Charley told them."

They emerged on the ground-floor level. Through the glass south wall of the library, the Humanities

Building loomed above the sycamores of the central mall, a monolithic sculpture against a dark-blue autumn sky. Usually Chee liked the building. Today it reminded him of tombstones.

"Why?" Mary said. "What can they possibly tell you that has anything to do with this?"

"Maybe nothing," Chee said. "But the killings grew out of the keepsake box, and stealing the keepsake box seems to have something to do somehow with Dillon Charley's peyote religion, and everything seems to lead back to what happened at the oil well."

"Or maybe you're just curious," Mary said. "Anyway, you won't be able to find them. It's been thirty years."

"It won't be so hard," Chee said. "They'll probably all be kinfolks of Dillon Charley. He hired them, so they'll be kinfolks. Cousins, or uncles, or in-laws at least. The Navajos not only invented nepotism. We perfected it."

"But thirty years," Mary said. "They'll be dead. Or half of them will be."

"One or two, probably," Chee said. "We know Dillon Charley is. But the odds are about four of them are still around." They were outside now, walking across the bricked mall south of the library with the brittle sycamore leaves underfoot and the heatless light of the setting sun throwing their shadows a hundred yards ahead and turning the craggy east face of the Sandia Mountains the color of diluted blood. Chee thought of that, and of Hunt walking fifty feet behind them, and of the target they would make for someone standing at any of the walkways or balconies that overlooked the mall.

"And what can they remember about thirty years? Probably not much."

"Who knows?" Chee said. He thought. Probably nothing with any real accuracy. But there was no other lead to follow. And if nothing else, hunting survivors of the People of Darkness would take him out on the reservation. He would take Mary with him. On the reservation, the blond man would never know where to look for them.

≫ **22** ≪

A day later, Chee had taken a fruitless shot in the dark and added a few details to his list of names of Dillon Charley's People of Darkness.

The shot in the dark had taken him to the university's Geology Department library. With some help from a cooperative graduate student, he had found a copy of the geologist's log of the oil well. "It looks fairly typical of that area," the student told him. "There's been some shallow production from the Galisteo formation." He checked through it quickly. "Looks like they found the formation but not the oil."

"You see anything unusual about it?" Chee asked. The log was totally incomprehensible to him. He stared at the sheet of symbols and notations, feeling foolish.

"I'm no authority on Valencia County petroleum geology," the young man said. "But it looks like what I'd expect. What are you looking for?"

"That's the trouble," Chee said. "I don't know."

His luck in hunting Charley's roustabout crew had been only a little better. He and Mary had driven to the reservation and spent the remaining hours of daylight jolting over the washboard back roads and wagon trails of the Checkerboard, hunting information to go with the names extracted from the *Grants Beacon*. By nightfall the list had looked like this:

Roscoe Sam, Ojo Encino or Standing Rock. Mud Clan. Dead. Confirmed.

Joseph Sam, Ojo Encino or maybe Pueblo Pintado area. Mud Clan and married into Salt Clan. One report he died in the 1950s. Others say no.

Windy Tsossie. Mud Clan. Married into Standing Rock Clan. Used to live around Heart Butte? May be dead?

Rudolph Becenti. Mud Clan. Coyote Canyon? Married?

Woody Begay. Mud Clan. Sister lives at Borrego Pass?

It had been generally frustrating, except for Roscoe Sam who had got sick at Tuba City and died in the BIA hospital there, and was remembered as being dead. Joseph Sam was another matter. A distant cousin on the paternal side of the family thought, rather vaguely, that he, too, was dead. Another even more distant paternal-side cousin said he'd moved his wife's sheep and his own belongings over to the Cañoncito Reservation and probably still lived there. Dead or alive, no one had seen Joseph Sam for years. It was the same for the rest of them. An in-law remembered that Rudolph Becenti had moved to Los Angeles but had heard he'd come back again. Windy Tsossie was recalled dimly and unfavorably by a few of his contemporaries around Ambrosia Lakes as one of the Tsossie "outfit" which had lived at Coyote Canyon but had moved away a long time ago. Except for Roscoe Sam, definitely and specifically dead and buried, the day had produced nothing concrete. As for Woody Begay, there was only an old woman's memory that his sister lived north of the Borrego Pass chapter house, and his sister's name was Fannie Kinlicheenie.

The vagueness of it had puzzled Chee. It was almost as if these People of Darkness existed only in shadowy rumors and not as flesh and blood. Even the site of the oil well explosion eluded them. The hunt for Roscoe Sam had taken them near the place where Chee's notes said it had been. They found only the immense dusty hole that was the Red Deuce—a dozen gigantic power shovels eating the earth in a pit that was already two hundred yards deep and a half mile across. The oil well site, too, seemed part of a memory of something that never was.

But Fannie Kinlicheenie was definitely flesh and blood. She had looked out the doorway of her house at them when they drove up. Chee parked his patrol car a polite thirty yards from the residence, thereby respecting a modest people's tradition of privacy. When Fannie Kinlicheenie was ready to receive guests she would let them know. Meanwhile they would wait. Chee offered a cigaret to Mary, and she took it.

"I shouldn't smoke these things," she said, as he lit it for her.

"Neither should I," Chee said.

"This guy's going to be dead, too," Mary said. "Either that or moved way off somewhere."

Chee had a feeling she was right. Otherwise, someone would have remembered him.

"You're too pessimistic," Chee said.

"No. I'm a realist. There's four of them left. After thirty years, you'd have a mortality rate of about twenty-five percent. I think Woody Begay's the one."

Chee considered this logic. He exhaled a cloud of cigaret smoke.

"You started with six," he said. "We got Dillon Charley dead, and Roscoe Sam dead. That's already a thirty-three percent mortality."

Mary didn't comment for a moment.

Then she said, "If you think like that you should

avoid poker games. What happened in the past doesn't affect the mathematics. It doesn't affect the probabilities. Forget the other two. Now we have the names of four men who were alive thirty years ago. Chances are one of the four is dead now and three of them are alive."

"Okay," Chee said. "I'll buy that. Now tell me how you figure the dead one will be Woody Begay."

"That's intuition," Mary said. "Women have intuition."

Chee reached for the key in the ignition. "Any use sticking around, you think? Wasting Fannie's time."

Mary grinned at him. "As long as we've come this far, maybe we might as well confirm the hunch."

"I'd like to," Chee said. "Sure you won't be insulted?"

"Naw," she said. "I was wrong once."

"But not recently," Chee said.

"I think I was four." She paused. "No, as a matter of fact, make that twice I was wrong. The second time was being dumb enough to go along on this Great Jimmy Chee Manhunt. Boy, am I tired. How far did we drive today?"

"I don't know," Chee said. "Maybe two hundred and fifty miles. It just seems longer because a lot of it was dirt roads."

"It seems like a thousand," Mary said. "This thing rides like a truck. I think you have too much air in the tires."

"We put in the specified amount," Chee said. "It's

intended to jar us around enough so we don't doze off while driving."

"Come to think of it, there was another time I was wrong." She glanced at him and looked quickly away. "That was at the auction, when I got the impression you were interested in me."

"I am," Chee said.

"I mean romantically. You're interested in me because I'm an Anglo. Questions all day long. I feel like I'm being interviewed by a sociologist."

"Anthropologist," Chee said. "And that's the same reason you came along with me. 'What's this Navajo Indian really like?' You just won't admit it."

Mary laughed. "I admit it," she said. "Now I know what you're really like. You're weird."

"But who knows," Chee said. "Maybe something great will grow out of it. We had a Shakespeare teacher at UNM who said that Romeo was doing a paper on the Capulets for his social studies class. He just wanted to pick Juliet's mind."

"I think he was the Capulet," Mary said. "She was a Montague."

" 'What's in a name?' " Chee recited. " 'A rose by any other name . . . ' "

"So what's your secret name?" Mary asked.

"Rose," Chee said. "Something like that."

The Kinlicheenie house was of wood-frame construction, insulated with black tar paper. It sat on an expanse of sandstone elevated enough to offer a fine view of a rolling, eroded landscape—gray-silver sage and black creosote brush.

On the horizon Mount Taylor dominated, as it dominated everything in the Checkerboard. Its top was white, but its slopes were blue and serene. Behind the house was a circular stone hogan, its doorway facing properly eastward. And behind that stood a small Montgomery Ward steel storage shed and the humped roof of the dugout where the family took its sweat baths. "Ever notice how Navajos always build their houses where they have a view?" Chee asked.

"I've noticed that Navajos build their houses as far as they can possibly get from other Navajos," Mary said. "Any significance to that?"

"We don't like Indians," Chee said.

Mrs. Kinlicheenie was at the door now. Her hair was neatly tied in a bun, and she was wearing a heavy silver squash-blossom necklace and a wide silver-and-turquoise bracelet. Mrs. Kinlicheenie was ready to receive guests.

≫ 23 ≪

"**M**y brother?" Fannie Kinlicheenie's expression was puzzled. "You want to find him?"

They were in the front room of the house. The chair in which Jim Chee sat was covered with a stiff green plastic. He felt the chill of it through his uniform shirt. The house was the "summer hogan" of the Kinlicheenies. There was no heating stove in it. In a while, when the high country frost arrived full force, the family would shift its belongings into the old earth-and-stone "winter hogan" and abandon this poorly insulated structure to the cold. Until then, the problem of the chilly margin between the seasons was solved by wearing more layers of clothing. Fannie Kinlicheenie looked about eight layers deep. Chee wished he had worn his jacket in from the patrol car.

"We heard this man was your brother," Chee said. "We need some information from him."

"But he's dead," Fannie Kinlicheenie said. "He's been dead for . . ." She paused, trying to put a date on it. "Why, he was dead when I got married, and that was 1953."

Chee glanced at Mary. "I didn't know that," he said.

Fannie Kinlicheenie was frowning at him.

"Why did you want to talk to him?"

"He used to be a member of the peyote church. The one over by Grants. We wanted to ask him about that."

"Those sons-a-bitches," Fannie Kinlicheenie said in English. "What you want to know about them?"

"About something that happened way back. Your brother and some of them were working on an oil well. The peyote chief warned them not to go one day, and the well blew up while they were away."

"I know about that," Fannie said. "I was a girl then and I was in that peyote church, too. I was the water carrier. You know about that?"

"Yes," Chee said. He didn't know everything about the Native American Church, but he knew the water carrier, usually a woman, played a minor role in the ritual.

"Those sons-a-bitches," she repeated. "There was . . ." She paused, glanced at Mary, and back at Chee. They had been speaking in English, the language shared by all three. Now Fannie Kinlicheenie shifted languages. "There was witches in that church," she said in Navajo. One talked cautiously of witches. One discussed them with strangers reluctantly. One talked of them not at all in front of those who were not members of the People. Mary was not Dinetah—not of the People.

"How do you know they were witches?" Chee asked. He stuck to English. "Sometimes people get blamed for being skinwalkers when they're not."

Fannie Kinlicheenie answered in Navajo. "They gave my brother corpse sickness," she said.

"Maybe he ran into a witch somewhere else."

"It was them," she said. "There were other things. There was that oil well that blew up that year. They pretended the Lord Peyote told them it was going to happen. They told everybody that the Lord sent a vision to tell them not to go to work that day. But the witches blew up that oil well. That's how they knew it was going to happen."

"How do you know that?" Chee asked. He had forgotten to speak English. In fact, he had forgotten Mary, who sat there listening and looking puzzled.

"I just know it," Fannie Kinlicheenie said.

Chee considered this. An irrelevant thought intruded. In a white man's home there would not be this complete silence. There would be the ticking of a clock, the sounds refrigerators make, the noise of a TV coming from somewhere. Here there was no sound at all. No traffic noise. No sirens. Outside it was sunset now; even the breeze was still.

"My aunt," Chee said, using a young man's title of respect for an older woman, "I have come a long way to talk with you here because what you know may be very important. I think that something very bad happened at that oil well and that people may still die because of it. If Navajo Wolves did it, then I think we are still dealing with the same bunch of witches. Can you tell me how you knew Navajo Wolves blew up that oil well? Did somebody tell you?"

"Nobody told me. Just my own head."

"How was that?"

Fannie Kinlicheenie thought about how to answer.

"My brother got sick. He had pains in his middle here." Fannie indicated her stomach. "Where the spirit is. And pains in his legs. We got a hand trembler to come in and find out what was wrong. The hand trembler said a witch had done it to him. He found a little bump on the back of Woody's head where the witch had put the corpse powder in. Then another one of them got sick, and they got the hand trembler for him. And he'd been witched, too. And the hand trembler said to have an Enemy Way for both of them." Fannie Kinlicheenie paused, organizing what she wanted to say.

"What's going on?" Mary asked.

Chee held up his hand. "Just a minute," he said. And then to the Kinlicheenie woman: "Another one got sick, you said. You mean another member of the church?"

"It was Roscoe Sam," Fannie said. "One of the bunch that worked at the oil well with Woody. One of them that called themselves the People of Darkness."

"Ah," Chee said. He was speaking in English again, conscious of Mary's curiosity. "And the hand trembler said to have an Enemy Way? To do that right, you have to know who the witch is. Who . . ."

"That's right," Fannie Kinlicheenie said. "They did the Enemy Way for both of them, and it was done right. Both of them got better for a while, but then they had to take Woody off to the hospital at Gallup and he died."

"They don't much believe in Navajo Wolves at the hospital," Chee said. "What did they think he died of?"

"They said it was cancer," Fannie said. "Leukemia got in his blood."

"Does Joseph Sam still live around here?"

"He died too," Fannie Kinlicheenie said. "I heard it was the same thing. Leukemia."

"I'd say that the Enemy Way didn't work too well," Chee said.

"I think they waited too long. But part of it worked. It turned the evil around and pointed it at the Navajo Wolf." Fannie Kinlicheenie's smile was full of malice. "He died, too."

"Do you know who it was?" Chee knew he'd have to wait for an answer and that he might not get one. The Dinee didn't like to talk of the dead, or of witches. Speaking the name of a dead witch was doubly dangerous.

Fannie Kinlicheenie licked her lips.

"It was the peyote chief," she said.

And thus she avoided pronouncing the name of Dillon Charley.

> **24** <

They jolted down the dirt track toward the graded road that would take them to the asphalt pavement and back to Crownpoint. The sun was down now. High overhead a strip of feathery cirrus clouds glowed salmon pink in the afterglow. But all around them the landscape was dark. Mary had been saying almost nothing.

"Are you going to tell me what all that was about?" She asked it without looking at him.

Chee glanced at her profile. "The part where she started talking Navajo?"

"And you started talking Navajo. Yes. That part."

"She said some people in the Native American Church were witches, and they gave Woody Begay and Roscoe Sam corpse poisoning, and they both died. And before they died, they held an Enemy Way for them, and that turned the witching around against the witch. And the witch was Dillon Charley, and that's what killed Dillon."

Mary was looking at him now. "What do you think of all that?"

"And she said the witches made the oil well blow up," Chee added. "And that Joseph Sam is dead, too."

"Did she say why they wanted to do that?"

"No," Chee said.

"Did she know? Did you ask her?"

"No," Chee said. "You have to understand about our witches. They wouldn't need a motive in the normal sense. Do you know about Navajo Wolves?"

"I thought I did," Mary said. "Aren't they like the white man's witches, and witches in general, and our Laguna-Acoma witches?" She laughed. "Hyphenated witches," she said. "Only with the U.S. Bureau of Indian Affairs would you get hyphenated witches."

"The way it works with Navajos, witchcraft is the reversal of the Navajo Way. The way the Holy People taught us, the goal of life was *yo'zho'*. No word for it in English. Sort of a combination of beauty/harmony, being in tune, going with the flow, feeling peaceful, all wrapped up in a single concept. Witchcraft is the reverse of this concept, basically. There's a mythology built up around it, of course. You get to be a witch by violating the basic taboos— killing a relative, incest, so forth. And you get certain powers. You can turn yourself into a dog or a wolf. You can fly. And you have power to make people sick. That's the opposite of the good power the

Holy People gave us—to cure people by getting them back into *yo'zho'*. Back into beauty. So, to make a long story short, a witch wouldn't have a motive for blowing up an oil well. It's a bad thing to do, blowing people up. That's all the motive a skinwalker needs."

"And she said Dillon Charley was a witch?"

"That's what she said. The families had an Enemy Way and turned the witching spell around, and Dillon Charley died."

"That proves he was the witch?"

"Well, sort of," Chee said. "They'd have to already have him spotted as the witch. Then someone has to get something that belonged to a witch—hair, pair of socks, a hat, something personal. That represents the scalp in the Enemy Way ceremonial. On the last day of the ceremonial, the scalp is shot with an arrow. If everything has been properly done, and they have the right witch, this causes the witch to get sick and die from his own spell."

"And the patient gets well?"

"That's the way it works. But it didn't work for our friend Woody. And it didn't work for Roscoe Sam."

The patrol car jolted into a shallow wash and out again. The cloud overhead had changed from pink to a deep glowing red. "Two more dead," Mary Landon said. "Or three."

"You predicted Woody," Chee said.

"There were six of them to begin with," she said.

"Six People of Darkness. Six men who didn't go to work at the oil well. Now Roscoe Sam is dead, and Joseph Sam and Begay, and Dillon Charley."

"Leaves Windy Tsossie and Rudolph Becenti," Chee said. "And so far nobody knows where to find them."

"That's too many dead," Mary Landon said. "They wouldn't be all that old. Probably late middle age if they were alive now. But they died a long, long time ago. When they were pretty young. Just a few years after the oil well. That's too many to be dead." She looked at him thoughtfully. "You think somebody poisoned them all? Something like that? Maybe revenge?"

"As far as we know, Begay died of leukemia," Chee said. "Same thing with Roscoe Sam. Dillon Charley died in the hospital. Vines says he told him he had some sort of cancer. Anyway, in a hospital they'd have detected poison if it was that."

"With an autopsy?" Mary asked.

Chee drove a little while. "I think you're thinking the same thing I'm thinking," he said. "You're thinking about Emerson Charley."

"Yes," Mary said. "I'm thinking about how Emerson Charley didn't have an autopsy."

"Because somebody stole his body out of the cold room at BCMC," Chee said.

"Which seems a funny thing to steal."

"Right," Chee said.

"Unless you don't want an autopsy performed."

"Right," Chee said.

"Which is also what you'd get if you blow the guy into little pieces by bombing his truck. No autopsy. Right?"

"Yeah," Chee said.

"Yeah," Mary said. "Yeah, or maybe baloney. Why would anyone want to poison Emerson Charley? Or Dillon Charley? Or Woody Begay, or any of those guys?"

"No reason," Chee said. "But you know what? Let's go to Albuquerque and see what we can find out at the hospital."

"I don't know," Mary Landon said. "When I go places with you, it's no picnic." She hesitated. "Do you think he'll be there?" She didn't have to say the blond man. Chee knew what she meant.

"I've thought about that," Chee said. "If I was him, I wouldn't go near that hospital. And if I was looking for you and me, that would be the last place I'd look."

» 25 «

The doctor's name was Edith Vassa. The midmorning sun slanted through the window behind her desk and flashed through her short reddish hair. She was a young woman with that pink complexion which made Jimmy Chee wonder why the white men called Indians redskins. Dr. Vassa was the physician who had treated Emerson Charley at the University of New Mexico Cancer Research and Treatment Center. Thus she had been stuck with the job of trying to find out what had happened to the Charley corpse. It had been a frustrating, embarrassing dead end. Edith Vassa was sick of it. Her expression showed it.

"I can tell you everything I know in a very few words. Emerson Charley's vital signs ceased at approximately 5:13 P.M. The physician on duty made the usual examination and certified death. The body was tagged for autopsy and moved to the morgue cold room. The next morning, the morgue attendant noticed he had only one body instead of two.

He guessed the body had gone to the morphology laboratory without being properly checked out." Dr. Vassa made an impatient gesture with her hands. "To skip the unnecessary details, it was finally learned that the body had disappeared."

"You presume it was stolen?"

"I presume his relatives collected him," Dr. Vassa said. "The Albuquerque police thought we might have just misplaced it somewhere." She laughed, but she didn't think it was funny.

"All we actually know is that one of the morgue carts was found the next morning in the hallway near the loading dock. Presumably it was used to move the body. And we found that the bag of personal effects that belonged to a second body in the morgue was also missing. It seems safe to presume that someone got into the morgue, picked up the wrong bag of personal effects, put the bag on the cart with the body, rolled it down the hallway to the loading dock, and loaded everything into a car or something."

"It was being held for an autopsy?"

"It was supposed to be held for an autopsy."

"Why the autopsy?"

"It's the routine. We're studying cancer. How it affects cells. How treatment affects tumors. Effect of treatment on blood platelets. On bone marrow. Metastasis. So forth."

"Metastasis?"

"Spreading. How cancer spreads from one part of the body to another."

"You didn't suspect foul play?" Chee asked.

Dr. Vassa smiled, very faintly. "You don't get leukemia through foul play. It's not like a poison. And it's not like an infectious disease, which you could cause by inserting a bacteria. It's caused by . . ." Dr. Vassa hesitated.

Jimmy Chee waited, curious. How would this woman describe the origins of leukemia to a Navajo?

"We don't know exactly what causes it. Perhaps some sort of virus. Perhaps some malfunction in the bone marrow, where blood cells are produced."

Fair enough, Chee thought. He couldn't have done better himself.

"And it's rare, especially among adults?"

"Relatively," Dr. Vassa said. "I think the current case rate for all sorts of malignancies this year is less than three per thousand. Leukemic diseases are about one percent of that. Say three in a hundred thousand."

"Three per thousand?" Mary Landon said. "What would you think of a situation in which you had six men, friends, members of the same church, sort of distant relatives, and three of them die of cancer?"

"I'd be surprised," Dr. Vassa said.

"How surprised?" Mary Landon asked. "Three out of six instead of three out of a thousand."

"It would be quite a coincidence," Dr. Vassa said,

"but things like that can happen. Mathematical probabilities work in odd ways. Was Emerson one of the three?"

"He was the son of one of the three," Chee said.

"His father died of cancer?"

"That's what we're told," Mary said.

"But you don't know for sure?" Dr. Vassa asked. "Did they all live in the same area? Work at the same jobs? I think if they really did all die of cancer our epidemiology people would be interested." Dr. Vassa smiled. "Especially if it happened to be cancer of the gall bladder. They're fascinated by that." She reached for the phone. "I'll make you an appointment with Sherman Huff."

Sherman Huff's office was in the basement. Dr. Huff asked questions and took notes, and picked up the telephone. "Three out of six is unusual," he said. "So first we try to find out if the tumor registry has them." He spoke into the telephone, identifying himself and reading the names of Dillon Charley, Roscoe Sam, and Woody Begay off his notes. He kept the receiver pinned to his ear with a raised shoulder and turned back to Chee and Mary Landon.

"Just be a minute or two," he said. "It's a matter of checking the names with the computer. The registry tries to keep a file on every cancer case diagnosed in the state, but these were way back when they were first setting it up. And it could be they were out on the reservation, where they weren't diagnosed."

"In other words, if you don't have the names registered, it won't necessarily mean they didn't have cancer?"

"Not from the early 1950s it won't," Huff said. "And not from the Navajo reservation. However, even in those days, they were getting most of them. They had a pretty good . . ."

The telephone said something into Huff's ear. "Just a second," he said.

He made a note. "Okay," he said. He wrote again. "Thanks. Pull the folders for me. I'll want to look at them." He hung up and glanced at Chee.

"Dillon Charley, leukemia. Roscoe Sam, malignancy affecting liver and other vital organs. Woody Begay, leukemia." Huff's face was thoughtful. "That's a hell of a lot of cancer," he said. "And a lot of leukemia for men their ages."

"And Emerson Charley," Mary Landon added. "He also died of leukemia."

"That's what Vassa told me," Huff said. "Let's make sure. Let's get that folder, too." He dialed the phone again.

"While you have them, give them some more names," Chee said. "Give them Rudolph Becenti, Joseph Sam, and Windy Tsossie."

"Those the other three of the six? You hear they had cancer, too?"

"All we know is that Joseph Sam probably died

back in the 1950s, and we couldn't find Becenti or Tsossie," Chee said.

"Tumor registry data is confidential," Huff said. "I can confirm a cancer death for law enforcement. I'm not sure I can just go on a fishing expedition for you."

"I'm only trying to confirm that their cause of death was cancer. It saves me time. Otherwise, I'd have to go hunting for death certificates in county courthouses."

Huff talked into the telephone again. He asked for the Emerson Charley file and a check on Tsossie, Becenti, and Joseph Sam. Then he waited, phone to ear. He was a burly man, with a gray mustache merging into a bushy gray beard, sun-weathered skin, and bright blue eyes. Behind him, the wall was covered with posters: "Smoke Can Make Your Doctor Rich." "Little Orphan Annie's Parents Smoked." "Stamp Out Old Age: Smoke!" "To Kill a Mockingbird: Blow Smoke on It." In the silence, Chee became conscious of a tapping. Mary's little finger was drumming against the arm of her chair. The telephone receiver made a sound.

"Go ahead," Huff said. He wrote on his note pad. "Okay," he said. "I'd like to see them all." He hung up and sat for a moment looking silently at what he had written. "Well," he said.

"Another one?" Mary asked.

"Rudolph Becenti," Dr. Huff said. "Another form of leukemia."

"That's four out of six," Mary Landon said.

"That sure is," Dr. Huff said. "That's a hell of a high percentage."

"How about the other two?" Chee asked. "Tsossie and Joseph Sam?"

"Neither name showed up," Huff said. He was frowning. "Four out of six," he said. "What in the world could account for that? What were they doing?"

"In 1948 they were the members of a roustabout crew on an oil well out near Grants," Chee said. "The common labor. Beyond that they were all members of the same little cult in the Native American Church."

"They ever work in the uranium mines out there? We think we had a little increase from that. But that was lung cancer."

"Not as far as we know. And the mining was just getting well started in Ambrosia Lakes when these guys were dying," Chee said.

"How about asbestos? Were they installing insulation?" He shook his head. "No. Inhaled asbestos fiber is a carcinogen, but nothing like this. Nothing like four out of six. And not that quickly. And it's the wrong kind of cancer. You know anything else about them?"

"Damn little," Chee said.

"Did they ever work up at the Nevada test site? Did they work up there when we were doing that atmospheric testing of the bombs?"

"I don't know," Chee said. "It's not likely."

"That could explain it," Huff said. "We just found out this fall that we had a whole rash of leukemia fatalities downwind from the test site in the middle of the 1950s. We've pinned down twelve cases in one tiny little community. Blood cell formation is particularly sensitive to some forms of radiation."

"I know Dillon Charley didn't work anywhere near Nevada," Chee said. "He was working at Mount Taylor until just before he died."

"As for Emerson Charley," Mary said, "they stopped atmospheric testing years ago, and he just died."

Huff looked disappointed. "Yes," he said, "but sometimes it takes years to develop. And the cases might not all be connected." He produced a wry smile. "And also, of course, maybe none of them have been within a thousand miles of the test site. Do you think you could find the other two of the six?"

"We can keep trying on Tsossie," Chee said. "But Joseph Sam's dead. He won't do you any good."

"Actually, he might do us some good," Huff said. "Some kinds of cancers affect bone tissue. Some other kinds leave their traces in bone when they metastasize. You can often find the damage in ribs, or vertebrae, or sometimes large marrow bones. Do you know where he's buried?"

"We can try to find out," Chee said.

"And we'll try to find some sort of common denominator among them," Huff said. "How about this church they all belong to?"

"Native American Church," Chee said. "The peyote church."

Huff grinned through his beard. "If we suspected peyote of being carcinogenic, we'd have our mystery solved. But it isn't. Anything else? Anything that ties them all together?"

Chee told him of Dillon Charley's peyote vision, which had saved them all from the oil well explosion, and of the survivors being joined, or so it seemed, in their own cult—the People of Darkness.

"With a mole as their amulet figure? Isn't the fetish usually a predator? A mountain lion, or a bear, or something like that?" Huff asked.

"The mole's the predator of darkness," Chee said. "But it *is* unusual to use him for an amulet."

"So why did they pick the mole?" Huff asked.

"I've wondered," Chee said. And as he said it, he had a thought. "Whoever took Emerson Charley's body left his personal effects. Could we take a look at them?"

"Why not?" Huff said. "If we haven't lost them, too."

≫ 26 ≪

The red plastic bag was in a storage room on the second floor among scores of identical plastic bags, all arranged in alphabetical order.

"Bracken," the attendant said. "Caldwell. Charley. Here it is. Emerson Charley. You can take a look at it there on that table."

Chee removed a crushed black felt hat, a pair of cowboy boots which needed half soles, a denim jacket, a Timex watch with a steel band, a plaid cotton shirt, a T-shirt, a pair of jockey shorts, a pair of worn denim jeans, socks, a set of car keys, a pocket knife, a small leather pouch attached to a long leather thong, two blue shoestrings, a package of paper matches, and a billfold. He put the leather pouch and the billfold aside and quickly explored all the pockets. They were empty. Then he inspected the billfold. It contained a five, two ones, a driver's license, a social security card, and a card identifying the agent who had written the liability policy on Charley's pickup truck.

Then he picked up the leather pouch.

"What's that?" Mary asked. "What are you looking for?"

"It's where you carry your ceremonial stuff," Chee said. "Supposed to be made of the hide of a deer killed in the ritual fashion. It holds your gall medicine. What you use against witchcraft. A little pollen. Maybe a little ceremonial corn meal. . . ." He pulled open the draw cord and fished into the pouch with his fingers. "And it's where you carry your amulet, if you carry one."

The amulet he extracted was black, and dull, and shaped into the eyeless, sharp-nosed form of a mole. He held it up for Mary's inspection. It was heavy, formed from a soft stone. Some sort of shale, Chee guessed. "Here we have Dine'etse-tle," Chee said. "The predator of the nadir. The hunting spirit of the underworld. One of the People of Darkness."

He stared at it, heavy on his palm, hoping for some information. It was well formed—better than most amulets. Chee remembered the amateur sculpture in B. J. Vines' huge office. Had Vines made this? Was this formed from one of those fragments of black rock Emerson Charley had found in Vines' keepsake box? Perhaps. But what did that mean? He slipped the mole back into the pouch.

"Did it tell you anything?"

Chee recited two lines of Navajo. "That's from one of the blessing chants," he said.

The mole, his hunting place is darkness.
The mole, his hunting song is silence.

» 27 «

The secretary from Dr. Huff's office met them as they left the storage room. The message was from Chee's Crownpoint office. It told him to call Martin at Albuquerque FBI headquarters.

"I thought nobody knew where we are," Mary said. She was frowning. "Wasn't that how we were going to stay safe?"

"Nobody but my office," Chee said.

"But if your office knows, can't somebody else . . . ?"

"How?" Chee asked.

Mary thought about it, still frowning. She shrugged. "I guess you're right," she said. "But you know how people are."

Martin wanted to remind Chee that he was supposed to come in and look at photographs.

"Maybe in a day or two," Chee said. "To tell the truth, I'm going to stay away from places where this guy might be waiting around for me."

"I think you can relax a little now. He's gone."

"How do you know?"

"We made a clean sweep," Martin said. "Checked every motel, every hotel, every place he could be staying. We even checked new apartment rentals."

"Lot of work," Chee said.

"He's no place around here," Martin said. "And we found the green-and-white Plymouth. It was in a little garage in Gallup. The son of a bitch drove it in and told the mechanic it needed a valve job and he was in no hurry for it. That's why we didn't find it abandoned anywhere."

"That was smart," Chee said. "You know how he got out of Albuquerque this time?"

"We're pretty sure he stole a car. Just drove it somewhere. Maybe El Paso or Denver. Somewhere far enough to miss our stakeouts. And then he took a plane for wherever he goes."

"So he's not in Albuquerque?"

"Not unless he's staying with relatives," Martin said.

≫ 28 ≪

At the cost of hours of driving from here to there in search of older members of the Mud Clan, Jimmy Chee learned a little about Windy Tsossie. He learned that not long after the oil well explosion, Tsossie had married a daughter of Grace Yazzie of the Standing Rock Clan. He had moved northwestward to the Bisti country to join his new family. He had been seen around Ambrosia Lakes no more. Chee learned that Tsossie's wife was dead. He learned other things as well. Among the important ones was that Tsossie's sister-in-law, a woman named Ramona Musket, was alive and well and living between Thoreau and Crownpoint in the log house with the tin roof and the sheep pens behind it that was visible on the slope above the highway. Mrs. Musket seemed likely to know where Tsossie could be found, alive or dead. Chee had also learned that no one seemed to know for sure which one it would be. No one had heard Tsossie had died. On the other hand, Chee had found no one who had actually seen him for years. And finally Chee had accumulated a general impression of Windy Tsossie. It was a negative impression. His kinsmen and his clansmen, when they admitted remembering him at all, remembered him without fondness or respect. They talked of him reluctantly, vaguely, uneasily. No one put it in words. Since Chee was Navajo, no one needed to. Windy Tsossie did not "go in beauty." Windy Tsossie was not a good man. He did not follow those rules which Changing Woman had given the People. In a word, Windy Tsossie was believed by his kinsmen to be a witch.

"I don't see how you can say that," Mary said. "You told me what they said. Nobody even hinted at anything like that."

"They wouldn't," Chee said, "not to a stranger. I might be a witch myself. Or you might be. And witches don't like people talking about witches."

Mary yawned. "You're stretching things," she said.

"Did you notice that talking about Tsossie made them nervous? That's the tip-off."

"The thing that interests me is I think we're finally going to find one of them alive," she said. "What's he going to tell us? I really think now he's going to remember something."

"If he's alive."

"He will be."

"I have the same sort of hunch," Chee said.

They were driving the subagency's pickup truck,

having traded the relative comfort of the patrol car for the ability to follow wagon tracks. They drove northeastward, mostly in second gear, over a rutted road which now tilted downward. Chee flicked his lights to bright. The beams lit the broad, sandy bottom of an arroyo below. When they reached it, he stopped.

"Chaco Wash," he said. He switched on the dome light, unfolded his map, and examined it. The map was one entitled "Indian Country," produced by the Auto Club of Southern California; Chee had found it both accurate and detailed. It rated routes of travel in nine categories, ranging from Divided Limited Access Highways, down through Gravel, Graded Dirt, and Ungraded Dirt to Doubtful Dirt. For the last fifteen miles, they had been driving on Doubtful Dirt. According to the map, the Doubtful Dirt ended at Chaco Wash.

Chee folded the Indian Country map and extracted from his shirt pocket a lined sheet of notebook paper. It had come from a red-covered Big Chief notebook at the home of Mrs. Musket. On it, a grandson of Ramona Musket had drawn another map to show how to reach the hogan where Rudolph Charley was conducting a Peyote Way. His grandmother was attending the services. The grandson was about twelve. He wore a T-shirt with the S symbol of Superman decorating its front, and he drew the map carefully with a ballpoint pen, and while he drew he explained that Rudolph Charley was the new peyote chief because somebody had shot the old peyote chief, who was Rudolph Charley's older brother.

"Right at Chaco Wash the regular road got washed out," Supergrandson said. "You turn right there, and you drive up the sand if you want to, because it's smoother. You got to pay attention or you'll miss the turns. I'll put down some landmarks to look for." He glanced up and grinned at Mary, and switched politely to English. "If you're not careful out there you can get lost," he assured her.

On the Big Chief map, Supergrandson had penned in "salt cedars" at the point where the Doubtful Dirt road petered out at the wash bottom. Now, in the beam of his headlights, Chee could see a cluster of winter-bare salt cedar below. Chee let the truck roll forward again, past the trees and onto the smoothness of the arroyo floor.

"Here's where we get to the place where if we're not careful we can get lost," Mary said. "Is that right?"

"Right," Chee said.

"Let's not," Mary said. "I'm too tired. I'm flat out exhausted. It seems like we've been in this truck about seventeen days."

"Just since about sunrise," Chee said.

Mary turned suddenly and stared back out the rear window. "I get a feeling I'll look back there and see somebody following us," she said. "Not somebody. That blond man."

"How could he?" Chee asked. "There's no way he could know where we're going."

She shivered, and hugged herself. "Let's say he's smart," she said. "Or let's say he has some reason himself to go to this peyote ceremony."

"I can't think why he would."

"It's a memorial service for Tomas Charley, isn't it? Or something like that. Maybe he's looking for people, just as we are. Maybe we'll just run into him there."

"I doubt it," Chee said.

"I think you're like me. Too tired to care. You're so tired you're going to tell me your war name."

"It won't be much longer now," Chee said. "We want to be at Charley's place at midnight, and then Mrs. Musket will tell us that Windy is living in Grants and give us his address and telephone number. Then we go get some sleep and tomorrow we'll call Tsossie, and he'll tell us who blew up the oil well and why, and where to find the evidence to give to the grand jury, and who to arrest and why Emerson Charley's body was taken out of the hospital, and who hired the blond man to shoot Tomas Charley, and . . ."

"Oh, stop," Mary said. She yawned hugely behind her hand. "With the luck you and I have," she said through the end of the yawn, "that kid gave us the wrong address or the wrong night, or Mrs. Musket won't be there, or she never heard of Windy Tsossie, or she won't like your looks and won't talk to you, or she'll tell you Tsossie moved to Tanzania and didn't leave an address, or it's the wrong Tsossie, or the blond will be there and he'll shoot you. Or even worse, he'll shoot me."

Chee smiled. "Well," he said, "we'll soon know."

At seven minutes to midnight the track they were following skirted a rocky outcrop covered with stunted juniper. The truck's headlights reflected from a windshield, and then from the corrugated metal roof of a shack and the glass of the window below the roof. Chee slowed the truck to a crawl and examined what the headlights showed him. Three pickup trucks, an old white Chevy, and a wagon on which bales of hay served as seats. Twenty yards behind the shack was the round stone shape of a hogan, with a thin wisp of blue smoke emerging from the smoke hole in the center of its conical dirt-insulated roof. No one was in sight.

Chee parked the truck beside the newest of the pickups, flicked off the headlights, and stepped out into the darkness. The moon was down and the black sky was brilliant with a billion stars. He stood with face raised, drinking it in—the great fluorescent sweep of the Milky Way, the pattern of the winter constellations, the incredible silent brightness of the universe.

Mary was standing beside him now. "My God," she said in a hushed voice. "I never saw the sky like that."

"Altitude," Chee said. "We're almost at the Continental Divide here. Mile and a half above sea level; air's thin. And partly it's because there's no ground lights. Look," he said, pointing to the southeast. "See that little glow on the horizon? That's Albuquerque. Hundred miles away, but you can see what it does."

"It makes you forget for a minute how cold you are," Mary said. She shuddered. "The minute's up. I'm cold."

From the hogan came the sound of song and the tapping of a pot drum. Distance and the hogan walls muted it, and the singing was not much more than a rising and falling rhythm, part of the background of the windless night. Chee glanced at his watch. The followers of Lord Peyote wouldn't recess their ceremonial until midnight. They began at sunset after a prayer to inform the setting sun that their intentions were holy, and the ritual would not end until sunrise. But at midnight there was a break. And that meant another five minutes to wait.

"When I was a boy," Chee said, "sometimes my mother would wake me up in the darkest part of the night, and we'd go out away from the hogan, and she'd teach me star lore. How the constellations move and how you can tell the direction and the time of night if you know the time of year. And how it all began."

"How did it all begin?" Mary asked.

"There weren't any Navajos yet. Just Holy People. First Man, First Woman, Talking God, Gila Monster, Corn Beetle, all the various *yei* figures. At night, the sky was black and blank except for the moon. So First Man decided to hang out the stars. And he put up the Blue Flint Boys"—Chee pointed to Cepheus—"and the Bear, and the Stalking God, and all the rest. And along came Coyote, and he grabbed the blanket where First Man had the stars waiting to be hung, and he gave it a toss and threw all that were left out in one great swinging motion. That's what made the Milky Way."

"Quite a coyote," Mary said. She shivered again and hugged herself.

The hogan was silent now, and suddenly there was light at the doorway as the blankets hung across the opening were pulled back.

Chee reached into the cab of the truck and turned on the dome light. It was polite to let people know who was calling on them.

Contrary to Mary's pessimism, Mrs. Musket was there. She was a gray-haired, sturdy woman with a red-and-green mackinaw over the voluminous velveteen blouse and skirt of traditional Navajo womanhood. She wasn't sure she wanted to talk about Windy Tsossie.

Rudolph Charley invited them into the hogan out of the cold, and stood beside them listening. Rudolph Charley looked a lot like Tomas Charley. Just a little younger and even thinner.

"It all happened a long time ago," Chee was saying. "Before he married your sister. There was an explosion at an oil well where he worked. We want to see if he remembers what happened."

Mrs. Musket stared at Chee, glanced nervously at Mary, at Charley, and then back at Chee.

"He won't remember anything," Mrs. Musket said.

"It seems like just about everybody else who was working with Tsossie is dead," Chee said. "We can't talk to them. We want to talk to him."

"I think Windy is dead, too," Rudolph Charley said. "I think the witch got them all."

"Yes," Mrs. Musket said. "He's dead."

"When did he die?" Chee asked. He suspected Mrs. Musket was lying. Experience taught one to watch the face of a person being questioned. Lying made almost everyone nervous. Mrs. Musket was nervous. But then she would be nervous anyway, at being questioned by strangers who appeared out of the darkness to talk of death. And there was more to it than nervousness. Something vague and hard to define. And he thought that he knew what was causing it. Mrs. Musket had eaten peyote and drunk of the "black drink" of the ceremonial—peyote tea. She was in that dreamy world of the psychedelic. He glanced at Rudolph Charley. The road chief of his ceremonial, too, looked at Chee as if he wasn't sure that Chee existed.

"When did he die, then?" Chee repeated. "And where did they put the body?"

"Long time ago," Mrs. Musket said. She stood

looking at Chee and through Chee. The seconds ticked away. "They lived out behind Bisti in the badlands. I wasn't with them. But my sister's husband was a witch, and somebody turned the witching around against him. He got corpse sickness and he died."

"You weren't there, but you heard about it? Is that right? From your sister?" Chee asked.

"From my sister," Mrs. Musket agreed.

"He died of a sickness?"

"Corpse sickness," Mrs. Musket said.

"Where?"

"In my sister's hogan."

"And they buried him there?"

"They got a white man who worked there at Bisti to come and put the body out in the rocks. They told me that he put it in a little blowhole in the side of a cliff and covered it over with rocks."

"It's all starting up again," Rudolph Charley said suddenly. "More witching."

Chee looked at him. Charley's eyes were focused somewhere a long way off.

"The first time it killed my grandfather, and all the people who the Lord Peyote let see through the doorway. The witching killed all six of them. And now it has started up again. First it killed my grandfather. Now it has killed my father, and it killed my brother. Tonight we are asking the Lord Peyote to let us see what will happen next. . . ." His voice trailed off.

Mary began a word and bit it off. The four of them stood there, silently, waiting for the road chief to continue. Beyond Charley, Chee could see the room. The packed earthen floor had been cleared of furnishings. The peyote altar had been built across the back of it—a low crescent shape of hard-packed sand. The peyote moon, they called it. At its center, where the sand was perhaps six inches high, a cup-sized bed of cedar twigs had been built. In this nest the gnarled, hairy shape of a peyote button rested. On the sand beside it was a small silver box, lid open. Behind the peyote moon two zigzag lines were inscribed in the earth, representing the footprints of Christ. The Native American Church as it came to the Checkerboard was more or less Christian. Christ taught the white man only through the Bible, because the white man had crucified him. But the Navajo, who had not harmed Christ, God instructed directly through visions. And Lord Peyote was the instrument, the key to the door which led to reality.

Rudolph Charley still stood motionless, caught in some odd drug-induced expansion of time.

"Did he let you see?" Chee asked.

"I saw the mole," Rudolph Charley said. "The amulet that was my father's and my grandfather's."

"Nothing else?" Chee asked.

The door opened and two men ducked through—both young. They glanced at Chee and at Mary. One added sticks to the piñon fire which had burned to a bed of coals in the hogan fire pit. The other went to the back wall and squatted by the pot drum, watching and waiting. Rudolph Charley's mood changed.

"Nothing you would understand," he said. "We have to start again now. We have to finish the service."

"The man you want to talk to is dead," Mrs. Musket said.

"All right," Chee said. "Then tell me where to find the blowhole where they put his body."

≫ 29 ≪

Finally Colton Wolf was ready. He'd had both a CB radio and a radiotelephone installed in the cab of the pickup. He had driven up an arroyo east of the Sandia Mountains and refreshed his marksmanship with both his rifle and his .22 caliber pistol. The rifle was an expensive .30 caliber Ruger equipped with a scope. He'd fired off half the shells from a 100-round carton, adjusting the open sights for ranges up to 250 yards and the scope up to 800. Then he'd established with a telephone call to the hospital that Western Union couldn't deliver a telegram to Jim Chee because Jim Chee had checked out. That confirmed what Colton had expected. Next he called the city desk at the *Albuquerque Journal,* identified himself as a professor at the university, and got permission to do some research in the newspaper's library. An hour of reading through clippings of crime reports provided him with the names of FBI agents and sheriff's officers who worked on or around the Navajo reservation. He jotted the names and pertinent information into his notebook and then asked if there was a file on B. J. Vines. There was. The oldest clipping reported a transfer of uranium leases from Vines to a consortium of mining companies headed by Kennecott Copper and Kerrmac Nuclear Fuels. Another, a wire service story originating in New York, reported that Vines had won the Weatherby Trophy, the world championship of big-game hunting. The only substantial story was a feature, with photographs, of the construction of Vines' home on the slope of Mount Taylor. The residence was described as "probably the most expensive ever built in New Mexico." The man whose name Colton had found in the box he'd been hired to recover was obviously rich enough to pay the cost of recovering it. There was a good chance, then, that Vines was the client. Not a certainty, because someone else seemed to have wanted the box. But Vines seemed most likely. Colton added to his notes a description of the house and its location. If all else failed, that might be useful.

Colton's last stop was at the municipal library, where he checked through the file of telephone books and noted the numbers he might need. And then he drove westward from Albuquerque, climbing out of the Rio Grande valley, crossing the Rio Puerco breaks, and rolling at a steady fifty-five miles an hour across the empty mesa-butte landscape of west central New Mexico. As he drove, he tested his radio reception on the federal and law-enforcement channels. Reception was excellent. The technique and terminology of the radio dispatchers was no different from what he'd heard in other states. Then he tested the telephone connection by calling the U.S. Weather Service for the forecast. For the west central plateau of New Mexico, the forecast was for increasing afternoon cloudiness, periodic gusty winds, and colder temperatures through the afternoon, with a 60 percent chance of snow before midnight. The green interstate information sign told Colton that the Grants interchange was ahead. To his right, Mount Taylor rose against an unnaturally blue sky, its highest slopes white with snowbanks. He let the camper roll to a stop on the shoulder of the highway, picked up the phone, checked his notebook for the names he wanted, and placed a call to the Navajo Tribal Police subagency office at Crownpoint.

The voice that answered was a woman's.

"This is the Federal Bureau of Investigation," Colton said, "Albuquerque. Agent Martin. Is Captain Largo there?"

"He works out of Tuba City," the voice said. "That number . . ."

"I know that," Colton said, "but Largo told me he might stop in there today. How about Jim Chee, then?"

"Chee's not here, either," the voice said. "He's taking some time off."

"How's he feeling? Hope those ribs are healing up."

"Okay, I guess."

"I was calling about Chee," Colton said. "We got some things we want him to look at. About that shooting. How can I get hold of him?"

"Just a minute," the voice said. There was a pause.

Colton waited. This was the crucial moment. He would allow the delay to stretch four minutes. More than that would risk a successful trace. He couldn't chance the police learning that this was a radiotelephone call. The second hand on his watch dial swept into the second minute.

"We'll have to get him on the radio." It was a man's voice now. "What's the message?"

"Tell him Martin has some information for him, and I need to show him some pictures. Tell him I'm coming out to the reservation and have him call me on my car telephone." He provided a wrong number that sounded reasonable. "Is he near a telephone?"

"I doubt it," the voice said.

"Look," Colton said. "This is urgent. See if you can find him, and if he's a long ways from a telephone, can I get you to call me back and let me know how long it will be?"

"Sure," the voice said.

"Okay. Thanks," Colton said. He hung up, switched on the radio receiver, and pulled the truck back onto Interstate 25. He hadn't gone a mile before he monitored the first call from the Crownpoint dispatcher trying to reach Jimmy Chee.

Colton drove steadily westward, past Grants, past the uranium-processing mills of Ambrosia Lakes, into the rougher country which climbed toward the Continental Divide. Crownpoint was trying to reach Chee at ten-minute intervals. At the Thoreau interchange, Colton pulled off the highway and parked. It was here he had decided to wait. He had never thought there was a serious chance that Chee would run far after the fiasco in the hospital. There was no need to run. Where better to hide an Indian than on an Indian reservation?

He sat with his knees propped against the dash and put together a sandwich of the materials he had brought from the trailer. As always, he ate slowly. The mountain was miles to the east now, but it still dominated the landscape, cold and ominous. When this was over, when he had caught Jim Chee and killed him, and killed the woman; when his tracks were erased and he was once again secure, then he would find a better way to trace his mother. Perhaps a hypnotist could help him remember something he had forgotten. Something useful. There was that old woman in one of his earliest memories. She had put him on her lap and her breath had smelled of tobacco. He had always guessed she might be a grandmother. If he could remember that—or even the place where they had lived when he was very small—it might be helpful. He could remember so little of that. Only a sense of days of cold fog, days of rain, days in an upstairs apartment with his meals left in a refrigerator, his mother coming home in the mornings, his mother's hair damp against his face, his mother's hands cold against his skin. There were men then, too, but no particular man he could remember.

He was staring outward at the blank blue sky, but his thoughts were on that room. He could remember the cracks in the gray linoleum. He'd had two marbles then and the marbles would chase one another down the cracks. He could remember playing that game endlessly, day after day, and the grimy windows, but not the name of the town. Surely he had heard it. Surely, even at four or five, it had meant something to him. His mother had not talked to him often. She wouldn't have been likely to tell a child they were living in Seattle, or Portland, or wherever it was. But he must have heard it. He would find himself a hypnotist and maybe then he could remember something. Colton was aware that things were wrong with his memory. Gaps in it. He ran his thumb down his sweater, feeling the bump under the skin where the rib had healed crookedly. He could remember when he didn't have the bump—when they lived in San Diego. He could remember having it, already healed, in Bakersfield. But he couldn't remember the beating that produced it. It was the same with the ridge of thick white scar tissue under the hair above his left ear.

That also had grown from some blank spot in his childhood. The last time he had tried to remember about that was in Taylorville, but trying had made him sick and he had stopped.

His radio spoke again, the voice of the Crownpoint dispatcher called for Jim Chee.

This time, Chee answered. Colton put down his sandwich and picked up his notebook. Crownpoint relayed the message he had left.

"Well, hell," Chee's voice said. "We're way over here by the old Bisti trading post."

Colton jotted "We're by Bisti" on his pad. He underlined "We're."

"If you're away from the telephone, he wanted me to call him and let him know where he could meet you. He said he'd be coming to the reservation," the dispatcher said.

There was a pause. "Well," the voice of Chee said. "I guess he's going to have to wait, then. We're trying to find a hogan northwest of the old trading post. It's about nine miles back in there, and it'll take me a while to find it. Tell him I'll meet him at our office in Crownpoint tonight. Tell him I'll try to be there by nine, but I might be a little late."

"Ten-four," the dispatcher said. "You paying attention to the weather? It's supposed to snow."

"Right," Chee said. "We'll watch it."

Colton jotted "We" on his note pad. He also wrote "nine miles back in there." He didn't make a note of the nine o'clock meeting time at Crownpoint. By nine o'clock Jimmy Chee would be dead.

≫ 30 ≪

The Bisti trading post had burned years ago, with the thoroughness with which buildings burn when there is no fire department to interfere. The fire had left only the blackened stone foundation and odds and ends of melted glass and twisted metal. Years of casual Navajo scavengers had sorted through the ashes, and years of weather had piled tumbleweeds and dust against the ruins. The great cypresses imported to protect the post from the sun had long since starved for water, like town dogs abandoned in the desert. The row of bare dead trunks now served as an incongruous landmark for a ruin that had otherwise almost returned to nature.

Chee turned the pickup truck left beyond the dead trees, leaving a road marked "Graded Dirt" for a track his map did not show. It ran, fairly straight and fairly smooth, across an expanse of creosote brush.

"You sure this is the right way?" Mary asked.

"No," Chee said, "but I'm sure it's the right direction."

"And you still think we can find the hogan? After all these years?"

"Probably," Chee said. "She said nine miles northwest by north of the trading post, at the south side of an isolated butte. And she described the butte." He pointed ahead. "That must be it. And out here they'd have had to build the hogan of stone, so it's still there. It's just a matter of hunting it. And I'm pretty good at hunting." Chee paused, thinking about that statement. "Or I used to think I was."

The land sloped downward now, into an immensity of erosion. What once had been a sandstone plain had been carved into a grotesquerie of shapes—tables, heads, layer cakes, twisted spires, exposed ribs, serrations, and weird forms that suggested things to which Chee's imagination could not attach names. Wind and water had cut through the overlay into the blackness of coal deposits, into crimson clay, into the streaky blue of shale. Every color showed except green. This was the Bisti badlands. It stretched away for fifty miles under a sky in which clouds had been steadily building.

"I have a hunch he's not dead," Mary said. "I sort of sensed she was hiding something."

"She was nervous," Chee said. "Maybe she was lying and maybe there was another reason. But if the bones are there, we'll find them. And if they're not, we'll find Tsossie."

As he said it, his confidence surprised him. But he *was* confident. Finding Tsossie, skeletal or breathing, involved things purely Navajo—a pattern of thinking and behavior with which Chee was in intimate harmony. He felt no such harmony with the thinking of the whites who must be involved in this affair. For all enterprises, such harmony was essential. Especially for the hunter. And this was from the very start a hunt.

One of the prayers from the Stalking Way ran through his mind, and the voice of his uncle chanting:

I am the Black God as I sing this,
Black God I am. I come and I stand
beneath the East, beneath the Turquoise
*   Mountain.*
The crystal doe walks toward me,
as I call it, as I pray to it,
toward me it comes walking, understanding me
it walks this day into my right hand.
Pleasant, it comes to join me,
in its death it obeys the voice of my singing.
In its beauty I obey the crystal doe.

Perfect understanding, Chee thought. Harmony between deer and man. Harmony between Jim Chee and Tsossie, or the bones of Tsossie, and the thinking of those who had placed Tsossie's corpse among the rocks. But Jim Chee didn't understand the thinking of whites. Neither Changing Woman nor Talking God had given him a song to produce that understanding. What would his uncle say to that? Chee knew exactly what the old man would say. He could almost hear him, because he had heard him so often:

"Boy, when you understand the big, you understand the little. First understand the big."

And that would mean, in this case, that if Chee learned to understand all men (the big), he could understand white men (the little). His uncle would add that if a Navajo could find harmony with a deer, he could find equal harmony with a white man. Chee grimaced at the windshield. And then his uncle, who never failed to belabor a point, would add some wisdom about deer and men. He would say that the deer is much like the Navajo in fundamental ways. It loves its offspring and its mate, food, water, and its rest. And it hates cold, hunger, pain, and death. But the deer is also different. Its life is short. It builds no hogans. The Navajo is more like a white man than like a deer.

That's about what his uncle would say, Chee thought sourly. But his uncle had no dealings with the whites when he could avoid them. And how would his uncle explain the thinking of a white man who filled his home with mementos of his achievements but kept his greatest honors hidden away in a keepsake box? The medals Tomas Charley had described were a Bronze Star and a Silver Star, which—as the military encyclopedia in the university library had informed him—are awarded for deeds of courage in combat; and the Purple Heart, awarded to those wounded in action. You would expect to find them framed in places of prominence on Vines' wall, along with his other trophies. Why did he hide them away with a package of old boyhood photographs and a double handful of rock fragments? A Navajo might either advertise his exploits or modestly conceal them. Why would anyone hide some and advertise others?

The sky was darker now and the wind blew from the northwest. It gusted around the pickup, kicking up a flurry of sand and tumbleweeds.

"That has to be our butte," Chee said. He pointed through the right side of the windshield. "It's the only one within nine miles of the trading post. And it's in the right direction."

The track emerged on a great sheet of barren granite and skirted an island of overlaid sandstone. The island was capped by a slab of white limestone, which left a wide overhang where the softer rock had worn away. It suggested to Chee a table where giants dined. Suddenly, just beyond this landmark, he took his foot from the gas pedal and let the truck roll to a stop.

"What?" Mary asked.

Chee looked at her. "Boy," he said. "Am I stupid." He slammed his fist against the steering wheel. Two sets of keepsakes, he was thinking. One on the walls.

One hidden in the safe. What was the difference between them? The difference was in time.

Mary was staring at him. "Come on," she said. "Cut it out. Let me in on it."

"I'm still getting it sorted out," Chee said. "But what it boils down to is why a man who's very much into keeping mementos and showing them off would hide the best of them in his wall safe."

"Like those medals," Mary said.

"Like those and his high school football team picture, and a couple of athletic awards."

"And black rocks," Mary said.

"Let's get to those later. Stick to the easy stuff now."

"Easy if you've thought of the answer," Mary said. "Quit showing off, damn it. What have you thought of?"

"The only difference I can see is the ones in the safe were all from Vines' early life. Boyhood and young man in the military. The stuff on the wall is after he struck it rich."

Mary had her lower lip caught between her teeth. Her expression said she was looking for significance in this. "Before the oil well explosion and after the explosion. Is that it? And how about the rocks?"

"We better get moving," Chee said. "It's going to get dark." He put the pickup in gear.

"In other words, you don't know about the rocks."

"Somehow they had to be important. A memento

of something important," Chee said. "And from his early life."

"I'll buy that," Mary said. Moments ticked away as the pickup jolted over the rocky surface. "Hey," Mary said. "I know what. The rocks are from when he found the uranium deposit. They're his first ore samples. Don't you think?"

"That would fit," Chee said. "Sure. Why didn't you think of that earlier?"

"You didn't ask me," Mary said. "All you had to do was ask."

"Okay, then. Explain why he keeps those medals in the safe."

"Maybe he's keeping them for somebody else," Mary said.

The wind rocked the pickup again, buffeting it with a barrage of driven sand. Chee down-shifted to pull the truck up a steep incline.

"Mary," he said, "you're a genius." He switched on the transmitter and raised the dispatcher at Crownpoint. His instructions were specific. Call Martin at the FBI. Tell him to have the Veterans Administration make a high-priority emergency check on the military record of Benjamin J. Vines. Was he a first lieutenant in the 101st Airborne Division? Had he won the Silver Star, Bronze Star, and Purple Heart? What kind of discharge? Any criminal record in the service?

The dispatcher read the instructions back. "Anything else?"

"Tell Martin I'll explain it to him when I see him tonight. Tell him I'll be late. And . . . wait a minute." Chee fished out his notebook. "Give him these names, too." He read off the names of those killed in the oil well explosion. At the name of Carl Lebeck, he paused. Lebeck the geologist. Lebeck the well-logger. For a geologist, black rocks might be a memento. "Put the name of Lebeck first," Chee said. "Tell Martin that if Vines didn't win those decorations, to have the VA go down that list of names and see if Lebeck or any of the others won them."

"Got it," the dispatcher said. "You still at Bisti?"

"Northwest of the burned-out trading post," Chee said. "We'll be out here until after dark, the way it looks."

"Better watch the weather," the dispatcher said. "It's snowing some over on the west side. Inch on the ground at Ganado. Not supposed to amount to much, but you know how that is."

"We'll watch it," Chee said. He flicked the radio switch and put the pickup back into gear.

"What are you thinking?" Mary asked.

Chee frowned at the windshield. "Mostly, I'm just taking a shot in the dark."

"But just mostly," Mary said. "Have you figured a way that Vines and the oil well connect?"

"They must," Chee said. "They have to connect. If not Vines, then Gordo Sena. One or the other has to connect."

Mary laughed. "Sure," she said. "Now all you have to do is figure out how."

"I think I have," Chee said. "At least part of it."

The track angled to the right and up the slope of dark-blue shale marbled with reddish impurities. Above it, the top of the butte loomed, now no more than a thousand yards away. Chee shifted down. Mary was watching him impatiently.

"I'm waiting," she said.

"Okay," Chee said. "First we agree there has to be a reason. White man or Navajo, you do things for a reason. With a Navajo, something this bad—blowing up people wholesale—would have to be witch business. Irrational. Evil for the sake of evil. No other motive would make sense. For the white man, I think it would be greed." He glanced at her. "All right so far?"

Mary looked puzzled. "I guess so," she said.

"If we're dealing with witchcraft, what's happened since doesn't connect. Maybe a Navajo would want to kill the Charleys if he knew they were witches who'd done him harm. That's happened. But he would do it in the heat of rage, not years later. So let's set that aside."

Mary shrugged.

"So we're dealing with a white man's crime," Chee continued. "The motive's greed. Who gains by blowing up an oil well? You have to remember where that well was. We couldn't find the remains because the Red Deuce has swallowed up the site. So the oil company drilling the well had a mineral rights lease on that piece of land. If the well produces oil, the lease is extended as long as production lasts. That's the standard oil lease form. So let's say somebody knows there's a uranium deposit under the well. Who'd benefit?"

"You mean the Senas? Because it was on their ranch?"

"Maybe the Senas," Chee said. "When it finally did happen, uranium made Gordo Sena rich. But something doesn't fit with thinking Gordo did it."

"You mean like killing his own brother?" Mary asked. "Maybe Robert Sena planned it himself and then something went wrong and he killed himself, too."

"I didn't mean that," Chee said. "I meant the Sena ranch is like most ranches out here. It's a little bit of privately owned land connected to a big spread of federal Bureau of Land Management land. Most of what you own is a permit to graze your cattle on BLM land. That's where the well was drilling. On federal land. The Senas had the grazing lease, but it was about a quarter of a mile from the boundary of their own land. So they wouldn't benefit directly from either an oil strike or a uranium find. Sena got rich because the uranium deposit spread over onto his family property."

"So you rule out Sena," Mary said. "Who then?"

"I don't quite rule out the Senas," Chee said.

"There's a piece missing somewhere. I can't think it through."

The pickup tilted abruptly downward into a narrow wash. Chee shifted into his lowest gear, braked to a stop, and inspected the arroyo. The problem would be pulling the truck up the other side. The arroyo carried very little water even after downpours, and a tall growth of mesquite and rabbit brush on both sides of the track had limited erosion. But still, years of cutting away had made the opposite bank steep enough so that getting traction to the pickup out of it looked chancy.

"Looks like the end of the line," Mary said. "But aren't we close enough to walk?"

"We'll try the pickup," Chee said. "If we don't make it, there's plenty of room down there to turn it around."

The vehicle produced a great shower of flying gravel, lost traction briefly, and skidded sideways. But it made the brief, steep climb. Ahead now, no more than four hundred yards away, they could see three gnarled cottonwoods. In a desert climate they signaled either a spring or a very shallow water sand that could be tapped by a well. And that in turn explained why this track led across the badlands and why the Tsossies had picked the site for their hogan. Chee and Mary could see the hogan now about twenty feet beyond the trees. It was a hexagon of stacked sandstone slabs, roofed with poles which radiated outward from a central smoke hole. The earth that once insulated the roof against cold and heat had long since washed away.

Chee pulled the pickup to a stop against an outcrop of cliff. He clipped on his holster and hung his binocular case around his neck. "Be prepared," he said, and stepped out into the wind.

The doorway of the hogan was closed with planks nailed across the lintel logs. The only opening now was on the north side—a hole knocked through the stone wall to provide an exit for the ghost and to warn strangers that this was a death hogan. Chee stood looking into the hole. The evening light that filtered through the latticework of roof showed nothing but odds and ends of junk too worthless to carry away even by an impoverished family. Dirt had blown in and tumbleweeds had bounced through the ghost hole, but the danger posed by the *chindi* had made the place secure from scavengers.

"If Tsossie didn't die here, someone did," Chee said. "Let's find the place the old lady said they put him."

Mary was staring at the hogan. "I've heard about this," she said, "about Navajos not using buildings after somebody dies in them. It seems awfully wasteful."

"Unless maybe they died of something contagious," Chee said. "When the custom started, I guess that was the purpose."

"They carry the body out the hole? Is that right? Always on the north side?"

Chee didn't want to talk about it now. The wind gusted again, carrying around a light load of dry, feathery snowflakes. "North is the direction of evil," he said.

Mrs. Musket had told them the blowhole was in the mesa wall, west of the hogan. The butte was formed of layers of geological formations, capped with a gray erosion-resistant granite. Below that was a stratum of red sandstone perhaps thirty feet deep, which covered porous, whitish volcanic tuft that had been riddled with wind pockets and seepage holes. Only two of these near the hogan were large enough for a burial. Chee examined both through the binoculars and saw nothing conclusive. They climbed the talus slope toward the nearest one. Against the perpendicular walls of the butte, sections of the soft perlite had been worn away, undermining the sandstone. A section of it had fallen in a clutter of blocks, each as large as a freight car. Chee scrambled up the sloping side of one of the blocks and looked into the blowhole. Rocks had been piled on its floor. From beneath one of them a ragged fragment of blue cloth protruded. The wind eddied into the hole. The cloth fluttered.

"Come on up," Chee said. "I guess we found Windy Tsossie."

Sometimes the dry cold of a desert winter will protect a corpse from decay and turn it into a desiccated mummy. Since the placement in the cliff and the covering of rocks had protected Tsossie from both animal predators and scavenger birds, this might have happened to him. But Tsossie, apparently, had died in the summer, and thirty years of insects had reduced what he had been to a clean white skeleton.

With the last rocks removed, Chee squatted in the low opening and looked at what remained. The skeleton was still wearing moccasins, put on the wrong feet to confuse any *chindi* that might follow the spirit into the darkness of the afterworld. The denim trousers Tsossie had worn had been reduced to scraps of decayed rags, but for some reason the shirt was about half intact. Two buttons still held it across the empty cage of ribs. Chee checked the skeleton's left hand. A finger was missing. Mrs. Musket had said Tsossie had lost a finger. The wind caught the shirttail and blew it against the ribs, revealing the dull silver of leather-strung conchas. The heavy belt that had once encircled a waistline now encircled only a row of whitened vertebrae. Under the concha buckle Chee saw a leather string, the thong of a medicine pouch. Pouch and belt lay just above the socket where the ball joint of Tsossie's thigh bone connected to the pelvic socket. The thigh bone was distorted by a heavy, unnatural growth of scar tissue, an ugly lesion which ran from the joint almost halfway down the heavy bone. It looked very much like the illustration Dr. Huff had pointed out to them in his medical text. Bone cancer. The sort of crazy growth that happens in bone tissue with the metastasis of cell malignancy.

Chee picked up the pouch and pried open the brittle leather.

"It's snowing again," Mary Landon said. She was sitting on the slab outside the cave entrance inspecting the landscape through the binoculars. "And it's getting dark."

"Just another minute or two," Chee said.

The leather broke apart under his fingernail. Inside there was a coating of yellow dust—what once had been sacred pollen. The pollen coated four small fragments of abalone shell, a gallstone taken from some small animal, two feathers, a withered bit of root, and the small stone shape of a mole.

Chee held the mole delicately and polished away the pollen dust. It looked just like the one he had found in Emerson Charley's medicine pouch. Almost identical.

"Jimmy. Somebody's coming."

It was as if they were the same mole. The same amulet. The feel under his fingers was the same. The same blunt legs, the same sloping, pointed snout.

The tone of Mary's voice cut through his concentration more than the meaning of the words. The tone was fear.

"What?" he asked. "Where?"

"There." She pointed over the open hogan roof, past the almost bare cottonwoods, down the track they had followed.

At first he saw nothing. Then a man wearing a navy-blue stocking cap and a heavy black windbreaker trotted into sight. He carried a rifle in his right hand and ran easily, in a low crouch. Chee could see just enough of his face to confirm what he instinctively knew. It was the blond man. In his crouching, careful trot, he was skirting Chee's pickup truck.

"Climb in here," Chee whispered. He helped pull Mary into the blowhole. "It's him," Chee said. "But I don't think he's seen us. He's looking for us around the truck."

"How could he have found us here?" Mary whispered.

"God knows," Chee said. The blond man was kneeling behind a growth of rabbit brush, apparently watching the truck. Chee lifted the binoculars and surveyed the landscape down the track. The man must have driven here and left his vehicle parked somewhere. Chee could see no sign of it. It was probably parked out of sight in the bottom of the arroyo they'd crossed.

Mary found a place behind the bones and the rocks that had covered them. She sat pressed against the sloping wall, looking first at Chee and then at the skeleton. The blowhole was an elongated circle perhaps six feet along its longest diameter and flattened at the bottom by fallen debris and accumulated dust. The wind had cut into the soft ash no more than four feet. If the man with the rifle learned they were there, the blowhole offered no safety.

Chee spoke in a very low voice. "We stay absolutely still until it gets dark. No motion. No sound. Nothing to attract attention. I want you to ease yourself down as flat as you can get. You're out of sight from where he is now, but do it slowly and carefully. I'm going to lay flat, too. Then he won't be able to see anything in here, even if he tries. Not without climbing up on the slab."

"And we can't see him, either," Mary said in a very faint voice. "We won't know where he is. We won't be able to do anything to defend ourselves."

"He has the rifle," Chee said. "We don't have any defense against that. Not until it gets dark."

Chee lay on his stomach, his left hand pressed against the tuft beneath him, his right hand gripping the butt of his revolver. Ready to move. There was the smell of dust and ashes in his nostrils. The wind picked up again and hooted through the blowhole opening. Grains of perlite fell against his cheek. The blowhole had become infinitesimally deeper. There was a sound outside. The blond man? The wind? A brushy branch scratching against stone?

Chee struggled against an overwhelming urge to run.

The sound came again. A creaking.

"What was that?" Mary asked. The question had

a frantic sound. Panic had come to her a little later than it had to him.

He reached across the bones for her, gripping her leg with his left hand. "The wind," he whispered. "Mary, listen. The way the owl hunts, he sits in a piñon and he hoots. He can't see the rabbits, and they can't see him. And that's the problem for the rabbits. He hoots. And he waits a little to let them think about it, and he hoots again. And the rabbits think. And one of them will think too much. He thinks the owl is getting closer and closer. He thinks the owl has found him. So he makes a run for it, and the owl has her meal for the night."

Mary moved his hand from her leg. "Okay, wise guy," she whispered. "I get your point."

A flurry of snow blew into the hole, the flakes cold against his face. Noises came again and with them a return of panic. He found himself imagining the blond man's face appearing suddenly over the rim of the hole behind the silenced .22 pistol. Chee found his muscles rigid with tension. He forced himself to think of other things. In three weeks he would go to Albuquerque and buy his ticket and report to the FBI Academy. Or he would drive out to the place of Hosteen Nakai and tell his uncle that he was ready to work with him—that Hosteen Nakai could count on him this winter when the calls came to conduct his sings. Which one would it be? He couldn't concentrate on the question. Instead he planned what he would do when darkness came. He would move when there was still a little light. He would find the blond man's car. If the blond man was in it, he would kill him. If he wasn't, then Chee would wait. He waited now, hearing the sound of the wind when it gusted and the sound of Mary breathing when it was silent. He had time now to add what Tsossie's bones and Tsossie's mole had told him to what he had already surmised. The People of Darkness had been murdered. Tsossie had been an unpleasant man, perhaps even a witch. But he had been reduced to bone for a motive that had nothing to do with the anger his unpleasantness had provoked. The motive was mathematical, not emotional. A simple matter of improving the odds against the future. A white man's crime.

Chee felt an impatience to move, to begin the contest. It was much darker, but not quite dark enough. Words from the Stalking Way ran through his memory, his uncle's husky voice singing them, his uncle's stubby fingers tapping rhythm on the pot drum.

I am the Black God, arising with twilight,
a part of the twilight.
Out from the West, out from the Darkness
Mountain, a buck of dark flint stands
out before me.
The best male game of darkness, it calls to me,
it hears my voice calling.
Our calls become one in beauty.

Our prayers become one in beauty.
As I, the Black God, go toward it.
   As the male game of darkness comes toward
   me.
With beauty before us, we come together.
   With beauty behind us, we come together.
That my arrow may free its sacred breath.
   That my arrow may bring its death in beauty.

The song ran on and on in Chee's mind, a pattern of repetitions, of slightly varied sounds and slightly varied meanings, exorcising the primal dread of death and preparing man and animal for the sacred hunt.

Jimmy Chee was ready. The wind gusted again, sucking into the blowhole, eroding away another thousand infinitesimal grains of ash and moving icy air up Chee's pant leg.

"I'm going now," Chee said. "Stay quiet for a few more minutes, until it's darker, and then slip out and find a sheltered place. But stay within shouting range. When it's safe, I'll call you."

He raised himself to a crouch, surprised at how stiff his muscles had already become.

"I've got a better idea," Mary whispered. "Give me the pistol, and I'll go out and see what I can do. I don't like this being the only one out here who can't shoot back."

Chee grinned. "No; it's my gun. I bought it with my own money."

And with that, he slipped quickly out of the hole, dropped to the slab, and from the slab to the brushy ground behind it. If the blond man had seen the motion, he hadn't seen it quickly enough to react.

Chee moved as fast as caution allowed. He made a wide circle away from the butte, angling on a course that would cross the little arroyo they'd had trouble traversing. That's where the blond man's vehicle would be and that's where Chee would find the blond man. Somehow, God knew how, he must have guessed the trail ended at the butte and that Chee would be there, and he hadn't risked the noise of trying to grind up the steep arroyo slope. He had parked and come for Chee on foot.

Chee had thought it through very carefully. The blond man had found Chee's pickup truck, but he hadn't found Chee. Hunting him in the brush and boulders around the butte would have been like searching the white man's proverbial haystack for a dangerous needle. So the blond man would opt for another solution. He'd return to his own vehicle and simply wait. When he heard the engine on Chee's pickup start and saw the reflection from Chee's headlights, he would have plenty of time to set up his ambush. The arroyo would be a perfect place for it. Chee's truck creeping down the steep arroyo bank. The blond man shooting Chee through the truck door. Shooting at point-blank range and with plenty of time for as many more shots as were needed if the first one didn't get the job done.

Where Chee reached the arroyo it was much shallower and broader. He hurried up it, moving silently on the sand. Wind and snow had almost stopped, but now the wind rose again, blowing in icy gusts against his face. The right direction for the hunter. Blowing scent and sound away from the prey. Even so, when the arroyo deepened, and when the dim light told him he was within a hundred yards of the point where the track dipped into it, he left the open bottom and moved slowly through the brush.

The vehicle was almost exactly where he'd thought it would be. The blond man had simply nosed it down the arroyo and left it far enough off the track to be out of sight. Chee moved carefully along the extreme edge of the arroyo bottom, slipping from one bit of brush cover to the next. He held the pistol in his right hand at full cock, so that a touch of his thumb to the safety would make it ready to fire.

The eastern sky was totally black now, but the west still filtered a dim twilight through the cloud cover. The blond man's vehicle was a dark-blue GMC pickup truck. From halfway up the arroyo bank where he was crouched, Chee could see the right front and side and look slightly downward into the cab. The cab seemed to be empty. It was empty unless the blond man was prone on the front seat or sitting on the floor. That seemed unlikely. A long willowy wand jutted upward from the back bumper—the antenna of a two-way radio. That was how the blond man had known he could find Chee at Bisti. He had monitored the Navajo Police radio calls.

With that thought came another. What had Chee said when he talked to Crownpoint? Had he mentioned Mary Landon in that call? Had he even said "we"? Had he said anything that would have told the blond man that Mary was with him? Chee squeezed his eyes shut, concentrating, trying to remember. As always, his memory served. He had said "we." "We're going nine miles northwest of the old trading post. We'll be there until after dark." Those had been his words. So the blond man knew Mary was with him.

Chee slouched back on his heels, his eyes still on the truck, and thought. He considered that the blond man—apparently, at least—was not waiting where Chee's good sense told him the blond man should be waiting. So where was the blond man? He was back at the butte, hunting Chee and Landon. Or he was back at the butte, staked out, watching for them to return to their pickup. Either way he might find Mary, or she might, cold and confused, walk into his trap.

Chee put the pistol carefully on a rock beside his boot. He extracted his billfold, and from the billfold the check Vines had given him. It was perfect for the message. The check itself would tell the blond man that Vines had been in contact with the police.

He wrote carefully, trying for legibility in the darkness.

> *KILLING US WON'T HELP. VINES IS*
> *DEALING WITH FBI. HE GETS OFF LIGHT.*

Chee pushed his hand back into his warm glove, picked up the pistol, and moved cautiously to the truck. The door on the driver's side was locked. Chee pulled out the wiper blade and wrapped the check around it securely. If the blond man got back to the truck, he couldn't miss seeing it. It appealed to Chee's Navajo sense of balance, order, and harmony—this business of using the check, the witch's own poison, to turn the evil back against its source. It was the way Changing Woman had taught. Chee trotted off in the darkness toward the butte.

An hour later there was no light at all left in the west. The snow was falling again, still dry, feathery flakes, now drifting almost vertically downward, now whipped by gusts which whistled and moaned around the cliffs of the butte and sent the snow stinging against the skin. Chee had scouted the ground carefully, using his pickup truck as a center and making cautious, time-consuming circles widening around it. He'd moved when the wind blew and crouched motionless, listening, when it dropped into calm. He'd checked every bit of cover that a man in ambush might use to watch the pickup. He'd found nothing. Now he squatted beside a scrubby juniper, thinking. He could see the shape of the pickup against the dark stone of the outcrop. Where could the blond man be? What was he doing? Chee reexamined everything he had been told of the man and everything he had observed himself. He considered the way the man had behaved on the malpais and in the hospital and what Martin had told him of his assassinations. Always meticulous care. Always caution. Never a chance taken. That was the key. No unnecessary chances. No overlooked possibilities. That was why Chee hadn't found him in the two places where the man might logically have been. Because the man had thought it through, had realized that he might have been seen, had realized that Chee might be smart enough to expect a trap or an ambush. Chee frowned into the darkness. The blond man would hardly be floundering around the butte in darkness. He had to be hiding somewhere, waiting. Waiting for what? Waiting for Mary and Chee to get into the pickup and drive into an ambush somewhere? Not if he suspected he had been seen. Then Chee would simply slip into the pickup and radio Crownpoint for assistance. The minute such a call was made, the blond man would be hopelessly trapped. Therefore, the blond man must keep him from his radio. Why isn't he doing that? Chee asked himself. What is to keep me from slipping into the front seat and calling for help? Perhaps he doesn't know that police disconnect the switch that turns on the courtesy light when the door opens. Perhaps he is somewhere, waiting for that flash of light. But no, Chee thought. The blond man would know that. Perhaps he is waiting inside the pickup? No. Chee had left the truck locked. Even if the man picked the lock, hiding inside would be risky.

So how was the blond man protecting himself against the radio call? Chee went over what he knew of the blond man again, incident by incident, from the hospital to the very beginning and the bombing of Emerson Charley's truck in the parking lot. When he reached that, he knew exactly what the blond man had done and what he was waiting for.

He had put a bomb in Chee's pickup. Now he was off somewhere in the darkness, out of the wind and totally unfindable, waiting patiently for Jim Chee and Mary Landon to blow themselves to pieces.

It took Chee only a few minutes to climb the outcrop. From atop that table of stone, he could look directly down into the bed of the truck thirty feet below. It was too dark to be sure, but he could see nothing in the pickup bed that hadn't been there before. If the blond man had placed a bomb, it wasn't likely he had put it in the same place he had used in his effort to kill Emerson Charley. Here, most likely, he would have placed it on the truck frame under the body. If the FBI knew what it was talking about, his bombs detonated when they were moved. Driving over the first bump would do the job. Under the cab, the effects would be certain.

The point where the outcrop jutted from the face

of the butte was littered with chunks of fallen stone. Chee picked up one that weighed perhaps twenty pounds and carried it to the edge. He placed himself carefully, over the center of the truck bed. In the same motion he tossed the boulder and jumped backward away from the edge.

The crash of the boulder striking metal was engulfed a minisecond later by a great flash of light and sound. Chee, already off balance, found himself sprawling on hands and knees, his ears ringing and his eyes seeing only the red and white circles imprinted on his retinas by the flash. He lowered himself on the surface of the stone, waiting for sight and hearing to recover.

Soon he could hear a second sound through the receding ringing and see a flickering light through the flash blindness. The truck was burning. At first the flames from the burning gasoline flared above the rim of the outcrop, but they quickly lost their force. Now Chee lay in the darkness looking out across a landscape illuminated by the fire. It was the ideal place to be. When the blond man came to make sure of his victims, Chee would shoot him. Chee lay on his stomach, the cocked pistol held in front of him, waiting.

The wind rose, fanned the flames into a roar, and then died away. The snow drifted straight down again, still dry and feathery. The rock around Chee, blown clear by the most recent gusts, collected another thin layer of snowflakes. Gasoline and oil were almost exhausted now, and the fire fed itself on rubber and upholstery. Chee could smell the rancid black smoke of burning tires and plastic. The landscape the blond man would be crossing was white now. He would be easy to see in the firelight. But the blond man did not come. Through the sound of the fire below him, Chee heard the sound of a starter, and then of a motor, grinding in low gear. Across the ridge where the blond man's pickup had been parked, there appeared a fan of light reflecting in the falling snow. Chee jumped to his feet. The light tilted upward, two visible beams jutting into the snowy sky. The truck was climbing out of the arroyo bottom. But the headlights were pointed away from the butte. The blond man was driving away.

> 31 <

They built the fire in the crevasse between two of the great fallen slabs in a sheltered cul-de-sac protected from the wind. Chee had picked the spot carefully and then had made a walking circuit, assuring himself that no light, even dimly reflected, was visible. The blond man had driven away toward the Bisti road. Chee had watched the truck lights moving eastward until finally they no longer reappeared through the falling snow. The blond man probably wouldn't return. There was no reason for him to do so. But he might.

Now, finally, they were out of the wind. Mary Landon sat across from him, back against the vertical stone, her denimed legs stretched straight in front of her. Above them the wind gusted past the butte top with a hooting noise. Between these walls of fallen stone, it only caused the fire to flicker. But Mary shivered and hugged herself.

"I think it was a mistake," she said, "leaving that note about Mr. Vines."

"Why?"

"Because," Mary said. "Because maybe he'll go and shoot Vines—and you don't know for sure Vines killed anyone. You don't have any proof."

"I know for sure," Chee said.

"You don't have anything to prove it with. You're not a judge."

Chee thought about that. The firelight was red, burning the rosin of dead piñon. It reflected on Mary Landon's face, casting deep shadows where her hair fell across her forehead.

"Yes," Chee said, "I am a judge. If the blond man kills Vines, then that's justice. But he's not going to kill Vines. He won't have time. He can't get there tonight because of the weather. If we get three inches of snow down here, there'll be two feet of it up on Mount Taylor. The road won't be open until they get a snowplow on it—and that won't be until tomorrow morning. They'll be using the snowplows where there's more traffic."

"Still, you don't have any right to . . ."

"We don't have much violence, we Navajos. What there is is mostly associated with witchcraft. Changing Woman taught us how to cope with the Navajo Wolves. We turn the evil around so it works against the witch."

"But first you have to know for sure he's the witch," Mary said.

The snow started again, larger flakes now. The wind moaned around the butte top and the snowflakes eddied and swirled above them, lit by the redness of the fire. Some settled into the cul-de-sac. They landed on Chee's knee, on Mary's hair, on stone surfaces. Some drifted into the fire and vanished—cold touched by the magic of heat.

It was going to be a long, frigid night, and there was nothing that could be done until there was a little light. When it was light, the pipeline companies would be scouting their collection systems to make sure the abrupt drop in temperature had cracked no exposed metal, separated no joints, jammed no valves. The little slow-flying planes would be up looking for signs of gas leaks. Whatever those signs were. Spurts of blowing dust, Chee guessed. He remembered they had crossed the El Paso Natural Gas trunkline between Bisti and the butte. When dawn came, they would walk to it and build a smoky fire and wait to be spotted. Until then there was nothing to be done, except help time pass, avoid freezing, and think.

"I am born a Slow Talking People," Chee said. "I'm also a member of the Red Forehead Clan because my father was one. And I'm connected with the Mud Clan, because my uncle—the one teaching me to be a singer—he's married into the Muds. All of those clans have the same tradition. To become a witch, to cross over from Navajo to Navajo Wolf, you have to break at least one of the most serious taboos. You have to commit incest, or you have to kill a close relative. But there's another story, very old, pretty much lost, which explains how First Man became a witch. Because he was first, he didn't have relatives to destroy. So he figured out a magic way to violate the strongest taboo of all. He destroyed himself and recreated himself, and that's the way he got the powers of evil."

"I never heard about that," Mary said. "I thought for a minute you were changing the subject. But you're not, are you?"

"I'm not," Chee said. "Lebeck decided to be a witch. He destroyed himself. And he came back."

Mary was frowning at him. "Lebeck? The geologist at the oil well?"

"Yes; the geologist," Chee said. "Think about what we know. We know the oil well was drilled through uranium, because the Red Deuce is now mining that deposit where the oil well stood. Lebeck was what they call the 'well logger'—the one who inspects samples of the rock they're drilling through and maps the deposits. Very shallow, maybe down just fifty feet or so, the bit goes through pitchblende, a thick layer of the very richest uranium ore. So Lebeck suddenly knows something that's worth hundreds of millions of dollars. How can he cash it in? He can cash it in only if this oil lease is allowed to expire. Then he can file his own mineral lease claim. So he falsifies the log."

Mary was leaning forward, intent. "Hey," she said. "You looked at the log. Did he? Why didn't you tell me? How could you tell?"

Chee made a wry face. "I couldn't tell," he said. "I checked out that log and a couple of other ones from other wells drilled in Valencia County, and they all looked about alike. The oil companies were all looking for a shallow oil sand, just down about two thousand feet. I was looking for God knows what down at the bottom of the well, down at the end where they were deciding to shoot the tubing with the nitro. I didn't know what I was looking for, and I didn't see anything."

"But you should have seen something," Mary said slowly. "You should have seen they'd drilled through the uranium ore."

"Exactly!" Chee said. "I've heard that Red Deuce deposit is a couple of hundred feet deep. It should have been noted on the log." Chee felt an overpowering urge to smoke. He hadn't had a possibility of lighting a cigaret since the blond man's arrival at the butte. He fished out a Pall Mall, offered it to Mary. She shook her head. He lit it.

"Those things will kill you," Mary said.

"Actually, I think now he must have falsified the log twice. Once when they drilled through the ore and again at the end. I think they found the oil sand they were looking for, and Lebeck put it down as something else and had them drill right through it. Or maybe he had the log show they were drilling into a geological formation which should be below the oil sand—which would mean the sand didn't exist at this particular place. Anyway, he wanted them to shut down the well and let the lease lapse, so he could get a lease on it himself. If they struck oil, the lease would be renewed by the oil company and he would never get the uranium. So when the company decided to shoot the well, Lebeck must have known there was a good chance that would start the oil flowing. He couldn't risk that." Chee inhaled a lungful of smoke and let it trickle from between his lips. It made blue swirls in the slowly moving air, drifting upward while the white flakes drifted down. Far above at the butte top, the north wind, the evil wind, began hooting again. Chee puffed out the last of the smoke, destroying the pattern with his breath. "And so Lebeck decided to blow everything, and everyone, sky high. Lebeck decided to become a witch."

He glanced at Mary.

"To die, or seem to die, and to come back as B. J. Vines," she said.

"Yes," Chee said.

"But when the nitro truck arrived, something went wrong. Dillon Charley's crew didn't show up for work."

"How did Dillon Charley know?"

"The Lord Peyote told him in a vision," Chee said. "Or perhaps Lebeck warned him—which I doubt. Or perhaps Dillon Charley saw things that made him nervous. I think Charley was a very perceptive man. Mrs. Vines told me that her husband and Dillon Charley were friends—had a sort of rapport.

Perhaps that was already true when Vines was Lebeck." Chee shrugged. "Who knows? Lord Peyote, or nervousness about nitroglycerin, or what? Anyway, he didn't show up that day, and he warned his crew away. I think Lebeck wanted them all there. No one else around here knew him. No one else would recognize him as Vines. But he didn't have any choice. The nitro truck came. He had to act then or never."

"How did he do it?" Mary asked.

"I have to guess. Obviously he left the rig. I'd say he probably got far enough away to be safe, and he had a rifle and fired a shot into the nitro bottle at the proper moment."

Mary Landon shivered again and hugged herself. "And then he just walked away, so he'd be counted among the dead. Didn't he have a family? A mother and father? People who loved him?"

"I don't know anything about Lebeck," Chee said.

"And then to come back here. Wouldn't he be afraid someone would recognize him?"

"Probably nobody knew him, or had even seen him much. Just the well crew. It was an isolated place. Hardly a road then, and the crew would have lived out at the well, where nobody saw them. And then he stayed away two years. Maybe a little more. Long enough for the mineral lease to expire. Long enough to grow a heavy beard. Who knows—maybe he did something else to change his looks. I said we didn't know anything about Lebeck, but we do know a little. You get into the paratroops by volunteering. And once he was in, he won two top decorations for courage. So I guess he wasn't afraid of taking chances. Or of killing, either. He must have done a lot of it." Chee paused, thinking about it. "I guess he knew he'd have some more to do."

"The People of Darkness," Mary said.

"Yeah. He couldn't count on Dillon Charley forgetting him."

"You think Dillon Charley saw Vines and recognized him as Lebeck?"

"Maybe. But I'll bet Lebeck didn't wait for that to happen. I'll bet he went looking for him. Maybe he told Charley the Lord Peyote had given him a vision, too. Or maybe he just offered him a job, money, so forth. He'd know Charley wouldn't tell the sheriff anything—not with the way Gordo was harassing him and his church. And besides, Charley wasn't going to live very long."

"Lebeck knew Dillon Charley had cancer?"

"Lebeck knew Charley was going to have cancer," Chee corrected. "That black rock, it must be pitchblende. When the oil well bit drilled through it, Lebeck recognized pitchblende, and that's the hottest kind of natural uranium deposit. He didn't put it on the log, but he saved a piece of the core to test and make sure. And then he kept it because he saved mementos, and this one was going to change his life. Maybe he already knew it was going to be useful to him."

"You're losing me," Mary said. "How do you know it's pitchblende? I never heard of it. How do you know so much about it?"

"Out here everybody is prospecting half the time," Chee said. "You learn about minerals, and mostly you learn about uranium-bearing minerals. I should have thought of it before. I think if we get a mineralogist to check those rock samples and those mole amulets, we're going to find they're radioactive. Vines gave Charley the mole knowing he would carry it in his medicine pouch—hanging from his waist under his clothing right against the groin."

"Dillon Charley, and Tsossie, and Begay, and Sam, and all of them," Mary said. She shivered again.

"He didn't overlook much," Chee said. "I think Dillon Charley must have been the first to die, and Vines got the body and buried it, just in case an autopsy would show something. But Navajos don't have much interest in bodies, and the authorities don't have much interest in dead Navajos, and people got scattered out, so after Dillon Charley it wasn't worth the trouble, I guess. It looked like he could quit worrying. Everybody on that work crew who had ever seen him as Lebeck was dead, or soon would be. Nothing to worry about for years."

"Not until Emerson Charley gets cancer," Mary Landon said.

"I think that's right," Chee said. "Old Dillon was

a pretty important religious leader, and people like that sometimes try to pass it along to their children. I guess he gave Emerson his medicine bundle, hoping he'd become the peyote chief, and one day, years later, Emerson decides to revive the cult. He starts wearing old Dillon's mole, and of course he gets sick. . . ."

Mary was leaning forward now. "And Vines gets nervous," she said. "Now it's 1980, and Vines doesn't want Emerson checking into a modern cancer research center, where he's sure to undergo an autopsy, and so he hires somebody to kill him."

"And to steal the body," Chee said.

"And probably to get the mole back. But the blond man missed the mole."

"And Tomas Charley was too suspicious. The Navajos around Mount Taylor may not know a lot about radioactive pathology, but they could count up the fact that people who associated with Vines seemed to die. They knew he was a witch. When Emerson Charley's truck was bombed, Tomas was suspicious. He wanted to prove Vines was a witch. He broke in and stole the box, and all Mrs. Vines knew was that the box was extremely important to Vines, so she asked me to get it back. I think she wanted to know Vines' secret."

The snow was falling more heavily now, drifting almost straight down out of an abruptly windless sky.

"Can't we build that fire a little higher?" Mary asked.

"A little," Chee said. He moved two chunks of piñon trunk into the blaze.

"You can't prove any of this, can you?" Mary said. It wasn't a question.

"I won't have to," Chee said. "I told the blond man. Tomorrow we'll tell Gordo Sena. Sena won't need proof either."

≫ 32 ≪

Chee passed the word to Sheriff Sena via the radio in an El Paso Natural Gas Company helicopter. The copter had found them where the EPNG collector pipe bridges Nagasi Wash. They had built a fire in the brush that flourishes there, and not ten minutes after the greasy smoke spiraled into the sky, the little Bell had puttered over the rise. The pilot was a young man with a scarred nose, a walrus mustache, and the emblem of a First Cavalry Division gunship unit sewed on his greasy flying jacket. He had already spotted their bombed pickup truck, and circled it curiously, and he was ready to believe Chee's story of a police emergency.

Chee told the sheriff's dispatcher at Grants no more than Gordo Sena would need to know.

"Tell him the man who killed Tomas Charley is headed for B. J. Vines' house. Tell him that Vines hired the man, and tell him that Vines' real name is Carl Lebeck."

"Lee what?" the dispatcher asked.

"Lebeck," Chee said. "Be sure to get that right. Carl Lebeck." Except for describing the truck, and the blond man, Chee offered no more details. They would be redundant. Gordo Sena had lived for thirty years with the details of that oil well explosion burning in his mind. He'd know instantly who Lebeck was, and he was smart enough to put it all together. The dispatcher had said Sena had left for the Anaconda Mine. The same road led through the fringes of the Laguna reservation toward the high slopes of Mount Taylor and Vines' place. About fifteen miles, Chee guessed, compared to the sixty they had to cover in the helicopter. But that last mile or two would be impassable to something on wheels. Sena would have to walk in. Chee would get there first.

The thought excited him. At one level he was afraid of the blond man. At another, he longed to find him. His broken rib ached, as it had ached all morning. But it was more than vengeance. The man had shot him once. He had twice hunted Chee down to kill him. The memory still rankled—of the interminable minutes spent on the metal duct above the hospital ceiling, of the helpless panic in the blowhole. Now he was the stalker. He tried to analyze the feeling. Expectant? Exultant? Something between, and something more. There was a mixture of fear and of the remembered childhood feeling of the hunt. The smell of smoke, of boiling coffee, the forest scents carried on the predawn dew. His uncle greeting the sun with the dawn chant and blessing them all with the sacred pollen and singing the final song to call the spirits of the deer. Through the scarred, oil-smeared Plexiglas he could see the Turquoise Mountain rushing toward them, its upper slopes a virginal white, glittering in the sunlight against a sky swept clean by the night's storm. The thump of the copter blades covered the words as he repeated the Stalking Song. Perhaps Mary heard them, jammed as she was between him and the pilot. She glanced at him curiously.

They found the blond man's pickup truck about three twisting miles below the Vines house. Chee examined it through his binoculars, and the tracks told a story that was easy to read. The truck had slid off the narrow forest service road, losing traction on an upslope, where its spinning rear wheels moved sideways into the ditch. The driver had emerged, walked uphill several hundred yards, and then returned to the truck. He'd done this while the snow was still falling heavily, and his tracks were half-filled depressions. Later, when the snow was no longer falling, he had emerged again, walking uphill through snow that now was perhaps two feet deep. The new tracks were easy to follow, but there was no reason to follow them. They would lead to Vines' house.

The only question was whether they had yet reached the house. How fast could the blond man struggle uphill through deep snow? A mile an hour?

At the butte the snowfall had stopped about 4:00 A.M. On the mountain, it would have lasted longer. Perhaps until 5:00 or 6:00.

"Let's take the shortest way to Vines'," Chee said. "When we're there, get close to the ground and try to keep behind the trees. They'll hear us, but I don't want them to know where you're letting me off."

"Letting you off?" Mary said. "You're out of your mind. We'll wait for the sheriff. He can't get away now."

"No," Chee said. "There's something I have to do."

The copter settled in a great cloud of feathery snow behind a cluster of blue spruce which screened off the garage. Chee dropped into a snowbank deeper than his knees and stood blinded for a moment while the copter pulled up and away. Then he ran, floundering, to the stone wall of the garage. The blond man, and Vines, and Mrs. Vines, anyone in the house, would have heard the copter, but they couldn't have seen it, and they wouldn't know it had dropped him. Still, he'd be careful. He stood against the wall, remembering the layout of the house. It sat with its back into the mountain slope, looking outward across the great panorama below. But the view was limited. Behind the house, the wall was low and windowless, and in many places one could step from the mountainside to the tile roof. Chee trotted around the garage. The tombstones of Dillon Charley and the first and faithful Mrs. Vines wore high white hats of snow. Behind the house, he stopped to listen. The stillness was almost total—the silence of a windless morning on a mountain buried under new white insulation. From somewhere back in the forest, a fir limb bent and gave up its bushels of snow with a sibilant sound. From the house, only silence.

Thirty feet ahead there was a doorway. Perhaps a laundry room, or some other sort of utility entrance. Chee moved toward it cautiously, keeping close to the wall, with the pistol, cocked, in his right hand. He tried the knob. Unlocked.

Over the roof he heard the sound of the copter. It was approaching fast. The sound peaked, receded, and returned. First Cavalry was creating a distraction for him, Chee realized. Mary's idea, probably. He pulled the door open and slipped inside.

The room seemed almost totally dark. He stood, back to the door, giving his eyes a chance to make the adjustment from the brilliance of sunlight off snow to the interior gloom. He was in a sort of washroom/supply room. Down a short, narrow hall he could see into the kitchen. His ears told him absolutely nothing. The house was as silent as the snow outside. But something reached his nose. Acrid. The smell of blue smoke produced by gunpowder. Chee leaned against the edge of the clothes drier, unlaced his wet boots and removed them. He moved silently down the hall, placing his stockinged feet noiselessly. The kitchen was empty. It was lighter. The room was lit by a row of small high windows and more light came in from the broad doorway, which opened into what seemed to be a game room. Chee moved through the kitchen, back to the wall, trying to see into the adjoining room without being seen himself. He edged past the door of what was probably a pantry. Then he froze.

From behind him came a quick gasping sound, a quick release of breath, a quick intake of breath. Someone was standing behind the door, inches away from his back.

Chee slid away from the door. He stood beside it. Listening. His pistol was cocked. The safety off. He squatted just to the left of the door, facing it. He reached across his body with his left hand and gripped the knob. Then he thought. This was not where he would find the blond man—not hiding in a closet. He heard the clamor of the helicopter again from the front of the house, and he jerked the door open.

The Acoma woman stood there. She looked startled, but she made no sound.

Chee put a finger to his lips, signaling silence. "Where is everyone?" he whispered in English.

The Acoma woman stared at his pistol. It was pointed at her stomach. Chee lowered it.

"A blond man came here," Chee said. "Is he here?"

She seemed not to understand. She appeared to be stunned. "Where is everyone?" Chee repeated.

The woman released another gasp of breath. *"El*

brujo esta muerto," she said. That was all she would say. She said it twice, and then she turned abruptly and walked silently down the hallway and disappeared into the laundry room. Chee heard the outside door open. And then close.

"The witch is dead." Did she mean the blond man? Did she mean Vines? Not Mrs. Vines. She had used the masculine noun. The dead witch was male.

Chee found him in Vines' study. He sat behind the great desk, still upright because the swivel chair had been tilted slightly backward, and the impact of the bullet had pushed his head against the leather cushion. The light from the sunny snow outside streamed through the shutters and lit his face and showed a spot low on the forehead just above the bridge of his nose. It hadn't bled much, but a trickle had run down across his cheek and into his white beard. B. J. Vines' eyes were still open, but the witch was forever dead.

Where was the blond man? Chee stood just inside the door, back to the wall, listening. He heard nothing. The copter had gone now. Had it landed? Vines' dead face wore a look of shocked surprise. He had seen death coming. A tigress looked over his shoulder, her glittering glass eyes staring at Chee. Where was the blond man? Chee found himself thinking instead of B. J. Vines' head mounted among those of the other predators, the blue eyes glittering. The blond man might have left. He would hardly stay after he had accomplished his purpose. Chee moved quickly around the desk. He put his finger against Vines' throat. The skin was still soft and warm. He touched the bloody streak that ran down the side of the nose. Not even sticky yet. Vines had been dead only minutes. No more than five or ten. The blond man was close. Then where was Rosemary Vines? Perhaps she was away from home.

Chee stood beside the desk, watching the door, listening. What would the blond man do? The copter thudded close again, hovering in front of the house. Mary trying to help. He remembered the blond man's rifle. Stay away, Mary. Stay out of range. She was a woman among women. She made him happy. She was a friend. She made him feel like singing. She deserved nothing but beauty all around her. But now, stay away. The blond man must be in the house. Close. Doing what? Looking for servants? Making sure he'd leave no one alive to report this visit? Chee's eyes rested on the telephone. The line would be cut. He picked up the receiver, expecting deadness. Instead he heard the buzzing dial tone. He dialed 0. It rang, and a woman's voice said, "Operator. Can I help you?"

"Sorry," Chee whispered. He hung up. Why had the blond man left the telephone intact? He hadn't got to it yet. Then he heard the sound. Someone coughed. And coughed again.

The blond man was sitting on the floor of the entrance foyer, his shoulder against the massive door. Blood was everywhere. It splashed across the polished wood, it soaked the blond man's trousers, it spread in a still-growing stain across the patterned ceramic tiles of the floor. A pistol lay in the blood, black, with the long cylinder of a silencer on its barrel. The blond man coughed again. He glanced at Chee, then focused his eyes on him. He moved his lips, tentatively. Then he said:

"It's cold."

Chee could see what had happened. The shot had hit the blond man as he reached the door. One of Vines' hunting rifles, probably. Something big. The slug had torn through him from the back, splashing the door with blood. It had broken the blond man as a stick is broken.

"Is there someplace warm?" the blond man asked.

"Maybe the fireplace," Chee said. He put his pistol in its holster, walked through the blood, and squatted beside the blond man. He put an arm under his legs and an arm behind his shoulders and lifted him—carefully because the blood was slippery under his socks, carefully because the man was dying.

In the big room, a log fire had burned itself down to flickering coals in the fireplace. Chee knelt in front of it and put the blond man on the skin of the polar bear. The man's back was broken somewhere between the shoulder blades. The blond man's head rolled toward the fire. His voice was small.

"There's this detective agency," he said. "Webster.

In Encino. He's going to find my mother. She'll know about the cemetery. She'll come and get me."

"All right," Chee said. "Don't worry."

"I thought I killed him," Rosemary Vines said. She was standing in the doorway, holding a long-barreled rifle. It was pointed roughly in Chee's direction.

"You did," Chee said. "It takes a few minutes."

Mrs. Vines' face was bloodless. The lipstick she wore made a grotesque contrast against chalky skin.

"Did you know who your husband was?" Chee asked.

Rosemary Vines stared past him, her eyes on the blond man. She's in shock, Chee thought. She didn't even hear me.

"I knew he'd had another life somewhere," she said slowly. "I suspected that even before we were married. He loved to talk about himself, but not back before a certain time. Earlier than that—when he was a boy, when he was in college, any of that time before he'd come out here and found his mine—any time before that it was all very vague. So he had to be hiding something. And finally he admitted he had his secrets. But he'd never tell me what. I told him it had to be criminal or he wouldn't be ashamed of it. But he'd just laugh."

On the pelt of the dead polar bear, the blond man was now quite motionless. Rosemary Vines still stared at his body, the rifle still ready.

"I knew it was in his safe. In his box. It had to be. That's the way B.J. was. Everything he did, he had to keep the evidence. Heads. Pelts. Photographs. He was compulsive about it. Like he had to have proof it had happened. He wouldn't take twenty-five years of his life and just throw it away. If I could get the box before he got back, there'd be things in there to tell me who B.J. had been when he was young. And there'd be something to tell me what it was he was so ashamed of."

The thought brought something like animation to her face—a look of triumph anticipated. It was a sort of smile. "Ashamed of, or afraid of," Mrs. Vines said, still smiling.

Jim Chee looked away from her, away from the body, and the white fur stained with red. Through the great soaring expanse of glass that lit the room he could see only sky and snow. Blue and white purity. Such beauty should have aroused in Jim Chee an exultation. Now he felt nothing. Only numb fatigue and a kind of sickness.

But he knew the cause, and the cure. Changing Woman had taught them about it when she formed the first clans of the Dinee from her own skin. The strange ways of strange people hurt the spirit, turned the Navajo away from beauty. Returning to beauty required a cure. He would go tomorrow to Hosteen Nakai and ask him to arrange an Enemy Way, to gather family, the interlinked relatives of the Slow Talking Dinee and the Red Forehead

Dinee—the brothers and sisters of his blood, his friends, his supporters. Then there would be another eight days for the songs and the poetry and the sand paintings to recreate the past and restore the spirit.

He would persuade Hosteen Nakai that Mary, too, should undergo the blessing even though she was not born Dinee. The arrangements would take weeks—picking the site, spreading the word, getting the proper singer, arranging the food. But when it was over, he would go again with beauty all around him.

Here's chapter one from Tony Hillerman's
Talking God,
on sale now from HarperPaperbacks.

≫ 1 ≪

Through the doorway which led from her receptionist-secretary's office into her own, Catherine Morris Perry instantly noticed the box on her desk. It was bulky—perhaps three feet long and almost as high. The legend printed on it said it had originally contained a microwave oven manufactured by General Electric. Strips of brown tape had been wrapped erratically around it. It was a crude box, incongruous amid the pale pastels and tasteful artifacts of Catherine Perry's stylish office.

"How was the weekend?" Markie said.

Catherine Morris Perry hung her raincoat on its peg, hung her rain hat over it, removed the transparent plastic from her shoes, and said, "Hello, Markie."

"How was Vermont?" Markie asked. "Wet up there, too?"

"Where'd that come from?" Catherine said, indicating the box.

"Federal Express," Markie said. "I signed for it."

"Am I expecting anything?"

"Not that you told me about. How was Vermont?"

"Wet," Catherine said. She did not wish to discuss Vermont, or anything else involving life outside this office, with Markie Bailey. What she did wish to discuss with Markie was taste. Or lack of taste. Putting the big box, brown and ugly, on her antique desk, as Markie had done, was typical of the problem. It squatted there, ugly, obscenely out of place. As out of place as Mrs. Bailey was in this office. But getting rid of her would be almost impossible. Certainly a huge amount of trouble under federal civil service rules. Mrs. Perry's specialty in law was not personnel, but she had learned something from the efforts to get rid of Henry Highhawk, that troublemaking conservator in the Museum of Natural History. What an unending fiasco that had been.

"You had a call," Markie said. "The cultural attaché's office at the Chilean embassy. He wanted an appointment."

"Later," Catherine Morris Perry said. "I'll return it later." She knew what that problem would be. Another Indian giver problem. General Something-or-Other wanting artifacts returned. He claimed his great-grandfather had only loaned them to some big shot in United Fruit, and he had no right to give them to the Smithsonian, and they were national treasures and must be returned. Incan, as she remembered. Gold, of course. Gold masks, encrusted with jewels, and the general would probably decide they were the general's personal treasure, if he could get his hands on them. And seeing that he didn't meant a huge amount of work for her, research into documents and into international law, which she should get working on right away.

But there sat the box taking up desk space. It was addressed to her as "Museum Spokesperson." Catherine Morris Perry didn't like being addressed as "Spokesperson." That she was so addressed probably stemmed from the statement she'd given the *Washington Post* on museum policy. It had been more or less an accident, the whole thing. The reporter's call had been referred to her only because someone was sick in the public affairs office, and someone else was away from his desk, and whoever had handled the call had decided a lawyer should deal with it. It concerned Henry Highhawk again, obliquely at least. It concerned the trouble he was stirring up about returning aboriginal skeletal remains. And the *Post* had called and identified her incorrectly as spokesperson, and quoted her when they should have quoted the museum board of directors. The policy on skeletons was, after all, official policy of the board. And a sound policy.

The Federal Express shipping order attached to the box was correct except for the erroneous title. She was "Temporary Assistant Counsel, Public Affairs" on loan from the Department of the Interior. She sat and flipped quickly through the remainder of her mail. Nothing much. What was probably an invitation from the National Ballet Guild to an upcoming fund-raiser. Something from the American Civil Liberties Union. A memo from the museum maintenance director telling her why it was impossible for him to deal with a personnel complaint as the law required him to. Another letter concerning insurance for borrowed items going into an exhibit opening next month, and three letters which seemed to be from private outside sources, none familiar.

Catherine Morris Perry put all the envelopes aside unopened, looked at the box, and made a wry face. She opened her desk drawer and extracted her letter opener. Then she buzzed Mrs. Bailey.

"Yes'um."

"Mrs. Bailey. When packages arrive like this, don't bring them in and put them on my desk. Open them and get the contents out."

"Okay," Mrs. Bailey said. "I'll open it now. It's a heavy thing." She paused. "Mrs. Paterson always wanted all the mail put in on her desk."

"I'll open it," Catherine said. "I meant from now on. And Mrs. Paterson is on leave. She is not in charge now."

"Okay," Mrs. Bailey said. "Did you notice the telephone messages? Two of them? On your desk, there?"

"No," Catherine said. They were probably under the box.

"Dr. Hebert called and just said he wanted to congratulate you on the way you handled the skeleton thing. On what you said in the *Post*."

With her free hand Catherine Perry was slicing the tape away with the letter opener. She thought that this box was probably a result of that story in the *Washington Post*. Any time the museum got into the news, it reminded a thousand old ladies of things in the attic that should be saved for posterity. Since she was quoted, one of them had sent this trash to her by name. What would it be? A dusty old butter churn? A set of family albums?

"The other one was somebody in the anthropology division. I put her name on the slip. Wants you to call. Said it was about the Indians wanting their skeletons back."

"Right," Catherine said. She pulled open the top flaps. Under them was a copy of the *Washington Post*, folded to expose the story that had quoted her. Part of it was circled in black.

MUSEUM OFFERS COMPROMISE
IN OLD BONE CONTROVERSY

The headline irritated Catherine. There had been no compromise. She had simply stated the museum's policy. If an Indian tribe wanted ancestral bones returned, it had only to ask for them and provide some acceptable proof that the bones in question had indeed been taken from a burial ground of the tribe. The entire argument was ridiculous and demeaning. In fact, even dealing with that Highhawk man was demeaning. Him and his Paho Society. A museum underling and an organization which, as far as anybody knew, existed only in his imagination. And only to create trouble. She glanced at the circled paragraph.

"Mrs. Catherine Perry, an attorney for the museum and its spokesperson on this issue, said the demand by the Paho Society for the reburial of the museum's entire collection of more than

18,000 Native American skeletons was 'simply not possible in light of the museum's purpose.'

"She said the museum is a research institution as well as a gallery for public display, and that the museum's collection of ancient human bones is a potentially important source of anthropological information. She said that Mr. Highhawk's suggestion that the museum make plaster casts of the skeletons and rebury the originals was not practical 'both because of research needs and because the public has the right to expect authenticity and not to be shown mere reproductions.' "

The clause "the right to expect authenticity" was underlined. Catherine Morris Perry frowned at it, sensing criticism. She picked up the newspaper. Under it, atop a sheet of brown wrapping paper, lay an envelope. Her name had been written neatly on it. She opened it and pulled out a single sheet of typing paper. While she read, her idle hand was pulling away the layer of wrapping paper which had separated the envelope from the contents of the box.

"Dear Mrs. Perry:

"You won't bury the bones of our ancestors because you say the public has the right to expect authenticity in the museum when it comes to look at skeletons.

Therefore I am sending you a couple of authentic skeletons of ancestors. I went to the cemetery in the woods behind the Episcopal Church of Saint Luke. I used authentic anthropological methods to locate the burials of authentic white Anglo types—"

Mrs. Morris Perry's fingers were under the wrapping paper now, feeling dirt, feeling smooth, cold surfaces.

"Mrs. Bailey!" she said. "Mrs. Bailey!" But her eyes moved to the end of the letter. It was signed "Henry Highhawk of the Bitter Water People."

"What?" Mrs. Bailey shouted. "What is it?"

"—and to make sure they would be perfectly authentic, I chose two whose identities you can personally confirm yourself. I ask that you accept these two skeletons for authentic display to your clients and release the bones of two of my ancestors so that they may be returned to their rightful place in Mother Earth. The names of these two authentic—"

Mrs. Bailey was standing beside her now. "Honey," she said. "What's wrong?" Mrs. Bailey paused. "There's bones in that box," she said. "All dirty, too."

Mrs. Morris Perry put the letter on the desk and looked into the box. From underneath a clutter of what seemed to be arm and leg bones a single empty eye socket stared back at her. She noticed that Mrs. Bailey had picked up the letter. She noticed dirt. Damp ugly little clods had scattered on the polished desk top.

"My God," Mrs. Bailey said. "John Neldine Burgoyne. Jane Burgoyne. Weren't those— Aren't these your grandparents?"